OUT OF THE BLUE

OUT OF THE BLUE

BELINDA JONES

ISIS
LARGE PRINT
Oxford

Copyright © Belinda Jones, 2008

First published in Great Britain 2008
by
Arrow Books
an imprint of
The Random House Book Group Limited ???

Published in Large Print 2009 by ISIS Publishing Ltd.,
7 Centremead, Osney Mead, Oxford OX2 0ES
by arrangement with
The Random House Book Group Limited

British Library Cataloguing in Publication Data
Jones, Belinda
 Out of the blue. – Large print ed.
 1. Cruise ships – Fiction
 2. Crete (Greece) – Fiction
 3. Love stories
 4. Large type books
 I. Title
 823.9'2 [F]

ISBN 978–0–7531–8206–2 (hb)
ISBN 978–0–7531–8207–9 (pb)

Printed and bound in Great Britain by
T. J. International Ltd., Padstow, Cornwall

To my editor Kate Elton
(This one's for you!)

Acknowledgements

Firstly, this story simply would not have existed were it not for the one and only Yiorgos Kakaroubas! Unlimited *filakia* for your divine character inspiration and commitment to this book!

Elegant *epharistos* to Greek goddess Lena Melidonioti of Helios Hotels, the smartest and swiftest marketing director in the business. And to Nikolaos Chronis for your amazing generosity with the heavenly Elounda Carob Tree Valley Villas.

Other stars of Elounda include Petros, Angelos, Birgit, Drew, Jack and Jessica. And in Athens: Athina, Sylvia Fierro and the wondrous Nia Vardalos.

Em and Graeme — thank you for sharing in the midday sun madness of it all! Raki toast to you both and blue cocktail chinkings to wonder-wit Dylan Callaghan and my able seamen Ian Nathan, Adam Smith and the irrepressible Jindrich. Carry on cruising!

Retsina all round for the Random House crew — Georgina, Rob, Oli, Laura, Claire, Louisa, Emma — and my agents Eugenie and Rowan at William Morris Associates — you all deserve a week on a Greek island for the hard work you put in!

There are always two people (and one cat) who go above and beyond the call of duty in terms of supporting me in the writing process and they are my mama mia Pamela and flatmate and head chef James.

Well, who can write on an empty stomach? And who enjoys a fish dinner more than Cabbage? Love you all. Finally, a sun-kissed infinity pool hug to Mr Dean Tony Joseph whose encouraging words kept me focussed until The End.

Special mention to the hilarious dream-energiser Barbara Sher and all my fellow Scanners worldwide!

CHAPTER
ONE

"We must free ourselves of the hope that the sea will ever rest. We must learn to sail in high winds."
— Aristotle Onassis

Oh no. Here he comes again.

Striding purposefully towards me in precision-pressed naval whites complete with rigid black epaulettes, soft white loafers and a patent peaked cap with nifty gold insignia. Even his Mediterranean tan and onyx-glow eyes look like they've been officially issued in a bid to create the ultimate cruiseship pin-up, all perfectly offset against an icy blue ocean backdrop.

I dart back along the corridor and into my cabin, leaning on the door like a fugitive. Ever since Officer Alekos Diamantakis boarded the ship in Alaska last month, my life has been one long Benny Hill sketch. I can honestly say that in my twelve years working in Shore Excursions, I have never been pursued so doggedly. I still can't fathom why someone several thousand leagues too good-looking for me is in such hot pursuit but in a matter of hours all speculation will be irrelevant as I am airlifted to safety — having completed my eight-month contract, I am about to get my standard two months off.

I am prone to end-of-an-era blues on my last night, bidding farewell to so many people I'll never see again, running a little flicker book in my mind of all the sights I've seen on this latest journey; I even get nostalgic about the soft furnishings. But tonight is different, for the very first time I've put in a request to return to the same ship. And it's not that this one is any more fabulous than the others, it's just that lately I seem to be having an uncharacteristic craving for familiarity. At least I think it's that. If I was going to attempt to define the exact sensation, I'd say I'm feeling homesick. But how is that possible when I have no home?

Last year my parents emigrated to New Zealand to be near my sister and her new baby. I did have a brief moment feeling like a child in an abandoned pram but I don't blame them. It's just possible that coastal Wellington, voted twelfth-best quality-of-living city in the world, has the edge over Watford and as my mum says, I'm never home anyway and just as likely to crop up in the southern hemisphere as the northern.

Besides, it's not like I'm going to miss out on my trips to the Harlequin shopping centre because my new best friend Jules lives just a few streets away from my parents' old house, so at least I can leave my homing device set to the same co-ordinates for now. She's who I'll be staying with on my shore leave. The fact that she's a former cruise staffer (we shared a cabin in Hawaii) really eases the transition back to dry land — she understands all the jargon and the nature of ship gossip. Not least because she was often the centre of it.

2

"Spa girls" (those working in beauty therapy and fitness), along with the female dancers, are the most sought-after women on the ship, especially among the highly competitive Greek officers. I did wonder if that was why Alekos homed in on me initially. I was up visiting my hairdresser friend Kirby when he made his first approach. Admittedly, when he found out I was more sightseeing than shiatsu, he didn't cast me aside, but the fact that he was loitering around the salon in the first place rang a few Tibetan tingsha bells.

Speaking of spas, Jules has already booked me in for a Jet Lag Body Wrap to eliminate the travel toxins accumulated on my ten-hour flight from Vancouver. This will be followed by a marathon catch-up of the last series of *Brothers & Sisters* while eating gluten-free home-made muffins. I know the gluten-free bit kind of kills the pampering vibe but, cocktails aside, Jules' body is a highly toned temple and I'm just grateful I won't be the one watching TV in an assortment of yoga poses. Plus, the fact that I won't have to make any decisions while I'm under her roof is the real holiday. All day long I'm super-organised, keeping track of numerous tour groups, but with Jules I get to set the paperwork aside and relax in the passenger seat. Quite literally, this coming week, as she's planned a little roadtrip to Brighton for my birthday, insisting we wear candy colours and wedge heels, even when we go paddling. I suppose her directional assertiveness spills over from her working life — calling out aerobic moves, correcting people's posture, making sure they are exercising correctly. She's equally opinionated when it comes to other people's love lives and heaven knows I need guidance there.

I remember when she first came on board and I was seeing the Norwegian Chief Radio Officer — Nils. Generally I don't like to get involved with fellow shipmates unless either myself or the other party only has a few weeks left of their contract. It's the first question I ask: "How much longer have you got?" Like we all have a terminal disease. It's just too risky otherwise — bad enough breaking up with someone in the same town, but on the same ship, with a maximum storm-off distance of three hundred metres? Hideous. But I hadn't been out with anyone in two years and he was so darn clean and courteous, I broke my rule. I did not choose well.

Unaware that Jules was my new cabin-mate, Nils made a play for her. She came straight to me requesting my permission to accept the invitation back to his cabin so she could infiltrate the emails on his laptop and suss him out. She took along a special spa treatment for him to use in the shower, insisting he try it immediately, thus giving her opportunity to snoop. Oh the humiliation when she revealed the magnitude and multiplicity of his cheating ways — forget his seafaring skills, this is a man you'd want in charge of flight paths at an airport, he was so unbelievably adept at keeping numerous affairs criss-crossing without clashing. Until that moment anyway. She copied every girl in on his mailbox and then forwarded the lot to her own account so she could show me: My darling Caterina ... My darling Ola ... My darling Narinda ... My darling

Sheila . . . Talk about a woman in every port, I think it was more literally every porthole. And they say men can't multitask.

I'm just grateful that she was there to give us all a wake-up call.

It's like that with Alekos; everyone else is trying to persuade me to give him a go whereas Jules, well actually she thinks I should sleep with him too but for a very different reason.

"It's the quickest way to get rid of him!" she told me when I first started to complain of his relentless wooing.

"Oh charming!" I retorted. "What exactly are you implying about my prowess in the boudoir?"

"Nooo!" she had laughed. "No personal slight intended. It's just that he's only lingering and fixating on you because you're resisting."

That's a good friend, one who'll tell you straight: "He's all about the chase!", not fill your head with nonsense about him being different to all the others and worth a chance.

Jules may not be one of life's romantics but she's never short of male attention. Despite all her offers from officers — and one indecent proposal from the captain — it was actually the ship's DJ who triumphed. Dominic was a reluctant sailor, not someone who had ever considered taking a cruise, let alone working on board, but his former girlfriend — an effervescent Entertainments Manager called Cherry — persuaded him to give up his job and flat in Ipswich and do a stint in the ship's nightclub. Within a matter of weeks she got a better offer, not from another man but another ship! It's lucky that Jules was there to comfort Dom after Cherry left. They soon became an item and when Jules' contract ended he cut his short and they went back to England together. That was nearly a year ago now.

I miss having her on board but cruising for Jules was just a way to get a really good tan; for me it's a way of life. It may not be perfect — a little too reminiscent of boarding school at times and not the best earner — but as far as I'm concerned it beats any alternative.

My mum likes to trace my career choice back to my mermaid-themed ninth birthday party and my sister attributes it to covert viewings of *The Love Boat* but in actuality it was *Shirley Valentine* that made me run off to sea.

I missed the film when it first came out, which is nearly twenty years ago if you can believe it. In fact, it wasn't until about eight years later when I was twenty myself that I saw it. At the time, I'd opted to forgo university (and my planned degree in Travel & Tourism) in favour of staying home with my boyfriend Ricky. I'll never forget how we met — I was washing my hands in this trendy restaurant bathroom when I felt another soapy set of fingers entwine with my own. I jumped back and looked below the mirror ledge and there was a scruffy blond head staring back at me, equally perturbed. Turns out the bathroom designer had thought it would be amusing to link the sinks between the Ladies and the Gents, but without any obvious indication that this had been done. We got talking, kept talking all weekend and by Sunday night

I'd lost my heart and mind. The sense of complete surrender felt nice in a way — in life there is so much deliberation, weighing things up, assessing worst-case scenarios, but for him I was willing to sacrifice all I had planned without question. Everything went blurry, he was my only focus. And when we moved in together my world shrank even more.

Cohabitation wasn't quite the non-stop cuddle I'd imagined it to be. He was working long hours in construction and when he got home he had no energy for anything except splaying in front of the TV, still covered in brick dust. Meanwhile, the summer job I'd taken in the local travel agent became full-time and though I loved nothing better than matchmaking holidaymaker and hotel, the irony wasn't lost on me that I had the power to send people whizzing all around the globe and yet couldn't get my own boyfriend off the sofa. Still. That's cosy isn't it? Snuggling up watching TV. It got a lot cosier when he lost his job. This was pre-Tivo and I found him so brain-dullingly indiscriminate about what he would watch. Even being a party to his mindless channel-hopping made me feel my life was slipping away from me. Despite my every encourage-ment he made no effort to look for a new job — well, why should we both suffer? Perhaps we'd take it in turns to work!

And then Marianne at the agency was offered a familiarisation trip to a new resort in Greece and she invited me around the night before for moussaka and *Shirley Valentine* on video, scandalised that I'd never seen it. Poor woman didn't bargain on my reaction. To

7

me this personable comedy was more chilling than any horror film because it could really happen, does happen all the time — women fall in love, get married, have children and lose themselves. And then they spend the rest of their lives searching for "The Girl Who Used To Be Me" as the theme song goes.

Watching it was like a flash to the future, a cautionary tale — at twenty I could already relate to the feelings of domestic drudgery and "Is this it?" resignation. Twenty years on would I be talking to the wall and wearing polyester housecoats? Would I have sent a thousand people on exotic adventures and not done a single sodding thing with my life? I went back to the flat in a daze. Without even looking up from the TV, Ricky said he needed me to leave him a fiver for lunch the next day. I explained that I hadn't been to the cashpoint and only had schrapnel in my purse. He promptly went ballistic, telling me how inconsiderate I was and what was he supposed to do, starve? At that point it struck me that actually I could be a little bit worse off than Shirley because at least her husband Joe had a job.

When I went into work the next day my first instinct was to follow Marianne to Mykonos. But I'd had a couple of dodgy family holidays in Greece in the past and even if this one went like a dream it would only save me for two weeks. I needed something more profoundly life-changing. Something I couldn't cop out of the second I had a pang for Ricky's heart-ensnaring kisses, which is what got me into the trouble in the first place. And that's when a couple came in to book a cruise.

They'd been every year for the past ten, got pally with staff in every department including the one that sold and arranged the trips in each port of call — i.e. Shore Excursions. Though obviously comparable to my own profession, what they described was the absolute antithesis of my current existence and light years away from suburbia.

"It's not just a job," the husband told me. "It's a radical change in lifestyle."

While I was aboard the ship I wouldn't have to cook or clean or commute. I wouldn't have to do laundry or be responsible for anyone else's stomach — if a man wanted his tea on the table at six he'd go to the canteen. It seemed too good to be true — no peeling spuds at the sink watching the rain drizzle down the window pane. No standing at bus stops with plastic carrier bags slicing into careworn hands. No torturing myself with posters for exotic destinations — I would be sipping Caribbean coconut water under that palm tree, touring those Mayan ruins, promoting that Polynesian snorkelling trip.

It sounded a lot better than being buried alive with a mean-mouthed couch potato. As I filled in my application, I vowed I would never again settle to the point of stagnation. I even decided I would never marry, just to be extra sure I would forever repel the label housewife. Instead my life would be one long honeymoon cruise. Albeit solo.

I remember my first day. I was so daunted. Instead of telling myself to just get through the next eight hours so I could go home and collapse, it felt like I had an eight-month-long day ahead of me. The commitment was huge but every time I thought of bailing, I would think about what I'd be going back to. And then, of course, when I did get to go back to England on my break, I was antsy within a fortnight. It was like I'd been given a ticket to a magical new world and I couldn't wait to see where it would take me next.

Most of my friends were excited for me but then I remember at a Christmas party a few years back we were picking songs for each other to karaoke to death and someone handed me Charlene's "I've Never Been to Me" . . . I wasn't quite sure how to take that. At the time I couldn't empathise with the regretful singer. What was she complaining about — if you've been to Nice and the "isle" of Greece and sipped champagne on a yacht, that's not a bad life. In fact she's probably quite similar to Joanna Lumley's character in *Shirley Valentine* — remember classmate Marjorie Majors who went on to become the jet-set high-class hooker? Well I've been to Georgia and California without having to resort to prostitution. I may not have been undressed by kings but I have had my share of international flings and though none of them have worked out at least it's been culturally educational.

Anyway, what Charlene seems to be saying is that she'd swap her misleadingly glamorous and ultimately lonely life for the day-to-day reality of a husband and baby. And what makes me wonder if this choice of song was somewhat barbed, is that the friend who handed me the lyrics was a mother of two.

I've been pondering the differences between us a lot lately. (It's amazing how that song catches me unawares in the strangest places — a supermarket in Barbados, a disco in Anchorage.) But I'm still not convinced about the trade-off. Whoever you are, you always feel something is missing, don't you? Isn't that just part of the human condition? And unlike Charlene, I *have* been to me. I know who I am. More or less. My only concern is that I'm running out of world to see because that's what keeps me going — the thrill of discovering something new.

At least that's what I've always felt. As someone with "Keep moving!" as their mantra, I keep doubting my decision to return to the same ship — I just hope it's not a slippery slope. Am I slowing down when actually what I need is another big shake-up? But what could that be? The most dramatic thing someone who is always on the move can do is stand still! And I can't possibly do that.

I partly blame Alekos for my current jarred equilibrium. When I first met him I was as intrigued and attracted as the rest of the ship, then came word of his reputation: heartbreaker of the first degree. Succumb at your peril. So I stepped back and shut down, which isn't easy when you've got all stirred up by the attentions of a wickedly handsome man. Holding strong (in a run-and-hide kind of way) I reminded myself how miserable I felt after the Norwegian — I didn't want that again. At least this one had come with a warning.

Of course intentions are one thing but it's not so easy to un-trigger your desire. Even if you've switched off to that particular person, you still can't help lying in bed wondering about alternatives . . . What if I did meet someone nice, someone Jules gave her seal of approval to? What if we moved in together and it deteriorated into sofa life again, would that be so bad now that I'd seen something of the world?

But then off I'd go on some tour and find myself brimming over with wonder as I beheld a two-hundred-foot-high glacier face glowing blue and I'd think, "I can't give up all this for a man, I just can't."

I even feel a little annoyed now — look at me cowering in my cabin when I should be having farewell Martinis with my friends. I'll give it two more minutes to be sure he's gone and then head out. Perhaps if I finish my packing I'll at least feel I've done something constructive . . .

I flip open my suitcase, tucking a few pairs of shoes down the sides, not that I'm short of space — now that I know I'm returning to the ship, I don't have to take any of my winter woolies or jackets back to England. I can't wait for the day when I can walk out the door in just a T-shirt. Well not literally — oop, that'll be the phone. "Selena?" It's Jules.

"Heyy!" I cheer. "I'm just packing!"

She giggles, knowing this is her cue to quote one of our favourite moments from *Desperate Housewives*. "Whoah! I told you to just pack essentials!" she channels Carlos addressing his high-maintenance wife Gabrielle. "Is that a *boa*?"

I clutch at an imaginary ruffle of black feathers and pout. "If you're taking me somewhere where I don't need a boa, then I don't want to go!"

We chuckle and then I huddle up for a gossip — even though I'll be seeing her in two days' time I have to bring her up to speed on the latest — and last — instalment with Alekos.

"Well, you say last but I bet you anything he'll be in the bar tonight and then giving it one last shot outside your cabin door at two a.m.!"

"Don't!" I wail. There's only so many times I can say no convincingly to that man.

"I expect you'll be glad to get away," Jules concludes.

"And even more glad to see you! So, what Duty Free booze should I bring?"

Silence.

"Jules?"

"Oh Selena! I don't even know how to tell you this . . ."

"Tell me what? You surely haven't quit drinking —"

"I'm getting married!"

My stomach drops all the way down to the engine room. "To Dom?" I don't know why I asked that, who else would it be? Clearly I'm stalling for time.

"Yes!" she exclaims. "It was supposed to be this big surprise but then I found the tickets for Mauritius —"

"You're doing the whole barefoot beach thing?" Now at least that makes perfect sense — Jules will make the ultimate bikini bride.

"Dom said we should do it naked but the hotel won't allow it."

"Spoilsports!"

"It's okay, they'll more than make it up to me in spa treatments — I've already booked in for the frangipani body float and there's this Exotic Moisture Dew facial that sounds divine!"

I know Jules loves her fancy gunks and pummellings but she actually sounds more excited about Elemis than becoming a Mrs.

"So when's the big day?" I ask. "Or should I say the big *holiday*?"

"We leave Sunday."

"Sunday Sunday? This Sunday?" Surely she can't mean the day I am due to arrive on her doorstep. "As in the day after tomorrow?"

"Sudden, huh? Good thing I had booked the time off work to be with you."

"Yes. Well. Wow." I sit down on the bed, accidentally flattening my straw cowboy hat. "So I take it it's just the two of you? Or is your family going?"

Suddenly I feel a total outsider — reminding me how recent a friendship this is.

"No, it's just the two of us. You're not miffed, are you — that it's ruined our plans?"

"Don't be silly," I tut. "I'm just shocked. I mean surprised." I scrunch my brow trying to come up with the appropriate phrase. "What I mean to say is that I'm delighted!" I conclude, only to add, "If this is what you want?"

She hasn't even mentioned Dom in any recent correspondence but I suppose that's a good sign — in my experience people generally have more to say about their partners when they're peeved with them and want to vent and gain support for their side of the argument — I remember bumping into an old friend on my last trip to the UK and asking how life was since his girlfriend moved in and he said, "Uneventful." And he meant it in a good way.

I decide to sidestep the emotional probing and cut to the crux of the matter — "What are you going to wear?"

"Well, for the old I have my nan's diamond earrings, new is going to be this amazing white sequin bikini I'm collecting tomorrow, and my mum is letting me borrow her Gucci sunglasses."

"What about the blue?"

"I'll just pick up something out there."

I listen to her talking about coconut-scented body shimmer and the possibility of using a wispy sarong as a veil while simultaneously trying to break down my feeling of unease.

Obviously I'm disappointed that I won't be seeing her and that our plans have gone awry and I can't help but feel snubbed by Dom — Jules took the week off to be with me and he's trumped my company with a marriage proposal and a spa-fest. I suddenly feel very dispensable. On the upside I don't have to worry about being homeless, at least initially, because she's kindly said I can stay at her flat while she's gone. But what about when they come back? Will he be moving in straight away? Where will I go? I shake my head — look at me selfishly considering all the repercussions in my life! This is supposed to be a time for celebration and, more significantly, jealousy. Well, I can certainly cop to a pang of the latter. It's not the marriage itself that gets me, just that partnership thing — being in cahoots, be it with a friend or a lover, moving forward in life with someone by your side. I sigh to myself. This really is the end of an era, only with Jules I don't have the benefit of a last-night party. When I see her next she will be someone's wife.

"Oooh, I've got to go," she suddenly blurts. "My sunrise pilates class is here!"

As I put down the phone, I turn my head to look out into the churning black abyss. Tomorrow I have a set schedule involving a bus, a plane and a couple of trains. Logistically I know exactly where I'm going and when. And yet the truth is, I've never felt more at sea.

CHAPTER
TWO

"The oldest, shortest words — yes and no — are those which require the most thought."
— Pythagoras

Passing laughter weaves under my cabin door reminding me that I'm letting my last night of guaranteed sociability slip away from me.

"Come on, Miss Harper — your guests are waiting!" I gee myself up, flouncing the netting of my skirt and checking on the elaborate up-do Kirby experimented with earlier. One more swish of Benefit blush and I'm on my way.

Normally I would walk the internal route to the bar but feeling in need of a quick blast of air, I tug open the glass side door and find myself caught in a salt-tinged twister. Instead of ducking back inside like a sane person, I step boldly into its midst, holding down my skirt, closing my eyes and letting the wind bluster and muss me, hoping it will buffet the queasiness from my body.

As I reach for the railing to steady myself, I find myself leaning over, concentrating on the water rushing below me.

"Don't do it!" Kirby is suddenly upon me, pretending to wrestle me back from the edge and

17

bundling me inside. "Christ, you look like Helena Bonham Carter!" he curses as he assesses the damage. "I've never seen such wilful wrecking of a hairdo. What were you thinking?"

Technically the answer would be, "*I don't want to leave — I've got nothing and no one to go back to!*", but I don't want his parting impression of me to be a moany no-mates so I tell him I was just thinking about Mrs Burrell's false teeth falling overboard while she was whale-watching.

"Don't worry," he says, smoothing my stray strands back into place before leading me onwards, "just one more night of this insanity and you're free!"

I force a smile but there it is again, that sinking feeling and a niggling query: "Free to do *what?*"

What choice could I possibly make now that would revive my deflated spirits?

"White Chocolate Martini or Peach Bellini?"

Well. Everything starts with baby steps.

I take a sip of my smooth, perfectly chilled cocktail and look around me. There's something so comforting about a cruiseship on formal night. With everyone putting on the ritz, it's as though we are all harking back to a more refined era.

People are so quick to dismiss cruises as full of newlyweds and "nearly deads" and even my own parents say they're saving it for their eighties "because there are doctors and coffins on board", but I say don't knock it until you've tried it. There's a camaraderie among the guests that you rarely find in hotels; a sense of shared experience. Here people actually talk to one another in the lift or at the café counter. That's one of the things I have to watch when I first get back to England — not saying good morning to every person I pass on the street. Maybe I'll solve that by not getting up till noon — oh glorious lie-ins here I come!

While Kirby goes in search of Lana the Lithuanian croupier who he sent in search of me, I approach the group of foxy fortysomething divorcees who chose Alaska based on the state's excess of single men.

"So, how's the manhunt going, ladies?"

"Oh that lumberjack show you sent us to was hilarious!" the ringleader raves. "All check shirts and whopping great axes!"

"We got pictures with them, look!" Her friend shows me on her camera — three strapping chaps with necks like tree trunks and one who looks like he'd be better suited to IT. "Well, you know what they say about Alaskan men — 'The odds may be good but the goods are odd!' " they all chorus and then fall about laughing.

"So you've had a fun time?" I conclude happily.

"The best!" they enthuse. "We've already booked the Southern Caribbean for Jen's fiftieth next year!"

I congratulate them though I am a little envious, imagining them all cavorting together when my own birthday plans have so recently gone awry. But I don't have time to ponder this further because two of my most adventurous customers are beckoning me over to the piano.

"We're so sorry you won't be with us next week." A liver-spotted hand caresses my wrist. "You've taken such good care of us!"

"It was my pleasure," I tell Mr and Mrs Sinclair. "You've been an inspiration — I hope I'm game for ziplining and canoe safaris when I retire!"

"We're just a little bit concerned about the choppier seas they are predicting."

"Just get a pair of those anti-seasickness wristbands," I tell them. "They really do work."

"What about acupuncture? I see they have a special on at the moment."

I pull a face. Each to their own but all I could think as I lay there covered in needles was that if the ship made a particularly violent pitch I'd be tossed from the treatment table to the floor and impaled, dying a thousand deaths like an Agatha Christie murder victim.

They look suitably stricken. "Ginger is supposed to be good for settling the stomach . . ." I try to temper my accidental scaremongering. "Oh, and by the way, I've left that book on totem poles at the Shore Excursions desk for you to have a look at."

This cheers them up no end. "You're a gem!" they say, kissing a cheek apiece before I move on, colliding with Dashing Danny from the Entertainments crew — dashing as in he's always running, as opposed to his being particularly debonair.

"Oh Selena! I'm glad I caught you!" His eyes are even brighter than normal. "I spoke to the boss and he's interested in your idea!"

"Really?" I gawp. Now this is unexpectedly good news.

"Which idea?" Kirby reappears, nosing in alongside me. "Voyager or Voyeur?"

Kirby has a natty label for everything. Voyager is what he calls my travel project, offering guests personally customised tours, and Voyeur is his name for my bid to get into guest speaking.

Every week we have an expert come on board and present three fifty-minute talks on a specialised subject, be it opera, astronomy or something more destination-related like the behaviours of Alaskan black bears. They don't actually get paid for this — the cruise itself is the fee — which is where my custom tour sideline would come in. I've actually had a fair bit of practice at the speaking part in that I do daily talks on stage in the theatre to showcase our range of upcoming tours — a combination of promotion and information and answering any questions the guests may have, however bizarre and unrelated. Anyway, I have boldly decided to become an "expert" on the one thing I probably know least about — love.

It all began on my last South America run. I met a beautiful Swiss lady of seventy who became a teenager before my very eyes as she spoke of a Peruvian man she'd fallen in love with in her youth and never forgotten. It really was captivating, being so close to such treasured emotions . . . I couldn't believe that over fifty years on — and now that her husband had passed away — she'd come to Lima in the hope that she might pass him in the street and have another chance . . .

It seemed incredibly romantic but also sad. I looked at her thinking, she'd spent her whole life missing him and it made me wonder, who does it really happen for, enduring love? I know I've never experienced it. But then I started looking around me — cruiseships are full of people celebrating twenty- and thirty- and even sixty-years anniversaries. I started listening to their stories and then when I was in Singapore I picked up a camcorder and began filming couples on location, talking about how they met and what has kept them in a state of bliss, as well as looking at the way different nationalities express and define love. Kirby calls it voyeurism because he says I'm all observation and no personal interaction. I can't argue with that. Meanwhile, Jules thinks I'm delusional. She says it's like I'm out collecting evidence so that one day when I've met enough happy couples I can present the film footage to the high court and say, *"I have proof! True love does exist!"* And then as a reward they will hand me over my man.

She could be right. Perhaps falling hopelessly in love again is my secret wish as well as my greatest fear.

Danny brings me back to business. "Have you filmed all sixteen of the couples you outlined in your proposal?"

"I've done fourteen," I tell him. "I was planning to do a British couple when I'm back home and then one more European couple to finish up."

"So it's feasible you could be good to go for the start of your next contract?"

"Absolutely!" I pip. "Are you really going to let me try this out on a live audience?"

He nods. "But as for the notion of offering guests sample aphrodisiacs from the countries you are featuring . . ."

"Oh jeez!" Kirby mutters. "If this boat's a-rocking!"

"Is that a no?" I look rueful.

"Well, we checked with the head chef and he said not enough research has been done into the potential effects of mixing, say, damiana tea with oysters or the borojo fruit of Colombia, so he suggested little heart-shaped cookies."

"That's a bit lame." Kirby grimaces. "What about chocolate-dipped strawberries?"

"Oooh, I like that!" Danny and I concur.

"Great, well, I've got to dash but have a safe flight and good luck finding true love!" He winks as he leaves.

Wow! I really am amazed. I was on the verge of a major mope but now I feel I have a little life raft to cling to in this sea of uncertainty!

Maybe it's even a good thing that Jules won't be around to lead me astray when I first get back. I still have a fair bit of editing to do on the other films, cutting hour-long interviews down to ten minutes or so, this way I can get straight down to it — prop myself out on Jules' patio with a flower behind my ear and a jug of fresh lemonade . . .

"Have you heard it's tipping down in England?" Lana ruins my fantasy as she appears with a new set of gaudily coloured cocktails. "They say it's set to be the wettest summer in fifty years."

"Who told you that?" I cry in dismay.

"One of my blackjack regulars — he called his daughter to arrange for her to pick him up at the airport."

Suddenly I feel a bit claustrophobic — shut away in a damp flat in Watford with only other people's love to keep me warm? I give an involuntary shiver.

"Cold?" Kirby enquires.

"I don't have toes any more," I complain. "Just ten little icicles. I was really looking forward to some heat . . ."

"I know someone who could defrost you . . ."

I give him a withering look but it doesn't stop him.

"Alekos Diamantakis." He gives his most seductive, dark-roast vocal impersonation as the man himself enters the room, causing my stomach to loop wildly.

"Lower!" Lana paws at his throat.

"Alekos Diamantakis!" He drops his chin to his chest.

"That's it!" she swoons. "Do you think all Greek men have such deep voices, or is it just the officers? When he speaks I don't hear him in my ears, I just get a rumble right here." She motions to her groin.

"I don't know how you can resist him, Selena, I really don't." Kirby pricks me with his swizzle stick. "I mean look how taut that material gets over his thighs . . ."

"You don't find it all a bit *Officer and a Gentleman* strippogram?" I cringe, refusing to even look in his direction.

24

"You say that like it's a bad thing!" Lana scoffs. "Do you know, sometimes I deliberately stand next to you when he's looking your way just to get the second-hand lust."

"You think that's bad!" Kirby toots. "I've been known to leave my client mid-blow just to get a sniff of him."

"Oh, he smells so good, doesn't he?" Lana rasps in rapture.

"Ay up — the OAPaparazzi are at it again." This is Kirby's name for the older ladies who get snapping every time Alekos passes. "Classic move!" he cheers as one woman drops her sequinned clutch, so that Alekos bends to retrieve it, giving her seated friend a faceful of his pert rear.

I can't help but smile — I suppose in some warped way it's been fun being the object of his affection. I mean, how often do you get to turn down someone that handsome? Or that resilient. Alekos obviously doesn't have the normal human issues with rejection. Mind you, I have recently evolved a theory on this, one I now share with my salivating colleagues.

"So it dawned on me this morning that in Greek 'neh' means yes," I begin, pausing to taking a slurp of pink Martini. "I say no to him but he hears neh, hence his confusion."

"So what's Greek for no?" Lana enquires.

"Well, I don't know how to spell it, but it's pronounced oh-hee."

"Sounds Chinese." She frowns.

"Or a bit Scottish, like och-aye!" offers Kirby. "Definitely too enthusiastic for a negative."

"Exactly. Do you wanna have sex with me? *Oh-hee!*" I chirrup. "Sounds like a cross between Okay and Oh yeah!"

"Talk about mixed messages."

Not that the language should really be a problem — I happen to know Alekos spent four years doing Maritime Studies in Merseyside before becoming an environmental officer and his English is so good he can even do the full Liverpudlian clicking in words such as "like" and "chicken". Less explicable is his liberal use of the cockney phrase "Innit?", though I actually find that oddly charming. It's his overpowering virility that's off-putting. Now some of my best friends are womanisers (well, ship life does seem to breed a "What happens mid-ocean, stays mid-ocean!" mindset) and provided you're not on the receiving end of their philanderings they can be fun people to be around — big appetite for life, whereas I sometimes feel I'm still nibbling at the doily. Anyway, I thought I'd try and parlay flirtation into friendship with Alekos but it just doesn't seem possible — one minute we're talking normally, and I'm thinking he's quite a reasonable chap, but then a shadow will pass over his eyes, his lids will lower, he'll study my mouth in a salacious way, and suddenly I can't think straight. I get panicky and on the defensive and I can't wait to get away, hence why I now try to avoid him altogether. Much to Kirby's annoyance.

"I think it's just plain selfish." He pouts with a blue curaçao-stained lip. "We all want to know what he's like in bed; you're the only one who can find out and you're cruelly withholding the experience from us all!"

"Yeah, selfish," Lana concurs.

"I very much doubt that I have exclusive access," I tut. "Besides, the second I'm gone he's bound to move on to someone else."

"Look, I know that Polish girl who worked with him last summer said she saw him with a different woman every hour and yes, he does always seem to be surrounded, but if he really was so rampant how come he turned me down?" she challenges.

This really is virtually inexplicable. No one turns Lana down. They just lie back and praise the deity from their part of the world.

"You must have just caught him on an off day," I mutter.

"Three off days in one week?" She's having none of it. "I don't think so. Anyway, you leave tomorrow, what harm could it possibly do now to have one night with him?"

"I just couldn't!" I protest, feeling more than a little hounded. "If I slept with him now I'd feel like he'd won in some way."

Lana throws her hands up in despair. "Why can't he be the notch on *your* bedpost? That's how I'd look at it!"

"Sweetie, you've got nothing left to notch," Kirby ribs her. "Last I heard you were sleeping on four toothpicks and a wafer."

"Oi!" She threatens to squirt him in the eye with a kumquat.

"I'm going to say goodbye to Jindrich," I excuse myself, pointing in the direction of my Czech waiter pal, but Lana pulls me back. "Selena, I know that whole episode with the Norwegian left you hyper-suspicious and cautious but that was over a year ago — you can't dismiss all the officers because of one man with a harem fixation."

"And as far as Alekos' reputation goes," Kirby adds his twopenn'orth, "let us bear in mind we have no hard evidence about his womanising; it could just be sour grapes — some gal he turned down bad-mouthing him. Yes, he does always appear to have a harlot on his arm but from what I see, they're going up to him." He gives me an earnest, if a little blurry, look. "There is a chance that he's actually as Cary Grant gorgeous as he seems."

"You're right," I say quite reasonably before shrugging. "It's just not a chance I'm prepared to take."

And then I turn and slam straight into Alekos' brass buttons.

As I reset my nose, I sense the tension around me — Kirby pretending to scan the cocktail menu (as if he didn't already know it off by heart) and Lana freezing like a street performer statue, only without the silver spray paint.

"Is it true?" he growls at me.

I take a breath. The only thing worse than talking to Alekos is talking to him when other people are listening. And looking. Even the lady who has finally won an audience with the captain is peering around the side of his head to have a good gawp. I decide to lead Alekos over to a private nook by the window, yet all those spying eyes in the bar are no match for the intensity of his greeny glinters. He could do keyhole surgery with that stare, it's just so invasive!

"Is what true?" I huff. Is this going to be a line?

"That you're leaving the ship tomorrow?"

"Oh. Yes," I say simply.

"So this is my last chance?"

I give a non-committal shrug. I was going to make some comment about "*no* chance" but there's no need for me to be rude — he'd probably mistake it for banter anyway.

He takes a step closer. His hand is beside mine on the ledge. His little finger steals closer. "You can't turn me down now!" he husks.

"Actually I can," I tell him matter-of-factly, folding my arms.

"You can't."

"I am."

"You're not."

"Really. Aleko. It's never going to happen."

"But why?" He looks absolutely dumbfounded.

At moments like this I half expect him to take out his diary and jab the page, "Look, I had you down as succumbing to my charms this evening, you can't go messing up my schedule!"

Anyone would think I was being deliberately obstreperous, just to vex him.

"I don't think you realise what you are turning down, just how good we would be together . . ."

Give me strength! "Do you know, I discovered the perfect word for you the other day." I smile sweetly. "Braggadocio."

He raises an eyebrow.

"It's someone who is full of empty boasts and swaggering self-aggrandisement." I give him the official definition.

"You think I swagger?"

Actually I like the way he walks, it's more about the way he sits — one arm slung behind the chair back, splayed out like lord of all he surveys. He's gone beyond the realms of superiority, straight to a Greek-god complex. Apparently it's typical of men from Crete — it's the biggest Greek island and they have an ego to match. Myth in his own lunchtime and all that.

"How can you possibly know if my boasts are empty, until you try me?" he wheedles.

I shake my head despairingly. "Wouldn't you rather someone slept with you because they liked you, not because you dared them to do it?" I enquire.

"I don't see the problem —"

"The problem," I cut in, "is that you won't take no for an answer."

It's almost as if the word has a perishable quality for him. He says, "Ah well, you say that *now!*" For Alekos every day is a new day — she didn't say no *today*. If he keeps going he'll eventually catch me in a different mood, wear me down . . .

"Persistence is an admirable quality," he says proudly.

"Not in this case. It's just annoying."

"But what if I know best — what if I know that we are meant to be together?"

"That's so romantic!" a random passer-by coos.

"No it's not!" I snap, outraged. "It's presumptuous and pompous and shows a total disregard for my feelings and opinions."

This is so typical of him. I remember one time I was sitting at the bar and he came up and ordered a drink for me. He didn't ask what I wanted, simply decided what would suit me best. I think he thought he was going to woo me with his taste in fine wine but from my reaction you'd think he'd offered me a poisoned chalice.

Alekos takes off his hat and gives his head a rub before giving me a pitying look. "I don't know why you think I can't be trusted."

"Because, frankly, it would be weird if you could!" I blurt out, trying to resist the temptation to fix the section of jet-black hair he's left skew-whiff. "A man with your looks in your position — endless offers from an ever-changing parade of women — why would you?"

In my mind there are two types of handsome men — the oblivious and the know-it — and Alekos is so self-aware he practically comes with wing mirrors. He really is the only person I know who would rush to get in that mirrored cubicle with Trinny & Susannah and relish seeing himself from every angle.

"Do I know I'm considered good-looking?" he asks, matching my exasperation. "Yes! Do I know women find me attractive? Yes. I'd have to be some kind of moron not to realise."

Finally some straight talk!

"Have I been with other women? Of course. But what does that matter now that I have met you?"

I roll my eyes. "I fail to see what could be so earth-shattering about meeting me! Which isn't to say I don't think I'm utterly fabulous, but you hardly know me."

"I know you better than you realise."

"What?" What does that mean?

"And if I don't know you well *enough*, it's because you won't let me."

"Because you're too pushy, too intense!" I rally.

"It's just . . ." For once he looks lost for words. "I have waited so long for this."

"A month. You've known me a month."

"Yes, but I've waited a lot longer than that, to feel this way . . ."

For a second he throws me. I don't know how to snub that. That actually did feel romantic.

"But what's the point?" I have to state the obvious. "I'm leaving tomorrow . . . and when I do come back, you'll be gone."

That's the other suspect thing about Alekos — he's a *relief* officer which means that whereas the rest of us do eight-month stints, he does short bursts of two. Wouldn't that suggest he has to keep switching ships to keep the women on the speediest possible turnover?

"I could change for you."

I know he's referring to his schedule but I can't help but think how men do change when you let them in . . .

When you've been hurt before you tread carefully, meanwhile they're doing this frantic dance trying to impress you. They spoil you, dote on you, tell you they love you . . . Gradually you start to believe them and you coax your heart into making itself vulnerable again and then the second you reciprocate, they change. I've seen this happen almost overnight — suddenly I'm a sure thing, someone who no longer requires the effort. And I'm not just talking about Ricky. And I'm not just talking about me. I see this happening all around me all the time.

Why would it be any different with Alekos, of all people? And, frankly, why am I even having this conversation with him? I'm ready to cut my losses and turn on my heel when he baits me one more time:

"What frustrates me the most is that you never gave me a chance."

Oh my god, the man is infuriating!

"You are so darn entitled!" I marvel. "That's not how it works. I can't go whining to Hugh Dancy that he's never given me a chance — these things have to start with some kind of mutual attraction."

His confidence, as ever, is unshakeable: "I know you like me really. I'm just a few steps ahead of you, that's all. It would come in time. Every day you spent with me it would get a little clearer and you'd trust me a little more."

I expel a weary sigh. "Well, I guess we'll never know."

And then I tell him *yassou,* which, in case you don't know, is Greek for goodbye.

Usually when I conclude a scenario with a man, I feel a sense of relief — I am out of the danger zone. My pact with myself to never marry is intact. All is well.

But as I walk away from Alekos I get a sense of unfinished business.

It's then I remember that "*yassou*" also means hello . . .

CHAPTER
THREE

Beware the barrenness of a busy life.
— Socrates

It's that classic morning-after cry — why did I have that last lychee Martini? I tut myself as I divide up my toiletries, adding Nurofen to the essentials for the flight and then placing them in a zip-loc sandwich bag. Ah, the glamour of modern-day travel.

It's funny, I actually feel nervous today. As I clatter my case down the metal gangway I see passengers lined up to board, twittering excitedly about leaving home to brave the wintry wilds of Alaska. Our positions seem curiously reversed — having done the circuit innumerable times this season I know every pebble on the beach at Icy Strait Point, where to go to measure my "wingspan" in Juneau and exactly what I'd order if I went back to the Twisted Fish Grill (baked salmon fillet served on a cedar plank with a bourbon-molasses sauce on the side). It's this trip back to England that feels like the real voyage into the unknown for me.

I turn back and give a wave to the ship, blowing a symbolic kiss to Kirby, Lana, Jindrich and Co. Oddly, I suspect I'll even miss Alekos — his attention, at least. How sad is that? Jules is getting married and all I have to show for myself is an amorous sailor.

"How many are we today?" I ask the driver, leaning on the front bumper of the bus waiting to take us to the airport.

"Twenty-seven," he tells me as he heaves my suitcase into the side storage unit.

I tip him two dollars and climb on board, scanning the seats for any familiar faces.

I recognise one of the guys from the reception desk and a girl I think works in the kiddy crèche but no one well enough to sit next to. But then I see a sight that has me tripping up the aisle.

"Aleko!" I exclaim. "What are you doing here? Don't you have another month?"

He looks profoundly pained as he mumbles, "I have to leave early."

"Sexual harassment?" I gasp, spouting the first thing that springs to my mind.

He spears me with a disapproving look. "No, of course not. I have an injury."

It's only now that I notice that his left arm is in a sling. "What did you do?" I frown, picturing the offending limb being slammed in a cabin door as a woman tries to escape his Mr Tickle arms.

"I don't want to talk about it." He averts his eyes — for once he's the one cutting our conversation short.

"Well, is it broken or sprained or severed?" Curiosity gets the better of me.

"Do you really care?"

Wow. He's obviously feeling very sorry for himself. I take the seat behind him muttering, "The things you do to be with me!" but he's not biting.

36

Ten minutes of trundling along pretty, leafy streets and he's still silent. This is most disconcerting. Last night he was begging for a chance to begin a life together and now he won't even speak to me?

"At least you get summer in Greece this way." I make another attempt to jolly him up. "You said you've been missing home."

He grudgingly concedes a nod. "In some ways the timing is perfect — my brother has to go to the mainland to assist our mother so he's asked me to oversee his watersport business."

"Well, that's handy," I chirrup. "No pun intended."

"Except what use am I, like this?" he sighs. "I can't windsurf with one hand, can't even paddle a kayak — the only thing I'm good for is the pedalo."

As demeaning as this might seem to someone so jet-powered as Alekos, his injury could be worse — I mean, he could have groin strain, then where would he be?

"Here we are!" I announce as we pull up in front of Vancouver airport.

He motions for me to go ahead of him but as he steps off the bus, the kiddy crèche girl accidentally collides with his arm and I see him blanche with pain. "You alright?" I wince, this time with genuine concern — it's so strange to see this usually full-on feisty man so wounded and withdrawn.

He nods gravely, again avoiding eye contact. Obviously he doesn't like to be seen at any disadvantage and my fussing seems to be making matters worse. I find this surprising in a way — not the machismo, obviously, but I would have thought he would be fully exploiting this opportunity to be fawned over and physically "assisted".

"Well, have a good trip!" I breeze onward, stopping off at the Ladies and the magazine stand, only to discover five minutes later that he's there in my check-in line — apparently due to change planes in London before he continues on to Greece.

As I take a step forward, I watch him struggle to negotiate his luggage as he tries in vain to locate his travel documents. Don't get involved! I tell myself. It's not your problem. I go to turn away but then the nudge he gives his leather sports bag sends it swinging too violently around his body and the strap catches at his throat, threatening to garrotte him. Before I know it my human empathy has kicked in.

"Jeez! We'll be here all flipping day if we wait for you." I lunge forward, relieving him of his bag and demanding, "Where's your passport?"

"Jacket pocket," he replies, too startled to protest.

I reach inside and pull out the burgundy booklet.

"Ticket?"

He hesitates.

I raise my brows in schoolmarmish warning, just in case he's tempted to have me rooting around his trouser pocket.

"Front zip of the bag." He nods to the hand luggage I have just nabbed.

"Got it."

"Are you travelling together?" the chap on the desk enquires. Before I can reply he adds, "Only, I have a two-seat pairing at the back of the plane — you won't be disturbed by other passengers there, less chance of your arm getting bashed." He looks at Alekos for instruction.

"Are we together?" he turns to me.

This is the first time since I've known him that he hasn't been presumptuous. I look at his all-too-vulnerable arm and find myself muttering, "Yes."

It's no big deal. I'll just watch the movies — nothing gets through my noise-cancelling headphones.

By Security I'm already having regrets — why, why, why is today the day I get selected for an all-too-thorough pat-down by the female official? With Alekos watching this feels like a set-up for a porn movie.

"Legs further apart," she barks.

I'm rigid with mortification. It doesn't help that Alekos emits an audible moan as she brushes my inner thighs.

"Don't say a word," I caution him as we move on.

"What?" he splutters.

"No '*I bet you liked that!*' or '*Did it feel gooood?*'"

"I wasn't going to say anything!" he protests before adding under his breath, "I just can't believe she beat me to it."

I hang back for a second, wondering at the wisdom of this seating arrangement. I am feeling increasingly trepidatious but at the same time a little foolish at my level of resistance. It's just a flight. I mean really, how much trouble can you get into in a confined space at thirty thousand feet?

"Would you like the window seat?" Alekos attempts to be gallant but I decline — his arm will be better protected if I act as a buffer between him and the aisle walkers. Of course, I don't want to come across as caring, so I snip, "No thanks, I'm not sitting next to your good hand with all its fully functional fingers, *if you know what I mean . . .*"

"Once! I grabbed your boob once!" he protests.

The lady across from us looks up, slightly perturbed.

"And look what happened as a result!" I tease, motioning to his bandage. "You don't want to lose the use of your other arm, do you?"

We have actually established that Alekos was swatting a bug off my chest — as borne out by the squidge of green left on my shirt — but I think it's important to establish boundaries, especially when we are going to be in such close proximity.

"Allow me," I say as he tries in vain to do up his seatbelt single-handed. As I reach over him I feel like I'm clicking a kiddy into a car seat. An image I don't think he'd be too happy with.

"Thank you," he mumbles.

"You're welcome," I say, snatching up the in-flight magazine so I can busy myself with selecting my ideal sequence of movies. I won't be able to sleep a wink knowing he's next to me.

I'm just deciding whether to start with the quality drama that will make me feel grown-up and smart or the crass but prettily dressed comedy, when Alekos' trousers start ringing. Naturally it's the left pocket. He tries to reach across but the angle is all wrong for him to burrow within.

"Why did you put it on this side?" I despair as I am compelled to reach down inside, feeling the hairs on his granite thigh through the silky lining.

"The ship's doctor helped me dress this morning — we didn't have a strict masterplan," he replies tartly before flipping open the phone and barking, *"Yassou?"*

He speaks in grumpy, gruff Greek — a series of staccato exchanges, followed by a brow-furrowing barrage of what I can only interpret as complaint. I am forced to bite back a smile at his excessive manliness. Having spent most of my spare time on the cruiseship with Kirby, the contrast is really quite extreme.

As Alekos concludes the conversation, he seems resigned to whatever the disappointment might be. But seconds later he gives a frustrated biff at the seat in front — unleashing the clipped tray, which duly smacks down on his injured hand. He turns away to conceal his yelp but I know his eyes are smarting in agony.

Today is not a good day for Alekos Diamantakis.

"Something wrong?" I ask lightly.

"It's nothing," he sighs heavily.

"You react like that to nothing?" My eyebrows hoik high.

He seems in two minds about whether to admit he's experiencing any further difficulty but finally reveals, "My friend, he cannot help me this week."

"At the watersport place?"

He nods.

"That's a shame."

"Yes. It is." He flips open his phone again and starts scanning through alternative names to call but before he can press dial, out blares the tannoy announcement requesting passengers to turn off their mobile phones for the duration of the flight.

"Perfect!" He pouts.

"You'll still have time to call ahead when you get to London," I suggest in my most appeasing voice. Yes, it is high season in the Greek islands, but how busy can the locals be?

During take-off Alekos stares pensively out the window. I'm now on to the Duty Free magazine wishing the perfume section had scratch-and-sniff patches and wondering why Sarah Jessica Parker's Covet ended up in such an uncovetable bottle when I become aware that he is now looking at me. In a very particular way.

"What?"

"What are you doing this week?"

"Oh no." I retreat as far as I can within the confines of my seat.

"But —"

"No!" I chortle, amazed that he would even consider asking me.

"You have plans, of course." He turns away, dejected.

I say nothing. I've done my good citizen bit. Anything more would be way beyond the call of duty.

"What are they exactly?" He turns back. "Your plans?"

I thank my lucky stars I have a ready response. "Not that I need to justify myself to you," I begin, "but I shall be very busy editing reams and reams of video footage."

"Of what?" He looks confused. "Your excursions?"

"Actually, it's a kind of side project I'm working on," I explain somewhat reluctantly. "I've interviewed couples from all over the world and their stories need cutting down to ten-minute segments."

"Oh. Is this digital?"

"Yes," I reply. Typical man interested in the technical side rather than the stories themselves.

"And you have to go into a studio editing suite to do that?"

"No, it's brilliant, I can do everything on the iMovie package on my laptop now," I pip.

His face changes. "Really?"

Oh no! What have I said?

He leans closer. "So on a practical level, you could do that anywhere?"

"In theory," I grant, "but obviously I need absolute peace and quiet to concentrate."

"Crete is peaceful."

I give him a patient smile. "I'm sure it is. But I don't see water and computers being too compatible, do you?"

"Most of the time we would be on dry land. You could be *all* of the time if you prefer. We even have a big desk you could sit at. In the shade, overlooking the bay, very inspirational, very peaceful . . ."

"Until a parade of holidaymakers comes by, all clamouring for a ride on your inflatable banana." I give him a knowing look.

"There are not so many." He tries to play down the success of the business. "And it would really help to have you there — my brother's girlfriend Birgit has gone away with him so I am without a French-speaker . . ."

My eyes narrow. "How do you know I speak French?" I don't remember doing any "ooh-la-la"s in front of him.

He gives me one of his hefty shrugs before enquiring, "So, what do you say?"

I shake my head — giving a decisive. "I don't think so" — and then turn to watch the woman ahead of me snagging the complimentary socks on her gnarly feet, while wondering if I could ask the air steward to pluck my eyebrows as expertly as he has his own.

"So what are these stories that have been told to you?" Alekos is not so easily distracted.

"Love stories," I say, bluntly, without looking at him.

"Love stories?" he repeats, all too intrigued.

I don't really want to get into this with him so I just give him the run-through of the countries I shall be featuring — Japan, Russia, Croatia, South Africa, Argentina, etc. etc.

"And Greece?"

I blink back at him. "Actually, so far, no."

He looks scandalised. "How can you speak of love and not of Greece? What of Aphrodite, Eros . . .?"

I smile, ready to enrage him more with my dismissal: "Those are just mythical figures, Alekos. I need real people. Besides, those tales of gods and nymphs, they're all a bit acrimonious and tragic, aren't they?"

I half expect his breathing apparatus to unravel from the ceiling in response to the stricken look on his face.

44

"So you are only interested in happy endings?" he splutters.

"Honestly? Yes. That's what people want to hear."

"Do you really think these myths would have endured if people didn't want to hear something more dramatic? If they didn't find them fascinating and meaningful, would they have repeated them and passed them on through generations?"

"Well, there's a bit of a discrepancy between the listening ears of ancient Greeks and your average cruise-ship guest," I explain. "I'm targeting people on honeymoons and anniversaries. They want to feel optimistic and encouraged about love."

"Well, maybe they would hear the stories of Echo and Narcissus or Eros and Psyche and realise how lucky they are to have found it."

"Maybe," I concede.

He gives me a sideways glance. "Are you familiar with those stories?"

I open my mouth to see if a convincing phrase might arise but nothing is forthcoming.

"As I suspected." His jaw juts proudly.

I study my seat-back screen. The first film is about to start, providing me with the perfect get-out clause. And yet I hesitate — I love movies, but what are they if not stories? And there's a story I haven't heard sitting right next to me . . .

I set down my headphones and turn to Alekos. "So, this Narcissus . . ."

"Yes?" He looks hopeful.

"Did you mention him because you feel a certain empathy there?" I bite my lip at my own cheek.

He twists around to fully face me. "You are deliberately trying to antagonise me, aren't you, Miss Harper?"

I grin broadly. I can't deny it.

"Why?" he asks, plainly.

I give a nonchalant shrug. "Because, all of a sudden, I can!"

The truth is, it never really occurred to me before. All my energy was taken up with trying to wriggle away from him. But now we're committed to sitting together for ten hours and I've got him on the defensive, well, it seems a good opportunity to get my own back.

"Do you mind?" I ask, all wide-eyed and innocent.

He considers my question for a moment, allows his eyes to rove around my face and then softens his voice as he declares, "How can I complain when I have waited so long for the pleasure of your company?"

Flustered by the twinge of intimacy, I quickly caution, "Well, you have my company but I think we'll keep the pleasure part to a minimum, shall we?"

"You always have to have the last word, don't you?" he notes, tapping his lips with his forefinger. "I think the story of Echo and Narcissus is most apt." He clears his throat in preparation.

"Aren't you going to ask me if I'm sitting comfortably?" I jump in before he begins.

He gives me a supercilious look worthy of Simon Cowell. "We're travelling economy, I hardly think that's relevant."

46

I can't help but chuckle. He may be opinionated but he's entertaining, I'll give him that.

Echo, Alekos reveals, was a chatterbox nymph whose incessant babbling got her into trouble with the gods. By way of punishment her power of independent speech was removed — she could no longer initiate conversation, all she could do was repeat back what someone else had already said.

One day out frolicking in nature she spied the handsome but heartless Narcissus and, transfixed by his beauty, followed him for miles, desperate to engage him in conversation but unable to. Eventually, he became concerned that he'd strayed too far from his hunting party and called out, "Is anyone here?"

"Here!" Echo replied, seizing the opportunity to reveal herself, arms flung wide ready to embrace him but he rudely pushed her away, spitting, "I would rather die than let you make love to me!"

"Make love to me!" she wailed but he was already gone.

So wretched from the rejection she wasted away there on the mountainside, her body withering until it turned to stone, only her voice lingered on . . .

"Unrequited love," I rue its cruelty.

"Well, it was to be the ruin of him too," Alekos informs me. "In arrogance he had spurned so many offers of love that the gods sought to give him a taste of his own medicine . . ."

Out hunting another day, he stooped beside a pool of water to relieve his thirst and fell instantly in love with his own reflection. But every time he leaned in for a kiss or a caress the image dispersed. His curse was that although he knew he could never hold his love, he could not tear himself away, so he, too, wasted away until he cried out with his last breath, "Beloved in vain, farewell!"

"Beloved in vain, farewell!" Echo called as Narcissus' beauty was put to better use and made eternal in the form of a flower.

Alekos turns to me. "Obviously you don't have Echo's problem," he teases. "You say exactly as you please."

"And unlike Narcissus, you are happy to kiss a lot more than your reflection."

He shakes his head. "This bitterness does not become you."

"Excuse me?" The mood just went from light banter to heavy judgement.

"These comments that you make," he expands, "you say them thinking that you expose me, to show that you know what nature of man I am. But you are mistaken. And in truth they reveal a lot more about you. And your mistrust."

Though I feel I've just been slapped, I still muster a retort. "Ah yes, it's all my issues. Nothing to do with your ego."

"How do you mean?"

"You are absolutely incredulous, aren't you, that any woman could turn you down?"

"Well, don't you think you could have any man you want?" he demands.

"No! Of course not!"

He looks at me as if to say, "Well, that's your problem!" and it makes me want to slap him.

Well, that didn't take long — we're both all riled up and irritated with each other and not even an hour has passed.

But then comes the wine.

It falls to me to unscrew our individual bottles but Alekos insists on pouring both, as if we're cosied up in a velvet booth on the Champs-Élysées. "Do you feel like we're on a date?" he enquires as I take a sip of the blackcurranty Shiraz.

"Honestly? I feel like a guard escorting a prisoner to his new jail — handcuffs and all." I nod to his bound wrist.

"It's such a curse!" He pouts as he watches me peel back the foil from his meal.

"One person's curse is another's blessing . . ." I mutter under my breath as I cut up his chicken for him. I didn't realise I had a cruel streak but I do seem to be enjoying the minor humiliations he is having to endure — it feels like the only way I can get back at him. Does he really think I'm bitter? That's so harsh. And so unattractive. I'll admit I've been hurt. Disappointed. Crushed. And yes, it's made me a little wary. But bitter? He's just trying to wind me up, I decide, as I lodge on my headphones.

When the second round of films fires up I choose *Feast of Love* only to hear Morgan Freeman growl, "There is a story about the Greek gods: they were bored so they invented human beings. But they were still bored so they invented love. Then they weren't bored any longer. So they decided to try love for themselves. And finally they invented laughter, so they could stand it."

I become aware that Alekos is watching the same film and that everyone in the ensemble cast seems to be getting their own sex scenes so as soon as I've finished my brownie desert I release myself from the seat and do a circuit of the cabin. I see a few familiar faces from the ship but no one I think will be using the in-flight phone to send back gossip about the uptight Shore Excursions Manager canoodling in the back row with the sexy Greek officer. Round I go again. People are starting to drop off to sleep now, in various states of rumpled contortion, but when I do finally return to 60B, I find Alekos still perky.

"I thought maybe the captain made you a better offer!" he comments as I climb back into my seat.

"He did," I tease, pretending to realign my clothing. See, that's what I don't like about being around people like Alekos — it brings out the sleazy side in me. "Oh my god, you're freezing!" I gasp as my arm brushes his. "You need a blanket!"

"I'm fine!" Once again he tries to act all manly but I'm already putting in a request with the flight attendant.

"This is our last one, I'm afraid, you'll have to share!"

"You take it!"

"No you!" We squabble until I exclaim, "Aleko, you've got goosebumps the size of falafels!"

"Falafels aren't Greek," he gives me a withering look, "they are Middle Eastern in origin."

"Either way, what kind of nursemaid would I be if I let my patient shiver the flight away?" I reach across him and tuck the blanket around his far shoulder in my most patronising, babying way.

We sit for a while in silence. It's a strange thing, whenever he stops attacking me I find myself tiptoeing back towards him to prod him with a stick.

"So, have you got any more stories?"

He gives me a sideways smirk. Apparently he can't stay sulky either.

As he speaks of Muses and Graces, soothsayers and sorceresses, reality is once again suspended and anything seems possible up here amid the clouds.

Talk of Odysseus inevitably leads to our own salty tales. We've had our fair share of storms. Alekos tells me about the night everyone lost their dinner — in all senses of the word — as the entire dining room tilted sending china, wine and marinated pork flying across the room, like a fairground ride, but with really messy props.

"See this?" He shows me a tiny crescent-shaped scar on his forehead. "That was actually from the stiletto heel of a guest — her chair tipped back, leg came up and bam, she branded me for life!"

"Ouch!" I wince, mentally tracing the indentation with my fingertip. I noticed it the first day we met; funny that it's taken this flight together to discover its origin.

"What about you?" He looks into my eyes. "When have you been most scared?"

I think for a moment. "Well, oddly, I would say it was when we were just a few metres away from land in Sorrento on the Italian coast . . ."

I was sent to collect a group who had tried in vain to get the hydrofoil to Capri and were standing drenched and shivering on the pier when the canopy roof blew off. I had to get them back on the ship pronto as the captain had decided that it wasn't even safe for seventy thousand tons of cruiseship to stay put — he would have to relocate to Naples. It's not easy identifying passengers when your eyes are so full of rainwater you can't see out and you can't raise your voice above the howl of the wind but I managed to get them on the tender, only to spend a full hour attempting to make the five-minute transition back to the ship — the water levels were fluctuating so wildly there was no way we could reach the step to clamber on board. I feared it was curtains for us but being the person in charge you can't be the one screaming, "We're all going to die!" or push anyone else out of the way so you can press your mouth up to the crack in the window to suck in some desperately needed fresh air. Anyway, eventually the captain swung the ship around to offer us some shelter (and thus calmer waters) and we made it on board, where we were met with blankets and huddled through to the dining room to get a warming cup of tea. I expected all the other guests to be rallying round us in a state of *Titanic*-style anxiety but instead they were all chattering normally and tucking into huge plates of local pasta, absolutely oblivious to our peril.

"Nothing comes between a cruiseship guest and their buffet!" I conclude.

"I like hearing your stories," he tells me as he pours the last of the wine. "I don't have so much interaction with the passengers as you."

"So where do you spend a typical day?" I ask, realising I don't really know much about the manoeuvres of an Environmental Officer.

"Well, I do general walk arounds and check the quality of the drinking water and in the pool but much of my time I am in my office near the bridge, or doing crew training, or visiting the chemical storerooms or incinerator room." He pulls a face.

"If it's any consolation, it's not all fun and games for me — a good portion of my time is spent dealing with complaints!" I grimace. "If I could change one thing about my job it would be less accounting and more escorting the actual tours . . ."

"I saw you on the dog-sledding one, with the huskies."

I grin. "That was amazing, wasn't it?" I say, having a recollection of him being there, though in a different group to me. "If there's anything animal — or mammal — related and it coincides with my day off, I'm there."

"Do you have any pets at home?" he asks, twisting to face me more.

"No, obviously it's not really practical. I'd like to have a dog. One day . . ."

"If you came to Crete you could have custody of Loulou for ten days, she's my brother's dog. And in fact her daughter has just had puppies . . ."

I give him a sly look. Puppies? Is he for real?

"I could take you to see them," he offers and then gives a wistful sigh. "I think you would really love it there. And we're only talking about ten days out of the sixty you have off . . ."

I give him a dubious look.

"None of what you call 'funny business'. Not least because physically I can't."

I smile. I do seem to like him better now that he's incapacitated.

"What do you say?"

Our faces are closer now. Our bodies warmer. It's amazing the bond you can create when you are so unavoidably up in someone's personal space. I don't know any other occasion that you would be so physically close to someone for such an extended length of time, other than in bed.

"Thanks but no thanks." I try to sound assertive but the truth is I'm not as sure as I was when I first boarded the plane. The last few hours have passed so quickly and comfortably. I even feel a sense of dismay when we touch down in London. And not just because it's bleak and drizzly outside. For possibly the first time ever, I don't want the flight to end.

Everyone else springs to their feet the nanosecond the seatbelt sign pings off but my legs are leaden. I turn to an equally static Alekos.

"Shall we go round again?" he asks, almost hopefully.

I smile, first fondly and then awkwardly. All I can think to do now is grab my bag and join the shuffle to the exit.

Once through Customs he stops and faces me. "Well, I guess this is goodbye. Good luck with your editing."

"You don't get rid of me that easily," I tap his good arm with my passport, "I'm coming with you to baggage claim."

There is the strangest tug of war going on within me. It's probably just nerves at the prospect of being alone — properly alone — for the first time in eight months. Coupled with the thought of heading back to Jules' flat in the rain only to be greeted by cupboards full of healthfood — such a grim thought that even touting pedalos with Alekos seems preferable.

I turn to speak to him but he's on the phone, still trying to arrange a helping hand. He's getting on with his life. I should look like I am too. So who can I call? I know, Michelle! She's always perky.

"Oh my god! It's so brilliant to hear you! Where are you?"

"The luggage carousel at Gatwick airport!" I sing back to her.

"You're back in the country! Too exciting! I can't wait to hear about your travels! In fact, I could do with a cosmopolitan eye to help me pick out some wallpaper samplings . . ."

"You got the house you wanted?"

"Yes! We're moving right now — still got three rooms' worth of stuff to shift today and all this in the rain, can you imagine?"

All too well. And then I get a stab of guilt. "Oh Michelle, have you had to lug my gubbins over there too?"

When my mum and dad moved to New Zealand, Michelle kindly offered to house all my worldly goods in lieu of me renting a storage unit. She said she'd rather I spent the money taking her to a West End musical once every eight months.

"Don't you worry about that — Ian's already got all your stuff up in the new loft. You know it was only two boxes in the end?"

"Really? I don't take up much space in this world, do I?" I can't help but sound forlorn. "So, it's *Jersey Boys* you want to see this time, right?"

"It was but Ian actually fancied that so we went about a month ago. He's been serenading me ever since, which would be lovely if he could hold a tune . . ." She groans, adding, "I'm desperate to see *Wicked* again but I honestly don't know if I'll have an evening spare . . ."

"That's okay," I breeze. "I'll just spend the equivalent on cakes when I come by for the wallpaper consultation. How's Hazel?" I enquire, considering my other options.

"She starts her new job on Monday. It's a fantastic promotion but she's going to be working all hours."

Oh. "Roxy?"

"You know she's about to pop?"

"Pop what?"

"Oh my god, did you not know she was pregnant?"

"What?" Now that really is shocking. Roxy is party central.

"She's moved back in with her parents in Scarborough so she'll have some help for the first few months. If you can get up there to visit I know she'd be thrilled —"

"But!" I cut in. "I mean . . . who's is it?" I still can't believe my ears.

"No idea."

"You mean you don't know or she doesn't know?"

"Both! Isn't she brave, going it alone?"

I nod into the phone but I can't find any words. I always thought I was the one whose life was skidding along apace, while back home nothing much changed. But everyone seems to be busily getting stuck into the next phase of their life.

"Roxy. Motherhood," I test out the combination. "I can't believe it!"

"I know! I went to see her last week, you wouldn't even recognise her. But I'll tell you all the details in person — how soon can you get here?"

The truth is, I could be with her in a couple of hours but I find myself saying, "Hold on a minute, Mish, I think I've seen my case!"

I put the phone receiver against my chest and take a step towards Alekos. "Any luck?"

He shakes his head. "All my friends are too busy with their own lives."

I know the feeling.

"So you still need someone to help you?" I need to be clear.

He nods.

I put the phone back up to my ear.

"Ten days," I tell Michelle though I am still looking at Alekos. "I'll be there in ten days."

CHAPTER
FOUR

For mine own part, it was Greek to me.
— William Shakespeare

If anyone had waved me off the ship with the words, "Have fun in Crete with Alekos!" I would have thought they had lost their mind. Or stumbled upon a plot to drug and origami me into his carry-on case. But I've done this out of my own free will. He wasn't even begging me at the time. *I chose this!*

The heat that rushes to embrace us as we step out from Heraklion airport makes me feel like I made the right choice. I need to feel the sun on my skin after months trawling around assorted icebergs with a pink nose and a puffa jacket. Gleefully I shake off all superfluous layers and follow Alekos to where his brother has left the car for him, or more accurately *me*, to drive.

"Ah." I stall beside the dusty Fiat Bravo.

"What?"

"I don't do gears."

"What do you mean?" Alekos frowns.

"I've only ever driven an automatic."

He looks at me like I've just revealed I have a negative IQ.

"Frankly, I don't understand why they still make cars *with* them," I babble. "Why make life harder than it already is?"

It doesn't help any that the driving seat is, of course, on the left with the gear stick to the right which means that in order for Alekos to assist me he would have to contort and reach over his bad arm. Funny how quickly a good mood can be dispelled. He ends up driving, using his knee to steady the wheel when he changes gears. Now I'm the one who feels inadequate and a burden. And not a little anxious — his driving is competitive to say the least.

"What's up with the road markings?" I gulp as we merge on to a motorway painted with lines that look more like an optical puzzle than lane delineation, leading the cars a merry, side-panel-grazing dance.

This merely elicits a grunt so I wait until the traffic thins out and then try a more straightforward approach: "So, Mr Diamantakis, where exactly are we going?"

After all the excitement of making The Rash Decision in London we both zonked out on the four-hour flight to Greece and it's only now that I am thinking of asking all the practical questions that got shunted in the hustle to get me on the plane.

"Elounda," he replies. "It's a small fishing town on the northern coast. Very popular with a celebrity clientele."

"Really?" I nod, sagely. "Is fishing the new rehab?"

Alekos smirks. "No. They seem to like the luxury resorts there."

"Ah."

"You haven't heard of it?" He seems almost perplexed.

"No," I claim my ignorance.

"Agios Nikolaos?" he tries for the next biggest town along.

"Actually, I have heard of that!" I surprise myself. "My parents went there the summer before they emigrated." I chuckle to myself remembering out loud a story my father told me: every day they would lunch at this same taverna, shaded with a pretty vine-entwined roof trellis, and they'd watch the kittens playing above them like they were doing a kitty assault course clambering over all the leaves and branches and then, one day, one of them slipped through and landed in someone's soup!

I get the first full grin from Alekos since we left the airport. "Well, perhaps we will go there for lunch. See what's on the menu."

I chuckle. "So how far is that?"

"From Elounda, just twenty minutes. About an hour from where we are now." He looks over to his left. "It's a pity it's so dark, the coastal aspect is really stunning."

Personally I'm glad I can't make out any hazardous cliff-drops and decide instead to engage my other senses: winding down the window, I inhale the warm, thyme-scented breeze and marvel, "I didn't think I'd ever come back to Greece."

"You have been before?" Now he sounds surprised.

"A few times, actually. Hasn't every Brit?"

"But never to Crete?"

"No. It was Paxos when I was five. Corfu as a teenager. And Athens in my twenties. All harrowing experiences in their own way," I breeze.

Alekos gives me a dubious look. "Isn't 'harrowing' a word usually reserved for war zones and places of extreme poverty?"

"Well, perhaps I should say eventful. When I was five I nearly drowned —"

"A wave washed over you," he tuts.

"No, my family was travelling to the island on a boat and a storm blew in so they battened down the hatches which basically left my dad all cosy downstairs having a brandy with my sister — well, obviously she wasn't having a brandy —"

"I understand."

"And I was left up on deck thrashing around with my mum. There was nothing either parent could do — they couldn't let him up or her down for fear of the ship filling up with water and well, sinking, I suppose."

"But you survived."

"Yes, but that wasn't the worst of it," I tell him gravely. "I fell in love for the first time."

"Aged five?"

"Yes, and to look at our holiday snaps you might suspect it was the little blond boy from Yorkshire with the pudding-bowl haircut and velour hoodie but in fact it was a middle-aged hotel manager called Dimitri. He said I was the daughter he always wished he'd had and I took a massive shine to him. Even now I still feel a bond. My mum says that when we left I said nothing but I had tears streaming down my face."

Alekos smiles knowingly.

"What?"

"You were destined to love a Greek man, even as a child."

"Well, I don't know about that," I snort. "My teen romance wasn't so successful."

Alekos' face darkens and his worry beads take on all the menace of numchuckers. "Who was he?" he growls.

"I don't remember his name," I answer truthfully. "He was one of the hotel waiters — naturally — but the romance wasn't the big hoo-har of the trip. The real disaster was the intake of the local firewater."

"Oooohh." Alekos cringes.

"Zohhh," I confirm. "I'll spare you the details . . ."

"Thank you," he says, sounding genuinely grateful. "Though if you feel another episode like that coming on you would feel at home in this next town." Alekos nods to the sign for Malia. "A lot of drinking here. A lot of English."

"In the eighteen to thirty age bracket?" I make a daring supposition.

He nods confirmation.

"I went on one of those holidays once," I confess. "Bodrum, Turkey."

"Why?"

"That was the first word that sprang from my lips when my friend Roxy revealed the details of the trip. Can you believe there was actually a couple there on their honeymoon? I can't think of anything less romantic. I didn't drink a drop the whole time —

getting yelled at to do shots at breakfast made me all contrary and I went teetotal."

"For how long?"

"The whole week," I reply as I spy a series of frazzle-haired girls lurching down the road with linked arms and strappy stilettos, serenaded by the lewd hecklings of three shirtless, scorch-chested boys. "Thank god we're away from all this."

"Well, not entirely."

"What do you mean?" I feel a chill to my core.

"You'll see soon enough."

He won't say any more. Probably afraid I'll hurl myself from the speeding car, though obviously not immediately or I'd be stranded right in the thick of it.

"So what happened on your third trip?" Alekos prompts me to complete the Greek trilogy.

"Oh no," I swipe away his interest. "It's just another catalogue of crapness."

There's no denying I've been talking too much, desperately trying to cover my realisation that I'm about to spend a week sleeping, waking, eating and working under the same roof as a man I typically go out of my way to avoid. But despite my protestations, Alekos won't let it go. It's as though he feels entitled to know everything that has happened to me in Greece simply by virtue of it being his homeland.

"Besides, you have to tell me so that I can ensure none of the bad things are repeated on this trip," he wheedles.

"They couldn't be. It was almost all down to my own stupidity."

"Tell me anyway," he insists.

I heave a long sigh. This was not my finest hour.

"Well, first I have to mention that a week before I left I met a man. It was all very intense, he even cried when I left for the airport."

"Cried?"

It was true. I'd never experienced anything quite like it before. I suppose it was quite emotional parting so soon after finding each other, plus we hadn't slept because we wanted to savour every last moment together. It was only when I got back that I discovered just how poignant the farewell was for him. Anyway, basically the plane was delayed, twice. Once they even boarded us and then discovered a fault and disembarked us again at which point I did wonder if the universe was offering me multiple opportunities to turn back, but I continued on regardless, arriving in Athens in the middle of the night and thus unable to get the required ferry to Poros. Half the other passengers kipped right there in Arrivals, heads on luggage, but as I was alone I didn't dare sleep so that was night two. By sunrise I was delirious and decided I couldn't wait another hour for the bus to Piraeus so I got a taxi. I remember the driver looked like an escaped convict and had a bloodied bandage unravelling from his wrist. When he announced that the fare was roughly half the money I had brought for the whole week, I didn't argue. I was just grateful to get out of his vehicle alive. It was then a stray dog (along with his flea posse) attached himself to me — wherever I dragged my suitcase, he would follow. I would have appreciated the company had he been able to speak Greek — I remember going into one café but all the food was completely alien to me and I felt so self-conscious I left empty-handed. Much to the dismay of the dog.

Finally it was time for the ferry. The sea air felt good but I spent the whole time watching a canoodling couple thinking, "I could be doing that right now if I'd stayed home," and wondering about the wisdom of breaking our romantic flow. When I arrived on the island I discovered there wasn't a single room to be had. I hadn't booked anywhere because I had naively decided to be spontaneous and see which way the wind blew me. Not a smart decision in July. The neighbouring islands of Spetses and Hydra were also chock-a-block. It was nearly a hundred degrees and I was unwashed and overheated and so I put down my case and walked into the sea, fully clothed, and then walked out again, changed my clothes, counted what was left of my money, and realised I had just enough to buy a flight back home.

"So you just turned around and came back?"

"Tried to. I got to the airport, sat down to wait the three hours till the flight and fell asleep."

"Please don't tell me you slept through the departure," Alekos despairs.

I nod. "Well, at least I would have done had it not been delayed."

"So you made it?" He looks relieved until he adds, "And back you went to the arms of your beloved."

"Well, that was the idea . . ."

Alekos shoots me a concerned look.

"I went directly from the airport to his house, all 'Surprise!' on his doorstep, and he bundled me around the corner and revealed that he actually lived with his girlfriend."

Perhaps that's the origin of me never doing follow-up romance — however keen I am on the fellas I meet on board, I never look beyond our time on the ocean wave: I'd rather be thought of as the one that got away than the one that showed up again at an inconvenient moment.

"I don't like that story." Alekos frowns, looking more than a little disgruntled.

"I'm not so keen on it myself."

"So we must rewrite it," he decides.

"What?" I laugh.

"Here's what I think happened . . ." he says, swiftly conjuring an alternative. "Selena is sitting on the beach with her suitcase. Alekos is on his uncle's yacht, bored. They both decide to go for a swim, her wading in from the shore, him diving in from the deck. About halfway between the two points, they turn on to their backs and float, squinting up at the sun. For a brief moment they feel contentment and then their heads collide. They swirl around and face each other . . ."

"What happens then?" I gasp, rapt.

"The rest is up to you." He shrugs. "But I have a feeling that he takes her to his brother's watersport base in Crete . . ."

I chuckle. "Wouldn't it be nice if we could wipe out the grizzly bits of the past just like that?"

He nods, looking serious for a moment, and then reaches to give my knee a comforting squeeze. "Nothing bad will happen to you this time — I will be your guardian angel."

I can't help but emit a sigh — I'll say one thing for charmers like Alekos, they sure know what women want to hear.

Five minutes down the road I tell him, "You can let go of my leg now!" in response to which he swerves into a gravelly lay-by, throws open his car door and bounds out into the night.

"What's the matter?" I call after him. I find it hard to believe it's the rejection, he's already had so much of it from me.

"I always stop here on my way home," he finally reveals.

Oh. I sit and drum my fingers on the dashboard. I really know nothing of Greek customs other than the ritual smashing of plates on the dance floor. I try to rack my brain for insights from *My Big Fat Greek Wedding* but the only thing that springs to mind is the dad spraying Windex on every ailment from psoriasis to burnt fingers. The fact is, he's probably just having a welcome-home wee.

"Are you coming?" Alekos startles me as he leans in my window, seemingly bemused that I am still in the car.

"Coming where?" I ask. I can see nothing but blackness for miles.

"To the monastery."

It's only now that I see a set of broad flagstone steps leading up to an open courtyard. As I follow Alekos, pacing heavenward, I am momentarily distracted by the stars — I don't remember the last time I saw such a dusty diamond scattering — and when I tear my eyes away I find him gone.

"Aleko!" I hiss, tiptoeing forward, a little unnerved.

I check each archway of the galleried arcade to my left, and every outsize plant pot bursting with peek-a-boo foliage, but there's no sign of him.

It's then I spy a small chapel to my right with the door ajar. "Are you in here?" I whisper as I peer tentatively inside.

As my eyes adjust to the darkness I begin to make out the most incredible religious art — striking, stylised images of saints and sinners, painted directly on to the walls and over the domed ceilings in flat, matt terracottas, burgundies and grey-blues, branded with Greek lettering in white. To me, the tiny room has the feel of an ancient treasure box with its chandeliers of dark, jewel-coloured glass, incense-wafters in tarnished gold and a wooden altar intricately carved with long-tailed birds and grapevines, inset with gilded panels.

Alekos is indeed here, facing the centrepiece, holding the pendant around his neck with one hand and crossing himself with the other as he murmurs a prayer. I feel mildly in awe of the understated mystique of the scene, not to mention the unexpected revelation of humility and faith — I didn't expect Alekos to stand in reverence of anything except his own reflection.

"This is St George," he introduces me to his pendant in hushed tones. I step closer to peer at the coin-size metal disc. I've never noticed this on him before, probably because I've never seen beneath his officer's uniform. Incredibly, after all these hours of travelling he still smells good.

As we step back out into the courtyard, I sense a figure moving in the shadows and freeze wide-eyed as its form is revealed — it's a monk! A real-live monk in a long, brown hooded robe! While I continue to behave like I've just spotted an aardvark on a night safari in the Kalahari, Alekos nods polite acknowledgement to him and then guides me on my way.

"Is that allowed, what we just did? Are we trespassing?" I hiss as I scurry along beside him.

He doesn't even bother to reply, just gives me a "don't be so absurd" tsk as we return to the car. As if the great Alekos is governed by any rules!

"That was wonderful," I can't help but enthuse as he starts the engine. Something that I would never have experienced alone. Perhaps I might even enjoy myself from time to time this week, who knows!

We're just about to pull back on to the main road when a woman driver screeches into the lay-by, cutting off our exit route and barking at us in fraught Greek. So much for serenity. I start winding up my window and brace myself for some defensive driving but Alekos surprises me by responding in a masterfully calm, firm manner before waving her on.

"What was that?" I puff relief, still a little shaken.

"She was asking if we had a cigarette."

I look incredulous. "You're kidding?" My jaw gapes further. "She pulled off the road like that to ask for nicotine?"

He nods.

"Do you know her?" I ask.

"No." He pauses then adds, "You don't smoke, do you?"

"No," I confirm, wondering if he'd suggest we chase her down if I did. It's a good thing I'm travelling with a local this time, these Greek foibles are going to take a bit of getting used to.

There's just one more stop en route, though with my nerves still jangling, I'm not thrilled that it involves standing at the unfenced edge of a rocky jut.

"This is it," he says, breathing in, all sparkly-eyed as he makes an expansive gesture with his good hand. "This is Elounda . . ."

I'm sure I'd be filled with wonder too, if I could make anything out. To me there's just a mass of blackness dotted with limpid blue swimming pools. I have to dig my heels in to avoid following a few displaced stones down into the Jacuzzi where some rock star is no doubt enjoying the view with a pair of complimentary night-vision binoculars.

"I take it that's the sea there." I motion to the empty expanse of jet, trying my best to join in.

He nods, still transfixed. It's then I feel a pang of envy — he's got that *coming home* feeling, I can sense it. For weeks he's been sailing the Pacific Ocean but this, the Aegean, is his sea.

As I continue to study him surreptitiously, I wonder if it's possible to get homesick for a body of water and if so, what would you call that, other than seasick?

"Come on, nearly there now."

Rolling down the hill we pass roadside tavernas named Ariadne and Andreas and shops adorned with bejewelled flip-flops and intricate shell wall-hangings. Every boutique and bar appears to be individually owned. Remember what that was like? Life before Starbucks. The large town square has a pretty domed church and infinite cafés and bars with terraces overlooking a cute collection of moorings but zero gin palaces. It's almost a relief not to be dazzled. I've seen too many sights lately, I'm pleased that there will be very little here to distract me from my editing.

Pausing to let some contentedly ambling tourists cross the road, Alekos points out a restaurant called Ferryman. He tells me it was made famous in the Seventies TV series *Who Pays the Ferryman*, and looks pleased as punch that nothing more notable has occurred here since that era. I do enjoy a bit of national pride. I spend so little time in England now, I don't particularly feel British any more and rarely brimmed over with patriotism when I was resident, but that's part of the Brit charm, isn't it? Self-depreciating to the point of ridiculing and despairing of our dear nation.

"You're surely not lost?" I can't help but notice that Alekos is making a second circuit of the square.

72

"I thought we might stop for a drink!" He nods to one of the chicer establishments.

"*Now?*" I gasp, gawping at my watch. "It's one a.m.!" Not to mention the travel exhaustion factor!

He gives an all-too-relaxed shrug as he pulls into an oceanview parking spot. "We're on holiday now!"

CHAPTER
FIVE

A woman who sleeps alone puts shame on all men.
— Zorba the Greek

It's alright for men, isn't it? Travel doesn't mar them in the same way. Alekos' shirt may be crumpled, his face stubbly, yet, if anything, he looks even sexier dishevelled. Personally I could do with a good spritz and change of clothes — it really is such a warm night — but I can't let my hygiene concerns stand in the way of the homecoming of Elounda's favourite son. So many people call out to him from bars and doorways I expect children to start clustering around his kneecaps waving flags.

"Popular fellow," I mumble.

He shrugs. "I have been coming here for thirty years. I know everyone," he says, before stopping short to chat to a man in a dusty truck. They speak darkly, conspiratorially, intently. It sounds like espionage. Then just as suddenly they bid a cheery goodbye and he picks up where he left off, inviting me to select one of the stylish seating options at a bar called Friends.

"I used to work over there," he tells me, pointing across to a younger-looking joint. "It's where I met my first English love."

And no doubt his first Italian, Swiss, Bahranian, yada yada . . .

"Well?" After all my stories in the car, I expect details.

He speaks of falling madly in love one summer, exchanging letters with this girl for a year and then excitedly styling the bar for her return, filling the otherwise minimalist surfaces with fresh flowers and writing "Welcome Back, Sweetie" on the window using the owner's wife's lipstick!

"Wow! What did she say to that?"

"She didn't turn up."

"What?"

"Not until the following summer."

"Was there some misunderstanding about the year?" I reel — twelve months is a long time to keep someone waiting.

"That wasn't the bad bit," he tells me. "When she came back we started up again and this time she invited me to spend Christmas with her family in England."

"And you went?"

"Yes."

"Please tell me she was there when you arrived!"

"Just long enough to dump me."

"What did you do?" I splutter. This is actually far worse than my story, I'd only been building up the guy for a couple of days.

"She told me I could still stay at her parents' house, while she went to stay with a friend."

This is just too bizarre. "So how did it end?"

"Her dad sat me down and had a talk with me. He basically told me she had a life there — a job with prospects and I was, well, essentially a Greek barman with none."

"What a cheek!"

"Well, they were right and, honestly, I think that talk changed the course of my life. I wanted to prove that I was more than what they predicted for me so I applied for maritime studies in Liverpool, graduated top of my class, and you know the rest."

I can't help but feel a tingle of pride. I think of all the people calling out to welcome him home, people who live here all year round, he's the special one now — off seeing the world on some glamorous cruiseship. She's probably married to a photocopier salesman. Of course in this particular case she could have made the right choice.

All the same, I can't help but wonder what impact this early broken heart may have had on him. I'd ask but now the waitress has come to take our order. My finger is in position on the cocktail menu but apparently first she needs to have an extensive catch-up with Alekos. In Greek. I'm trying to adopt a "don't mind me" expression but my face is too tired to hold it together and I can feel myself glazing over. I wonder if it would seem rude if I took this opportunity to text Jules?

"If you think your sudden wedding plans were shocking, get this: I've gone to Greece with Alekos!"

No one seems concerned — they don't seem to go much for overly formal introductions here, though the waitress does at one point reach over to shake my hand. I hope she doesn't think I'm one of his conquests. If I could I'd take her to one side and explain that I am independent, that my presence here is an act of kindness at best, pity for the most part. But she's off to rustle up our order.

Just the two of us again, I look up at Alekos as brightly as I can, ready to engage, only to find him eyeing up two miniskirted girls giggling into their frosted beer glasses. My heart sinks. Just as I suspected. I can hold his attention in an area with thirty-two inches of leg room but widen the arena and look what happens. I know I've made it clear I don't like him in that way but I still find it rude. I wonder if he'd feel the same way, if the situation were reversed . . .

"Wow, he's attractive." I point to a passing guy with a jaw-length man mane. "Do you know him?"

"He's too tall for you," Alekos dismisses him in a trice.

"No he's not!" I laugh, a little taken aback by the absoluteness of his reaction.

Alekos merely shrugs — apparently the subject is closed simply because he has decreed it so.

I look back at the girls he was eyeing and taunt, "Don't you think they're a bit *young* for you?"

"Too young and too cheap," he agrees, throwing me completely.

"Really?" I do a double-take. "You mean you wouldn't —"

He shakes his head.

"Well, who would you go for?" I'm curious as I look around the bar, ironically now actively encouraging him to gawp at other women.

"Of course it would be you."

"Tell me why!" I challenge him, expecting him to flounder but he answers without hesitation.

"You don't have to try so hard. You don't exploit yourself to get male attention. You have class."

I don't even get to revel in this compliment for a full minute. All my supposed class is kicked to the kerb with the arrival of my cocktail — it's not enough that it's vast and luminous blue with multicoloured paper fans crowding the rim, but it's also sporting a giant Rio Carnival sparkler.

"Oh great," I mutter, quickly trying to dismantle it before the people of Malia hear that this is where the real party is. "Where's yours?" I ask as the waitress sets a dessert bowl before him.

"I'm not having one, I ordered kataifi instead."

It's one of my quirks that I find men with a sweet tooth a turn-on. I don't know if it's because it takes all the guilt away from my own calorific indulgences but I can feel myself warming to him further as I witness his obvious pleasure.

"You have to try it!"

I grab the spoon from him before he attempts to feed me. "Mmm!" I'm surprised by the texture. "It's like shredded wheat with golden syrup on top."

"Try it with the ice cream!" he enthuses.

"Aleko!" I hear his name called from across the street. In seconds three burly blokes have crowded

78

around and I've lost him again. I wonder if its a cultural thing, these men ignoring me, or whether any woman with Alekos is not really worth the investment of a pleasantry because surely they'll be disposed of within a week or two? I could just be letting paranoia get the better of me, but suddenly ten days seems like an awfully long time. Especially since what little advantage I had on the plane appears to be evaporating by the second. I have entered his world now. And that makes me uneasy.

Come on, Miss Harper! Keep positive!

I try to tell myself that sipping cocktails al fresco on a balmy night beats lolling in Jules' flat, but does it? Aside from *Brothers & Sisters*, she would have recorded *Ugly Betty* and *Strictly Come Dancing*. Plus there would be a stack of *Psychologies* magazine and that lovely Thai takeaway around the corner from her . . .

"Are you ready to go home?" Alekos appears to have read my mind.

It takes me a second to realise that he means *his* home.

After returning to the car, we weave along the coastal road, glinting water splaying out to our right, commercial properties thinning out to our left. The night is so quiet, I should just let my grievances waft out to sea but the excess of food colouring in my drink means I just can't keep my mouth shut.

"So how come you didn't introduce me to your friends?"

He frowns deeply. "I thought I did."

"Not to the majority of them, not to those last guys . . ."

"Not all of the people I spoke to tonight are my friends." He gives me a significant look. "I don't want everyone knowing my business."

"Oh. Well." I hadn't thought of that. "I just found it a little impolite."

"Really?"

"Yes. You know how we English love our manners . . ."

"Okay." He nods as if he's actually taking on board what I am saying. "Do you want me to take you to see the puppies now?"

I can't help but laugh. Is that his idea of a peace offering? "How about tomorrow?" I reason. "Seriously, I'm dying now. Aren't you tired?"

"I'm happy." He shrugs. As if the two things are mutually exclusive.

Veering away from the coast, we weave up a haphazard collection of dirt roads until Alekos halts beside a multilevelled angular block with a brick chimney-stack sticking up through a corrugated iron canopy. Surely not?

The front is more picturesque with patchwork stonework, foliage draped around the arched window and a stable-style door.

"After you." He allows me to step first on to the marble-slabbed floor. The kitchen-dining area is directly ahead, with an Aga, woven fabric rug and dark wooden table that could comfortably seat eight.

"This is typical of a Cretan home." Alekos draws my attention to the stone arch dividing the main room and enhancing the sense of cave dwelling.

"I keep thinking you're saying cretin," I snigger as I run my hand over the rough walls. "I am."

"No, not Cretan, *cretin* — you know, as in imbecile."

Again the look on his face suggests that he's in no doubt which of the two of us best fits that label.

I turn my attention to a photo magnetised to the fridge.

"That's my brother, Angelos." He points to a face that couldn't be more different to his own — whereas Alekos has a square-jawed Bond quality, Angelos is more lean and Wolverine.

"Is this his girlfriend?" I ask, somewhat rhetorically as they are lovingly entwined.

He nods. "Birgit. She's Belgian."

"She's beautiful," I coo. She looks almost ethereal, like a water sprite or a woodland fairy with the most delicately sculpted features, gamine haircut and pretty cotton sundress.

I can see this rustic environment suiting them but I'm having trouble picturing Alekos here — on the ship I always perceived him as quite the metrosexual: so groomed and fragrant, Kirby even saw him getting a manicure once. But this is no place for cufflinks and cuticle cream. Even Loulou the dog is wonderfully dishevelled — a scrappy, grey-whiskered, dreadlocked creature — rub her head and the fur in question instantly becomes a backcombed nest.

"You can have the upstairs room," he nods to the wooden staircase, "it has its own bathroom and terrace."

"Sounds great."

"I'll be down here," he says as he nudges his case behind the curtain that separates his camp bed from where we stand. "I hope to have my own place here soon," he says wistfully. "Some of the guys I spoke to tonight have places for me to view — once my brother gets back and I have time to go shopping."

I do my best to muster a smile — I'd love to stay and chat about the Greek mortgage system but I really do need to get to bed.

"What time is kick-off tomorrow?" I ask as I head for the stairs.

"We'll leave around nine."

"Great, see you in the morning!" I exit with the merest flutter of fingers as a goodnight gesture. Nightie on, horizontal position, out.

If only.

Lying in the dark in an unfamiliar bed in an unfamiliar room brings home to me that I really don't have a clue where I am. It was so dark on the way here I may as well have been blindfolded in the trunk of the car. You'd think I'd be used to feeling displaced but typically I'm never further than a life-ring's sling from the ship: no matter how exotic my day's excursion — from some temple heady with incense or a vast expanse of wilderness, I go back to my own little personalised bunk at night. This situation feels particularly odd, not just because I'm sleeping in someone else's home, but because I feel like I'm trespassing in someone else's life.

"*Selena!*"

Oh here we go. The night call of the amorous Greek.

"Are you sleeping?" His voice wends up the stairs to me.

"What do you want?" I grizzle back to him.

He sighs before replying. "I know this sounds ridiculous but I am having trouble getting undressed."

I roll my eyes but simultaneously swing my legs out of bed. I should have thought of this before I slipped into something diaphanous. "Hold on a minute!" I reach for my dressing gown and then creak across the rough floorboards, regretting not having packed my slippers.

"I managed the first two buttons but the rest are resisting my touch," he explains, awaiting my assistance beneath the Cretan arch.

Avoiding eye contact, I duly release the rest of his tiny pearlised shackles and part his shirt.

"Oh!" I find myself saying out loud.

"Oh what?" he looks curious.

"Nothing!" I flush.

"You thought I would be hairier, didn't you?" He tilts his head to the side. This obviously isn't the first time he's had this reaction.

"Maybe," I concede, toes scrunching in embarrassment. Certainly the black tufts escaping his cuffs had led me to presume a furry bear of a man lurked beneath. In reality, aside from the strokeable forearms, a pleasant whisking on his pecs and a fine trail leading down to his belly button, his torso is polished-toffee smooth. Not that I'm peering closely or anything.

"I'm going to undo the sling," I inform him, getting back to business.

Gingerly I unclick the clip, cradling his elbow until his arm is resting safely. Now for the grand unveiling. "Right arm first," I say, lifting the material away from his skin and allowing him to shrug free of the first sleeve. I then walk the fabric around to his now bare back.

"One moment!" I put him on pause on the pretext of figuring out my next manoeuvre but really I just need a second to take in all the contours of his back. I didn't expect him to be so elegantly defined or to have such incredibly sheer skin. Though his body is emanating a warmth that invites touch, I continue to behave like I am doing one of those steady hand, loop-over-a-wiggly-wire tests, never letting my fingers stray from his shirt, even over the bandaged area.

One part of me may be whispering, *You're alone on a hilltop undressing a Greek officer in the moonlight!* but the more dominant part appears to be channelling a department store shop assistant: "Is there anything else I can help you with, sir?"

"Well . . ." He looks sheepishly at his navel.

"I am not unzipping your fly!" I splutter in protest.

"I'm not asking you to, just the button above it. It's a little stiff," he explains, with the faintest hint of mischief.

84

I take a deep breath and manhandle the metal stud free. "There!" I announce.

"Thank you. I should be fine now."

Is that a twinge of disappointment I just experienced? "Well, if you have any issues with pyjama buttons —"

"Pyjamas?" he scoffs. "In this heat?"

"I was only asking," I pout. "I realise you're not really the type."

"I sleep naked."

"Of course you do."

I turn to leave but he halts me with the words, *"Don't you?"*

I tug at a swatch of my nightie: "Exhibit A. Nope."

"How very puritanical of you."

I should just let this comment go but a combination of lack of sleep and intense irritation at myself for admiring his bare-chested charms magnifies his patronising tone tenfold and sends me over my overtired edge.

"Do you have any idea how judgemental you are?" I switch back to face him. "You presume that just because a girl prefers to wear a nightie she doesn't know how to have a good time in bed?" I snort with derision. "I hate that you address me like I'm some kind of repressed prude!"

"Well, you are a little that way!" He can't hide his smile.

"How would you know?" I gasp, outraged. "You've never even slept with me!"

"Exactly!"

"What?" I reel. This man really is the giddy limit.

"If you weren't such a prude we would have had sex by now," he reasons.

"Oh my god, you are amazing! I mean really, the arrogance of you!"

"You said yourself you find me sexually intimidating!"

"Yes, in a totally off-putting, turn-off kind of way!" I'm all up in his face now. "Have you ever heard the fable about the sun and the moon competing to get the traveller's coat off?" Before he can answer I'm in full flow. "The more the wind blows, the tighter he clings to his coat but when the sun gently warms him, he voluntarily disrobes." I give him a loaded look. "It's no wonder women load on the layers around you!" I say, tugging my dressing gown tighter and flouncing out of the room with a highly ineffective parting cry of: "*You are the wind!*"

Unfortunately I'm still within earshot as he informs me that Aesop, originator of the fable, was Greek.

Aaagghhh! I simply can't win with him. What was I thinking coming here? Before today I hardly knew this man and what little I did know I didn't like. I hear a few ancient yarns over a couple of glasses of wine and board a plane with him to another country! I must be mad. I don't even really like beaches. Not like Jules. God, if only she wasn't already in Mauritius, I'd insist she took the first flight over. She'd make mincemeat of him.

I reach for my phone and text her furiously. *I need your man-squishing skills! The Greek is proving seriously offensive. May be at your flat sooner than expected. Sx*

Setting the phone on the floor beside me I try to steady my breathing, lying flat out with my palms to the mattress. But then I hear footsteps on the stairs.

"You've got to be kidding me!"

I'm about to reach for the nearby bouzouki to clout him over the head when Loulou jumps up on to the foot of the bed.

"Oh it's you!" I can't help but smile, giving her straggly head a rumple. Maybe I have an ally after all. "That's right," I tell her as we both snuggle down. "Us girls have got to stick together."

CHAPTER
SIX

The unexamined life is not worth living.
— Socrates

No engine burr, no message from the captain announcing our arrival into a new port, no room-mate squealing that she's late for the art auction and can't find her name badge or her left shoe. I listen more closely. The only sound I can hear is Loulou's nails clicking around the slate floor of the kitchen. Alekos must still be sleeping. I don't want to risk waking him so I tiptoe to the terrace to get some air.

The view widens my scrunched eyes even in the face of blinding sunlight. Last night I thought we'd edged up some enclosed alley; I had no sense of how high we'd climbed and I was hardly expecting a full spin-around panorama to greet me this morning.

The first thing to zap my vision is the electric blue of the sea, tantalising the half-parched land surrounding it. At the farthest ebb, the mountains recline long and lazy, trimming the horizon with gentle undulations, contrasting directly with the angular jiggle of unfinished-looking houses tumbling down to the water's edge through patches of defiant greenery. I've seen more lush and lavish views in my travels but this vista has a certain unfussed-with, take-me-as-I-am charm and I find myself leaning in the doorframe gazing lovingly upon the sea, just as Shirley Valentine did that first morning beyond her package tour. She looked so sun-kissed serene in her lemon and lavender silk kimono donated by Gillian from across the road, in honour of her pursuit of passion. Now that comparison I wouldn't mind a bit.

In fact, without Alekos affecting my mood, I feel almost at ease with myself in this moment. Nothing seems as scary or daunting in the sunlight. My only regret now is biting his head off last night. I think of his self-satisfied smirk and kick myself all the more — he was being deliberately provocative and I was a fool to react.

Back in the room, I reach for my phone — if only I could get Jules' input. She's two hours ahead but is it too early to call her? Oh! She's just texted me! I quickly press the appropriate button, delighted to be connected to my other world.

Sorry didn't get chance to reply last night — went to sleep with a hibiscus flower behind my ear and now my cheek is stained yellow. How's everything look with you in the morning light?

I grin at her message — life's awkward moments are so much more bearable when you've got a friend enquiring after your well-being! *Haven't seen him yet but dreading it. Was such a screechy harpy last night. All very embarrassing.*

Fret ye not! she taps back. *He's totally baiting you — however neurotic you were before bed you get a fresh chance this morning. Greet him all smiles, if he makes* any comment act like you don't remember what was said because, really he barely registers with you, RIGHT?

If only this were true. *He couldn't be of less consequence!* I mirror my guru. *I'm just here for the taramasalata.*

That's my girl! Keep the updates coming!

I'm about to tap back, eager to hear how she's getting on in Mauritius, when I hear Alekos address Loulou. I'd like to face him while Jules is still "around" so quickly discard the troublesome nightie, opting instead for my most Amish beachwear. Which is more than I can say for him.

"Oh dear god, do you have to?" I lose my footing and practically fall off the staircase at the sight of his stark nakedness at the sink.

"Oh! I didn't realise you were up!"

I open my eyes presuming he's covered himself but instead he has merely turned to face me!

"Could you *please* put some clothes on!" I implore, staring intently at the wall.

"What's the problem — I'm in my own home!"

"You have guests!" I exclaim.

"Guests?" he mocks.

"Okay, one guest but a very prudish, repressed one, remember?"

He sighs heavily. "Okay, if you insist."

As he slips behind the curtain to rifle through his suitcase I realise I've fallen at the first hurdle — I reacted! Jules wouldn't have batted an eyelid. Still, something tells me I'll have plenty more chances to practise curbing my disdain before the day is out.

"Happy?" he challenges as he reappears sporting a pair of red boardshorts.

"Happy that you didn't need me to help you get them on, yes." God bless Velcro.

He gives me an enormous grin, apparently harbouring no ill will from last night, and enquires, "So, how did you sleep?"

"Amazingly well," I only now realise. "What about you?"

"I woke myself a couple of times when I lent on this." He nods to his arm. "Apart from that, good. You hungry?"

"Starving."

He looks apologetic. "With my hand like this I can't do anything in the kitchen."

"Well, frankly even with two hands neither can I," I confess, eager to get out into a public arena. "How about I take us for breakfast?"

"I know just the place!" He smiles.

Initially I wonder if he might exploit my offer by suggesting one of the five-star resorts draped so elegantly along the prime aspects of coastline, but instead he leads me to a backstreet bakery and suggests I try a flattened pastry envelope seemingly filled with semolina.

My first bite is tentative but oh my! "It's so melt-in-your-mouth flaky!" I enthuse. "Like porridge and a croissant all in one!"

"You like?"

"Love it!"

Darn it! I'm so easily won over! Must try harder to hold a grudge!

Once we're done he dips into a scrappy little grocer's a couple of doors down offering to get some fruit for the beach. I follow behind, intrigued to discover a Greek Bobby Ball smoking behind the tatty counter. The fruit looks pretty misshapen and manky by M&S flawless standards but Alekos sniffs and squeezes his way to a bag full of perfectly ripe produce, at which point a second Bobby Ball appears, equally furry of moustache, to take his money.

"Twins?" I enquire as we exit.

He nods. "They have two other brothers, also twins."

"Must be something in the water here. You're not —"

"No," he shakes his head, "it's just me and Angelos," he says, putting paid to a brief fantasy of a shy, humble version of Alekos waiting in the wings.

Funnily enough the Norwegian was a twin. I never did find out if his brother was good to his evil or whether they were in cahoots as far as the womanising went. Mind you, with all the ladies he had on the go, he'd really need to be part of a set of quadruplets. Or more appropriately sextuplets.

"You really are a morning person, aren't you?" I observe as Alekos taps along to a jubilantly jingly Greek tune on the drive to the beach.

"It just feels so good to be back here," he beams, hailing another pal on a passing motorbike.

"You really do know everyone here!" I marvel.

"I should know him — he's my father."

"What?" I experience an instantaneous stab of meet-the-parents anxiety — heightened by the fact that Alekos then pulls over beside a hotel jetty and announces, "This is where he works."

He gets out of the car but as usual there is no corresponding instruction for me. Am I supposed to wait or follow?

He's halfway down the slope to the beach before he turns back and exclaims, "Selena!"

I take it that means I should join him. As I close the car door behind me I watch him greet the man with the motorcycle helmet: despite his dodgy arm they still manage to have a hearty, if sideways-on, embrace. The older man then pulls back and cups his son's face, looking at him with such twinkly-eyed affection it takes my breath away. I have only ever pictured Alekos being adored by women, never by a father figure. And whereas I would have predicted a Greek George Hamilton, this man is actually gauntly rugged and whiskery like Angelos.

As he enquires after his son's injury, I edge closer, extending my hand to greet him.

"This is Selena!" Alekos quickly remembers his introduction duties.

"*Yassou!*" He grins, introducing himself as Petros though for me it's like beholding my beloved Dimitri all over again. He's just so overwhelmingly warm and likeable. I don't feel I have to say anything fascinating to impress him, which is just as well because even if I had my wits about me, there simply isn't time to exhibit them.

"He seems so nice!" I mutter, stunned, as Alekos marches me back to the car.

"He *is* nice. Why do you sound so surprised?"

"I just thought —"

"Yes?"

"Nothing."

I don't really know why I'm so thrown. I suppose bad boys don't necessarily have lothario fathers. Just as runaways such as myself can have very stay-at-home parents. Even if they are now staying at home on the other side of the world from where they grew up.

We drive on for a few minutes in silence, both thinking our own thoughts, until some flags flag up our next stop — Driros Beach.

"This is us!" Alekos informs me, gathering up our wares and then eagerly leading me down the scuffly, skiddy pathway.

Just as I'm wondering if my flimsy flip-flops are up to the task, one sole catches on a rock and bends back on itself, thus propelling me forward and yanking the strap from its socket. Well, if I will wear footwear that comes free with magazines.

I hobble onward barefoot, with the inevitable *oo-ee-aah-arrghh!* soundtrack as the flintier gravel nips at my toes.

"Please do not injure yourself as well!" Alekos cautions as he reaches back to help me make the last and trickiest leap. "It is true that we overlook a former leper colony but we don't want to sit here with a row of arm-slings and crutches in a line between us. It does not give the right impression."

"Are you serious, about the leper colony?"

He nods and points across the water to a bijou island with a Venetian fortress, encircled by a protective wall. "Spinalonga," he says with appropriate gravitas. "They had patients there right up until the 1950s. A lot of our business is boat trips there. We take people over, leave them to explore for an hour and then go back to pick them up. Alternatively they can pedalo there in about ten minutes."

"It's really that close?" I marvel, stepping towards the shoreline and then letting my eye wander across to the lean stretch of land directly opposite us. "What's over there?" I ask, spying no discernible features.

"Well, in truth that is Spinalonga — meaning 'long thorn' — but the names got switched and it is now known as Kalidon but really there is nothing to see there."

"I guess the sea is the real attraction," I decide as I contemplate the narrow band of unpretty shingle with a gritty pathway that Alekos tells me leads to a taverna with a large water-lapped patio. Already I can't wait for lunch. Is there anything nicer than eating al fresco with a sea breeze? Maybe a little slurp of wine from a handcrafted jug? But of course there's work to be done first.

"This will be our base!" My new boss pads over to a raised area paved with flagstones, sheltered with palm-frond raffia and dominated by a vast wooden office desk painted bright blue. "This is where you can set up your laptop and this is where you can lock it up if we're both out at sea," he says, tapping a metal locker set against the back wall alongside further storage units and a small fridge.

"When you say at sea . . ." I look a little concerned, "just how far out are we likely to go?" I've only been here for a matter of minutes but already I'm finding the quiet, secluded vibe soothing — do we really have to venture back out into the big wide world?

He gives me a look of bemusement. "You have been on cruiseships days from land in far more forbidding waters than this, I don't think you've got anything to worry about."

"Yes, but I wasn't captaining any of those cruiseships!" I reason.

"You don't captain a speedboat, you just drive it."

"Whatever!" I huff. "I'm just trying to get my bearings."

"Most of the action will take place within the area you can see," he says, addressing the bay. "If we get requests for trips around the island or to go octopus hunting —"

"Octopus hunting!" I cut in with a splutter. "You're kidding, right?"

"No," he says simply.

"Well, what exactly does that entail?"

"If my arm was working I'd show you."

"I bet you would," I can't help but mutter. Even though we've established that the boob grab was an accident, I still feel I have to make the odd disparaging remark just to stop myself getting any funny ideas. I mean, look at him — there's no denying his absurd good looks, a fact currently amplified by the removal of his shirt.

It may be an inelegant manoeuvre, what with his sore arm to consider, but the final effect is the same. After last night's close encounter by moonlight, you'd think I'd be prepared for that defined torso, but in the shimmering beach-light it's hard not to want to throw him down on the sand and have a *From Here to Eternity* moment. Only there's not really much in the way of surf here. And the immediate water does seem a bit congealed with slimy frills of seaweed.

Just as well, I think to myself as I try to focus on the job in hand — namely dragging assorted floatation devices out of the wooden storage shed.

Kayaks come first. They may only weigh about a few stone but even pulling a twelve-foot ostrich feather along the sand would be too much effort in this heat.

"It doesn't seem right to have you do this . . ." Alekos grimaces as I struggle along.

"Oh come on, I bet you've let women do all the work a few times before!" I tease through my puffing.

"The pedalos are heavier," he warns. "They will take two of us."

I shuffle backwards guiding the front as he hoiks up the back with one hand, a funny look on his face.

By the third trip it dawns on me what is going on. "Are you looking down my top?" I accuse him.

"Only because you expect me to," he chuckles. "You're the prude and I'm the pervert, remember?"

"Right," I grumble as I wipe off my hands. "Maybe I'll get T-shirts made up for us, just so we don't forget."

The lifejackets come as a light relief — we sling them over the branches of the tree like we're hanging laundry out to dry. I have a brief moment of housewifey anxiety but the setting is so far removed from a suburban washing line I manage to push on through.

Thankfully the windsurf equipment is already in position in its own slatted letter-rack unit but though the boards look the most robust, they are the items I am to keep the closest eye on, in terms of protecting them from wreckage on the shoreline rocks. "Make sure no one sails them closer than fifty metres in," he explains. "From that point they need to be carried. Got that?"

"Got it!" I say, wading ankle-deep into the sea in a bid to cool down.

"And at the end of the day we have to hose the saltwater off all the equipment."

"Right! So now what?"

"We wait for a customer."

"No appointments? No schedule?" On the cruiseship everything is allocated a strict time-frame, usually designed around the customers' desire to be back on board for lunch. Here it's apparently a little more unpredictable.

"We're wide open until three p.m.," Alekos confirms.

"And what's happening at three p.m.?"

"We are going on a little excursion. You'll see."

I get the feeling I'm going to hear a lot of his "You'll see" phrase this week. But then it's probably a novelty for him to be able to act laissez-faire after his own regimented schedule on the cruiseship. He definitely seems more relaxed here.

While he ambles off to stretch his good arm on a waterski rope attached to a pole, I survey the beach for prospective clients — I see a family with three frolicking nippers, two fiftysomething women gossiping animatedly, a skinny young couple as flat and featureless as the sunloungers on which they are pasted, and a single man conspicuous in that he's even more covered up and studious-looking than me. Sitting in the shade, he seems to be favouring a bulky-looking reference book over the latest Robert Harris. I wonder what the subject is — there appear to be several photos but I can't make out the details. Still, I'm glad to see I won't be the only one at work on the beach and reach for my laptop.

"You're not going swimming?" Alekos sounds scandalised.

"Not right now, no."

"Don't feel you can't because I am unable to," he says, acknowledging his bandages. Poor fellow, he's obviously desperate to plunge into the cooling waters.

"It's not that," I assure him. "I just thought I'd get a bit of work done first." A reasonable enough explanation, though not entirely true. I'm self-conscious on the beach at the best of times but I can't think of anything worse than stripping down to a bikini in front of someone so naturally toned as Alekos. Of course I shouldn't care what he thinks but some warped part of me doesn't want him to stop fancying me. Not because I want anything to happen, because I don't. It's just vanity, I know, but it is what it is and I'm not dunking myself until he's off on some boat trip.

I open my laptop. Right, shall I start with the lovebirds from Latvia or the couple kissing at the Kremlin? Suddenly I couldn't feel less inclined to work. I want a customer! I want someone to stroll up to me and ask me how much it is to go skimming across the water on an inflatable ring. Which reminds me . . .

"Gosh, these prices are very reasonable," I say, perusing the chart.

Alekos concurs mid-sinew extension. "My brother's not into ripping people off. He just wants to make a living."

"I suppose I'm used to some major mark-ups," I say, thinking of what we charge for our ship's excursions. It's actually one of the reasons I try so hard to ensure people have a good time — I know what the real local cost is and thus I have to make my service worth the extra dosh.

"What about you?" I ask. Something tells me Alekos is not on this earth to simply make a living. "What's your strategy?"

"I'm going to retire at forty-five."

"In ten years' time? That's ambitious! How do you plan to do that?"

"I have a few business ideas that I am exploring. In fact" — he releases the rope and reaches for the galia melon he purchased earlier — "I'll show you one right now." He approaches the table with two plates and has me hold the melon steady as he starts neatly slicing it with a knife.

"You're going to make your fortune from diced melon?" I ask, taking over the chopping, keen to retain my fingertips.

He gives me one of his withering looks. "The secret isn't in the melon, it's this!" At which point he pulls what looks like a dull gold credit card from his pocket and places it under one of the plates.

"Is this some kind of magic trick?"

"You'll see. We just have to give it a few minutes."

I look at him and then back at the melon. He really is not a predictable man. Perhaps I will be able to last a week after all — how could I possibly leave not knowing what bizarre behaviour may occur tomorrow, and the day after that?

"Ready yet?" I'm impatient to see the results.

"Five more minutes." He leans on the corner of the desk. "What about you? What are your plans for the future?"

"Keep moving," I give my standard reply, only to mumble a less assured, "at least that's always been the plan."

"You don't ever want to stop?" He sounds almost concerned. "I mean, it's wonderful being on the cruise-ships but I also want to make a home for myself here sometime soon."

Home? This subject matter is so delicate, so pertinent to me at the moment I can't help but feel unsettled. "I don't know, lately . . ." I trail off.

"Lately . . ." he repeats.

I can't look him in the eye so I stare out to sea as I say, "I've thought about stopping but I'm not sure I know how to. In fact, I may have passed the point where I could." My eyes flick to him for just a second. "I understand your bond with this place but nowhere feels like home to me any more. And I don't mean that in a self-pitying way!" I try to shrug off my emotion. "I just think, ultimately, I belong in transit." I conclude with what I hope is a confident smile but I know I'm not convincing.

"So long as you're happy," he says, before husking:

"Are you?"

I take an elongated breath. Alekos is the last person I'd expect to get deep and meaningful before noon.

Nevertheless, I look him in his green eyes and say in all honesty, "I have no idea."

CHAPTER
SEVEN

"You can discover more about a person in an hour of play than in a year of conversation." — Plato

"Melon!" I suddenly exclaim.

"What?" It takes Alekos a second to realise I am urging him to resume his demonstration. "Oh, yes." He picks up a fork. "Are you ready?"

"Absolutely!" I chirp, keen to move on from the soul-searching. "If the melon's ready, I'm ready!"

Having reminded himself which plate the magic card was under, he bids me taste the untampered section first.

I concentrate hard — "Mmm-hmm, juicy, nice . . ." — wondering if I'll be able to spot any difference on cue.

"Now try this one."

I do so with a degree of suspicion.

"Well?"

I speak cautiously. "I could be imagining this but the flavour seems stronger, more intense."

He looks delighted. "Exactly! It's called a vitalisation card and it restores the fruit to its original freshness, as if it had just been picked."

"How is that possible?" I gasp as I inspect the groovings etched on the metal card.

"Well, it is encoded with the harmonising frequencies of oxygen and sunlight . . ."

The second he starts talking biosystems and reactivation, all I hear is blah-blah-blah. But I can't deny what my tastebuds are telling me.

"So does it just work on melon?" I want to know.

"No, all fruit and salad — you can put it in the fridge to keep vegetables fresh, it even revives flowers, keeps them blooming longer. You can really taste the difference with wine, white especially, it makes it smoother somehow. We'll have some later and you'll see."

"What about water?"

"Yes, we can try that now," he says, slopping out two samples.

"And this is really how you see yourself making your fortune?"

He doesn't strike me as a high-tech Del Boy type. But then he explains that he's really just helping a friend spread the word.

"If you discover something good, you want to share it, don't you?"

"Absolutely." I nod in agreement. "And for the record — I'm sold. Aside from all the revitalising properties, it makes a great party trick!"

"*Excusez-moi?*" a French voice interrupts us with a modicum of concern, probably wondering why we are staring so intently at a glass of water. "We would like the boat ride to Spinalonga?"

"Of course!" Alekos jumps at the first business of the day. "You alright holding the fort?" he checks with me as he grabs the appropriate set of keys.

"Of course, but are you alright driving a speedboat with one hand?" I ask out of the corner of my mouth.

"The ride won't be so smooth but I'll get them there." He turns to find the girl strapping on a lifejacket. Did she hear our exchange?

"Are you planning to waterski on the way?" Alekos enquires.

"I don't swim," she explains nervously. "Is okay, yes?"

"Bien sûr," I assure her, stepping forward to find her a better fit.

"You could learn right now," he says, motioning to the water. "It's very shallow here, no waves. Want to try?"

"Non, non." She backs away, plainly terrified.

"Go on," he says, reaching for her.

"Aleko, leave her alone!" I tut, knowing all too well how intimidating he can be in persuasion mode. "I'm sorry about him." I roll my eyes at the boyfriend, telling him in French that sometimes Alekos' enthusiasm can come across a little bullish.

"What are you saying?" Alekos' eyes narrow at me.

"I just told them you want everyone to enjoy the water as much as you do." I smile sweetly.

He goes to speak again but I shut him up with a simple, "Just drive the boat!"

That boy needs a taste of his own bossiness and apparently I might be just the person to oblige!

It's weird to find myself completely in charge of the business within an hour of arriving at the beach and I set about speed-reading every scrap of literature in the desk drawers before giving myself a quick test on the price list. Got that down at least. I smile encouragingly as a family stroll past but forgo the hard sell, not least because I can't recognise their accent. There seems to be quite a mix here. Quite an appropriate international setting for me to do some editing.

I open my laptop ready to get going only to discover that the mature student has prised his nose from his book and is now standing beside the desk.

"Um. Do you speak English?" he begins uncertainly.

"Pretty well, yes," I tell him.

"Great." He takes a bolstering breath. "I was wondering if I might hire a kayak."

"Of course. That's ten euros an hour."

"Marvellous," he says, handing me the money.

We both stand there. It's hard to get a proper look at him with his floppy hat and sunglasses — I'm basically addressing a broad, friendly-looking mouth.

"So?" He looks expectantly at me.

"Go ahead, help yourself." I smile encouragingly. "Pick any one you like the look of!"

He hesitates. "I don't want to sound a complete imbecile but I actually haven't done this before."

Ah.

"Okay. Well." I walk boldly over to them. "Let's get one in the water and take it from there."

We slide in the one featuring the greenish palette and then contemplate it again.

"Is there a best way to mount it?" he enquires, edging into the water, T-shirt and all.

"We're very freestyle here." I shrug. "No rules!"

"You don't know, do you?" He susses me.

"No clue," I crumple, realising I can fake it no longer. "Sorry! It's my first day."

"That's okay," he smiles kindly, "it's my first holiday so I really don't know any better."

"This is your first holiday?" I gasp. Though I can only judge him by his jawline, he's got to be at least thirty.

"Well, my first abroad. I mean, obviously you can get kayaks in England, I just never have — my daughters are strictly lilo girls."

"Are they with you?" I look around. "Your daughters?"

"No. They were supposed to be but they're in Disneyland. With their mother."

"Ohh — she made them a better offer?" I joke, in what I hope is not terrible taste.

"Fairy castles trump sandcastles," he confirms.

I nod. Not sure what to say next; all my follow-up questions seem too nosy and personal. I return my attention to the kayak.

"Perhaps if I hold it steady, you can just clamber on? Let me just do a quick change . . ."

I nip back to the shelter to drop my skirt — board-shorts at the ready underneath — and then wade in beside him. The water really is so refreshing and this time I even go so far as to splash a little on my arms while I have the chance.

"Right! Let's give this a go."

There then follow several bungled attempts to board. First off he tries to jog himself on, bottom first, but slides directly off. With increased force he goes right over the other side. He tries to lift one leg over but it turns into an ungainly hopping motion that, too, ends in a dunking and some strainage.

"Do you know, we might be better off waiting until my colleague gets back," I decide, concerned at the amount of bruises he could be notching up on my watch.

"Or we could just pretend it never happened."

"No, no, we'll get there," I insist. I can't have my first customer going home unsatisfied. "So what made you pick Greece for your first outing?" I try to distract him with chit-chat.

"Well, it wasn't exactly my choice. My wife, my ex-wife," he corrects himself, "booked this villa for us last year and then . . . some things changed," he says, choosing his words carefully, "but she insisted I come anyway and bring some friends, which I did."

"Oh!"

"But they found Elounda a little quiet and so they've relocated to Malia."

"Oh no!" I can't help groan.

"I tried it for a night but . . ." He pulls a face. "They forget that I've spent years being vomited on as the parent of two daughters with delicate stomachs, the novelty of adults spewing up is lost on me."

"Oh don't!" I shake my head, thinking what a horrendous impression of Brits abroad that would be for a newbie. "I think you're much better off staying here."

He nods. "I'm ticking off the sights — Lake Voulismini yesterday, Knossos tomorrow, but today I thought I'd humiliate myself with some watersports."

I chuckle along with him and then suddenly I feel sad. This is his first ever trip abroad, he thought it was going to be all good, clean family fun but his wife and kids ditched him for Disneyland and so he came with his mates probably expecting some beer and bonding and they ditched him too. I wish there was something I could do to guarantee him at least one memorable day but looking at the unfamiliar props I've got to work with I'm stumped.

And then a thought crosses my mind. "How long before you go back to England?"

"I've got another week," he says, looking slightly daunted.

"Ever been octopus hunting?" I find myself asking.

"Wh-what? No!" He laughs.

"Well, if my colleague's hand gets better before you go we should do that."

"Really?" He looks unconvinced.

"Yeah, it's always good to try something you've never done before when you're abroad, something you wouldn't get the chance to do when you're at home."

He nods before tentatively offering, "We did try some Greek dancing, me and my friends, on the first night we were here . . ."

"How did that go?"

"Well," he looks ever more sheepish, "they were a bit wrong-footed but I had been practising before I came away."

My eyes widen.

"Well, you see all these sportsmen on *Strictly Come Dancing* . . ." He looks embarrassed.

"No, I think it's brilliant!" I assure him. "I'm just curious about how you went about practising, other than mimicking the moves in *Zorba the Greek!*"

"That's exactly what I did — that scene where Anthony Quinn teaches Alan Bates to dance? Brilliant! I watched anything and everything set in Greece before I came out here — *Never On Sunday, Captain Corelli's Mandolin, Mamma Mia* . . . I'm sounding gayer by the second, aren't I?" He laughs at himself, giving me the confidence to venture, "How about *Shirley Valentine?*"

"Of course!" he enthuses. "It's a classic."

"Did you relate to it at all?" Curiosity wins over discretion. (I have to know — it sounds like he ended up living the very life I was hell-bent on avoiding — housebound with kids, foreign holidays a distant dream!)

"Well, my situation was a little different," he says, expanding. "My wife wasn't holding me back from going abroad, it's just that she travelled so much with her job she couldn't bear the thought of any more flights on her time off, which I can understand. And with young kids . . ."

I nod vigorously; he shouldn't feel like he has to justify himself to me.

"As far as the rest of the film goes, I guess I've been ditched by my mates but I'm still waiting for my female Costas to come along!"

I laugh delightedly, brimming with a million more questions, but suddenly I become aware of my own Greek bristling beside me.

"What's going on?" Alekos asks, so gruff he sounds almost accusatory.

"We were just trying to work out how to board the kayak!" We both titter at our lack of know-how.

Alekos does not. "You're in too deep, bring it shallower and hold it steady," he orders me, wasting no time on pleasantries. "Now you grip here," he tells male Shirley. "Bring your leg over. There." He nods to me to hand over the paddle.

"Is there anything else he should know before he heads off?"

"Just paddle steady, avoid going in front of any boats or swimmers and away from the rocks."

"Okay, see you in an hour!" I pat the tail to send him on his way. "What?" I squeak as Alekos continues to give me a stern look. "He's all by himself, I was just trying to be nice."

"When I come back with the boat, I need someone to throw the rope to pull her back in to the jetty. I was calling to you."

"Oh. Sorry. I didn't hear you."

"Also, you're not going to get much editing done if you chat that much with everyone."

Aha! So he is a little jealous. "I'm a very service-orientated person," I try to explain as we head back to HQ.

"And that's very nice but just remember, we'll be away most of the afternoon."

Ah yes, the mystery 3p.m. excursion. Since reading the tour leaflets I suspect he might be sneaking me off to the sunken city of Olous. It sounds so mystical and romantic — if I was a womaniser, that's where I'd take me. Of course I do have my editing to be getting on with but technically I have nearly seven more weeks to complete it when I get back to England and, really, a good shore excursions rep has to experience everything her clients might have an interest in first-hand . . .

The next few hours pass relatively uneventfully: when Alekos returns with the French Spinalonga trippers I make sure I'm there to catch the rope. When male Shirley wobbles back into view I congratulate him on another first and then resume my post at the desk. I do mildly offend one man by offering him pink flippers instead of black but generally things go pretty smoothly.

Finally, there's a lull. I'm just watching my laptop screen flick back to life when Alekos kneels beside me with a grave look on his face.

"The time has come."

"For what?" I palpitate. Something in his tone suggests skinny-dipping with sharks. But in fact it's far worse . . .

"The booze cruise." His voice curdles.

I look at my watch — 3p.m. already! This is our afternoon delight? "We're going on a booze cruise?" My brows interlock in confusion.

"Not exactly. Well, I suppose technically *you* are . . ."

I quickly shut down my computer, aware that I need to be clear about what I'm letting myself in for.

"Basically, the party boat sets out from Malia for an afternoon cruise and then stops in the middle of the bay so we can meet them and offer rides on the inflatables. In a few minutes we're going to load up the speedboat with lifejackets and head out to the party ship, dragging the mattress and a squid behind us. We tie the one we're not using to the side of the boat. You board —"

"I board?" Oh I don't know if I like the sound of this — do I really want to be left unattended at a floating retsina-fuelled rave?

"Your job is to assign the lifejackets and tell the people when to jump in the water ready for the ride. The rep will take the money — ten euros a person — so you just need to keep a note of how many people take rides and then tally up at the end. Do you think you'll be able to manage?"

"What kind of numbers are we dealing with?"

"Well, I don't have the figures for the passengers on board but we won't be taking out more than a hundred, total."

"Oh that's alright," I sigh, relieved, reminding him I've dealt with way more than that on the cruiseship — when we gather all the day-trippers in the theatre, there can be up to eight hundred going off in all different directions.

"Of course these may be a little livelier than you're used to."

"And a lot drunker. I know."

"I'm sorry to have to subject you to this but it's the best money-earner our business has." Alekos looks quite earnest in his apology.

"It's fine, I'll be fine," I assure him.

"Good girl," he praises my bravado. "Come on, let's lock up your computer and get going."

I feel like a rogue pirate attempting an upgrade to a bigger ship as Alekos aligns the speedboat with the booze cruise ladder and bids me climb aboard. I pause a moment on the top step feeling like I should flail my beaded dreadlocks, brandish a sword and announce that they're all under my command now, but there's no time — Alekos has already started hurling the lifejackets up to me in clusters according to size. Next comes a rope attached to the squid.

"Tie it around there!" He motions to one of the metal girders. I hear him tell me to knot it a certain way but the adjectives are lost to the sea.

"What? How?" I fiddle around ineffectually until a swarthy Greek man appears and ties it properly for me.

"*Epharisto,*" I mumble, getting back in position.

Only now do I get a proper look at the twentysomethings thronging around me getting booze literally funnelled down their necks by a man in a fluorescent lime Borat costume. I do a double-take — the straps stretching up from his groin to his shoulders are so taut it looks as though he's planning to slingshot his own genitals into the sky. I've never felt more prim or sober. The sound system is already deafening and distorted and now the rep is bellowing into her mike announcing that the joy-riding is about to commence.

114

"So if you're going to jump off the boat do it on the right-hand side or you could get mowed down by a speedboat."

"The speedboat *is* on the right-hand side," one of the more savvy chaps points out.

"Not my right." She shrugs irresponsibly.

Ah. I can see there's going to be a more cavalier approach to safety than I'm used to on the cruiseships. Nevertheless, I smile cheerily as I go to introduce myself: "Hi, I'm . . ."

"The first five are ready to go," she cuts me off, no interest in pleasantries.

"Right!" I turn around to greet them but they've already started grabbing at random lifejackets. "Hold on, that'll be way too big for you, try this," I tell the first girl. "You can adjust the buckles," I advise the boy who's about to discard his good fit. "Erm, you might want to go up a size," I encourage the curvaceous creature whose boobs are up by her chin on account of her lifejacket having a corset effect.

Already I can hear Alekos calling impatiently for me to get them in the water. Apparently this is to be treated as a lifeboat drill rather than a leisure activity. "Jump!" I tell them. "*Now!*"

As they flounder around trying to board the mattress, Alekos reminds me to keep note of the numbers.

"Could I borrow your pen for a second?" I ask the rep.

"I need it," she says, without looking up.

"Literally just for a second," I persist.

"Ask at the bar," she gruffs.

I forgive her curtness, deciding she's probably had the hangover from Hades since the summer season began. Besides, the next five customers are already in line.

"Medium," says one girl, optimistically.

"Why don't you try this one, they come up on the small side," I say, feeling terrible that I'm having to hand her an XL.

It's equally awkward when a shrimpy guy can barely fill the children's size. All his beefy mates tease him and knock him around, in that adorable way men do. I can't help but wonder if any of them are pals of the male Shirley Valentine — or MSV, as I shall call him until I find out his real name . . .

"Next!" Alekos is back and apparently one of the girls from the first ride has taken a shine to him as she has now transferred into the boat for the next round. Naturally she is the one with the jiggliest boobs and smallest bikini. All I can do is congratulate myself on having the good judgement not to have succumbed to the bare-chested temptation of him last night. Being involved with him in this situation would be a living nightmare — he couldn't be surrounded by more willing, inhibition-free flesh.

I realise just how much they've had to drink when one good-looking blond even tries to get a bit frisky with me.

"Can you do up the buckles for me?" he asks, oh-so-coyly.

"Of course." I play straight into his hands as he then starts to gyrate and give me a standing lap-dance.

"Alright, that's enough!" I bark.

"Can you come with me?" he says wrapping his arms around my back. "I need something to hold on to!"

Out of the corner of my eye I see Alekos beckoning to me. Extracting myself, I lean over the side to get my next set of instructions but instead he says, "I see you — flirting with him."

"I wasn't —" I go to protest but Alekos has found the perfect way to get back at me — blowing a kiss at a girl who's lifting up her tankini top for him. Nice.

"Listen," he calls to me as I turn away in disgust, "my father is coming in another boat with the banana. Do the same for him but keep the list separate."

"What?"

"You've got it. The banana takes six, get them ready now."

No sooner has he gone, than Petros draws up.

"Yassou, Selena!"

From this point on its mayhem. Dripping bodies are coming and going, flinging down lifejackets willy-nilly, totally disregarding my size system. I'm trying to get everyone kitted out well in advance but the majority of girls appear to have ordered their bodies from the petite catalogue and there's rarely enough smalls to go round.

"You'll have to wait until the next lot come back and then have one of theirs," I find myself explaining to at least one of each group.

"What?" they gasp horrified — from the look on their faces you'd think I'd just told them there was no more room in the lifeboat.

As a result I get adept at unclipping those reboarding with one hand and passing the jacket to the appropriate body with the other. Having handled so many sopping items, I am now soaked through.

"There you go, one extra-small." I hand the lifejacket to an Eva Longoria cupcake of a girl in a sparkly thong.

"Ewww, it's all wet," she complains, apparently having missed the point of a watersport activity.

Wow! Her bottom is minuscule, I can't help but note as she steps over the side. Mine was never that size even when I was four. And look at that guy's arms — you could paddle all the way back to the mainland with them.

It's hard not to check out all the bodies lurching around me. The vast majority of girls have figures I would kill for. I'm always telling myself that I'm not alone in my all-too-human imperfections but the statistics on board don't bear me out. Mind you, they are a fair few years younger than me. And what of their personalities? I can't help but register that some of the most stunning girls are also the spikiest and the ones with the sweeter temperaments start to look a lot prettier after a brief exchange. Equally the boys with the hottest bods disappointingly have egos and attitudes in direct proportion to their biceps. With one notable exception — one tall, brown-eyed vision has the best manners on the whole boat. Luke. He's so darn nice I want to tell him to jump right now — *and to keep swimming till he reaches dry land.* I can't bear to think of him being corrupted by the rougher element on the boat, and by that I mean the girls, like this one with a big scab on her chin where she no doubt fell face-first into the kerb last night. Whereas everyone else comes back from the ride bedraggled but exhilarated she loudly declares, "That was shit."

Though judging by the rest of her conversation, I think that's her idea of an endorsement.

"Ohhh, I'm so scared!" whimpers one cute freckle-faced girl. "What if I come off?"

"You'll be fine," I assure her. "Just make sure you sit in the middle and get a firm grip on the handles."

"Is it as bad as it looks?"

I daren't reveal I haven't tried it myself — hardly confidence-instilling — so I tell her instead it'll be an unforgettable holiday memory.

Rather like the guy with the cropped hair who's just thrown up to my left.

"Will the couple who are currently shagging on the top deck —" the rep pauses for dramatic effect, "please carry on so we can all come and watch!"

I imagine the only person in danger of being asked to leave the ship is me — for being over the age limit. As is Alekos, I console myself as I hear two girls commenting on what they'd like to do with him and a tub of tzatziki.

"Next group!"

Oh god, the banana's back again. I count my six into the sea and then run back to the bar to write down the numbers, realising I haven't logged the last outing. Now is it the fifth or sixth round for the mattress? I'm normally so on top of things but I'm not used to working with a soundtrack that is the musical equivalent of the Kama Sutra. If only I had my little clicker with me. And a pair of earplugs.

As I correct my notes, I find myself eyeing the spirits behind the bar. If I had any money on me I'd do a swift shot to un-twang my nerves.

"Right, ladies, who's next?"

Two groups of five promptly get into a screaming match, both insisting they're first. I try to soothe them but it's like trying to be heard over a double dose of Girls Aloud.

"Okay, more of the group to my right have got their lifejackets on so they're going first," I tell the group to my left.

"It's not fair! We paid first. We're on the list first!" they protest agitatedly.

"It's just a matter of minutes," I reason.

"No way. We're first." The ringleader reaches to spring her counterpart from her lifejacket.

It all gets pretty nasty, with one group being a lot more foul-mouthed and aggressive to the other. And then one girl stings me with the cruellest insult, snapping: "You need to be better organised!"

Excuse me?

I waste no time signalling to Alekos to give the nice girls extra time, and the baddies a good dunking.

This is fun! I never get to play revenge games on the ship.

My formerly high standards have now settled to a level befitting my circumstance. At one point I have no choice but to kit out a guy in a lifejacket two sizes too big.

"This doesn't fit right," he complains.

With Alekos baying for bodies, I have no time to cosset him. "You can swim, can't you?" I ask him.

"Yes," he confirms.

"Well, then, what's the problem?" I say as I nudge him overboard.

An hour later we are done. I am absolutely exhausted.

As I collapse back into the speedboat in a nest of lifejackets Alekos attempts to high-five me but I haven't the strength. Besides, I don't feel like completing any action that would fit with the word "Dude!"

"How are you feeling?" he asks as we whip through the water, heading back to base.

Spent. Sullied. Wronged.

"Like I need a drink!" I admit.

"A strong one?"

"A very, very strong one."

"I think you need raki," he opines.

"Whatever you say."

He grins smugly. "That's right, I know best!"

"You know breast, that's for sure," I mutter under my breath.

"What did you say?"

"Nothing, it's just the booze cruise talking. I feel like I need to undergo some kind of purification process."

"The raki will do that," he promises. "It cures all ills."

And you know what? He's right.

CHAPTER
EIGHT

Experience, travel — these are as education in themselves.
— Euripides

"So let me get this straight!" Jules is summarising my day back to me. "He flashed you before you'd even had breakfast, then he took you on a booze cruise where women were flashing him, and now he's trying to get you drunk?"

"No, *I'm* trying to get me drunk," I correct her. "He's trying to get me to take tiny little sips between food, which is really good by the way — there's this thing called dakus, it's á bit like bruschetta but the hunks of bread are really coarse and crunchy and they sprinkle feta on top of the diced tomatoes —"

"Yeah, yeah — if we could just flash-back — pardon the pun — to the nakedness, I need details!"

"Well, I can't get too anatomical," I say casting a furtive glance around the other diners — I've just grabbed this chance to call Jules while Alekos is chatting with the owner of Peuko (meaning Pinenut in Greek), a cute street-corner bar with al fresco tables on the slant leading down to the sea. "But I'll tell you one thing — he has a really sweet tooth."

"Only you, Selena, could behold a naked man and be checking out his teeth!"

"I mean his taste in desserts is impeccable," I say, thinking of last night's kataifi and this morning's cream pie and now the backlava that has just arrived on the table.

"Sounds like he's found your weak spot . . ." Jules tuts.

"You don't have to worry," I say, taking another slug of the lethal liquid. "I would never succumb. Not that he's not attractive. Really attractive," I say as I watch Alekos weaving through the tables towards me. "But he totally knows it."

"Is that a crime? I'm gorgeous and I know it and you don't hate me!"

"Oop, gotta go!" I clip the phone closed as he sits back down beside me. "Can I have another?" I hold up my glass to the waiter.

"Was it really that bad today?" Alekos looks concerned.

"I believe I am now officially allowed to use the word *harrowing*. I'll tell you something though — it's made me realise just how much I love old people."

Alekos smiles, offering me a little toast. "Well, I thought you did a great job."

"I didn't. Apparently I wasn't organised enough." I pull a face.

"Who said that?"

"The girl with the Shrek tattoo."

"The one you asked me to drown?"

"Not drown, *dunk!*" I clarify. "You didn't, did you?"

"Of course, ditched the whole lot of them."

"Oh I love you!" I exclaim.

"What?"

Oh no I didn't. My cheeks instantly rage red.

"Interesting how people tell the truth after a few drinks . . ." He gives me a knowing look.

"That's not the truth, it's a figure of speech."

"Whatever you say."

I look away desperately trying to reverse the progress of the alcohol through mind power alone. Perhaps I did drink too much too fast but the warming sensation was so irresistible! When I sneak a look back at Alekos I see him wincing as he attempts to shift his arm.

"Is your hand hurting?"

"A little. I jolted it around a bit today."

"You probably shouldn't be doing half of what you are doing," I note, a little after the fact.

"Probably not," he concedes. "You all set?"

"Are we leaving?"

"I thought you said you were exhausted?"

"I am. To the degree that I was actually planning on sleeping right here in this chair." I honestly don't think I have it in me to get up, not without a stumble at least.

"Well, I just need to get a newspaper from the store." He nods across the street. "Join me when you're ready."

"Okay!" I wave him off and then down a whole glass of water and snaffle all the leftovers on the table in a desperate bid to absorb the excess raki in my system. If he needs undressing again tonight I could be in real trouble . . .

When I do make it over to the shop, Alekos is yapping intently to the owner so I start leafing through a book on Greek mythology, getting quite involved in a

124

story about the creation of the world's first woman — Pandora — though it takes me twice as long to read, what with the words merging in and out of focus.

"Do you want that?" Alekos calls over to me.

I nod and then lurch over to the till.

"Anything else?"

"Perhaps something for breakfast?" It's then I notice his line-up of yoghurt, cereal, juices, et al. "Oh. You seem to have that covered."

He pays for everything and then guides me to the car. I am so ready for bed now, I suspect I'll be climbing the staircase on my hands and knees.

"Is this the right way?" I query as we seem to be turning off way too early.

"Well, that all depends on where you want to go."

"Do you ever take a night off from being a smartass?" I querie.

"Not often," he admits as he pulls over into a shadowy car park and switches off the engine.

"Where are we?" I ask, checking for cars with steamed-up windows, but we're the only vehicle around.

"Still in Plaka. I just wanted to show you the beach here; it's such a lovely spot." He gets out of the car and heads towards some trees.

"What is it with you and sightseeing in the pitch-black darkness?" I despair as I stumble after him.

"Tonight is clear so it will be brighter," he insists, continuing onwards.

I want to tell him that I'm simply too tired and blurry to care but decide it'll be quicker to coo a few compliments than argue with him.

"Careful!" he cautions my bare feet as I stumble along the wooden slats leading to this most secretive and sheltered cove. As I come to a halt behind him, a few metres from the water's edge, he sighs, "Isn't it beautiful?"

I was planning to say, "Yes, yes. lovely, now can we go?" but the sincerity in his voice stalls me.

I don't know many men who pause in awe of nature like Alekos does. So many of my co-workers would barely give our surroundings a cursory glance — once they've gone around the block a few times they're all too blasé. I like the way he takes the time to show due appreciation. There's a stillness and tranquillity to him now that I was unaware of on the ship. I feel as though my own heartbeat is slowing, encouraging me to take a moment to look around me . . .

With the piercing bright stars, black sky and liquid-platinum waters, I feel like I'm contemplating a monochrome set for an old musical number. I almost expect to look up and see Pierrot swinging his satin pumps from his moon perch.

It's hard to ignore all the cues that would normally lead to a kiss — there's even some soft music wending through the leaves of the trees — but I find that picturing all the other women Alekos has no doubt brought here helps to kill the mood.

126

"One day I'd like to sit here all night, not saying a word, just waiting for the sun to come up." He turns to me. "You're very quiet . . ."

"I'm fine," I grunt. "Meanwhile, the yoghurts are going off in the back of the car!"

He bursts out laughing, defeated. "Okay. I get it. Let's go home."

Home. He said it so naturally, like it was a place we both shared. Which, I suppose in a weird way, we do right now.

"Are you coming?" he asks.

"I'll be there in one minute."

Just because I have a "no funny business" policy with the man who brought me here doesn't mean I don't want to revel in the romance of this setting. I take a step forward and tune in to the swish and sigh of the waves as they overturn a few pebbles in their wake. Breathing in, breathing out . . .

"Selena?"

Apparently my sixty seconds are up.

Back at the Cretan love shack, as I like to call it, I quickly check that I won't be recalled for further duties: "You don't need your bandage changing or anything, do you?" I squint at him.

"Not until tomorrow."

"And clothing-wise, nothing peeled off or unbuttoned?"

He assesses his outfit. "I think I can manage. Unless you have a Velcro fetish?" He studies his fly.

127

I can't help but imagine the rip of fuzzy white fibres and the tantalising glimpse of his lower navel.

"What was that?" he asks.

I turn my inadvertent whimper of lust into an exaggerated yawn and head for the stairs.

"Do I take that as a no?" he calls after me.

"*Ohee!*" I call back.

I sleep long and wake up ravenous. Remembering the stash of breakfast goodies, I head straight for the kitchen and help myself to a bowl of cereal. The kettle is just boiling for the camomile and aniseed tea when I hear Alekos cursing in Greek from the next room. From the additional sound effects I'm guessing he's had a bit of trouble squeezing his toothpaste on to his toothbrush one-handed, and then knocked the whole lot down the sink.

"Everything alright?" I call.

He appears a few minutes later looking a little frustrated but claiming all is well. "If you could just open these for me?" It's his painkillers. I feel a pang of sympathy — he doesn't look like he slept well — but I know he doesn't like to be fussed over so I simply offer him some tea and then, seeing as I'm up, breakfast.

"Thank you," he says, taking a seat at the table.

I find myself flashing to MSV as I place each item before him — he must have to do this for his kids every morning whereas I'm a little out of practice, the last man I served breakfast to was Ricky, twelve years ago.

"Er, could you open the yoghurt for me?" he asks.

"No problem," I say, peeling back the lid.

"And I'll need a spoon?"

"Oh yes."

"And if you could cut up the nectarine so I can have it with my cereal?"

Darn, I haven't really thought this through. I can see why he ordered a meze last night — if he relied on me to prep his food he'd starve.

"All set?" I ask, hoping there's nothing more I've forgotten.

"You're not going to eat with me?"

"I already had some cereal — I was going to jump in the shower . . ."

"Oh." He looks a little put out. "Okay."

Oh dear. Was that very rude of me to go ahead without him? On the ship I'm so used to scooting solo through the buffet, grabbing a perfectly sectioned pink grapefruit and a bowl of pre-mulched muesli and chowing down as I go over my schedule for the day. As many colleagues as there are in the canteen breakfast, it has never been a social meal for me — it's more about speed-eating and mild indigestion, on my feet before I've swallowed my last bite. Nevertheless, perhaps tomorrow I'll try exhibiting a little more etiquette.

As for today, once I'm all spruced and Alekos is out of sight, I sneak back to the kitchen to do the washing-up. I feel so furtive you'd think I was planning to make off with the family silver. Frankly, I'd rather he walked in on me in the shower than mid-domestic duty but luckily I manage to get it all done before he reappears.

"By the way, I meant to give you this . . ." Alekos hands me a phone number with the names Nikos and Athina scribbled beside it. "They are a Greek couple I think you should interview for your presentation. Married thirty-five years. Nice story. They are based in Athens, but that is only a fifty-minute flight from here."

"A mere hop."

He nods. "Their apartment overlooks the marina — I thought a bit of Greek shipping would be appropriate, seeing as this will be broadcast on a cruiseship."

"No doubt with a Greek captain at the helm!" I concur, touched that he's been thinking about my project. "Thank you very much."

"No problem. Ready to go?"

"Yes," I say, gathering up my bag and towel. "I quite fancy the beach today!" I jest with him. Like I have a choice.

"Really? That sounds nice," he plays along. "Actually, I think it's time for you to learn to drive a speedboat."

CHAPTER
NINE

The beginning is half of every action.
— Greek proverb

You know how you should never get a friend or family member to teach you to drive a car because you'll both end up all tense and tetchy? Same applies to speedboats. At least it does when the teacher is as brusque and bullish as Alekos. He's clearly of the "throw you in at the deep end" mode of education.

"Go on, then," he urges, offering me zero instruction.

"Aren't you going to —"

"I'm sure you can work it out."

I survey the dashboard area with all its dials and then look, in vain, to the floor for pedals — there are none. Is he really going to let me loose like this? Oh well, here goes nothing — I turn on the engine. I look at him, he looks at me, and then at the lever to my right.

"Do I push the handle forward or pull it back?"

"Think!" he barks.

"Excuse me?"

"What would be logical?" He cocks his head.

"Forward to go forward?" I venture.

"Precisely!"

I give him a withering forgive-me-for-being-a-little-cautious-my-very-first-time! look. "I just don't want to damage the boat," I explain.

"I won't allow you to. GO!"

I wish I had the nerve to throw it forward and thus send him flying but I don't. This is a lot less smooth than driving a car — the waves seem to be the equivalent of great ruts and potholes in the road and I don't feel entirely in control.

"I'm not sure this is my thing," I quaver.

"You'll get used to it."

Alekos is not a quitter and nor will he allow me to be.

As we roam around the bay he finally gives me some guidance and, better yet, some praise: "Good!" he encourages. "You're getting the hang of this now."

As my confidence grows so does my speed. I'm starting to feel like a female action hero, especially when I stand up to the wheel. Any minute now I'm going to do one of those tidal wave turns, then dive in and wrestle with some villain underwater.

"Looks like we've got some customers, we should head back." Alekos throws cold water on my fantasy.

"Can we come out again later?" I'm surprisingly eager for a reprise.

"Of course."

"Great!" I say, heading back to the jetty.

"Start turning," Alekos advises as we approach his brother's other boat.

"I've got plenty of room," I assure him, a little cocky now, already wondering what it would be like to handle an outboard motor.

"Turn! Turn!" He goes to grab the wheel but in releasing the hand that was steadying him he falls back on to the deck. Oops.

As I yank the steering wheel down to the left I realise now why he was being so premature; it's not like speedboats have tread that grips to the tarmac — we continue to glide, burrowing deep in the water, giving me horrible visions of the two vessels smashing together and exploding. When we come to a sloppy halt with only a fraction of a millimetre to spare I am shaking inside and out. I can't believe we didn't collide. And judging by Alekos' blanched face, neither can he.

I know he wants to give me a verbal lashing but he's obliged to bite his tongue in front of the customers. All he says is: "That would have been a very expensive mistake."

"Don't worry," I brazen, determined not to let him know how utterly freaked out I am. "I would have just had you dress up in your uniform and charged holidaymakers five euros for a Polaroid; we'd have made the money back in no time."

I step jelly-legged from the boat and pretend to be busying myself at the desk until the rest of my body stops juddering. I wonder if I could sneak off to the taverna and down a quick shot of raki. It worked so well last night. But then being drunk on the job probably isn't the way to restore Alekos' faith in me.

I expel a wobbly sigh. That's the last speedboat I'm ever driving. Not that he'd let me near the controls again. It's his fault really, I decide, poutily. He shouldn't have got me so geed up, egging me on, *"Faster! Faster!"* I would have been quite content with a steady putter; he's the one who brought out the girl racer in me.

I reach for my phone and fire off a few outraged texts to Jules when really I'm feeling slightly ashamed of myself — he told me to turn and I didn't listen. I didn't even apologise for nearly wrecking thousands of pounds' worth of equipment, just gave him lip. I wonder if he's going to have a proper go at me when the customers have gone. I feel queasy dread at the prospect. Alekos is not someone I'd care to get on the wrong side of — last night in Plaka it sounded like he was berating the waiter and all he was doing was placing the order; I can't begin to think what a genuine Greek tirade would sound like. I might never recover.

And another thing, I tap a third complaining message to Jules, this one reiterating what an exhibitionist Alekos is — he's just this minute elected to change into his boardshorts without the aid of a concealing towel — dropping his trunks right here in full view! Not that this part of the beach is busy right now but he's certainly given a passing middle-aged woman a thrill.

"What?" He catches my disapproving look.

I go to ask him whether that was entirely necessary but catch myself deciding that a) I'm not really in any position to be critical and b) it's possible that I'm the one with the problem. Maybe such things are considered a normal and natural part of island life? I certainly envy his lack of inhibition — can you imagine what life would be like with no body hang-ups? Oh the liberation!

"I need to pick something up from my father, I'll be back in half an hour," he gruffs as he heads off to the boat. But then he turns back — I suspect he's going to tell me not to touch or break anything but instead says, "Call me if there are any problems," and holds his mobile aloft.

I give a cursory nod and then take a moment to slump back in the chair — I need this time just to be dazed at the near-miss. How strange that both Jules and I are currently on a beach with a man, yet our situations couldn't be more different. She's about to start a new life; I nearly just ended mine.

We to and fro a bit more, and I'm just chuckling at a particularly unfortunate error of predictive text when I realise a father and son are waiting for me to serve them.

"Oh — sorry!" I exclaim, jumping up. "I was in another world!"

"You're like my daughter." The dad grins. "Put her on the back of a jet ski and she'd still be texting her mates!"

"You're English!" I almost cheer.

"Essex," he confirms.

"So what can I do you for?"

"My son here wants to go windsurfing." He places his hand on the shoulder of the blond boy beside him.

The family resemblance is quite striking — both have a thick mop of hair (though the father's is tawnier), golden complexions and crystal blue eyes.

"No problem," I tell them. "The instructor should be back in about ten minutes or so —"

"No need — we don't need lessons; my boy had dozens last year. He just needs to practise."

"Oh! Perfect! What size sail are you after?"

"Four metres square please," he replies.

"Okay," I say, realising I have no idea which one that would be. "Why don't you go ahead and pick it out!"

The father — who introduces himself as Mick — looks on proudly as his son moves the cumbersome item to the water's edge.

"You have to be careful of —"

"The rocks, I know."

"Okay!"

"He just loves being in that water," Mick beams, explaining that whereas his daughter Brooke is super-smart academically, his son Ben finds school more of a struggle. "This is his thing."

I can't help but feel a little pang, so happy that he has found a passion. School takes up such a chunk of your young life and when it doesn't accommodate any of your interests, it's hard to feel motivated or good about yourself. I watched my sister go through a similar thing but at least she enjoyed athletics. And look at her now — stretching her legs in New Zealand!

"What about you, what do you do?"

"You're looking at the chief toastie maker at the Olive Grove Apartments." He adjusts an imaginary collar. "I think I might have found my calling — two people ordered them yesterday and lived."

"New to the toastie-making trade are you?" I grin.

"Yesterday was my first day."

"And today?"

"I've got the day off."

"*After a day?*"

"Well, you don't want to burn out — a talent like mine needs to be savoured."

It turns out that Mick has done a bit of everything workwise, even chauffeuring Barry White's limo. "Not with him in it," he hastens to add. "I bought it after he died."

More amazing to me is the fact that he actually now lives here in Elounda — and daughter Brooke attends school via video link-up to her classroom back in England.

We chatter on about the differences in lifestyle until I'm obliged to tend to some new customers — it's a great booking: three families' worth of kids all wanting to go out on the inflatables later this afternoon.

"What are you looking so pleased about?" Alekos enquires upon his return.

I go to hand him the booking details and as I do so the piece of paper seemingly morphs into an olive branch.

"I am so sorry about earlier," I find myself blurting, all former bravado instantly turning to remorse. "I was being reckless — I should have listened to you."

His jaw juts forward. "I do know best."

I purse my lips. Considering the circumstances, I'll let that slide. "I can't believe I could have obliterated half your brother's business in under a minute." I slump. "I had visions of you yoking me to the inflatables and making me pull them around under my own steam."

"I didn't realise you were such a strong swimmer . . ." He near-twinkles.

"I'm not," I sigh, frowning back at him. "You're not mad at me?" I can't believe he's not milking this.

"I was" — he looks up the coast in the direction of his father, as if to say, That's why I took a breather — "but not any more."

"So there's no chance you're going to suddenly start yelling?"

"Do you want me to?"

"No, no, no!" I insist.

He gives a cross between a nod and a shrug and then sits on the edge of the desk to watch Ben and Mick at play.

"Aren't they great together?" I smile. "The son was just giving his dad a windsurf lesson and Mick was all, 'Did I do alright?' like he was seeking his son's approval. Isn't that sweet?"

I continue to give Alekos their potted history and when I'm done he reaches over and gives my hair a tousle.

"What's that for?"

"Nothing." He smiles. "You like chatting to the customers, don't you?"

"I know, I talk too much."

"No, it's good. You're good with them."

Apparently it's just MSV he doesn't like me yapping to.

"Well, it's all part of the service," I tell him.

"Ah yes, I forgot you're a professional. I should probably think about paying you more."

"I didn't realise you were paying me at all!"

"Don't you worry," Alekos winks, "I'll take care of you."

There it is again, one of those little heart dips when he says something nice. How is it possible that he can be so bristly one minute and so gentlemanly the next?

"The boy is pretty good . . ." Alekos' attention has returned to Ben. "I wonder . . ."

I study him. "What is your evil mind plotting now?"

"He could be the extra pair of hands we need."

I blink at him. "You do realise he's only twelve!"

He shrugs, unfazed. "You say he's really into watersports, it's the summer so no school, he'd get to use all the equipment — I think it could be a good arrangement."

"Am I about to be made redundant?" I can't help but sound a little forlorn.

"Oh no!" He grins. "My brother has been on the lookout for an assistant since the season began. And from next week things will get really busy."

I watch as Alekos wades over to approach Mick and Ben — the three of them talking business knee-deep in the sea. Alekos looks as intense as ever, the father receptive, the son a mixture of chuffed and embarrassed. I edge a little closer, curiosity getting the better of me.

"So what do you think?" I hear Alekos ask.

"Up to you, son."

Ben gives an eyes-averted shrug. "Alright!"

I can't help but feel a surge of excitement for Ben — he's just received his first vote of confidence from the working world! I look around me, wishing I had someone to squeeze, feeling like I may have just witnessed a formative moment — maybe it's because I have stories in mind from my editing but already I'm flash-forwarding to September when this shy boy's self-esteem has flourished to the point that he can foresee a bright future for himself!

"Well, I think it's ice creams all round!" I cheer, setting off for the taverna fuelled by my premature sense of community. It must be all those years of having to make instant friends on the ship regardless of location or destination, I guess I'm more adaptable than I realised.

"*Yassou!*" I grin, using up fifty per cent of my Greek as I greet the young chap serving the Mr Whippy-style cones. "Four!" I say, holding up the corresponding number of fingers.

"*Tessera,*" he educates me.

"*Tessera!*" I repeat. "*Epharisto.*"

Yesterday I felt like a fish out of water — actually that's a bad analogy; what I mean is that I felt an uncertain fit for this place, but now I am starting to understand my role and be less wary of Alekos. I can feel this parched environment growing on me. Even if it is so meltingly hot that by the time I rejoin the chaps I have milky rivulets down to my elbows.

"Quick! Grab the ice creams!"

Mick and Ben do so in a respectable manner but Alekos reaches for my arm and licks the overflow directly from my skin.

"Ewww! Gross!" I recoil from the sensation of his tongue. "What did you do that for?"

"It's my ice cream," he reasons with a twinkle.

"On my arm!" I protest.

"I didn't want to waste any!"

I roll my eyes at him before flouncing off to the water's edge to clean myself up. There was a time when I would have slapped him for less. Yet in this context his behaviour seems more playful than salacious. Especially when, as I crouch down to swish my fingers in the cool water, I notice a bright red plastic clothing peg sticking out from the side of my shirt.

"What the —"

I look back and see Alekos tittering. "I did that!" he calls, sounding no more than six years old.

I turn away so he can't see my smile. My initial thought is to remove the peg but then I hesitate — something about it has the sweetness of a school playground love token. I sigh and rifle through a handful of pebbles, concentrating on the detailing of each one. This is a little something I do when I'm feeling overwhelmed — I focus on minutiae. It usually helps calm me, stops my mind from racing to places it shouldn't go . . .

Business picks up after lunch and already I'm grateful that Ben is here to lift the kayaks in and out of the water, not to mention answer any windsurf questions. Even by Alekos' admission, that is his brother's forte, not his. He's all about monoskiing, another thing he'll show me just as soon as his hand is better.

Which reminds me. "You never did tell me how you damaged your wrist . . ." I prompt him as we prepare for the multiple inflatable booking.

Alekos wipes his brow and heaves a sigh. "I wish I had some dramatic story about catching a passenger who fell overboard and for nearly an hour holding them dangling — my powerful hand the only thing between him and the icy depths . . ."

"Not quite so heroic?"

He shakes his head. "It was just a silly accident. Don't make me tell you."

I look at him. "Okay."

"Okay?" He does a double-take.

"Yeah, it's no big deal." After him letting me off the hook with the speedboat, this is the least I can do. "Come on." I nudge him. "Let's see how loud we can make these kids scream."

Naturally one ride is not enough so each little tinker gets a second turn (with even louder screamage). Consequently, come 4p.m., we find ourselves dragging. Fortunately, there follows a lull and Alekos intends to take full advantage of it — leaving Ben in charge and positioning two sunloungers under the tree at the water's edge and inviting me to join him. I notice the

142

metal frames are perfectly aligned, creating a double-bed effect, but accept that this is the only way to fit both in the shade.

"The breeze here is heavenly," I acknowledge as I approach.

"It's the coolest spot at the beach," he informs me as he collapses on to the lounger nearest the tree.

Almost instantly, he's out.

I sit down on the edge of mine, wondering if I'll be able to surrender to sleep in such an exposed environment. At least I can rest my eyes, I decide as I recline, tuning into the lap of the water, the distant sound of children playing and some island commentary wafting in from a pleasure boat. Gradually I feel myself drifting . . . and then something lands on my chest with a thud.

At first I think one of the lifejackets has dropped from the tree on me but then I realise it's Alekos' right hand. Instead of throwing it off me with a karate move and a curse, I study his position — he's rolled over on to his side and flung his arm over in my direction. As if we were in bed together. And yet the motion is entirely innocent — he's fast asleep.

Without wishing to disturb him, I coax his hand upwards, a little closer to my collarbone in the name of public decency, but I don't remove it. It feels oddly comforting to breath in and out feeling his weighty connection to me. And I don't have to worry about him reading anything into this because he's not conscious. For five minutes I lie still and then surreptitiously I turn my head so I can take in his face. We haven't been this close since the plane.

Is it possible that I've read Alekos wrong and that he's actually a good guy? He does have his infuriating, brusque side but I was unaware of his other more fun qualities on the ship. I suppose he had to maintain a sense of decorum there, yet I must say I prefer this more relaxed, natural version of him.

As I shift again, the clothes peg digs in me. A-ha! The perfect chance to get him back. Oh-so-slowly I unclip it and then reach over and pinch it to the cuff of his boardshorts. But as I remove my hand, it falls on to his leg and his eyes flicker open — caught in the act!

I bite my lip nervously, fearing what mischief this might unleash, but he just smiles sleepily at me and husks, "You love me a little bit, don't you?"

My heart is beating wildly as I attempt to combat my blush by arching a disdainful brow: "You amuse me, I'll give you that."

Revitalised from our kip, we manage to keep our eyes open for the remaining hours of daylight, working side by side without any further spats. I really like having Ben here, he's a very easygoing presence — kind of like a twelve-year-old version of an old man rocking on a porch — and thus a nice balance for Alekos' energy surges.

With the extra pair of hands, closing up is swift and soon my boss and I are stepping out of the car beside the love shack. Only this time Alekos is marching off to his left.

Here we go again.

"Isn't the house this way?" I point to the right.

"I thought you would like to see the puppies," he says casually, continuing on his way.

I am clearly dealing with a man given to spontaneous diversions. Not someone I'm likely to catch saying: "But I always have steak on a Monday . . ."

I chuckle as I think of Shirley V giving the "vegetarian" bloodhound Joe's dinner in lieu of its usual bowl of muesli. And then gasp out loud at the sheer contrast between that droopy-jawed bounder and the snub-nosed velvet beanbags that await us, swaddled in an orange blanket.

"They sound just like squeaky toys!" I decide as they snuffle a chorus of whinnies and yelps.

About to take a step closer, I'm practically knocked over by the mother, a sleek black Labrador.

"This is Loulou's daughter, Roubas," Alekos introduces us.

My ears must be playing tricks. "The scrawny dreadlocked one gave birth to this glossy creature? How is that possible?!"

Alekos shrugs. "Just as one of these puppies is blond and the other two are black," he says, handing me a contrasting pair.

"Their eyes are still closed!" I gawp, amazed at how they look like they've been cross-bred with baby seals. "How old are they?"

"A week or so." He shrugs.

"And they still can't see?"

He tilts his head to one side. "You have never encountered a puppy before?"

"No, never. Look at their tiny Fuzzy Felt ears!"

Alekos looks delighted, plumping with pride as he decrees: "This is your first time."

It really does seem to matter to him that I have a special experience in his hometown! I can't help but find that endearing and feel sufficiently motivated to record the moment for posterity.

"Can you hold them up for me?" I ask, heaping two Ebonies and the one Ivory on to his good arm as I reach for my camera phone.

"Of course." They squirm adorably, showing off the miniature leather pincushions on the soles of their tiddly paws. I do one shot close in on their suckling faces and then take a step back so I can include Alekos in frame.

"Smile, Aleko!" a voice instructs from behind me, somewhat giving the game away. It's his father Petros, laden with groceries.

"Oh hello!" I greet him shyly.

"Now with the two of you." He sets down his shopping and takes the phone from me.

"Oh, well —" I fluster.

"Come on!" Alekos beckons me over, offloading the squeaky bundle so he can put his now free arm around me.

"Hold the puppies higher," Petros directs me. "That's right, now bring your faces closer."

I can feel Alekos' jaw at my temple, his stubble lightly grooving my scalp, although frankly, any form of

146

contact with him has my nerve-endings on hyper-alert. Even in front of his dad it feels dangerous being within kissing distance of him. I just hope none of this is showing in my face. The second I hear the camera click I pull away, and go about gently setting the wee pups back with their mum, watching as they scrabble blindly for the milk source.

"What about you?" Petros enquires as he returns my phone to me. "You hungry?"

"You should say yes," Alekos instructs. "My father is a good cook."

"Oh, that's so kind but I —" I motion to the door.

"You have a prior engagement?" Alekos looks bemused.

"No, I just — I think it would be better if you and your father had some quality time together. I've got leftovers from lunch I'll be quite happy with."

They both protest but I don't want them forced to make small talk in English when they could be having a proper catch-up in Greek so I insist that I have work to be getting on with, until they finally let me off the hook.

"If you're sure?" Alekos seems reluctant to let me go.

"Absolutely, just bring a little doggy bag home with you!" I wait for him to get the pun. "Doggy bag?"

"I get it." He smiles and I can't help but wonder if he also noticed that I said "home" just like he did yesterday.

"Oh!" He catches me turning to leave. "Would you mind feeding Loulou? Her food is on the side."

"No problem," I chime, feeling a little lift in the knowledge that there will be a friendly face waiting for me.

Having had our respective dinners, we settle on the sofa and I show Loulou the pictures of her three gorgeous grandkids.

"I'd say they had your eyes but I don't know yet," I say as I tousle her.

She pants appreciatively and then loses interest and rests her head on my thigh as I start flicking through the previous non-canine shots. My snaps literally take me from one of the Seven Wonders of the World — the Great Wall of China — to one of the seven deadly sins — the Norwegian. Look at those devilish eyes! I've tried so many times to delete his face but something always stops me.

Until now.

I can't believe it! I've pressed the button before I've even fully registered my intention to do so. Finally, *finally*, he's gone!

I get up to pour myself an eggcup of wine to toast his departure and then, as the next picture comes into view, my heart gives a little squeeze — it's my mum, dad, sister and her husband and baby Betsy. Five faces crammed into one frame. A family portrait. Flicking directly from that back to the most recent shot — me and Alekos and three furry, squealing faces — I find myself smiling unexpectedly and decide to text it to my mum. It may be a less conventional ensemble but you've got to work with what you've got.

148

For a second I think about forwarding the image to Jules but she'll think I've gone all Andrex-puppy soppy and lost my mind. I can just imagine her responding text: *What next, the two of you drawing each other's names in the sand?*

Right. Tea. Laptop. Editing.

Suddenly I feel incredibly tired.

Perhaps I'd be better off having a wee peruse of my mythology book? I mean, it could vaguely count as research for the interview with the Greek couple. I must give them a call in the next day or two, to see if they're up for being filmed. Nice of Alekos to sort that out. In some aspects he is a man of his word. Unlike Hermes who apparently was a terrible fibber before he got into the handbag and silk scarf trade.

I also read about the pre-brand-name existence of Ajax and Nike. (I didn't realise until now that the personification of victory was a woman! Excellent!)

Every time I hear a noise I get a little internal flurry thinking that it's Alekos and prepare to jump up and have a little nightcap chat but it's just the wind or a neighbour or Loulou moving around.

So I return to my book and turn another page.

CHAPTER
TEN

Pray thee, O god, that I may be beautiful within.
— Socrates

I'm half awake, half dreaming of Apollo, appealing to him as the Greek god of medicine to ease the pain in Alekos' hand, when I sense a presence beside me in the room. With my eyes still closed I extend a foot to the end of the bed and meet matted fur. It's not Loulou, she's still in position.

"Aleko?" I croak.

"Did I wake you?" He sounds concerned.

"What is it?" I daren't look in his direction — his naked groin could well be at eye level.

"There's something I want to show you."

Oh here we go. "Please tell me you've got some clothes on."

"Of course! Come with me . . ." His hand locates mine beneath the sheet and draws me from the bed, knocking my mythology book to the floor.

In my mind it's roughly 3 a.m. but as he opens the French windows I am instantly infused with the burnished glow of sunrise.

I move in a trance to the furthermost edge of the roof terrace and behold the searing globe of gold as it hovers above the horizon, diffusing a peachy light into the air-force-blue sky. "Mmmm!" I murmur, breathing it all in.

Turning to face my early morning caller, I notice he has a very specific look in his eyes. Only then does it dawn on me that, backlit by sunlight, my nightdress now has all the silhouette-shielding properties of cellophane. I'm about to clutch at myself and run inside when I realise his eyes are not roving lasciviously over my body, but simply studying my face.

"You look so pretty," he sighs.

I gaze at him in disbelief. First thing in the morning he says this? This light must be ultra-flattering to skin tone as well as scenery.

"Do you think you will return to sleep?" He tilts his head at me.

I look at my watch — there're nearly three hours before we're due at the beach. "I don't know." I look back at the view — the sun itself seems to be sending out a golden runway across the water to meet me. "Suddenly I feel like I want to get out and explore!"

A beam spreads across his face. "Good. Then I shall take you to the cave where Zeus got born."

"Got born?" I grin back at him. A night spent dreaming in Greek has obviously tweaked his near-perfect English.

"Anyway," he shrugs, "considering your new interest in mythology, I would think this trip was essential."

"Essential," I echo. Well, how can I resist? "I'll be ready in ten."

Ordinarily I'd rush to the mirror to inspect my newfound prettiness but today I avoid the potentially disappointing reality, preferring to go with the look in his eyes — it made me feel so much better on the inside.

With just a quick stop for pastries, we're on our way to the region known as the Lasithi Plateau.

It's a novelty for me to be on an excursion I didn't arrange myself — I really have no clue what lies ahead. That said, as we climb the hill taking us out of town, I have a distinct moment of déjà vu.

"Is this where we stopped on the first night?" I ask. "You know, for you to show me the view?"

He nods.

"*Now I get it!*" I coo. This is such a different experience to that initial blackness. Back then I could barely distinguish between land and sea, now I see Elounda Bay in all its languorous beauty, including the necklace-like isthmus reaching out towards the uninhabited island that creates the shelter for our watersporters. It occurs to me that I am also seeing Alekos in a different light. Yes, he continues to infuriate and provoke me but it's hard not to like someone brimming with such impulse and energy, especially when they seem so eager to please you.

Of course, *like* plus *fancy* could equal a whole lot of *trouble* so I decide to try to focus on the mythology.

"So tell me all about Zeus," I request.

"Zeus?" he begins. "Zeus was the ultimate womaniser."

My heart sinks. Of all the things he could have said about him — *Most powerful of all Olympian gods!*

Supreme ruler of the universe! God of thunder and lightning! — did he just choose the quality he identifies with the most?

"He had such an insatiable lust that his mother could foresee only problems for him and any future wife so she forbade him to ever marry."

"Is that why you haven't married?" I ask.

From the look on his face, I'm guessing it's a little early for personal interrogations. I attempt to soften my line of questioning by adding, "What I meant to ask was, did your mother give you any advice about women when you were growing up?"

"I thought you wanted to hear about Zeus."

"I do. Kind of. I was just curious, while we were on the subject."

"She thinks I should try a Greek girl," he deadpans.

"You mean you haven't?" I gasp.

"Yes, but not so often."

"Any particular reason for that?" This is fascinating to me.

He looks a little awkward as he reveals, "When I was at school in Athens I could not get a date; when I came to Elounda in the summer and there were girls on holiday from other countries . . ."

"Better luck?"

He nods.

How interesting. There are several ways you could interpret that. Mind you, the same could be said of me: I've never fared well with my fellow countrymen. Apparently Alekos and I have something in common after all.

"So, you were saying," I try to get back on track. "Zeus' mother banned him from marrying . . ."

"Yes, and he was so incensed he violated her."

"Oh." I recoil, setting down my pastry. "That's not very nice."

"No, but they were both transformed into serpents at the time," he says, as if this makes it less of a crime. "His first real lover was a shape-shifter called Metis who conceived the goddess Athena but I'll tell you more about that when we're at the cave."

He goes on to list a whole catalogue of Zeus' other conquests, including two aunts and his sister Demeter, resulting in offspring such as Persephone, Queen of the Underworld, and the nine Muses, conceived from nine straight nights of making love.

"How did he ever have time to rule the universe?" I marvel.

Alekos shrugs. "I don't know, but he was considered a very fair ruler."

"Any more children?"

"Plenty. Including the two most beautiful Olympians of all — Apollo and Artemis." He looks at me. "You are connected to Artemis, you know?"

"I am?"

"She's the virgin goddess of the hunt but also strongly associated with the moon."

"And?" I'm missing the connection.

"Selene was goddess of the moon." His brow furrows. "You know 'selene' is the Greek word for the moon?"

154

"Really?" I can't believe it's taken me thirty-two years to discover my name has a Greek origin!

"I've never told you that?" He looks astounded that he missed such a good line. "Oh well." He smiles apologetically. "You are the moon."

Despite the inopportune daylight delivery, I can't help but feel imbued with extra allure and practise seductively mouthing, "I am the moon!" to myself before enquiring, "What does your name mean?"

He mumbles something I mishear as predator.

"No, *protector*," he corrects me.

There it is again. The niggling sensation that I may have misjudged him. The truth is I do feel in safe hands with him. Or at least safe *hand*. Even though we are winding up and up ever more precarious cliff roads devoid of any barriers, I'm not worried.

At least not until I notice the Low Petrol sign flashing.

"Oh no," he starts to laugh.

"You think this is funny?" I snort, contemplating the ever-increasing gradient of the mod-con-free wilderness surrounding us. "Funny is me trying to push the car up these vertical slopes!"

Still we continue on, weaving higher and higher. Every time there's any kind of dip or downturn he switches off the engine so we can glide and conserve what little fuel remains. Though my stomach is twitching with anxiety, I find it hard to believe that something so mundane as running out of petrol could happen to Alekos, the man with a plan. *The protector . . .*

"I thought the whole deal with a plateau is that it's flat!" I'm getting impatient now. "Why do we keep going *up?!*"

He gives one of his classic "don't know" shrugs, adding, "I've never been here before."

I may be relieved that the birthplace of the most womanising god isn't on Alekos' regular pilgrimage route like St George's monastery, but this is tempered by the greater odds of getting stranded. The mountain range is visually dramatic but excessively bleak. It doesn't help that I spy a vulture circling us, the only car on the road.

"Am I seeing things?" I gasp, suddenly erect in my seat.

"What?" Alekos squints ahead.

I point to a small sign over to our left. "Petrol eight kilometres!" I whoop.

"Hermes has saved us!" Alekos winks.

I watch the odometer intently but it clicks to eight and then nine and ten kilometres and there's still no petrol pump in sight. "It doesn't make any sense!" I despair. "There were no turnings, no off-roads . . ." And then I remember that Hermes was the greatest fibber of the gods.

We trickle on, in silence now as the potential repercussions of breaking down hit home. Just when I'm about to call "Lunch is served!" to the vulture, a garage appears. And not just a solitary pump but a full service station with all the bells and whistles and teeth-rotting snacks you'd find on the M25. I'm so happy I'm tempted to change the oil and rotate the tyres just for the hell of it.

"You were really worried there, weren't you?" Alekos leans on the car as the petrol chugs into the tank.

"Weren't you?" I ask.

"I always have faith that things will work out in the end," he replies, holding my gaze, no jiggling of eyebrows, just steady.

Apparently it's not just the car shifting gears. Alekos was always so full speed ahead in his attentiveness on the ship, but perhaps because he knows we still have a week of quality time ahead of us, he knows he can ease off the accelerator, take the time to cruise a little. Or perhaps he's simply preoccupied with finding Zeus' cave, which continues to elude us.

We see a sign confirming we're on the right road but then every time the road splits there are no markings to guide us, so we have to make a choice and then, five miles or so along, we find out if it was the right one.

"Is this a Greek thing?" I wonder out loud.

Alekos doesn't reply and the mythology lesson is suspended as he's now spending more time leaning out the window asking directions than he is in the car. He asks the man riding side-saddle on a donkey, the woman on the olive oil stall, and a youth, so eager to help us that he literally runs to our aid. They babble feverishly back and forth, but when I ask Alekos to translate he simply says, "They said we're going the right way."

We're buzzing through villages now, every one with a wizened couple squatting by the roadside, seemingly with the express purpose of staring glassy-eyed at us as we pass.

"You know, I forgot to mention that Zeus had an affair with Selene," Alekos remarks as we pass for the third time through a narrow passage between two buildings layered with embroidered tablecloths, price tags wafting in the breeze.

"The womaniser and the moon?" I ponder, significantly. "How did that end?"

"Well, it wasn't ideal . . ."

"I suppose he ran off with another goddess?" I predict. "Perhaps a niece this time?"

"Actually she was in love with someone else."

"Really?" I wasn't expecting that. "Who?"

"Endymion — a king or a shepherd depending on the version of the story. Left or right?"

"Left," I pick randomly; it doesn't seem to make much difference.

"Either way he was an extremely handsome mortal, but vain — when Zeus offered him the chance to determine his own fate he chose to preserve his looks by sleeping for all eternity without ageing. They say Selene visited him every night and kissed him with her moon rays but, in essence, she was alone from then on."

I sigh. How frustrating lying next to someone, able to feel their breath and their skin but unable to interact or even look in their eyes. "I don't suppose the insatiable Mr Zeus mooned over Selene for too long, pardon the pun . . ."

158

He shakes his head. "For him the list goes on and on. What about you, have you had many sexual partners?"

"What?" I laugh. Did he really just ask me that? Surely that's my question for him!

"You heard me," he persists.

I think for a moment, pretending to be counting. "Well, more than Artemis but less than Zeus," I say, giving him a figure between nought and about a billion. "What about you?"

It's the million-euro question, neatly avoided as we unexpectedly arrive at the cave car park, along with coachloads of tourists. Where did they all come from?

Alekos goes to step out of the car but I put my hand on his good arm. "You didn't answer."

"Neither did you, not really." He shrugs. "Anyway, does it matter?"

I can't help but feel it does. If he was wired to a lie detector right now and the truth was twenty women I would have a whole different take on him. My current perception of him lies more around the two hundred mark. I tell him someone's past doesn't matter to me as much as how they're planning to behave in the future but I have to be realistic: "As Dr Phil says, the past is the best predictor of future behaviour."

"And every day is a new beginning," Alekos counters. "A chance to start afresh, to reinvent yourself."

"I think you've been reading too many stories of shape-shifters," I tell him.

"Perhaps," he concedes. "But watch me become a Cretan goat as I climb this hill!"

The metamorphosis is convincing. He is sure-footed and steady as he progresses up the flagstone pathway. Meanwhile, I more closely resemble a waddling sea lion. I haven't been going more than five minutes but already my back is streaming with sweat, my heart is yammering and my tendons are twanging audibly. A total workout in this heat is just too much.

"Aleko!" I wheeze ahead to him in anguish. He trots back down towards me. "I hate to be a bore," I pant, "but the leaflet says there's a gentler path to the cave. Do you think we could take that?"

"This is the gentler one," a middle-aged Brit tells me, on her way down.

"Really?" I gulp, horrified.

"I know!" she sympathises, flush-faced even from the descent.

"Is it worth it?" I cut to the chase.

She pauses to reply. "Well, put it this way, I'm glad I did it but I wouldn't do it again."

We have a brief confab and then I turn to Alekos. "Listen, I don't mean to be ungrateful and I've loved the drive but —"

His brow furrows. "What are you saying?"

"I don't think I can make it. This certainly isn't something I'd put my cruise groups through. I'd have to grade it *strenuous* —"

"Come on," he says, turning back up the path.

"Wait! I'm serious! It's at least another twenty minutes' trek and I honestly would expire before we got there."

"You just need some water. There's a spring right here."

"Where?"

He points ahead.

"I can't see it."

It's then he produces a bottle of water from his side pocket. And refuses to give me a sip until I've taken another ten paces. And then another ten. It's pure torture — the chasm between our physical ability has never been greater. I try to imagine a situation in which I'd have the upper hand and he'd be struggling as I am now but I can't come up with one. Already he's on the next loop. It's then I decide to cut barefoot through the brambles and the rocks to the next level. Any injuries I sustain in the process will heal, but if my heart explodes that's it, I'm done.

"Well, hello!" he greets me with a grin, seemingly impressed by my ingenuity. "Who's the mountain goat now?"

We continue on, him snaking up the path, me clawing up the short cuts. He is now carrying my bag for me, and looks most fetching accessorised with pistachio-green leather.

"You can do it!" he encourages as I make my last undignified stagger to the cave mouth.

Though I'm barely able to hear myself over the throbbing in my head, I thank him for persuading me to see it through.

"You haven't seen the cave yet!"

"That's irrelevant. I would have been annoyed with myself for giving up," I tell him. "Besides, look at all this!" I use my last scrap of energy to make a grand sweep at the vista. Finally I get to see the plateau!

Extending for miles in every direction, the fields of gold, tan and textured amber — bobbled intermittently with green — are the perfect match for that sunrise feeling. It's just so *expansive* here. I take it Alekos is feeling the same way because he climbs up on the wall and throws his good arm wide — lord of all he surveys! Look at him! There's arrogance you despise and arrogance that makes you smile. Or maybe it's not arrogance at all, just a wholehearted lust for life.

"Take a picture!" he demands, gleeful as a child.

As I raise my camera to capture his pose, I have an unexpected thought — namely, what a good father Alekos would make. He's clearly an effective disciplinarian — Supernanny could rent him out as a role model for all those fathers who give in to infant demands and protestations. Look at the trip up here — without him I certainly would have caved. And that would have meant forgoing this tawny majesty, all because I got a bit hot and bothered. So not only does he see things through, he believes you can too. He eggs you on to have a go — like driving the speedboat and making me try taramasalata for the first time in Plaka. Maybe it's not just kids he'd be good to have around. Maybe he's good for adults too. Maybe he's good for me!

I catch myself feeling quite giddy and decide it must be the altitude — the sooner I lower myself into the dank depths of the cave the better.

The stone steps are slicked with moss so I keep my feet bare as I descend, wobbly-legged, into the craggy green-lit hollow. Ridged and layered with stalactites, it strikes me more as a place of goblins and ghouls than gods.

"So this is where Zeus got born?"

Alekos nods, edging me to our own private nook, out of the path of the tour groups. "There's a story behind it."

"Of course there is." I smile receptively at him.

"First you need to know that prior to the conception of Zeus, his father Cronus had eaten all five of Zeus' brothers and sisters —"

"*Eaten them?*" I interrupt, thinking the quirky acoustics must surely have distorted his words.

"Yes, eaten them — Cronus had been warned that he would one day be overthrown by his own son and he didn't want this to happen so every time his wife Rhea gave birth, he would swallow the baby whole."

"Oh, I see," I say, as if this makes perfect sense now.

"But by the time Rhea was pregnant with child number six she'd had enough and implored her all-powerful parents to find a way to conceal him, so they sent her to Crete to give birth in secret in a cave . . ."

"Oh my god!" I exclaim. "They made her walk all the way up here *pregnant?*"

Alekos disregards my outrage and continues, "She left baby Zeus to be raised by Gaia, Mother Earth in essence, and then returned to Cronus with a rock wrapped in swaddling clothes. Without checking first, he swallowed the rock whole!"

And to think I have a problem with pips in grapes.

"Years later Zeus met his father for the first time, taking employment as his cupbearer so that he could serve him a potion to make him vomit."

"I suppose he drank that down in one?"

"Yes, and he promptly threw up all five of Zeus' brothers and sisters — each emerging unharmed. Naturally they teamed up with Zeus to overthrow Cronus and his Titans and, with a little help from the Cyclopes and the Hundred-Handed Giants, they were victorious!"

"Oh, I do like a happy ending!" I deadpan. "Let's take another picture!"

This time I try for an end-of-the-arm shot of us both but all I get is an eerie blur.

"Let me see that." Alekos tinkers with the camera, finding some hitherto undiscovered setting that solves the lighting issues. I can't bear it — he's good at everything. The only thing he can't do is extend his arm the extra foot needed to capture our faces *and* the other misshapen formations that surround us.

"Would you like me to take a picture of the two of you?" an elderly gentleman with a German accent offers.

It's such a simple enquiry but it prompts an involuntary shiver in me. All morning I've been studying Alekos as a separate entity, periodically wondering what it might be like to merge with him, yet as far as everyone else is concerned we're already

164

together. And they don't seem shocked by the match —
I don't hear any mutterings, "But he's a total playboy!
Can't she see?"

Mind you, he's wearing a bumbag, maybe that's
what's throwing them off.

Our great pilgrimage completed and the nourishment
from our morning pastry long gone, we head for the
mid-mountain taverna we spotted on the way up and
sit on the shady terrace and eat papery-thin courgette
blossoms stuffed with juicy rice and thick wedges of
potato in a tangy tomato sauce.

I hate to sound like a broken record but this might
be the best meal I've ever eaten.

"You do realise we're going to be really late opening
up today?" I say as I mop up the last of the sauce with
a hunk of bread. "I hope we don't piss off any
watersporters."

Alekos shrugs, cowing to no man. "Who are they
going to complain to?"

"Poseidon?" I suggest.

"Oh yes, he's going to be so angered by the lack of
pedalos smacking at his surface!"

We sit there for a further ten minutes, finishing up
with fresh fruit and a lesson in how to write my name
in Greek and then, as if to underline his lack of haste,
Alekos insists upon making two further stops.

The first is at a roadside stall — initially we pass it,
then he screeches to a halt and sets the car in reverse.
Full action-movie drama, all for a jar of honey.

As I step out of the passenger side, my skirt tangles in the bushes and I get into a tussle with the cat's-claw prickles, much to the amusement of the lady stallholder. Normally I'd be embarrassed, but she's laughing in the most sympathetic way and as I approach she holds out a wooden toothpick with a shiny bead of dark honey on its end. I taste it — so rich and earthy; sold to the lady in the shredded skirt! Next comes the raki sample. It's a bit early for cocktails but when I see Alekos accept, I do too. And immediately get a buzz.

"*Epharisto!*" I sing my thank-you as I squeeze back into the car.

"This is what I love most about Greece," Alekos sighs contentedly as we pass a man hand-whittling wooden sticks into salad servers. "Its simplicity. The world is changing so fast but you will always find villagers living this way. They will never change."

I inhale contentedly. I love that he loves that! He's such a modern, forward-looking fellow and yet . . .

Twenty minutes on we stop again, this time at a wondrous edge-of-forever viewpoint set with the dinkiest little whitewashed church, offset with three dark green poplars. I immediately reach for my camera but Alekos has something else in mind, having spied some tempting-looking grapes in the vines up a chalky verge. The average man impeded by a bound arm wouldn't consider scrabbling up and grappling with the branches to grab a bunch of tiny dusty-purple baubles, but Alekos, clearly, is not an average man.

166

"Careful!" I call, somewhat redundantly as he disappears into the undergrowth.

I wait a moment in case he tumbles straight back out but when the rustlings and manly strainings grow faint, I decide to take a proper look around and gingerly edge out into the road — it snakes a little here and I don't want to be surprised and flattened by a coach, our bodies discovered months from now — me as roadkill, him suspended with a withered bunch of grapes in his hand. But I do want to stand where I can see for miles and take a breath. There are no sounds at all now. All is silent. All is still. Perfect peace. This is one of those moments where you feel obliged to have a profound thought.

What I hear myself say surprises me. It's something I haven't heard for a long time. I'm happy. In this moment, I'm really happy.

I'm just inspecting some plump green teardrops, wondering if they are young figs, when I hear a mini-avalanche of rocks and see Alekos skidding precariously down the verge.

"Quick, give me the grapes!" I relieve him of his burden and then rush back to him instructing, "Now put your hand on my shoulder so you can jump down."

He follows both directives without question and I enjoy the sense of teamwork. Especially when he rumples my hair by way of a thank-you. There's no more denying it — I'm infatuated with this version of Alekos — Alekos the adventurer! Alekos who's so caught up in his environment that he forgets to flirt. I suppose it also helps that there's no attractive women for miles, no competition — just me and him and the fruits of nature. A peachy scenario if impractical in the long term. I can't see him wanting to live a remote mountain existence, though quite clearly he could. He's just too worldly. Seen too much, been to too many places. As have I.

Perhaps that's the thing that truly bonds us — we're always looking for something new.

"Ready to go?" he asks, his eyes warm and relaxed.

I hesitate, part of me doesn't want to leave, but the other part? I know it must be the raki talking but right now, the truth is, I'm ready to go anywhere with this man.

CHAPTER
ELEVEN

"It is the mark of an educated mind to be able to entertain a thought without accepting it."
— Aristotle

Back at the beach I feel like the keeper of a beautiful secret: *No one knows! No one knows what Alekos and I have just shared!* They probably think we overslept or had to run some nautical errand — if they only knew that we've driven up into the clouds and back down again!

Not that anyone else would be particularly wowed, I suppose. I try to convey the magic of the excursion in a text to Jules but struggle to find the words. She's used to hearing about Machu Picchu and Chichén Itzá. Only last week I was hiking on a glacier when a snowstorm blew in and we were left clinging together like tiny figurines in a snowglobe. She loved hearing about the drama. The first thing she'll ask is, "Did anything happen?" And what can I say to that? Well, we had a slight petrol scare, got a bit lost then a bit hot and a bit damp. Saw nice views. Ate stuffed courgette blossoms . . . My thumb hovers over the keys. It wasn't so much eventful as meaningful. Yet how can I explain the subtleties of the internal shift I experienced in four hundred characters?

Instead I write: *Day 3 at the beach. Got him feeding me grapes now!* That much is true — he's literally just popped one in my mouth.

She bleeps straight back. *Make sure they haven't been injected with Rohypnol!*

All is well, I reply. *I was there when he plucked them from the vine!*

Sounds a bit reverse Adam & Eve! she taps back. *Proceed with caution or you might have an unwelcome encounter with a serpent!!!*

Ordinarily I would cackle at that comment but today I find myself almost regretting discussing him. I don't want to be cautious any more. I don't want to think of Alekos as someone to guard against. I was rather enjoying the giddier raki-before-noon alternative.

So, how are the wedding plans going? I ask, eager to change the subject. I know she wanted the chance to top up her tan before she said I do but it must be happening any day now . . .

Well, currently number one on my to-do list is remembering why we got together in the first place, she texts, adding a sudden, *Gotta go!*

Oh! Do I detect a little trouble in paradise? Or is she just trying to revisit her initial attraction to help write her vows? Either way, it makes me question my situation from the opposite perspective, as in: what is really holding me back from getting it together with Alekos?

When I made my "No way, never!" statement it was based on the two-dimensional version of the man. Now I have seen so many different sides to his character it is making me reassess my reluctance to get involved. I mean really, what's the worst that could happen? Well, of course it could all blow up in my face and I could end up hurt and humiliated, but I've been hurt and humiliated before and survived!

Part of me can't quite believe that I'm giving this serious consideration — before I came to Greece he seemed such a joke! — but now I've got this new suspicion that he could be worth the risk. I'll admit there's a good chance this could be explained away by the microcosm theory — my world has shrunk down to this little beach resort and I am away from all things and people familiar to me. He has taken the role of leading man whereas before he was purely peripheral chorus. A lot of what I'm feeling could be the setting, the thyme-scented breeze, *those arms* . . . I think as I watch him flexing on the waterski rope again — bless, he's so eager to get out on that water.

Of course, hormones aside, there's no real need to rush into anything. In many ways this is the ideal courtship scenario — it's not often you have the chance to get to know someone with this much intensive quality time without the complication of sex. It's just that tomorrow is my birthday and birthdays always give me that sense of standing at a crossroads and being given the opportunity to make a different choice. I've been wondering lately if it might be possible to change course — could Alekos be a key player in that action?

He doesn't actually know how significant a day it is for me; I'd almost be embarrassed to tell him because there's this presumption that a person should spend their birthday with loved ones or at least their favourite people and I don't want him to feel burdened in terms of trying to make it special for me. Anyway, regardless of any birthday superstitions, this could be a good chance to experiment with advancing our relationship. See how logical I can make this all sound? I heave a muddled sigh — what it really boils down to is this: I find the notion of receiving a birthday kiss from Alekos highly appealing.

"Are you drunk?"

"Excuse me?" For a second I think it's my conscience talking, but the voice is male and coming from a body beside me . . .

"You look a bit squiffy!" I turn to find MSV, sporting a new pair of aviator sunglasses. "No offence, takes one to know one — I just tried some of that retsina at lunch."

"Ohhh." I nod, noticing his slightly unbalanced stance, and then confess, "Actually, I did have a small raki earlier."

He taps his nose as if to say he won't tell anyone and then frowns. "That's basically moonshine, isn't it?"

"Now you come to mention it, it was from a little roadside stall in an unmarked bottle . . ."

"Really? Whereabouts?" He looks vaguely interested in sampling some for himself.

"Have you heard of the Lasithi Plateau?" I ask, perking up, realising there is someone I could tell who I think would get it — not the stuff to do with Alekos, obviously, but the overall experience. In return he tells me about Knossos and the legend of the original labyrinth, designed to hold the ferocious Minotaur.

"As in half-man, half-bull?"

"Exactly."

"Sounds rather thrilling!"

"My days have been pretty interesting, actually," he agrees.

"And the evenings?"

"Well." He appears to think for a minute about whether he actually wants to reveal the details before continuing, "I've been downloading Greek recipes and trying them out at the villa — it has this amazingly slick kitchen so I thought I'd make the most of it. I mean, eating out by yourself in the day isn't so bad, but at night . . ."

"I know just what you mean. I've done it a hundred times but I always feel too self-conscious to really enjoy the food!" I wrinkle my nose. "Anyway, I think that's an inspired idea. I don't cook at all any more, so I'm in awe."

"A lot of the recipes are surprisingly simple — I could show you. In fact . . ." He looks across to where Ben and Alekos are now doing a little maintenance on the speedboat. "I could try cooking something for your team, after a long day's work you must be tired . . ."

"Well, tonight I suspect I'd just fall face first into the moussaka and start snoring —"

"Ah yes, you had a particularly early start . . ." His shoulders slump.

"But any other night?" I encourage him.

"Great!" He looks pleased at the prospect of some company. "I'd love to test my cooking out on a real Greek."

"Great!" I echo back at him, though I can't help but wonder what Alekos will make of this invitation. No doubt he'll bring along his card and stick it under the aubergines.

A couple of customers are hovering so MSV bids me good afternoon and goes on his slightly staggery way. Funny how you feel so at ease with some people. I only met him two days ago, but in terms of my new Elounda Beach World, he's one of my oldest friends.

I must remember to ask his name next time I see him . . .

I turn my attention to the young Czech couple before me. From their body language they seem obviously smitten but I've already got Eastern Europe covered for my project so I let them sail off to Spinalonga without quizzing them about their love life. However, upon their return, they manage to get me feeling pretty vexed about my own.

It begins with an innocent enough enquiry about whether they enjoyed their visit. Fascinating, they tell me.

"I must make a point to go," I tell them.

"You haven't been?" The girl looks absolutely scandalised.

"Well, this is only my third day, so —"

"Oh, oh." She calms down. "I thought . . ." She looks at the desk area as if comparing me to the other

174

permanent fixtures. "We were going to ask you about Zeus' cave, but —"

"Oh, I've been there!" I pip, triumphant. I can't believe my luck at getting to talk about it again.

They ask how it was and I'm about to complain wildly about the hike but clocking their smooth athletic limbs I focus more on the views and Zeus himself, which is what gets them all stirred up. "She's a student of Greek mythology." The guy nods to his girlfriend.

"Oh, me too! Well, I mean, I'm reading a book." I need to calm down. "You know the story?"

We banter back and forth about vomiting previously eaten children et al. and then she says, in all seriousness, "I'm not sure I approve of Zeus — all those affairs!"

"Apparently he was a fair ruler," I counter, surprised to find myself defending him now.

"Ah yes, the king of compromise," she sneers. "But it's Hera I feel sorry for."

"Hera?" I don't recall that name. "Who's that?"

"Zeus' wife," she replies.

Hold on a minute! "I thought his mother banned him from marrying?"

"She did but he went ahead and married his sister anyway."

"*His sister?* Oh, I bet Mum was thrilled about that!"

"The sister wasn't too keen either. But Zeus tricked her into it and though he seemed like a changed god initially, he soon began innumerable affairs and she became consumed with jealousy — all her energy went into avenging the women he'd slept with. Hence my pity. Anyway, we should go."

And off they stroll, leaving me on a total downer — I can't think of anything worse than being a woman whose life is defined by her man's infidelities. That to me is a true Greek tragedy. And perhaps a timely cautionary tale for me — it certainly plays to all my greatest fears about Alekos at a point when I was on the verge of shrugging them off.

"What's that look for?" Alekos complains as he finds himself on the receiving end of my disapproving scowl.

"So Zeus' mother was right about him not getting married." I pout. "You didn't tell me about Hera." From my tone of voice you'd think he'd been keeping an ex from me.

"We got distracted . . . besides, it wasn't all bad — their wedding night lasted three hundred years."

I roll my eyes and stomp back to the desk and pretend to be working. I'm fully aware that I'm being unreasonable and this is most likely just jitters about the force of my attraction to Alekos. But I can't help but fear that I am about to make another colossal mistake. That's the worst thing about all those dud men who do you wrong; it's not just the heartbreak at the time but the legacy of suspicion and loss of faith they leave you with.

"You know what they argued about the most?" Alekos saunters over and perches on the edge of the desk, oblivious to the fact that I'd be better avoided. "Who took more pleasure from sex, men or women.

176

They both insisted the other got the better deal. What do you think?"

I look up at him and, with my best Oscar Wilde delivery, tell him, "I think that if both parties are arguing so strongly then no one is having as much fun as the other presumes!"

He laughs. "Good point."

I should just leave it there but curiosity gets the better of me and I find myself enquiring, "Did they ever settle the argument?"

"Well, they called upon the great seer Teiresias and she stated that a woman's pleasure is nine times that of a man."

I can't help but snort in derision.

"Hera felt the same way — she was so infuriated by Teiresias' proclamation that she blinded her."

"Gotta love these myths," I mutter. "No pressure in those days to have a happy ending."

I'm feeling very conflicted. As much as I say I want to move forward with Alekos, right now I'd really rather he left me to my editing. I don't know how Jules can be so blasé about committing her life to someone when even setting a toe back in the dating pool has me so twitchy and on edge. It doesn't help that Alekos is so close now that I can smell his gorgeous scent.

"Do you like to be massaged?"

"Oh for god's sake, Aleko!" I throw up my hands, unable to take another second of sexual tension.

"What? I'm just asking —"

"You can only be a normal human being for so long, can't you?" I snap. "And then, sure enough, the urge to conquest —"

"Is that what you really think?" he cuts me off, looking genuinely hurt.

I open my mouth and close it. Is it? I don't even know any more.

"You know, Selena, if I'm really this sexual predator you believe me to be, why are you here?"

I think for a moment and then say, in a small voice, "Because your other qualities redeem you." It's meant to be a compliment but I suspect it just sounds patronising.

Fortunately, distraction has arrived in the form of a petite Chinese man.

"Oh, this is Chan," he tells me, when I point him out. His voice is subdued as he goes on to explain, "I booked you a massage. I know how much you strained your legs on the hike to the cave; I thought it might ease the tension."

Oh no. Now I feel terrible. Why did I have to open my big conclusion-jumping mouth?

"That's very kind," I say sheepishly, taking note of Chan's basket of assorted balms. "Does he do it right here on the beach?"

"Yes, but I've made a little treatment area for you; here, between the windsurf sails, so you have some privacy."

Great. He's just made the situation ten times worse — considerate and accommodating of my prudishness.

"Of course it's not compulsory . . ."

178

"No, it's really very thoughtful of you, thank you," I say sincerely.

"So, yes?"

"Yes," I say, forcing a smile. "Make sure you wake me if I nod off."

"Oh you won't sleep," he says, somewhat ominously.

I feel like the universe has just given me a big old slap. At the point when I was doubting Alekos the most, he did something incredibly thoughtful, leaving me feeling thoroughly ashamed. Again.

Ouch! Jeez. I was anticipating a smoothing, relaxing sensation, but this is pure Chinese torture. Chan's fingers pinch and penetrate so deep that if I had any government secrets I'd be listing them all and offering to type them up on my laptop.

"OW!" I yelp out loud.

"How are you getting on?" Alekos checks on me.

"Did you tell him to be extra mean to get me back?"

"No," he chuckles. "Is it too much?"

"A little," I say, just before Chan starts drilling his fingers into my temples so hard that I want to punch him. "*Aaaarrrghh!*"

"It's good for you."

"How can having your brain squeezed out be therapeutic? It's just not right."

It's even more agonising when he starts on my calves and shins. "I tell you, after this, every minute with you is going to feel like a skip through a field of cornflowers," I call out.

Alekos laughs heartily and suddenly my body stops resisting. I love that sound, love to hear him laugh.

It's hard to believe that a matter of minutes ago we were so tense. All thanks to me. I must say, I like this Greek way of arguing — you flare up, get it all out and then thirty seconds later, as he says, "It's done."

"Finished!" the Chinese man echoes the sentiment.

It seems odd to thank someone for putting you through new levels of discomfort but that's the English for you, whether it's a bad haircut or an inedible meal, we'll just mutter thanks very much and be on our way.

I'm vaguely gratified to hear Alekos cry out a few times when he takes his turn. Peeking around the screens I see his face contorting in agony as he bites down on the towel.

"It's good for you," I tell him with a wink before I start to pack away the lifejackets.

Back at the desk I find a new text from Jules.

Are you still a member of the Greek resistance? she asks me.

I think all his physical urges have just been sated by a Chinese beach masseur, I tap back as I wave the man with the demon fingers on his way.

As soon as I send it, I realise it sounds a little dodgy but I'm too hungry to send an explanation. I need to finish packing up and then get some delicious vine-leaf-clad snacks down me.

"Aleko, are you ready to go?"

There's no reply from between the windsurf sails. Surely he can't have dropped off? I creep in and kneel beside him in the dusky light. He has indeed. I do enjoy watching him while he's sleeping. I'm just thinking of Selene, her drowsy lover Endymion and the moon-ray kisses she sent to his lips when he stirs suddenly.

It takes him a second to realise where he is and then he croaks, "What do you say to a quick gyro and an early night?"

"If by gyro you mean kebab . . ." I begin.

"I do," he confirms.

I beam from ear to ear.

He looks surprised. "I finally said the right thing, didn't I?"

I nod approvingly. "Yes you did!"

CHAPTER
TWELVE

Live today, forget the cares of the past.
— Epicurus

This couldn't be any more of a contrast to dining out with Jules — we have as much fun getting ready as we do going out. Look at me now, not only am I salt-encrusted and smudged of eye but the tips of my tangled tendrils are coated in pungent massage oil. And yet nobody seems to mind. Least of all Alekos. On the ship, in his uniform, he looked like the type who'd insist upon high-heeled arm candy. I never would have predicted this laissez-faire side to his nature. Or mine for that matter.

We pass several candlelit fine-dining establishments on the way to Andreas, where I'm relieved to find paper tablecloths, plastic chairs and sport on the TV. I recognise the owner as probably the friendliest of Alekos' pals from our first night. He's also the man with the fanciest chip cutter in town. I get chatting to the chef while Alekos is talking Andreas through our order and before I know it I'm washing my hands, donning an apron and pushing a peeled potato through a razor-sharp gadget.

"This is such fun!" I rave, wondering if Shirley Valentine had the benefit of one of these wondrous machines behind the scenes at Costas' taverna in Mykonos.

"Mind your fingers!" Alekos cautions when he realises what I'm up to.

"Can I do another?" I request excitably.

"Of course." The chef smiles.

"Turn to me as you pull the lever!" Alekos instructs as he positions his camera phone.

Of all the ways to be immortalised — in a pinny prepping his dinner! And yet in this context it doesn't seem such a bad thing.

"You're so lovable." He beams, helping me down from the step.

My little housewife heart skips a beat — he's called me pretty and lovable in one day, it's a wonder I'm still vertical.

As he shows me to our table I find myself smiling at everyone and everyone smiles back. They all seem friendlier than on that first night. But then maybe I'm sending out different vibes now I'm starting to relax and get the lie of the land.

"What would you like to drink?" Alekos enquires.

I see Andreas is serving him a beer so I decide to have the same local brew — Mythos!

"*Yamas!*" Alekos grins. "That's Greek for cheers."

We chink glasses, including Andreas, who is pulling up a chair to join us. "So where did you two meet?" he wants to know.

"On the cruiseship," I say simply, sticking my fork into the plate of coleslaw he's brought for us to share.

"I remember the first time I saw her." Alekos takes a more leisurely approach. "I was getting my orientation tour and as we approached the Shore Excursions desk I could hear this lady ranting, red in the face, about the lack of penguins on her glacier trek. Selena was completely unfazed, calmly explaining that she too had once muddled Alaska with Antarctica but seeing as this lady was clearly such an animal-lover, she would be happy to arrange a visit for her to the zoo in Anchorage — all without any sarcasm."

Andreas gives me a respectful nod.

"And then, instead of rolling her eyes when the lady left, she simply moved on to her next client, coming out from behind the counter to save this old man from getting up from the sofa. But as soon as she was within reach he scooped her up in his arms and waltzed her around the office. She was laughing so freely. So sweetly," he sighs. "I remember standing there, looking at the way the sun glinted off his bald spot, and I thought, I want to be him — I want to be seventy years old and still holding that woman in my arms."

I may have taken a bite but I haven't managed to chew it yet. I wasn't expecting such tender detail. His account really reminded me of someone. But who? And then it hits me — he sounded exactly like the subjects from my love videos.

"Uh-huh." Andreas nods along. "So how long have you been together now?"

Alekos looks to me to explain, presumably since I'm the one holding out.

184

"Actually, we're not an item," I say, hopping up to grab some paper napkins from the side table.

"You mean you've never . . .?" Andreas looks searchingly at Alekos.

"Never!" Alekos confirms, in his most mournful voice. "She's coming round to me though, aren't you?" He gives his lap a playful tap and reaches for my hand.

Oh no. I'm not putting on a cutsie show for the boys. Maybe later when we're alone.

"I don't think so," I resist, returning to my own seat.

"Why not?" he asks, wide-eyed.

"You know why not," I say, eyes flitting to Andreas.

He shakes his head and adopts his most imperious tone as he demands: "How can you refuse a Greek god?"

I am aware that a couple of his waiter pals are now in earshot as I carefully announce, "You, of all people, should know the fate of mortals who sleep with gods."

He raises a curious brow. His pals shuffle closer, eager to hear what the Brit will say next.

"Go on," he encourages.

"Well, look at poor Semele," I begin. "Zapped by lightning when Zeus revealed himself to her. The once-pretty Medusa gets it on with Poseidon, next thing you know she's a hideous serpent-haired Gorgon." I've read this section earlier today so I'm good to go. "And what about Leucothoe — she has an affair with Helios, the sun god, her dad finds out and he is so peeved he buries her alive! Not exactly what you'd call happy endings."

Andreas chuckles and slaps the palm of the waiter delivering our platters before looking expectantly to Alekos for a comeback.

He shakes his head at me. "You have become too educated."

I'm about to tuck in when I notice Alekos has raised a finger: "You do of course realise that all the best offspring come from a god — mortal alliance."

"Oh really?" I say, setting down my gyro to give him a "convince me!" look.

"Well, Hercules for one, probably the greatest Greek hero."

This illicits much appreciative murmuring. "Yes. It's true."

"And?" I challenge him to give me more examples.

He pulls a face. "Perseus, Pegasus, Dionysus . . ."

"Ah yes, where would we be without the god of wine and revelry?" I say, encouraging everyone to raise their glasses.

"Well, for one thing he wouldn't have been around to father Priapus," he replies.

This evokes much tittering. Unfortunately I know just why.

"I don't know how you do it," I despair. "You can bring every subject back to —"

"Yes?" Now everyone is on tenterhooks.

"You know," I mutter and lunge at my gyro, naturally causing it to spill forth streamers of lettuce and meat shavings.

"You still can't even say it!" he hoots, stamping the ground.

"I'm eating!" I protest, trying to squish an overhanging tomato into my mouth. "Besides, you say it enough for both of us."

"So what do you know of Priapus?" He sits back in his chair, refusing to let the subject drop.

"Priapus?" I feign innocence as I take a slurp of beer. "Wasn't he the son of Dionysus and Aphrodite?"

"Yeess. What else do you know of him?" He leers closer.

"He was no oil painting," I say, fixing him with a significant look, though these words could never apply to Alekos.

"And . . ."

"Oh, for god's sake!" I exclaim, banging the tabletop a little too hard.

"Just say it!" he rallies.

"He had unfeasibly large genitals!" I throw my hands up in despair.

All the non-mythologically savvy diners in the place switch round to look at me, including one woman who consequently pushes her plate of meatballs aside.

"Happy now?" I hiss, mortified as Andreas rushes to find her an alternative dish.

Alekos nods delighted, topping up my glass of Mythos before pondering out loud: "I wonder what *our* children would be like?"

I can't help but wince at the thought of a two-year-old Alekos terrorising me with creatures from the deep, freaking me out with his daredevil tendencies and refusing ever ever *ever* to wear clothes.

"Uncontrollable. Incorrigible. Borderline feral," I decide.

"And what about if the child took after *me*?"

I can't help but laugh, now sending beer froth flying across the table. (What is up with my table manners tonight?) Once again, just at the point where I'm about to scream, Alekos has me giggling.

He takes another sip of Mythos and then says, oh-so-gently, "I think you'd make a very good mother; you're very caring." His tone is so cashmere soft, I'm thrown. I don't even know what I've done to make him think I'm caring.

"Well ..." I'm lost for words. Even though motherhood isn't something I have ever particularly aspired to, it still seems like one of the greatest compliments you could be paid.

"Ready to go?" he asks, summoning the bill and paying for the whole thing with a ten-euro note.

Back at the love shack Alekos tells me he's got to quickly run something over to his father so it falls to me to feed Loulou the leftover gyro meat. "Is it because of you that he thinks I'm caring?" I ask the straggly head I'm so very besotted with. "Doesn't he realise I could never be this sweet to a human being? At least not while they're awake ..."

She makes a sympathetic whine and then backs into me for a cuddle. I sigh as I give her a good rub down. I'd like to be. I'd like to be able to wrap myself around a man like this, to rest my head on his shoulder and let go. But that is going to require trust. Of course there are trustworthy men out there but I have to be realistic — I've never attracted any of them before.

Alekos returns, looks at me and Loulou and then helps himself to a glass of water. "Want one?"

I nod.

He comes over and hands me my glass, continuing to hold on even though I have it in my grasp. "Earlier, when I said I was a god, I wasn't implying that I had higher status to you."

My mouth twists in a smirk. "So you're saying I'm a goddess?"

"Not far off," he chuckles. "I really am grateful for all that you're doing here."

Oh. That's not quite the tone I was hoping to elicit.

"See you in the morning."

"You're going to bed?" I blurt as he turns to retreat.

"Yes."

"Now?"

He cocks his head. "I thought you wanted an early night."

"Well, yes but . . ." My eyes flick to the clock on the kitchen wall. Just two hours until my birthday. And then I look back at him — the poor guy is swaying he's so exhausted: up late with his father last night, up early with me this morning, hectic day on the beach. Not that he'd ever admit to any form of weakness — I know he'd stay up and keep me company if I asked him to but that would just be cruel on my part. Besides, when we do finally collide, I want us both to be fully present, and fully functioning . . .

"You're right. Goodnight!" I chirrup and then turn away.

Even though I know it's the right thing to do, I can no longer look at him and not want him — desire overrides logic. I sit down at the table and find an old song weaving its way into my consciousness . . . "I've Grown Accustomed to His Face". But it's not just his face. I'm getting accustomed to his ways, his company, even to his culture. I haven't felt this sense of contentment and belonging in years. I know this is dangerous and potentially disturbing to my equilibrium, but I'm ready now, to take the ultimate step towards him. I can't believe that the next time I see him —

"Oh!" I gasp as he reappears.

"Forgot my water," he explains, nodding to the glass beside the sink.

"Oh! Oh, yes." I jump up and hand it to him. This time it's me leaving my fingers lingering after he has it in his grasp.

"Everything alright?" he enquires.

"Just wanted to be sure you had a firm grip," I say, finally releasing it.

As he stumbles off towards his room, he waves the back of his fingers at me, muttering, *"Filakia!"*

"What's *filakia*?" I call after him, wondering if he's just dismissed me with the Greek equivalent of *"Whatever!"*

"Kisses," he sighs as he disappears behind the curtain.

At which point my knees actually give way.

190

CHAPTER
THIRTEEN

Be as you wish to seem.
— Socrates

Happy birthday to me, happy birthday to me, happy birthday dear moon goddess, happy birthday to me! I wake up with a tingle of anticipation for the day ahead. I went to bed auditioning assorted scenarios for our first kiss — beneath the Cretan arch here in the love shack? At the end of the jetty at the beach? After a tongue-tingling shot of raki in Plaka? But then I realised I can't schedule it like I'm putting together a tour package — "After visiting the local archaeological museum there will be half an hour allotted for kissing." I'm going to have to go with the flow. It's time I made some changes.

To mark my intention that this year will be different from all others, I decide to make breakfast. Yes, me. In the kitchen. Chopping, whisking, toasting and imbuing every fresh item with superpowers from Alekos' magic card . . .

Well, yesterday he went out of his way to take me to Zeus' cave. Today I want to do something nice for him.

A couple of times I try texting Jules for guidance but there's no reply and ultimately I'm glad I'm forced to work things out for myself. Who knew there could be so much satisfaction in fanning out nectarine slices or squeezing an orange till it's naught but pith? No doubt it's the novelty factor but, for now, I couldn't think of a nicer way to start the day.

I'm about to set everything out on the kitchen table when I get a better idea and begin transporting the wares up the stairs and out on to the roof terrace. I find a bright yellow tablecloth, dress the plastic chairs with cushions from my room, and even set a little glass of flowers as the centrepiece, between the Greek yoghurt and the sliced banana. I'm heading down for the honey we got from the roadside stall when Alekos appears all tousled and yawny.

"Hungry?" I enquire enticingly.

"Mmmm," he says, paw on his bare tummy.

"Follow me . . ." I say, licking my honey-dipped finger and heading for the stairs.

"Selena!" He looks quite taken aback.

"No, not in that way!" I tut as I continue on my way. "Just follow me, you'll see!"

"You did all this?" he exclaims as he surveys the breakfast banquet.

"Yes!" I beam. From the way my chest is plumping up you'd think I was the beekeeper and yoghurt-strainer to boot.

"And you're going to sit down and join me?"

"Of course!" I trill.

We both take a seat and tuck in. As do several wasps.

"Don't bother them," he says as I try to switch them away. "And they won't bother you."

"But that one is stuck in the yoghurt!" I protest.

Alekos reaches in the bowl and daintily plucks it by its wing and flings it on its way. Just like that!

But the real fly in the ointment, so to speak, is my sudden attack of first-date nerves. It's a terrible thing when you realise how much you like someone. Suddenly I feel all self-conscious and vulnerable and all last night's cheeky banter is gone. I don't quite know how to behave with him now that I am open to the thing I've been resisting since we met. Can he tell? I wonder. Does he know?

I try to sneak an assessing peek but only conclude that he gets more handsome by the day. I daren't look at him for too long for fear of looking too blatantly dreamy and malleable.

"How's your hand today?" I ask, defaulting to polite small talk.

"Getting better, I think," he says as he reaches for the butter. "I have a doctor's appointment today at eleven a.m. so hopefully he can give me an update."

"Good." I take a sip of tea. "So you slept alright?"

He nods. "All the way through."

"Good, good." I contemplate the view, the balmy breeze and the flawless blue sky. "Lovely day today . . ."

He looks askance at me as he takes a bite of toast. "Are you okay?"

"Yes, yes, of course."

We sit there for nearly an hour. I love how unrushed he is. This has the potential to be my most leisurely and enjoyable breakfast of all time. Shame I can't actually eat anything I've prepared — my stomach is in too much of a twirl.

I feel a little more relaxed at the beach now Ben is buzzing around us, but not a lot. I suspect I'm not really going to get anywhere until the evening when I can summon a little Greek courage with a Mythos or two, so for now I concentrate on boarding the latest kayak renters. Once they're on their way I venture a little deeper into the water, up to my waist now. Perhaps later I'll have a swim, to mark that this is indeed the first day of the rest of my life.

"Selena!" Alekos is trying to get my attention from the shore. "Your phone!"

"Who is it?" I call back.

"Ma!" he reads from the display.

My mum calling from New Zealand! "Answer it! Answer it!" I bleat, sploshing excitedly out of the water.

I hear him exchange a few words and then, as he hands me the phone, he tells me he's off to the doctor's.

"Okay!" I wave him off, delighted that I'll be able to speak freely. "Hello?"

"Happy birthday, darling! Happy birthday, sis!" Assorted voices come down the line to greet me.

"Was that the sexy Greek?" My sister wastes no time cutting to the chase. "Who is he and what's with all the puppies?"

I laugh out loud. "The puppies belong to his dad."
"So you've already met the parents! Things must be going well . . . Hold on, Betsy wants to say hello!"

There's a cutesy burbling down the phone. I feel a pang. I am so far behind in the family lark, will I ever be able to catch up?

194

"Oh great, she just puked on my new suede shoes, I'm handing you back to Mum."

"So, darling, are you having a lovely day?"

"So far it's been perfect," I say. "And it looks like it's going to stay that way!" I cheer as Ben hands me an ice cream. "Thank you!" I mouth to him as I listen to my mother explaining that she sent my card to Jules' thinking I'd be there.

"Well, that was the plan but she went to Mauritius to get married —"

"Married?" my mum gasps.

"It's all happening today. I've tried getting hold of her but I suppose she's all tied up with beautifications."

"It won't last."

"Mum!" I squeak. "Don't curse it before it even begins!"

"I meant her looks. As many beauty treatments as she has, she can only rely on them for so long. She really should look into developing some other aspects of her personality."

My mouth opens and then closes. I don't know what to say; Jules does seem to bring out the catty side in my mother. They only met once just before Mum emigrated but somehow Jules got her bristling within minutes. And apparently she's not done yet: "I don't hold out much hope for the marriage either, now you come to mention it."

"Why ever not?" I ask.

"You've interviewed enough golden anniversary couples to be able to spot the difference in traits, surely?"

"Hard to tell." I shrug. "Jules is never that bothered, regardless of who she goes out with; I don't think it's any different with Dom."

"Precisely!" she toots. "When you meet The One, it has to feel different, or how else would you know?"

Well, it's certainly different with Alekos, I decide. Maybe that's a good thing after all. Seeing as my mother is feeling so forthcoming on potential unions, I can't help but enquire: "So what did you think of him, Alekos . . . from speaking to him?"

"Well, judging from the picture and the voice, I'd say things would never be dull around him."

"What do you mean by that? Do you think he's giving me the runaround?" Oh please say no! Say no!

"I didn't say that," she tuts. "Yes, there's an element of mischief to him, but he does seem to genuinely care for you."

"Really? What makes you say that? What did he say?"

"Well, we only exchanged a few words, it was more his tone . . ."

I'm desperately scrabbling around for confirmation that I'm doing the right thing but of course, in love, there are no guarantees. I end up coming off the phone even more nervous. Now Team New Zealand have a vested interest in what's going on. I should have at least waited until I saw how tonight went before getting their hopes up. I've long stopped referencing any men to my family, my encounters are always so fleeting that come the next time they enquire after Gustav or Pablo I would invariably have no idea who they were talking about. And that's not good for a lady's reputation. I would have made an exception and told them about the Norwegian if I hadn't been completely out of signal range for those heady first weeks, but I'm glad I didn't. It's much easier to pretend nothing bad ever happened when no one else knows about it. What I'm finding now is how much harder it is to keep your mouth shut when you are excited about someone. I try Jules again. Still nothing. Perhaps she's taking that step-pause, step-pause walk across a sand dune now.

I know she has something old, new and borrowed, but I wonder if she has something blue yet? I could certainly supply that — switching my phone to the camera function, I turn and snap a half-and-half shot of the dazzling sapphire sea and cobalt sky. I press send and then lean back on the desk and look around me, imagining my own wedding on this very beach . . .

I wonder if I'm allowing myself to think about those things in relation to Alekos because it is still so farfetched it could never become a reality. As my mum says, there's nothing dull about him. He's not a pipe-and-slippers kind of guy. I don't get that fear of getting trapped when I think of him. I would never have to be submissive to his rules. If this week is anything to go by, we'd make quite a team. Perhaps we'd spend our summers here at the beach and the winters cruising, him with ever more stripes on his epaulettes, me working as the highly in-demand guest speaker.

Well, if I want that fantasy to become a reality, I'm going to have to work harder at getting my video presentation together. I look around. Ben has everything under control. Finally I can get out my laptop . . .

I'm just experimenting with a sepia effect on the Egyptian couple I filmed in a desert setting when a body presses hard into my back and a familiar voice growls: "Guess which part of me is exposed!"

"Aleko!" I despair, though not without a thrill. But when I turn around to berate him, I find it's his left arm that is laid bare. "I can't believe it!" I gasp. "You're free!"

"I am!" he confirms. "And it works!" He jiggles his pale fingers.

I reach to touch the one part of him I haven't been ogling these past few days. "Welcome back!" I say as I lean forward and press my lips to his knuckles.

Alekos looks amazed. As am I. Did I really just kiss his hand?

"So, erm, we had three more kayaks go out but other than that, it's been very quiet." I turn away, pretending to busy myself with some leaflets.

Fortunately he doesn't notice my awkwardness because he's already shrugging off his sandals and shedding his shirt ready for his first official dip in the sea.

"Finally!" he cheers as he races into the water.

My heart leaps for him as he dives in and then rises up euphoric. Must remember to drop Apollo a quick thank-you note when I get a moment.

I stroll down to the water's edge to get a closer look.

198

"Did I ever do my crocodile impression for you?" he asks, looking playful.

"No . . ." I reply, tentatively wondering if a ravaging is coming sooner than I think.

But instead of surging towards me and nipping at my ankles, he simply submerges his hand and then slowly lets only his knuckles bump up to the surface. He holds them there for a second and then submerges them once more, before looking expectantly at me.

"That's it?" I laugh.

He grins, for once the picture of innocence, and then flips back and powers into the blue. I look on fondly and then realise I have exactly the same pose as the woman next to me watching her five-year-old revel in the water.

When he finally emerges, the drip that falls from his face on to mine feels as personal as a kiss. I love him wet! His eyes seem greener than ever but it's his body that is showing the greatest variation in colour, from the Alaskan white of his newly unbound hand to the nut-brown of his face and feet and, in between, an assortment of hues resulting from the varying cover-ups of boardshorts, T-shirts, etc. He looks like an amalgamation of body parts from different nationalities.

"You might want to spend the afternoon working on that patchwork tan of yours!" I tease. "It'll be like a science project trying to work out which SPF to put where . . ."

"Oh no, I have a better idea. Now that my hand is better, you know what we can do?"

I shake my head though in fact I'm just thinking how timely it is that he's no longer physically restricted.

He bites his lip, barely able to contain his excitement. "I'm going to take you octopus hunting!"

CHAPTER
FOURTEEN

One must not tie a ship to a single anchor, nor life to a single hope.
— Epictetus

"What are you waiting for?" he whoops. "Grab your flippers and let's go!"

"Just give me a second to save my edits . . ." I make busy-sounding faux clicks on my keyboard with my nail tips.

I'm stalling partly in the hope that MSV will suddenly appear — didn't I say he should experience something he'd never get the chance to at home? — and partly because I simply don't want to go. Yes, I want to spend time alone with Alekos, but I'm thinking three's a crowd with some slimy creature from the deep. Not to mention the whole issue of what they do to the octopus when they catch it. Ben was filling me in on that earlier. Suffice it to say that if I'd have had any breakfast this morning, I would surely have lost it.

"Are you sure you don't need me to stay here?" I adopt my most self-sacrificing expression. "I understand if you'd rather take Ben . . ."

"I'll take him next time," he dismisses my offer. "Get that laptop shut down. The customers will be here any minute."

"Customers?"

"Yeah, I took the booking from this English couple on my way back from the doctor's. Don't mention the octopus bit, though, it's a surprise. I'm just going to prep the boat. Come straight over when they arrive."

I'm wondering if this makes things better or worse when I spy a minxy blonde with Heidi plaits, "man overboard!" cleavage and scarlet shorts complete with "stripper zipper" — a term I gleaned from the booze cruise. I'd expect her other half to be some tango-tanned wide boy but in fact he's a tall, pale, bespectacled Englishman dressed as the male equivalent of me: i.e. entirely inappropriately for the beach in long trousers and a freshly pressed shirt.

"Er, hello," he smiles awkwardly, offering me his hand, "I'm Graeme, this is Emily. We booked a boat trip?"

He has the kindest faded-denim-blue eyes I ever saw and I find myself liking him instantly. And the fact that Emily has chosen a genuine sweetie, over all the good-time guys that must surely sleaze her way, makes me kind of like her too.

"Won't be long," I inform them. "He's just topping up the petrol tank now."

Emily follows my line of vision to the jetty. "That's the guy who's taking us?" Her face falls in dismay — not the typical female reaction to Alekos.

"Something wrong?" I enquire.

She tugs her boyfriend to one side and hisses, "I don't trust him."

"Join the club," I mutter as I file their euros in the appropriate drawer. And then it dawns on me — I actually very nearly do now.

"Can't we just get a pedalo?" Emily, however, is still resisting.

"Babe —" He looks crestfallen.

"It's just that when you said a boat trip, I envisioned puttering around with some old walnut-skinned fisherman," she reasons, "not some hotshot that'll have the boat vertical at the first vroom."

The boyfriend sighs patiently. "I'm sure he's a very safe driver, isn't he?" He turns to me for reassurance.

"Of course. Alekos is very experienced. And not nearly as reckless as he appears." That didn't come out quite as placating as I intended, so I quickly add, "Also, I could ask him to go extra slow, if that would make you feel better?" Like he'll take a blind bit of notice of me. If only I knew the Greek god of little-old-lady driving . . .

"Well, if you're sure . . ." She sounds utterly unconvinced as I escort them to the boat.

"This may seem strange advice," I say as they hop down into the moulded frame. "But you might be better off with your back to the direction we're headed — something about not seeing the nose of the boat repeatedly rearing up —" I stop myself — once again I seem to be making things worse.

"I'm going to have my eyes closed anyway so it doesn't really matter," Emily informs me as she takes a seat.

"Actually, if you start to feel seasick, you should stare at a fixed point on the horizon and sing loudly."

"I only sing for money," she mumbles, focussing intently on her toe-ring.

"We're in a cover band," Graeme addresses my quizzical look. "Wedding receptions, corporate dos, Legoland, whoever will hire us, basically."

"What do you play?" I ask.

"Keyboard," he replies.

"He sings too," Emily adds, without looking up. "If he's had enough to drink. My nan thinks he's great — her very own Matt Monro! Whoah!"

Alekos boards with too much vigour, setting the boat pitching from side to side. "Ready to have some fun?" he says as he revs the outboard motor at the back of the boat.

"*Noooo!*" Emily grips the sides like we're in the midst of a tempest.

I can't help but be amused — her body may be built for high-speed hedonism but she has a surprisingly cautious sensibility.

"Just take it slow." I back her with as much gravitas as I can muster.

"Well, I have to go a little bit fast or we'll get smacked around by the waves," Alekos reasons, letting the shell of the boat bounce and bellyflop to make his point.

"Oooh, I don't like this," Emily quavers, looking ever more uncomfortable as he forges ahead.

"You wanted to see Spinalonga up close," Graeme reminds her.

"A postcard would have been fine," she mutters, body now rigid with tension.

"You look good up there, Miss Emily," Alekos tries to loosen her up with a little flattery. "Like the figurehead on a ship."

"Just keep your eyes on the road," she snarls, clearly immune to his charms, making me like her even more.

A full thirty seconds of shrill engine noise and hair-tangling breeze pass before she bleats, "Are we nearly there?"

"I'm taking you to the other side of the island." Alekos nods ahead.

"The other side?" she despairs. "Can't we just pull over here?" She points to the nearest bit of land.

"No, it's much better where we are going. Right, Graeme?"

"What?" She looks further agitated. *"What have you done?"* Her eyes bore into him like instruments of torture.

"You'll like it," he assures her. I believe him. He surely wouldn't risk upsetting her this much for no good reason.

We continue on with the occasional comedy bucket of water seemingly thrown over us by a stagehand.

"Pah!" Emily spits out a mouthful of seawater.

"How are you feeling now?" Alekos enquires.

"So miserable I'm actually getting *angry*!" she rages.

"Really?" he says, completely unaffected. "It'll be worth it. You're going to love it."

"No I'm not," she lashes back. "I'm not going to love anything until I'm back on dry land!"

I wish there was something I could do to make her feel better. There's still quite a way to go. Perhaps if I got her chatting on a non-nautical topic?

"So, who was your last gig for before you came away?" I venture.

She and Graeme exchange a look. "Four hundred Wandsworth prison guards!"

"Really?" I hoot. "You played a gig in a prison? How very Johnny Cash!"

"Actually, it was at the Hurlingham Club. Which does rather beg the question: *who was guarding the prisoners . . .?*"

I chuckle as she tells me about their Groovie Movie Band incarnation — with her dressed as Catwoman and Graeme in a furry Pink Panther costume.

"Do you do 'Kung Fu Fighting'?" I ask, starting to get a feel for their repertoire.

"Of course, and 'It's Not Unusual', 'Wake Me Up Before You Go-Go', 'Hot Stuff' . . ." Rather like people count sheep to help them get to sleep, Emily appears to have found a new cure for her sailing phobia. "'Boogie Oogie Oogie', 'Love Train' . . ." she continues as if in a trance.

Alekos catches my eye, giving me an approving nod as if to say, "Good work."

I feel so proud. We really are an excellent team.

But then, mid-recitation, the boat starts to slow.

"Are we here?" She looks around, suddenly remembering her dire circumstances. "Where's the beach?"

"That's not what we've come for." Alekos cuts the motor beside some particularly craggy rocks.

I can tell she's on the verge of panic mode again but this time I don't know what to say. Fortunately, Alekos does.

"Emily, I need you to be Anchor Girl," he commands, nodding to the great thunk of metal beside her feet.

"Me?"

"Yes," he says, going straight into the instructions which, amazingly, she follows without debate. Chains unravelled and rope uncoiled, she is now in position at the front of the boat. "Good. Now on the count of three I want you to throw it overboard, feeding it through your hands until you start to feel it getting slack."

She nods, poised for duty.

"Okay." He takes a breath. "One, two, *three*!"

Over the edge it goes, and down and down, taking the heavy chains and rope with it. But mercifully not Emily.

"Has the rope stopped pulling?"

She nods affirmation.

Alekos moves the boat away from the anchor so that it locks on to the seabed and then cheers, "Good work, Anchor Girl!"

She looks pleased with herself. I'm pleased with him. He's actually made her feel good about being on the boat. What an old pro.

"So, seriously, what happens now?"

"We dive for octopus."

Oh no, my eyes scrunch shut as I await the howls. I wait. And wait. But none are forthcoming. Is she in silent scream mode? Gingerly I open my wincing eyes, only to find Emily's face lit with rapture and Graeme beaming proudly. The boy done good!

"You like octopus?" I gawp.

"Love them!" she pips, yanking down the shoulder of her top to reveal a simple black tattoo. "You know octopus is a Greek word? Means eight legs," she mimics Alekos without even realising.

"Okay! So put on your mask and flippers and we'll go catch one," he instructs.

"Oh no, no," she tuts. "*You* catch it. I'll sit here, catching rays!"

"You don't want to snorkel?" Alekos can't believe his ears. "Look at this water . . ." He directs our attention to the jewel-like clarity of the aquamarine depths.

I, too, blink in wonder at the bedazzled surface — a million bright white glitterspots ricocheting from the sun into our eyes.

"It's absolutely lovely but I don't care," she chirrups, lowering her shades.

"Graeme?"

"I'm happy staying with Emily." He also defers.

Which just leaves me.

"I'm fine too." If it worked for them . . .

Alekos leans close to my ear. "They might want some privacy."

I turn back. They are already looking a little cosy. Oh dear. There's nothing else for it, I'm going to have to jump ship.

"Man overboard!" Alekos winks, about to flip backwards from the edge of the boat.

"Wait!" I grab his arm.

"What now?"

"Well. I mean ... how big are these octopus exactly?"

I see his eyes roll behind the mask and then he's gone, tipping backwards into the icy green.

Great. There's no getting out of this now. My first swim since I've been here and I couldn't be doing it in worse company — Emily may resemble a figurehead but I'm more bulkhead, which, technically, is a partition in a ship but you get the idea.

I shed my outer garments and try to sound breezy as I tell the couple, "See you in a bit!" before making a far less sporting entrance into the water — hobbling over the side, catching my foot on the metal rail and then plunging too deep.

The water is exquisitely refreshing but there's no time to revel in the sensation — I didn't put my mask on before I got in so now I'm jiggling my feet like crazy to keep my head above water as I try and stretch the rubber strap around my head and position the mouthpiece, which feels most unnatural and distorting. Have I got it in right? I look around for Alekos to consult but he's nowhere to be seen, setting me hyperventilating, wondering what dreadful underwater angle he could be viewing me from right now. Vanity is such a debilitating trait.

Puffing in and out of the breathing pipe, I try to remember the procedure I haven't practised since I was a child. Face in the water, breathe through the mouth. Mercifully, the second I glimpse the sandy bottom of the ocean and take in the flutterings of five or six small black fish quietly going about their business, I'm fine — another world has opened up to me and fascination overcomes my fears.

Until, that is, Alekos looms into view motioning crossly to my flipperless feet. Darn. I knew I'd forgotten something. But instead of having a Greek strop, he reaches for my hand, aligns my body with his, and uses his set of flippers to power us both along. It's a simple enough act — the waterworld version of taking a stroll hand-in-hand — but from the way I feel, you'd think the Man from Atlantis himself had singled me out for a private swoosh through his kingdom.

I am now officially floating internally as well as externally. I honestly don't think a more romantic thing has happened to me in my life and he's not even meaning it that way.

Somehow, within this surge of pleasure, I manage to feel a little bit guilty that this is Emily and Graeme's paid trip and I'm the one who's getting all the thrills. Mind you, I don't know what's going on in that boat.

Even underwater there is nothing disco-flashy about Greece, none of the technicolour tropicals on view at your local aquarium/Chinese takeaway, just muted neutrals and soft metallics. It's the simplicity motif again: these fish are designed for the dinner table, not your screensaver. Periodically, Alekos swoops down and scoops up a handful of delicate pumpkin-shaped shells in matt plum, greengage and brick-dust orange, each accented with tiny dots of white.

"Sea urchins with no more spines," he tells me as he makes a rare appearance above water.

They are so pincushion pretty we decide to take a few as keepsakes and he loads up the pockets of his boardshorts and mine.

Watching him move around, as confident in this sub-aqua realm as he is on dry land, I wonder if there are any Greek people who don't like the sea. They could be on to something — life is just better wet!

Just as I'm feeling at my most dreamy and sublime, Alekos motions animatedly to the seabed. Unable to identify what he's pointing to, I get a bit panicky. It looks like a rock, but is it about to rear up and start snapping at us? I try to manoeuvre so I can see if his expression is one of excitement or dread but he's already on his way — making a perfectly streamlined descent through the milky mint waters. How do people do this? Dive with a mask and tube on? I'm utterly rapt and almost expect all the local fish to clamour round to watch the show with me.

As his hand disappears into a nook at the base of the rock there's rummaging, then a tussle that gets me quite agitated: what if the thing clamps on to him and he becomes trapped down there? There's absolutely nothing I could do, I wouldn't even know how to make my body go down so many flights of seawater, let alone transfer any oxygen! Still, he remains there. Does he not need to breathe at all?

Suddenly his body is rushing back towards me. I'd feel relief were it not for the fact I now detect something sinewy and slimy dripping from his hand, in eight distinct strands, with a vile wobbling testicle-like sack on top. I scramble backwards, lifting my face out of the water so I can release a scream, only now of course I've taken my eye off the beastie so all I can think to do is start doggy-paddling away like crazy.

"Come back!" Alekos calls after me.

With his flipper power he's upon me in a second and I instinctively recoil, thrashing around blindly. "Get it away from me!" I beg, revulsed.

"Selena, calm down!"

"Do they bite? Do they sting?" I gasp, still back-paddling.

He gives me a weary look. "Touch it."

"No way!"

"*Touch it!*"

"Just let me look at it first!" I beg.

From a safe distance I can take in the proportions a little better. At full stretch its legs are no longer than my forearm. Alekos seems to have a fairly firm grip on its head. I take a steadying breath. I wouldn't do this for anyone else, but something about this man is so commanding, he makes me want to overcome my fear. Tentatively — or should that be tentaclely? — I reach out, but my hand springs back before I make contact. I can't do it! I'm squirming more than the octopus itself! Still Alekos holds it out towards me. I tell myself I might never get an opportunity like this again — though why I'd want one is another matter — and this

212

time I do it. It's slippery and gel-like on the surface, the arms are firmer than I imagined, and more serpentine, but the freakiest sensation is when its suction cups adhere to my skin.

"It's tasting you now," Alekos tells me.

"Let's go and show the others," I say, as an excuse to pull free and have a good shudder.

Back at the boat Emily astounds me further by cooing and stroking our friend like it's a little tinkerbell of a kitten. Appropriate behaviour considering her next comment: "Did you know that intelligence-wise octopuses are considered to be on a par with a domestic cat?"

"I did not," I tell her as I rhythmically tread water.

"Aside from marine mammals they're the smartest thing in the sea."

"Not counting me and Alekos, obviously," I tell her.

"Obviously." She grins.

"And they have three hearts," Graeme chips in. "That's my favourite fact."

"Really?" I look at the octopus with new-found curiosity. I could do with a couple of spares myself. "Do they fall in love?" I find myself asking out loud.

"I don't know about that." Emily frowns. "But their mating process is pretty bizarre — the male uses one specialised arm to insert the sperm into the female and then the arm detaches! Imagine if your wotsit dropped off after insemination!" she addresses Graeme, who looks suitably uncomfortable. "You wouldn't be so keen then, would you?" she chuckles. "Plus males can only live a few months after mating and females die once their eggs are hatched."

"Wow. No such thing as 'casual' sex in their world." I give Alekos a significant look.

"You do it, you die," Emily confirms.

Alekos' eyes remain upon me. "Ahhh, but what a way to go . . ."

"Let's take a picture!"

Alekos attempts to get the octopus to pose and in response it inks us — a big black pouff of liquid splattering us full in the face, a trick no doubt a few celebs would like to pull on the paparazzi. Emily and Graeme hoot delightedly and snap away. At least now I feel like we've put on a good show. Our work is done.

Better yet, Alekos announces that he's returning the octopus to its nest. What a nice thing to do, I think to myself, as I attempt to heave myself back on board, feeling like I have twelve anchors attached to my extremities.

"Graeme! Give her a tug!" Emily instructs her fella to help me over the final hurdle.

"Thanks!" I collapse panting, grateful for the orange soda Emily is offering me. "This doesn't come as naturally to me as some!" I cast a rueful glance in Alekos' direction.

"Don't worry, I'm a great believer in opposites attracting." She gives me a knowing wink.

"Really?" I look up at her, eager as ever to peek behind the scenes at a relationship. "How long have you two been together? If you don't mind me asking . . ."

214

"Four years," she replies, looking suitably impressed with herself. "He took a bit of persuading at first but I finally won him over."

Graeme gives me a sheepish smile. "She's quite a force to be reckoned with."

"Sounds like me and Alekos in reverse," I reveal. "Only we're still just . . ." I falter, unable to find the right words.

"You mean you haven't?" Emily looks as shocked as Andreas did last night. "What's holding you back?"

Funny that she knows I'm the issue.

"Well, I was very wary of him at first. I couldn't understand why he was coming on so strong, it was all a bit much for me."

Graeme nods understandingly.

"But then I got to spend a few days with him here at the beach and . . ." How embarrassing — I know my face has just gone all teenage besotted.

Emily gives me an impish smile. "Now you're thinking of succumbing?"

"Don't do it!" Graeme suddenly yelps.

"Are you crazy?" Emily turns on him.

"I'm not, but *he* is . . ." he says, pointing behind us.

Instead of returning to the boat, Alekos has made for the rocks and is now clawing his way higher and higher up the pale grey-gold surface like a tufty-haired lizard in Hawaiian-print shorts.

"He's going to jump," Graeme confirms our worst fears. "He said something about this on the phone; I didn't realise how dangerous it would be . . ."

"Oh no," Emily and I groan in unison.

Higher he goes, up angular juttings, hooking his nails into tiny crevices, higher still. I'm starting to get more than a bit apprehensive now. Is he planning to outdo the cliff-divers of Acapulco?

"I hope he doesn't injure himself," Emily frets. I'm thinking the same thing, quite earnestly, when she adds: "I mean, if he smashes himself on the rocks, we'll be stranded here."

"Ready?" Alekos calls down, making sure he has our full attention.

I hold my breath. It's all so precarious. He does realise there's another rock in the water, tucked out of view from the ledge he's standing upon? Of course he does. He must know every fluid ounce of this water. Right? But what if he hit it? Or what if he disappeared into the water with such force he just kept going? How would I feel if I never saw him again?

The truth is, I'd miss everything — the wild hand movements, the shrugs, the impatience, even our silly bickering . . . Yesterday I virtually accused him of being a sleaze but told him his other qualities redeem him. Well, they do more than that. They send him soaring into a stratosphere of his own creation. I sigh to myself — I am officially ruined! How is any man going to compare with this daredevil merman?

Just when I think he's lost his nerve he lets go and plunges downwards, creating a perfect hula-hoop of white froth as he hits the navy waters. At the same time as he impacts, I find myself saying, "I love him!"

216

I didn't mean to. I wouldn't have even thought it was possible. But I do. I don't know the last time I felt this feeling, right the way through me, inside and out.

Graeme and Emily are now cheering and whistling so I don't look out of place hooting wildly as he bobs back to the surface.

"Okay, Anchor Girl," he says as he climbs deftly back on board. "Time to pull her up!"

On the return journey Emily and Graeme sit comfortably together at the front of the boat, this time embracing the spritzing and spattering as well as the sunshine. Meanwhile, every icy flick makes me shiver more. I was too long in the cool water and wrap a towel cape-like around my shoulders, hunching against the buffeting breeze, about as un-siren-like as you can get.

"Why don't you come here?" Alekos beckons me to sit beside him and then takes my hand and places it over his, on the rod connected to the motor. "Pull to the right if you want to turn to the left." He demonstrates the counter-intuitive system without letting go.

I like this kind of tuition better. It could just be that after the speedboat fiasco he wouldn't trust me solo with the controls but, whatever his motivation, it feels so unbelievably good holding his hand I don't mind. I take a deep breath. How it is possible that a man I used to run from could possibly infuse me with such a sense of unity and harmony with a simple touch? Perhaps it's the liberation factor of embracing your emotions. I'm not afraid of them — or him — any more. "Together" seems a real possibility. Exhilarating and comforting at the same time.

I know I have new-found confidence in our potential relationship when I emerge from the water and see the ultimate swimsuit bod sashaying towards me and, instead of feeling threatened or gripped by a sudden need to slap my palms over Alekos' eyes, I am almost tempted to nudge him and say, "Check her out!"

She reminds me of Jules — at least five-foot nine with long perfectly tapered legs, boobs that wobble enough to let you know they're real and a whittled-in skittle-like waist in between. She's even sporting a twinkly bellychain — and you know there aren't too many women who want to draw attention to that area of their body . . .

And then she tilts back the brim of her sunhat — oh my god, oh my GOD!

"Jules?!" I squint — surely I must be seeing things?

"Sleee-naaa!" she whoops, suddenly animated. "Where've you been?" It's then I feel her bionic body upon my soft flesh, squeezing me tight as her breath tickles my ear with the words, "I've come to save you!"

CHAPTER
FIFTEEN

Envy is the ulcer of the soul.
— Socrates

I stumble back, still having trouble believing my eyes:
Jules, last heard of picking out tropical corsages in
Mauritius, is now standing before me. "How . . .?
What . . .?"

She takes a deep breath. "I've left him."

"*Dom?*" I gasp. "You've split up?"

She nods emphatically, if not a little manically.

"What happened?"

"I, I can't —" she gulps, shaking her head. Clearly
she's not ready to turn the pain into a quick anecdote.

"No rush," I insist, still feeling like I've been struck
on the head with one of our kayak paddles. "Talk about
a bombshell! Or should that be a *Dom*shell?" I try to
make a little joke.

Jules forces a smile then reaches for my hand. "So
there I was sobbing my lungs out when I thought
what's the point of you and I both suffering on separate
beaches when we could be happy together — so here I
am!"

Did I really give the impression that I was suffering?
That seems such a long-ago emotion . . .

"You poor thing!" I sympathise. "I wish there was something I could do to make you feel better . . ."

"Well, you know what they say — the best way to get over a man is to get under another!"

Apparently Jules is planning to take the bungee approach to rebounding. As her eyes scan the shore for options, I try to process what her presence means to me: I know I should be pleased to see her but I actually feel totally sideswiped — I had plans for today, very particular plans. And now all my attention will be required to go in a very different direction.

"He'll do!" she exclaims with a noticeable dilation of pupils.

I follow her gaze to a dewy and glinting Alekos, bidding farewell to Emily and Graeme. "Oh no. *No, no, no.*" I shake my head.

"Yes, yes, yes," Jules insists, eyes locked on her target.

"No, that's *him*!" I protest. "That's Alekos!"

"The Heartbreaker? That's okay," she shrugs, still not getting it, "I'm not planning on marrying him! I mean, can you see me with a man who drags people around on an inflatable banana for a living?"

I feel a little snubbed on his behalf and remind her of his officer status. But of course this has entirely the wrong affect: "Oh yess!" she gurgles. "Does he have his uniform with him?"

I roll my eyes — if only I thought she could be satisfied with a quick Polaroid.

Before I can expand on my protestations Alekos is beside us — "*Yassou!*" He nods in her direction.

220

"*Yassou* to you too," she growls, biting her lower lip in unashamed animalistic desire.

Alekos falters, looking a little bemused. Presumably he can't believe his luck — for once the chase has come to him.

"This is my friend Julie," I say, somewhat grudgingly. "Jules."

He reaches for her hand but she immediately swoops in for a cheek-to-cheek kiss, wasting no time getting the maximum body contact going. Did her boob just "accidentally" touch his pectoral? Nooo! I want to squeal — this is all the wrong way round — it's my birthday, but he's the one who's getting the present!

I try to give her a discreet "back off!" pinch but she seems to mistake this for encouragement — after all, I did once wish out loud that she could come and torment him . . .

"I hear you've been working Selena really hard!" She purrs mischievously. "I've come to offer some relief."

He looks confused. "You're taking over from her?"

"Not taking over, taking away . . ."

"What?" I startle. If she's come to take me to Brighton, she's too late.

"You don't need her any more, do you?" She cocks her head at Alekos.

He opens his mouth but no sound comes out.

"I mean, your hand is all better now, I see."

He flexes his fingers. "Yes, I suppose so."

"Wait until you see the hotel!" She turns her attention to me. "Total five-star deluxe!"

"But —"

She links her arm in mine. "Come on, let's get going!"

"NO!" I blurt suddenly, literally digging my heels into the sand. I don't care if Nana Mouskouri has come out of retirement just to give us a private concert; this is not what I want.

What I want is to blink and find Jules back in Mauritius and my day going ahead as planned.

"What do you mean, no?" Jules laughs. "The resort is known as 'heaven at sea level' for good reason!" Then she leans in to whisper, "And the sand on their beach is a lot blonder than here!" She turns her nose up at the grit I have come to love.

"I — I can't leave now," I stammer.

"Why not?"

"Well, for one thing I have to translate for Ben, he has a windsurf lesson with this little girl who only speaks French — look, here she comes now!" I point up the beach as a *petite fille* in a lilac bandana is waved off by her mum.

"Well, alright." Jules shrugs. "I don't mind hanging here for a bit, we're not due at the spa until five p.m."

"*The spa?*" I can't believe she's gone ahead and made all these arrangements without consulting me first! Other than that's what I normally love about her.

"I booked us in as soon as I got there," she explains. "You know how I love Espa."

"Yes, yes, but I don't finish here until seven p.m., so it's probably best if you go on ahead —"

222

"It's okay," Alekos assures me, all too graciously. "I don't mind if you leave early today. But maybe later we could all —"

I hold up my hand to halt his merry threesome plan.

"Do you know what I think would work best? Jules, you go back to the hotel, have your treatments and an early night, and then I'll be over first thing in the morning and we can have a good ol' chat over some Greek yoghurt —"

She shakes her head. "You have to come tonight."

Oh god. "Surely you're exhausted after your flight?" I reason, desperate to not let go of my fantasy. "Not to mention all the trauma . . ."

She steps closer, eyes welling up for maximum guilt-trip effect. "I can't be alone right now, not after . . ." She trails off. *Please, Selena.*

Oh marvellous. Now I look like I'm trying to ditch my friend in need. The little French girl is waiting patiently for me to do the right thing. As is Alekos. I can't help but crumple. Look how selfish I'm being — I'm entirely focussed on preserving the possibility of a birthday kiss when poor Jules has just called off her wedding! Imagine how wretched she must be feeling to have flown all this way for some sympathy and support from her best friend, and what does she get?

"Of course," I give her hand a reassuring squeeze, "just let me take this windsurf lesson and then I'm all yours."

The next sixty minutes are nigh on unbearable for me. All my new-found confidence about the bond Alekos and I have forged over the past few days appears to be evaporating in the all-too-intense sun. I'm trying to concentrate on translating Ben's instructions into French but out of the corner of my eye I can see Jules having a private tutorial of her own. I know she knows perfectly well what to do with a windsurf board but she's persuaded Alekos to stand behind her so she can jut that perfect stress-ball bottom of hers into his groin and then, yup, classic, tumble back into the water and clamber all over him as she rights herself. I feel utterly sick. Is this behaviour befitting a jilted bride? Of course she will desist the second I get the chance to explain that I actually like him now, but what if it's already too late? I can't think of anything more humiliating than informing her that Alekos and I have "special" feelings for each other, only to have to watch him salivate all over her. But I'm being silly. He's just accommodating her now because she's my friend. It's me he likes. Admittedly, he's stopped propositioning me lately but that's out of respect, not dwindling desire. Right?

"Selena! Selena?"

I return to my present position. "Sorry, Ben, what was that?"

"Can you just keep an eye on Chloe while I run up to the car to get the rest of the bottled water? I forgot to get it earlier . . ."

"Of course. No problem." I give Chloe a little wave. She really is doing a sterling job — she's only a slip of a thing, no more than eight years old, but she has great strength in her arms and natural control. She'll definitely be impressing the boys when she's older.

Mind you, apparently some girls think it's best to feign L-plates. My eyes narrow as Jules splashes backward into Alekos again, only this time the sail has landed on top of them. I wait for them to emerge. Nothing happens. Instant suspicion — what's going on? Why are they still under there? I start to feel all panicky and agitated. What if they're already kissing? "Those are my lips!" I want to scream. Still nothing. *She wouldn't.* She so would! Look how psyched she was on arrival — she's going to grab the first opportunity she gets and he's hardly going to turn her down; all he's had from me is rejection. Oh, if he only knew what awaited him tonight! Though, realistically, even if he did know, would he choose me? Suddenly I'm not so sure.

"Selena!" I hear my name again but this time Ben's call is not so casual. I turn to find him pointing wildly at Chloe who's now way out of her depth, being blasted along the surface of the water by an all-too-hearty gust.

Merde! I wave my arms but of course she can't see or hear me, every ounce of her being is focussed on corralling the wind and staying upright — she must be terrified! "Get the speedboat ready!" I yell to Ben, racing him to the platform.

As we scrabble to untie the rope, Alekos bounds ahead of us and grabs the steering wheel, simultaneously turning on the engine. "Get in!" he barks at me, surging off the instant I'm aboard.

"How did this happen?" he calls against the wind as we chase Chloe down the bay.

"I — I just looked away for a second . . ." I flounder. "I'm so sorry."

"You must always keep your eyes on them, *always*."

"I know, I'm sorry." I'd apologise a thousand times more if I thought it would help but, realistically, all I can do is brace myself against the pounding surf and pray she's not scarred for life — this has got to be the watersport equivalent of a bolting horse. Her mother is going to kill me.

"Ready?"

We're drawing level with her now and I need to put our rescue plan into action. "Chloe!" I call, trying to get the little purple bandanaed head to look in our direction. *"Laissez-tomber la voile!"*

Alekos is ready to dive in after her but as she turns I get a shock — her knuckles may be white but her face is alive with exhilaration. *"Non, non! Je l'aime!"* she calls to me.

"What's that?" Alekos can't hear her.

"She says she loves it!" I marvel. "She doesn't want to stop."

I see his shoulders relax and his eyes closing in blessed relief. But my anxiety does not ebb away. Even when we've got her safely back to land and she's pogoing around telling her mother she had the best surf of her life, I still feel wretched. My jealousy put a little life in peril.

Clearly this crush on Alekos is bringing out the most vile traits in me, just like Hera. I'm even resentful of my best friend. I should be ecstatic to see her, glad I can return the favour and be there in her hour of need, but instead I'm wishing she'd never come.

It doesn't help that I then knock over one of the bottles of water Ben brought down from the car and drench a customer's backpack.

"Ready to go now?" Jules enquires.

I nod, defeated. I can't believe I've just shown myself in my worst possible light at such a crucial time. I need to get away before I accidentally puncture all the inflatables with a ragged fingernail.

"Do you have the key to the house, so I can get my stuff?"

Alekos hesitates. "Why don't I bring it over for you after I've closed up?"

Great, he doesn't even trust me in his home now.

"Okay." I'm too weak to argue. "See you later."

Some birthday this has turned out to be. I hope this doesn't set the tone for the year ahead.

Even in my state of utter despondency, I'm still desperate to know just what happened under that windsurf sail but the second we're in the car Jules gets a call from her brother and spends the duration of the journey arranging to have the locks changed on the flat back home, presumably so Dom won't be able to get back in before her. Whatever happened must be serious. Hopefully the spa treatment will act as a salve, not that she looks exactly bereft . . . I suppose everyone handles these things differently. She's certainly a high-functioning dumpee, I'll give her that. If indeed it was him that did the dumping. Which seems unlikely considering he was the one who proposed. Either way, I have more pressing concerns — like nipping her Alekos infatuation in the bud.

Still she yaps on.

And with every tyre rotation that takes me further away from him, the discomfort in my chest and stomach grows — it's almost as if the springy band of elastic connecting us is now being stretched to its limit. I stare out at the racing shoreline and try to remind myself that, technically, she hasn't done anything wrong — as far as she's concerned he was there to be messed with and is fair game sexually. When I had the chance, my great protestation was, "No, that's Alekos!" not "No, I like him now!"

The sooner I speak up the better. Wait — is this her rounding off the conversation now?

"Yes, yes, well, just hang on to it until I get back. I'm not sure, I'll keep you posted. And don't go nicking any of my Le Mer face cream while you're there — I know exactly how much is left in the jar!"

"All sorted?" I ask as she snaps the phone closed.

"It will be by tonight," she replies.

"Good, good." I feel a little swirl of nerves as I venture, in my most sing-song voice: "Sooo, what went on with you and Alekos under that sail? You were submerged a long ol' time."

"Oh god!" she hoots, flicking her hair back. "He did this freaky thing where he expelled all his breath and sunk right down to the ocean floor like a dead body! I

228

thought I'd clunked him unconscious with the frame — and then what good would he be to me?!" she giggles.

"So there was no kissing?" I confirm, hope flaring within me.

"Give a girl a chance!" she says as she turns off the dusty main road and begins sloping down a lushly tropical driveway.

Oh thank god. It's not too late! It doesn't have to be him! I can find her a replacement! And soon, judging by the upscale upturn in our environment. Everything within the hotel grounds appears to be saturated with colour and flourishing in the most artful way. As we're helped from the car, I find myself assessing the broad-shouldered porter and the *Desperate Housewives*-style gardener trimming the hedges and then, inside the cool of the lobby, I eye the groomed men on reception with their aquamarine silk ties and discreetly check out the potential millionaire checking in beside us. "He's nice!" I say five times before we've even been handed the room key.

"You know, Selena," Jules turns to face me, "for one night only, let's not talk about men."

"What?" I splutter. This is a first. Besides, surely she's bursting to get the saga with Dom off her chest? "Do you really mean that?" I can't help but question her.

She nods, looking fragile for the first time today. "I know I was all bravado at the beach but now we're here . . ." she looks around her, "I just want our thoughts to be as beautiful as our surroundings!"

I blink back at her in amazement. And then I consider the bird of paradise flowers and the vivid blue ocean and I think, She does have a point . . . Besides, the last thing you want to hear when you've broken up with someone is that your best mate has found the man of her dreams. To tell her tonight about my newfound bliss with Alekos would just be cruel. The least I can do is respect her wishes and hold off until tomorrow.

"I'm really glad you're here with me." She smiles earnestly.

I'm not quite ready to say the same so I give her what I hope is a comforting hug.

"So!" she says, releasing me and clapping her hands together. "I say we go straight up to the spa, release all our toxins, and then enjoy a champagne dinner and some scandalously calorific dessert." She gives my chin a pinch. "It is your birthday after all!"

She remembered! Suddenly the niggly knotting within me unfurls. I've no reason to fret. Jules is not the enemy! I was just having a funny five minutes at the beach. We're in a safe haven now.

"That sounds *perfect!*" I enthuse, as we step forward, this time volunteering to link my arm in hers.

Tomorrow I'll explain about Alekos in a way that doesn't make her feel like I've found my love just as she's lost hers, then I'll suggest a night out in Ayios Nikolaos where we can mingle with some future prospects. Or, if she's in a real hurry, we can go to Malia . . .

CHAPTER
SIXTEEN

Do not speak of your happiness to one less fortunate than
yourself.
— Plutarch

So many spas I have visited with Jules have been down
in the dungeons so I'm pleased to discover the uplifting
and expansive rooftop location at the Elounda Beach.
The predominantly white design is a wonderful mix of
space-age serene and falling-leaf motif with an exquisite
touch of amethyst, the hue of which seems to have been
selected to perfectly complement the skin tone of the
handsome spa manager Yiorgos. He looks like he's been
hand-picked from an aftershave ad and I'm secretly
praying he turns out to be Jules' masseur but then he
introduces us to two petite girls who lead us away from
him for our respective treatments.

I've opted for the "Cretan Experience" which begins
with a foot exfoliation featuring locally gathered sea
salts, crushed thyme and rich Cretan olive oil.

"No arches?" I joke as I survey the pristine room she
has guided me to.

She looks apologetic. "Sorry, no, but we can adjust
the colour of the lighting to match your aura and we
have a selection of soothing music —"

"That's okay," I reassure her. "For my last spa treatment I was on a sunlounger wedged between a couple of windsurf sails, so I think you've probably got everything covered."

I sigh contentedly as she begins cleansing my feet in warm water infused with revitalising peppermint and lemon. With the dimmed lights and her gentle touch, it is delightfully soporific. Even when she moves on to my back massage — using more Cretan olive oil, this time infused with chamomile and lavender — there is no pinching or grinding, just relaxing. I feel myself slipping into a state of contented surrender when suddenly I spring up, sending her bowl of potions flying.

"Oh my gosh, did I hurt you?" she gasps.

"No! No, I'm so sorry. I just realised something!"

"You're not allergic?"

"No, it's nothing really!" I try to calm myself but can't stop babbling. "It's just that a friend of mine is looking for a holiday romance and it's just dawned on me that I have the perfect guy for her!"

"Lucky girl!" she chimes.

And lucky MSV. I don't know why he didn't pop into my head sooner. I'm not saying that he and Jules are necessarily the best personality match but, in terms of circumstantial needs, they are perfect. She needs a reviving fling; he needs a post-wife-walkout ego boost. Imagine what his pals in Malia will say when they see he's hooked up with a hottie like Jules. And what's a first holiday without his first holiday romance? I can't believe I'm not allowed to talk about men until tomorrow! Not that I'm sure Jules will be able to stick

232

to her rule after the first glass of wine. We'll only be able to stay Zen for so long . . .

As soon as I'm done I skip out to reception with silky skin and a new world view.

"I'll have what she had!" a fellow guest jokes. "You look so refreshed!"

I beam back. Maybe it's the Cretan Experience. Maybe it's the matchmaking. Or maybe it's that good old-fashioned elixir love. There's no denying its transformative properties — one minute you're ticking over, borderline bored, and then suddenly you meet someone who awakens a dormant part of you and if they like you back you feel instantly energised, way more optimistic, even a little invincible! The most mundane chores can be completed with joy because now your life has this fabulous other dimension. And even when you're not with them it feels as if you are moving with a secret, internal ally.

My hearts skips a little as I realise that Alekos is all those things to me.

"A little tea while you await your friend?"

"Oh yes please!" I accept the fragrant cup and step out on to a balcony purpose-built for blissful thinking. Sleek white chaises, rustling bamboo leaves and the almost indistinguishable blue of sky and sea. How can you not believe in the sensual purity of life as you contemplate this? I watch a swallow in free fall swoop and glide and think of the line from the *Shirley Valentine* theme song — *"As long as the wind is fair, the sky is always there."*

Whatever happens, I'm going to be alright.

233

"Ms Harper?"

"Yes?" I look up.

"Ms Webb wanted me to let you know she's going to stay on for a second treatment so you may either pick another for yourself" — she offers me the list — "or meet her back at the suite." She presents me with the key card.

"Oh, great, thank you!"

I loll a while longer and then decide to take a meander through the gardens, only to find myself back in the hotel driveway.

"Lost?" enquires a smartly dressed taxi driver, leaning on the bonnet of his Mercedes.

"Little bit," I confess.

"What is your room number?"

"Sixty-three."

"Ah, one of the presidential suites. Let me organise you a buggy." He motions to a staff member.

"Er . . ." I go to correct him.

"It'll just be a moment."

"Oh, thank you very much." Probably easier if I just play along.

"First visit?" he enquires.

"To the hotel, yes, but actually I've been in Elounda since Sunday night."

"Oh, where were you staying until now?"

"At a friend's place, up on the hill." I point over yonder.

"A male friend?"

"Yes, actually."

"A Greek friend?" His voice gets all treacly.

"Yes." Where's he going with this?

He gives me a filthy smile. "Greek men, best sex!"

I gasp at his audaciousness.

"Here is your buggy."

"Th-thank you." I stumble as I climb in the golf cart.

Burring along the path I am once again struck by the expert way Greeks let nature do the talking. The roughhewn stone buildings here complement, never compete, with the landscape and, despite my awareness that no expense has been spared, the overriding impression is not of designer labels or fussing entourage but effortless class.

"It's funny," I find myself musing out loud, "I know that this is one of the ritziest resorts in Crete, but it actually feels more like its own little village."

"You are right!" He laughs. "Our regulars love to return to the familiar faces here. You see this couple approaching?" — he nods to a chic pair in breezy white linen — "that's Mr and Mrs Kakaroubas, they come every year for several months at a time."

"*Months?*" I gasp.

He nods. "People ask them why they don't buy their own villa in Elounda but they consider us their family and they like to chat with the bar manager and see how his grandchildren are doing, enjoy a little 'home cooking' from their favourite chef, you understand?"

I nod confirmation.

"Here we are!" He stalls beside an archway of cerise bougainvillea.

"Down the steps and the door is on the left before you hit the sea!"

"Thank you so much!" I call back as I eagerly trot on my way. All I want to do now is flop down on the bed and daydream about Alekos. Maybe even give him a quick call before Jules returns . . .

The key card instantly releases the lock on the bright blue door, a hefty push and I'm inside.

"Oh my god — you're kidding!" I gasp out loud, eyes widening in awe.

No wonder Jules was so effusive — she actually has her own infinity pool stretching the width of the extensive deck and directly overlooking the sea. Perhaps it's something to do with this most glamorous vantage point but I don't think I have ever seen a body of water look so bling — it's almost as if all the off-duty stars are resting on the surface, glinting and bobbing and playing happily until their night-time shift.

I step forward to admire the pair of wooden sunloungers last seen on a 1920s cruiseship. They have the kind of padding that loves you back, big puffa jacket pockets of cushion in vibrant blue. There are also two canvas-backed chairs and a two-seater sofa the colour of crème caramel, set beside a low table displaying a potted orchid, its delicate petals belying its heady perfume.

As I stand there, bathed in pale turquoise light, I can only assume that Dom must have been a very bad boy and that Jules has drained every last penny from his bank account.

236

Or maybe she had to leave Mauritius in such a hurry because she did a bank job there — this new theory seems perfectly viable as I slide back the patio doors and venture inside, first encountering a full lounge area with soft cream sofas, a desk with its own computer and a cinemascope-screen TV. I pluck a few grapes from the fruit bowl and stumble up the steps to the vast bed. Even if Jules happened to be a basketball player prone to sleeping in the starfish position there would still be plenty of room for me.

Where does this door lead? Ah, to a walk-in wardrobe the size of a small boutique.

Flowers abound. There are three vases in the bathroom alone, lined up along the countertop beside a mirror so long it could house an entire chorus of showgirls, including plumage. To my right is a sunken tub with Jacuzzi jets and a picture window. I'm in danger of again losing myself to the view but then I see the reflection in the window — it can't be!

No! Noooo! I immediately convulse as I turn around. We have our own gym? A full-size running machine, a beast of a multi-function workout station, a full range of dumb-bells, wooden wall bars direct from my schoolgirl gym and — I kid you not — a boxer's punchball. It's probably this body-wrenching ensemble that sold the room to Jules. Another reminder of just how different we are.

Drifting back outside, I squish on to the sunlounger. As the light dims I find my gaze drawn to the distant somnolent mountains, now a soft pinkish-gold. I sigh, feeling positively dreamy with gratitude — grateful to

Jules for inviting me to share this incredible room but even more so to Alekos for introducing me to this landscape in the first place. I never would have experienced any of this magical island were it not for him. I have to call him before —

Oh no! I curse the rap at the door. I've left it too late — Jules is back already.

"Coming!" I call, psyching myself up to give her an overdue heartfelt hug. But as I haul back the blue door, I find my open arms greeting Alekos.

"You!" I gasp. I can't believe it — I've been given a second chance!

"Me!" He grins, wheeling my suitcase on to the deck and handing me my cabin bag.

"Th-thank you!" I don't know quite how to act but fortunately Alekos is equally overwhelmed by the suite, and his fascination buys me a few minutes to compose myself.

I decide I can't throw myself directly at him or he'd be like, "Oh, I see, your friend likes me and suddenly you're interested?" So how do I go about letting him know that I'm ready and that, although I've only been gone a couple of hours, I already miss him?

"This place is insane!" I hear the punchball reverberating in the gym area and then he returns to the deck, dipping down to feel the temperature of the water.

"Feel free to avail yourself of the facilities," I say, sounding like I am including myself in the invitation. Which, frankly, I am.

He doesn't need asking twice. His T-shirt is off, flip-flops discarded and, in one splash, he's in and under.

I love how he loves his water, I smile to myself as I sit on the edge of the pool swishing my feet as I watch my merman flip and glide. He looks so natural and free. Then suddenly he's on a mission, making straight for me, his hands encircling my ankles. Ordinarily I'd squeal and resist and pummel the water with my heels until I wriggled free, but today, despite the fact that I'm wearing one of my long, floaty dresses, I simply slide forward and sink down into the pool until I am in neck-deep. As his hands move to my hips my legs instinctively wrap around his waist, and my arms envelop his toned shoulders. He pulls me closer. Amazingly neither of us speaks. There are no smart remarks, no jibes, just breathing.

Without explanation he begins pacing the pool, moving steadily, calmly through the water so that it feels like a kind of ritual bonding ceremony. Though my dress is swishing around us I don't feel ridiculous, I feel strangely elegant and weightless. With each length he strides we press tighter together, his body the perfect fit for mine. Our faces are touching now, temple to temple and cheek to cheek like a pair of dancers locked in an Argentine tango.

As the sun sinks, the air cools and I shiver, feeling the chill of his own skin against mine, and yet neither of us lets go. There is something so unexpectedly intimate and tender taking place here. I don't want to move and disturb the trust but I am aware that all I would have to do for our lips to finally meet is twist my head a fraction. Does it fall to me to initiate the kiss? I have turned him down so many times I don't think he would presume to make a move any more. Not even when I am willing him to with every fibre. I am on the precipice now. Dare I take that next step?

Suddenly there's a banging at the door. We're so startled you'd think there was a shark in the water. I suppose, in a way, there is — it's Jules.

"Selena! Open up — I'm dripping Cretan oil!"

Before I can even locate the ladder, Alekos has lifted me up and on to the side in one smooth move — no grunting, literally a hand either side of my waist and I'm plonked on the edge.

"Coming!" I call as she rattles the handle.

But I don't find it quite so easy to get to my feet, what with sopping fabric suctioning in layers around my thighs.

"You really need to get yourself a decent swimsuit," Jules tuts, nearly skidding in the puddle I've created. "Oh! Alekos!"

"Hello," he says simply.

"I'm going to change," I excuse myself, heading straight for the shower — the furthest point away. I need a moment to process. To think. To claim what just happened.

I set the shower running, distracted for a second by the assorted jet and angle options. The cubicle doubles as a steam room and I'm grateful there is a seat, even though my naked bottom attaches to the blue marble like a plunger. Leaning forward I watch the water teem over my hands, hands that I'm looking at in a new light. These hands that were just traversing Alekos' body. I smile and clasp the memory to me. Bringing it closer. Trying to brand myself with the feeling.

Such harmony. It's as if we just reached a new level of understanding. Perhaps he had some kind of revelation about missing me too? Perhaps as he packed my things he paused and held my nightie to his face. Perhaps he had to sit down for a moment, so reluctant to remove all trace of me from his house?

As I wrap my de-chlorinated self in a towel, I feel a whisk of nerves — will that sensitive being still be there when I walk out or will his cocky alter ego have resumed control? When I step outside I find the pool empty, only the orange lifesaver ring remains on the surface. I turn back to the room, perhaps he's gone for a quick abseil in the walk-in closet . . .?

"Where's Alekos?" I ask, trying to sound casual.

"Gone. Is the bathroom free now?"

"Gone where?" I can't help but feel a little abandoned.

"He had to run some errand for his father."

"Is he coming back?"

Jules shakes her head. "He wanted to but I explained we need our girlie time. I'm starving, are you?"

"Mmm," I mumble absently.

"Why don't you look at the menus while I get in the shower?"

I sit down in a slump but quickly assure myself it's best that he left when he did, that way what happened between us stays pure. Yes, I would have liked to have spent my birthday with Alekos, but I'd almost rather not see him at all than with Jules in tow. I know she'll be fine when I explain everything but the spectre of her earlier carnivorous attitude towards him has left me a tad on edge. Besides, I still have four nights to go before I leave. Plenty of time. Tonight I will do the decent thing — friendship, loyalty and fine dining.

So let's see. I fan out the menus for restaurants named Argonaut and Artemis and Blue Lagoon, then have a *Shirley Valentine* chuckle discovering one simply called "F". Remember when Shirley's daughter Milandra storms out of the house in disgust that her mother is going on a "grab a granny" fortnight to Greece? Shirley is so insulted by her reaction that she leans out of the upstairs window and shouts after her that yes, she's going to Greece for the sex — sex for breakfast, sex for lunch and sex for dinner.

This outburst stops a passing delivery man in his tracks and he can't help but comment on what a wonderful diet it sounds.

To which Shirley replies: "It is. Have you never heard of it? It's called the F-Plan!"

Apparently in this instance the F stands for fusion.

I like the idea of a lamb tajine with ginger and sundried fruit chutney but I'm not so sure about it featuring the lamb's *knuckle*. Perhaps a little spaghetti with caviar over at the Italian or a seafood fantasy salad with grapefruit? I'm torn between all the options until I discover the dessert menu at Dionyssos: gazpacho of pineapple with lavender syrup, fondant of two chocolates upon a caramelised strawberry soup and

242

most intriguing of all — mille feuille of forest fruits in a mint chlorophyll sauce.

"That's a Greek word!" I joke with myself. "*Chloros* meaning green and *phyllon* meaning leaf." Alekos told me that yesterday on the long drive back from the Lasithi Plateau. Well, Jules said we can't talk about men, but that doesn't mean I can't secretly order desserts in his honour.

I call and book a table and then lie back and listen to the mesmerising swish of the sea below, letting my mind drift . . .

"Selena!" Jules tuts as she steps on to the deck. "Aren't you dressed yet?"

"Oh, I —" I turn around.

"You haven't even done your make-up!"

"Ten minutes and I'll be ready!" I jump to my feet and quickly go scavenging in my suitcase for something to wear.

"Did you book a table?" Jules calls over to me as she slides a number of metallic bracelets on to her wrist.

"Yes. At Dionyssos."

Her nose scrunches. "Is that Greek food?"

"*Gourmet* Greek." I get specific.

"I think there's a sushi place here . . ." She reaches for the menus.

"There is," I confirm. "Would you prefer that?"

She hesitates, remembering it's my birthday. "Another night. It's fine."

"Okay, well, I won't be a mo."

I hang my dress in the steam room to loosen out the creases and then confront my own facial variety. Only tonight there is no frowning and peering at my flaws, everything from my moisturiser to my eyeliner seems to glide on, as if that elusive inner glow has finally reached my surface.

Even my hair goes right with minimal effort. I pick my most glittery lipgloss to celebrate, blow my reflection a playful kiss, and step into the lounge.

"Okay! Ready!" I chime. "Let's eat!"

Silence.

"Jules?"

A slight rucked snore emanates from the bed area. Has she conked out for real or is this her teasing me for taking too long? I creep over and stand beside her. Her breathing is deep and slow. Poor girl probably hasn't slept in days. I feel torn. Should I wake her? Is that selfish? Or would she rather I did? I reach out and give her a gentle jiggle. "Jules!"

She wrenches open one eye. "Sorry, Selena . . ." she croaks, and then she's gone again.

Oh. I stand there feeling distinctly anticlimactic. And then increasingly peeved as realisation dawns: I've left Alekos for nothing. I thought I was doing the supportive friend thing but it's not like she's even allowed us any quality time together — on the drive she was on the phone to her brother, then we had separate spa treatments, she even extended hers, then we got ready in relays, and now she's out for the count. And I'm short of a dining companion on my birthday.

Great. Unless . . .

244

A thrilling notion bubbles up inside me — what if I called Alekos?

Suddenly I'm at great pains *not* to wake Jules. I back away from her fearing that the vibrations from the bongo drumming of my heart might cause her to stir.

If I can just get out the door.

I tiptoe across the room, picking up my handbag along the way.

Maybe I'll get my birthday wish after all!

CHAPTER
SEVENTEEN

Zeus does not bring all men's plans to fulfilment.
— Homer

I've done it! I've escaped the prison guard and entered a wonderland of twinkling lights and night-scented jasmine.

"Good evening!"

"Good evening to you!" I practically curtsey at the well-to-do couple passing me on their way to dinner.

This is such a civilised place; it seems a little uncouth to be yapping into a mobile phone, so I burrow into the nearest bougainvillea bush, forgetting just how prickly the stems can be. Still, no pain no gain.

My heart is yammering as I scroll through to find Alekos' number. As I press dial I get a further flurry of butterflies. *Answer! Answer! Answer!*

Nothing but a ring tone. I flip my phone closed and then redial just in case there was some faulty connection. Same thing. I get a little swirl of panic — what if I can't reach him? I can't let this perfect night go to waste! But then I take a calming breath. No need to freak out just yet. He could be in the shower or letting Loulou out or mid-conversation with his dad. I'll give it ten minutes and call back. Keep the faith!

I walk very slowly past the other villa-esque suites, encountering ever more elegantly attired guests, making me extremely glad I opted for my birthday best — a slinky teal silk dress I had handmade in Singapore. I wonder if Alekos has ever been there? There is so much to still discover about each other and I'm going to love every minute hearing all there is to know about him — a whole lifetime's worth of dinner conversation! And a few bedtime stories too, with any luck . . .

I look at my watch. It's nearly eight-thirty. Still his number just rings and rings. Perhaps I should send a text?

I opt for straightforward: *Scuse late notice but would you like to come to dinner at hotel?* I won't mention anything about Jules at this point. *Reservation at Dionyssos at 8.30p.m. but can hold the table until you get here. Call me!*

I press send and then the agonising wait begins.

It's the strangest thing with texting — the second you know your message has gone you are on tenterhooks. If you don't get a reply directly, your heart sinks a little more with every passing minute. In the good old days, if you left a message on someone's home answermachine and you didn't hear back, you'd simply presume they were out and that they'd get back to you the next day. With a mobile phone you can't help but think: it's right there with him — in his hand or his pocket — why isn't he replying? Even though it could be switched off or they could have no signal or be sitting in a cinema, you can't help but feel a little rejected. Are they ignoring me? I double-check the message status — definitely sent — and then skulk around for a bit and check the Inbox just in case it forgot to alert me to a new message. Nope. Perhaps he's asleep. I'd go for the cinema option, except Elounda doesn't have one. He could be in a noisy bar, however. It is the first night he's had off from me other than the dinner with his dad. He's probably out with his mates.

And then the paranoia begins. Maybe he's glad I'm gone. Maybe he needs this break. Maybe he's offended that I just dropped him like a hot potato when a better offer came in. No, no, no. Think of how we were in the pool. That was just divine. I have to have faith. He's not ignoring me, he just hasn't got the message yet. Got to keep positive.

I walk on, retracing the path of my earlier buggy ride until I reach the beach. Having studied the hotel map, I'm fairly certain I can cut through here, though I hadn't considered the practicalities of stilettos on the sand. I slip off my shoes and pad barefoot, experiencing a momentary sense of feeling grounded and at peace. Ahead of me is the most rustic of the hotel's restaurants — Kafenion — designed to look like a quaint beachside taverna. At a table with whitewashed banquette seating I see a youngish couple laughing together — he pulls her to him, kissing the side of her head as she pops a shrimp in her mouth, and I realise how much I want that easy affection in my life. Seeing Alekos suddenly seems more urgent than ever. I know the idea is that you release attachment and let the thing you want flow to you but I am working to a pretty tight time-frame here. Yes, I still have five more days, but what if Jules is planning on hanging around for the duration? It just won't be the same. Tonight has to be the night!

But what more can I do to make it happen? I've told him the name of the restaurant and said I'll hold the table so all I can do for now is get myself in position.

"*Yassas!*" I smile at the maître d' at Dionyssos. "I have a reservation under the name Julie Webb for two people but my guest may be a little late. Is it okay if I go ahead and wait at the table?"

"Of course, madam," he says, leading me through to a picturesque courtyard with lemon-plaid tablecloths, rattan chairs and a little blue fishing boat beached in the corner displaying a set of giant white shells.

A waiter helps me with my seat and napkin and informs me that tonight is Greek night.

"Isn't every night?"

"Greek dancing and Greek buffet," he expands, pointing through an archway to where tables are heaped with succulent goodies. "Would you like to see the wine list?"

"Oh, yes please!" I perk up. That should take the edge off.

I try and sip slowly but it's hard not to feel self-conscious and keep reaching for the glass when you are sitting alone at a table. I think of MSV and the conversation we had about dining solo at night. If I had his number I'd call him. But then how would that look if Alekos decided to show? I take a discreet peek at my fellow diners. Mercifully it's not all couples. The age groups are mixed and there're enough beautiful dresses to keep me visually entertained. Yikes! I wince as a new arrival weaves through the tables in a skintight leopard-print catsuit, so garishly Eurotrash amid all the streamlined elegance. Mind you, I'm a little bit leopard-print myself with all the bruises from assorted kayak bashings and clumsy speedboat reboarding. I really clunked my shin today. As I reach down to run my hand over the bump, I take a discreet look at my phone in my lap. How can a tiny metal object hold so much power? I feel like my entire destiny is caught up in telecommunication wiring right now.

Another sip of wine, perhaps?

In the absence of a dinner companion, I chink the display glass set with a single flamingo lily. Its red, heart-shaped petal seems a positive symbol of romance to come. Then again, you might also say that the yellow stamen is sticking its tongue out at me. Oh dear. All this switching between anticipatory excitement, impatience and disappointment is clearly taking its toll. I decide to distract myself with a perusal of the buffet.

I reel as I enter the second courtyard — there are so many platters, bowls and steaming tureens, it looks as if an entire village has got together and prepared a multitude of specialities for us.

But as I look around I find myself getting pangs — oh look! Mushed fava beans with diced onion like we ate at Plaka, tomatoey potato wedges akin to our *après*-Zeus-cave lunch, their version of the chickpea dish Alekos brought back from his father's the night we visited the puppies. Maybe I should have opted for the Blue Lagoon Polynesian Restaurant and Sushi Bar; I wouldn't be getting all nostalgic looking at a spicy tuna roll or a smear of wasabi.

Although my intention is to wait and eat with Alekos, I take a mixed plate back to the table as a prop. Fortunately, now the show is starting so all eyes are on the parade of dancers, not on the lone birthday girl.

Watching them bob and skip and stoop and flick, all interlocking arms and assisted leaps, all I can think is that I want to see my own Greek dance. Where is he? I rub the screen of my mobile phone as if the action might conjure a call. But none is forthcoming.

As the show progresses I learn that whereas the national costume for a male dancer is the white pleated skirt and dark red waistcoat, the Cretan man wears black, opting for knickerbockers instead of the ra-ra look and a raggedy tassled bandana. Their native dance — the *pentozalis* — seems more stompy-clappy in nature, culminating in a frantic double-speed dynamic. Apparently *zala* means dizzy in Greek. The dancers make it look effortless but as they take a bow I notice they are all steeped in sweat.

Giving them a well-deserved break, a singer takes centre-stage but all too soon the musicians begin plinking the infamous theme from *Zorba the Greek* and they're back for the grand finale.

Still no response from Alekos.

Unwilling to admit defeat and even less keen on returning to the suite, I loiter at the dessert table, getting an education on Greek biscuits — I can't decide on a favourite between the crispy-chewy *loukoumas* balls with their sticky sesame syrup and the sugar-dusted *kourabies* that crumble to the finest powder the instant they meet your mouth.

Each fingertip licked clean, I look at my watch: 10.50p.m. What now?

"Excuse me," I stop a passing waiter. "Could you recommend somewhere for a nightcap?"

Well, it's still early by Alekos' standards.

He directs me to the Veghera jetty bar — an open circular deck at the end of a rocky promontory, surrounded by swishy sea — such a magical setting I find myself hoping again. I can picture us here — the design emulates a ship with sails flaring taut from a central mast, multicoloured pulses racing the ropes and even a brass wheel for navigation.

"Champagne!" I order defiantly, taking a cushioned seat at the very edge of the decking so I can watch the tiny fish do their frenetic formation dance, made visible by underwater spotlights.

I sigh to myself.

There was a time when I would have sat here quite contentedly by myself but now I feel the absence of Alekos piercing into me. It seems scandalous now how dismissive I was of him on the ship — all that time we could have spent together that can never be regained . . .

"Selena!" I hear a familiar male voice. But not a Greek one.

"Graeme!" I gasp, recognising the chap from the octopus trip. "And Emily!" I cheer as she peeps out from behind him.

"What are you doing here?" we all ask at once.

It turns out they came in search of an unforgettable "last night of the holiday" dinner, opting for fish specialities at Thalassa, and now, like me, they are trying to prolong the evening as much as they can.

In turn I explain that I was kidnapped and brought here by Jules, who has since conked out, and I am currently trying in vain to get hold of Alekos so he can join me. (Though I do take this opportunity to text him one more time — *You'll never guess who I've just bumped into!* I don't mention to them that it's my birthday because if I get even a glimmer of pity at this point I'll probably burst into tears.)

"Well, as long as Alekos and Jules are not off together — you're sure she's asleep in the room?"

"Emily!" Graeme reprimands her.

"Actually, she's right to be suspicious — Jules did express a keen interest in him at the beach."

"Told you." Emily pokes Graeme. "We saw her all over him as we were leaving — talk about octopus hands! I wanted to turn the hose on her."

I laugh, loving having someone on my side. "It'll be okay as soon as I get the chance to explain the situation to her."

"You haven't told her yet?" Emily throws up her hands in horror. "What are you waiting for?"

"Well, it's complicated." I grimace. "She's just broken up with the man she was going to marry so I don't want to be completely insensitive and tell her that I'm wildly in love when she's at her lowest ebb."

"Yes, well, that's all very well but delay at your peril," Emily cautions.

"I know, honestly; first thing in the morning I'm telling her straight — she can have any man on the island so long as he's not Alekos!"

"Good thing we're leaving," Emily teases, putting a proprietorial hand on Graeme's knee.

We chat for a while until it dawns on me that I may be cramping the romance of the situation for them and bid them a most grateful goodnight — they were just the distraction I needed, I feel almost human again.

"Wait!" Emily calls me back. "Graeme, have you got one of your cards?"

He duly obliges.

"I'll give you my email address," she says, scribbling busily. "In case you want to keep in touch."

"That would be great!" I grin, smiling all the more as she draws three little hearts beside her message — "One for each of those octopus hearts!" She winks as I leave.

Strolling back to the suite I decide that, seeing as I only have one heart myself, I don't want it to be filled with anxiety and foreboding. I'd much rather it was brimming with love and optimism. So, yes, for whatever reason Alekos hasn't responded to my texts but these things always seem more dramatic and significant in the dark. It's not like I'll never see him again. Come morning, I know exactly where to find him, the sun will be shining and I'll tell him just how I feel. But first there's the small matter of getting through the night . . .

As I slip back into the suite, I first check on Jules — mercifully exactly where I left her — and then sit out on the deck listening to the breeze. I stay there until midnight. Only when my birthday is officially over can I finally retreat indoors and succumb to the unbelievable comfort of the pillowtop mattress and luxury cottons.

Lying there in the dark, I try to be grateful for all that is around me but all I can see in the blackness is the digital display of the running machine, reminding me just how far I am from the love shack.

CHAPTER
EIGHTEEN

"Everywhere man blames nature and fate, yet his fate is mostly but the echo of his character and passions, his mistakes and weaknesses."
— Democritus

My eyes ping open — I made it through the night!

I'm so raring to go I reckon I could project myself from the bed to the shower in one leap — even taking into account the solid wall between the two — but before I disturb Jules I sneak a surreptitious hand out to my phone. No messages, but then it's still early — Alekos would probably presume we were up all night talking, as girls are wont to do. Right. No more time to waste — I vowed I would take the very first opportunity to explain my change of heart to Jules and though it's going to be a shock, the good news is that she's already lying down. I take a breath and turn to face her.

Oh. She's already up.

"Jules!" I call, sitting up in bed.

No reply. I swing my feet on to the rattan mat and stagger through to the bathroom — she's not in the shower, bath or even dangling from the gym bars. I heave back the patio door. She's not on the deck, or in the pool. No doubt she woke up ravenous after missing dinner last night; she's probably already gone to breakfast. I'm surprised she didn't leave me a note, though . . . A-ha! It's then I spot a sheet of hotel notepaper held in place with a peach on the writing desk.

Wide awake at 1a.m., darn this jet lag! Have mad craving to see Alekos! If I'm not in bed with you in the morning, you know it went well . . .

What? One of Zeus' thunderbolts has just struck straight through my heart. She can't mean it! Surely she wouldn't have driven over there in the middle of the night? I look around the room for further evidence. Her handbag is gone and, more significantly, her makeup bag. Oh god no.

Instantly I'm shaking. It can't be, it just can't be! Why didn't I ignore her stupid "no talking about men" rule and tell her about Alekos when I had the chance? I feel panicky as I picture them together. Surely he wouldn't? Even if she is there, he couldn't possibly have slept with her after what we shared at the pool. I feel my legs giving way and fall back on the sofa.

Got to try to think rationally, keep the hysteria at bay — okay, so say she went there with a very specific sexual intention, it doesn't mean he would have obliged. If Hugh Dancy had propositioned me last night at the Veghera bar I would have told him his timing was terrible and that we'd have to take a raincheck. Maybe she felt humiliated by his rejection and went back into town and picked up some random holidaymaker? She's probably at his hotel room right now. Although he'd have to be quite something for her to give up this deluxe set-up. I take a wobbly breath. I refuse to react until I know exactly what has happened. The best thing I can do is pull myself together, get dressed and get to Driros so I can confront Alekos directly.

All the same, I find myself angrily ripping her note to shreds — she instigates a man-ban and then does this behind my back?

In the shower, I wash my hair and scrub my body with excessive vigour. I'm really seething now. I was so happy before she arrived — how dare she turn up here and ruin everything? This can't be happening. It just can't. I blast my hair with the hairdryer and apply my make-up double-speed. Gone is the dreamy gliding on of products from last night — then I took the time to smooth on some handcream, now I find myself making a fist and giving the punchball a good thwack.

I'm yanking a blue sundress from my suitcase with little concern for seams or stitching when I hear the door go and Jules call cooo-eee.

My heart stops. I'm going to find out the truth sooner than I thought.

Okay, there's no need to go out there all guns blazing. Anything could have happened. Alekos could actually have proved that he is trustworthy beyond my wildest dreams.

I take a deep breath and emerge from the wardrobe. "Hi!"

"There you are!" She skips over from the lounge area.

"I got your note." I stay rooted to the spot.

"Isn't that mad? Out for the count at eight and wide awake at one a.m.!"

"Did you really go and see Alekos?" I find myself shaking again.

She nods, looking positively devilish.

"And you stayed over?" This is absolute hell.

Again with the nodding.

"Did you have sex?" I know it's blunt but I have to know.

"Yes!" she squeaks, giddily doing a stupid celebratory, rub-my-nose-in-it dance.

I want to pass out. I want to drop to the floor and for my head to hit the wood panelling *hard*. But instead I duck back in the wardrobe. "Just give me a minute to jump into this!" I say, waving my dress at her.

Out of sight, I lean on the wall and try to withstand the flood of emotions. So he really is a lousy womaniser, no better than the Norwegian, no better than any other man. He did a few nice things and I dropped my guard — how could I have been so easily swayed? He booked me a massage and took me octopus hunting and I thought he must really love me! And now this. The ultimate betrayal. I close my eyes and try to wish myself numb. This is too much to bear. I have to get away from here. I have to get a flight or a bus or a buggy, whatever it takes — *just get me out of here!*

"Selena?" Jules pokes her head around the door.

"I hate all my clothes!" I say, throwing my sundress back at my suitcase.

"Oh, you're having one of those moments," she tuts. "Maybe you'd like to borrow something of mine?"

I look daggers at her. Is that how it works? She takes my man and in return I get a T-shirt? Why oh why didn't I say something last night? But what if I had? The fact that Alekos was willing to sleep with the first woman who offered herself to him — and at a time when I thought we were at our closest . . .

"Selena? Are you alright?"

"Actually, I feel a bit off." I pull my queasiest face and paw at my stomach.

"You do look pale."

I move away from her, afraid she'll touch me and I'll be forced to savage her. "Um, I don't know what your plans are for today . . .?"

Wherever she's going to be, I'm going in the opposite direction.

"Well, I just came back to have a shower — I don't know how you managed in the bathroom over there, it's so mank, isn't it?" She doesn't wait for my reply. "And then I was planning on going to the beach."

"Here or —"

"Driros. What about you?"

"Um. Well. If you're happy to hang out there I'd really like to take the chance to get some editing done. It's all been a bit hectic until now." Falling in love and all that.

"That's fine." She smiles. "I know the beach isn't really your thing. I don't know how you've stood it all this week!"

I give her a tight smile. "Honestly? If I had to go there today I'd probably throw myself chest-first on the harpoon."

260

She laughs. I don't.

"Have you eaten breakfast?" I ask, continuing to operate in survival mode.

She nods. "Alekos made it for me."

My heart sinks further into my boots. He never made breakfast for me. Admittedly I never lived with him when he had the use of both his hands — I gulp suddenly, trying to force back a violent reaction to the thoughts of his hands all over her perfect body.

"Well, do you mind if I rush out and grab something to eat? I'm starving!"

"I thought you were feeling nauseous?" Jules frowns.

"Yes, but I think I need something to settle my stomach. You know, dry toast or whatever."

"Oh, okay. Well, I have another treatment at six this evening so I should see you just before then. If you're sure you're going to be alright?"

"Nothing that a cream pie won't fix." And a drum of Valium, I think to myself as I stumble out the door.

I want to scrunch up and rock myself to oblivion but in my eagerness to get away from Jules, I have inadvertently exposed myself to a far broader audience. The hotel grounds are buzzing with people heading to the pool or the beach or breakfast. There's nothing for it but to squish down my emotions and put my hysteria on pause for half an hour, after which time I can return to the suite and howl like a banshee.

In a bid to occupy myself I file mindlessly around the breakfast buffet but it just puts me in mind of last night's dinner set-up and all my foolish hopes so I continue past the dried apricots and Cretan gruyère and keep walking. And walking. Down the path, back to the beach I cut across last night, up another path, just keep going. I propel myself onward until I inadvertently merge into the hotel's sister property, the Elounda Bay Palace, and find myself contemplating the waterside restaurant Thalassa with a pang — that's where Emily and Graeme dined last night. If only they were here now — Emily would understand my plight. She'd know what to do next. If I had their card on me I'd call, but I left it by the bedside, along with my phone, I now realise. I'm about to get even more stressed at my situation when I have a reality check — what could she, or anyone, possibly say to make me feel better?

I am now at the furthest point I can venture within the hotel grounds so I look around for somewhere to sit and try to form a plan. Opting for the informality of the beach, I forgo the sunloungers and slump directly on to the sand, raking my fingers back and forth through the warm blond granules in a daze. The tears are becoming more insistent now and I have to blink frantically to keep them at bay — I have no sunglasses to hide behind, I forgot to grab them in my eagerness to flee the suite. Oh why did I ever leave the shack? I wasn't "rescued" by Jules, I was untimely ripped. If I could only make her go away instead of me, could everything go back to how it was?

I snort at my own naivety. Maybe it's a good thing she showed up when she did — forcing Alekos to reveal his true colours. So much for him being a god; he's so patently just a man.

262

I am aware that the look of disgust and devastation on my face isn't a good fit with the rest of the sunny, contented expressions around me and decide to move on in search of somewhere less public, but where to go?

"Are you here for the tour?"

"Pardon?" I turn and see a shiny staff member beaming at me from a gateway.

"We're just showing a group our new Yachting Club Villas — you're just in time."

"Great!" I brighten, latching on to the distraction — anything that will compel me to maintain my brave face and get me out of the glare of the sun.

She leads us down a pathway, and into another world.

As with Jules' suite, Elounda Bay seems integrated into the villa itself; there's even a diving board and steps leading directly into the ocean lapping at the lower deck. (For the record there is also a middle and an upper deck, the latter with its own pool.) But as for the interior — I have never seen anything quite like it before. Our guide explains the concept of a contemporary loft with sliding wall partitions designed to create space changes to suit the guest. Apparently sometimes even the infinitely wealthy want to feel cosy.

"We fly our Yachting Club Villa guests in by private jet," she continues as she walks us through the Bond-esque living area complete with backlit map of the world.

I form my first almost-smile of the day — it comes to something when "presidential" feels like the poor relation.

As the group moves on to the bedroom area I find myself drifting on to the furthest jut of the deck. The aspect couldn't be any more stunning and still I feel like howling my heart out.

I don't understand why this situation with Alekos is having such a big impact on me. He's just a guy I met on the ship a month ago, 1 guy I spent an intense few days with. *Days.* Not months, not years. Why does the sense of loss so far exceed the hours spent?

And if everything happens for a reason, what was the purpose of our encounter? And while we're at it, what message is the universe trying to convey to me right now as I stand in this cross between bricks and mortar and a seafaring vessel? Go back to sea? Alekos was just a distraction, we have a millionaire lined up for you? There must be some positive spin I can put on this, but standing here broken-hearted in the midst of such privileged beauty, all that comes to mind is the title of the Christina Onassis biography I spied in the gift shop — *All the Pain that Money Can Buy.*

I need to excuse myself — surely Jules will have left by now? — but the guide is embroiled in a conversation with a pair of guests so I pretend to be studying the white leather recliner as I wait my turn.

"Yes, yes, well, we also have a property on the Athens coast — Grand Hotel Lagonissi. I will have a brochure sent to your room."

Athens! Suddenly I realise I have step one of my exit plan — interviewing the couple Alekos recommended! If I could set that up I would have the perfect excuse to run away. *"I'm just popping to Athens!"* isn't nearly so dramatic as, *"I'm leaving!"* It also buys me a bit of time to decide what to do next. And at least if I do the interview, I'll feel like this trip has served some purpose and then, when I'm ready, I can hop on a flight to London or maybe even Wellington. It might be fun to surprise my sister. I did think I'd wait until my next cruise took me a bit closer but if the fare isn't too excruciating, then why not now?

The thought of seeing my family brings some comfort and the second I am back in the suite I start frantically researching travel options on my laptop. Just as naming songs helped Emily distract her mind from her fear of drowning, so for me looking up every possible flight time and carrier to Athens gives me an all-consuming sense of a purpose. When I'm done with airlines I move on to hotels, analysing the facilities, location and decor of every hotel, including one that has a Mini Cooper sliced in half as its reception desk. It amuses me to note that selecting "complimentary newspaper" as an essential criteria reduces my options from ninety-seven to twenty-seven, like you'd forgo a view of the Acropolis for a copy of the *Daily Mail*.

Three hours pass in this numbing manner but before I commit to a booking I realise I should probably check the couple are willing to be interviewed, so I call the number Alekos gave me — there's no reply, but at least they have voicemail so I leave a message, hoping none of my loss of faith is conveyed in my voice. At least now I'm starting to feel more in control. This is what I do best: I move on.

As my stomach emits its own little war cry I realise I'm even ready to eat something. Striding purposefully over to Kafenion, I defiantly choose the exact banquette seat where I saw the young cuddling couple last night. I refuse to be terrorised by the fear of being alone. I look at the menu and completely over-order — crumby *dakos*, tangy sardines and juicy wild mountain vegetables. No meagre portions for me!

But all too soon the adrenalin rush of flights, hotels and new horizons starts to wear off. I can feel the energy seeping from my body and my heart begins to ache again. And not just for Alekos. Suddenly the thought of leaving this place for ever seems unfathomable. And yet how could I remain here without always feeling that something profound is missing?

I pay the bill and wander over to the tiny church in the square. It's just a little whitewashed affair from the outside but the inside, with its colourful saint portraits and incense wafters, catapults me directly back to the chapel at St George's monastery on the night we arrived in Crete.

I think of the man I saw crossing himself by candlelight and sigh — how little I knew of Alekos then. I got to see so much more over the past few days, and now it's all over.

In an instant my eyes well up and over — no holding back the tears now.

CHAPTER
NIINETEEN

"Suffering becomes beautiful when anyone bears great calamities with cheerfulness. not through insensibility but through greatness of mind."
— Aristotle

I run all the way back to the suite where the full eruption takes over my body, wracking it with sobbing self-pity.

Why is love never for me? Why does it come to taunt me only to be snatched away? I so wanted to believe this time! And now this . . .

As I angrily mop my streaming eyes, I look at the oh-so-exquisite infinity pool with a kind of contempt — as if it was part of the conspiracy. How can Alekos have held me so tenderly in that water and then slept with Jules? I don't understand. The rage and resentment is swamping me again and I find myself tearing off my clothes and then plunging into the water, thrashing around trying to purge myself of all this anguish.

How could I have got sucked into this? They said he was a heartbreaker, I heard it loud and clear and yet I allowed myself to become utterly deluded! Why would I do that to myself? Am I really so keen to prove to myself that I am better off being alone for all eternity?

The mountains remain unmoved by my tantrum.

Eventually, when I can't pummel the water any longer, I find myself leaning on the edge of the pool wall, staring out at those distant, slender land masses. Though my breath is still juddering from the tears, I know that I have got to try and find some dignity amidst this disappointment.

I try and bring my focus down to the minute detail of the Cretan stone walls, tracing the black veins of seaweed embedded in the rock, picking at the crystal encrustings and exfoliating my fingertips on the gritty grey and gold surface.

I think part of me is still in shock. It is so disconcerting to have the rug pulled from under you just when life appears to be about to take a wonderful upturn. It was a new experience for me to like myself so much better in the company of another. I was enjoying the upgraded version of myself I was becoming around Alekos — an odd mix of more adventurous and more domestic at the same time. I thought I was bringing out the best in him too. Obviously I was mistaken.

I can't bear that I'm already reverting to the stale, cautious version of myself. And worse yet, I can feel that nauseating adrift feeling returning.

"Phone!" I announce as I dredge myself out of the pool.

It's a text from the couple in Athens! The good news is that they've agreed to be filmed, the bad news is that they can't see me until noon on Sunday. Of course just because I don't have an appointment with them for two days doesn't mean I have to stick around here. I could say I want to spend tomorrow doing a location recce for the shoot or simply that I want to make the most of my first trip to Athens, do a bit of sightseeing while I'm there . . . anything but the truth.

As I take my laptop over to the bed to click in comfort, I wonder, are there people who would handle this differently? Would someone else have the guts to have said to Jules, "Actually, I'm going to have to ask you to not shag Alekos any more because it's really hurting my feelings"? But what would that achieve really? I'm not looking for pity or to guilt-trip her, that would just make me feel worse about myself and smack of "If I can't have him then no one can!" As for confronting *him,* what could I possibly say now? He's clearly not the man I thought he was. So what's the point?

The best I can do is keep my mouth shut and leave without any drama.

I pull my computer on to my lap. For a demi-second I wonder about asking Jules to come with me to Athens — she came to Greece to see me, after all, and that way I'd be killing two birds — and a fledgling relationship — with one stone. But then I think of this morning and how she'd already decided to spend the day at Driros, regardless of whether I was going to be there or not. Her priorities are clear. As are mine.

Right. There's a flight from Heraklion early tomorrow morning. That would mean just one more night here. I look up and around me — there are greater hardships. I can do this.

"Selena!"

Apparently my resolve is going to be tested.

269

"Oh dear, you don't look much better." Jules frowns at my puffy face.

"I'm still a bit iffy but it'll pass." I shrug, realising I now have a fantastic excuse for copping out of any activity she might propose for tonight. If, that is, she's thinking of including me . . . "You're back early!"

"Well, I've got some serious packing to do if I'm going to spend another night at that shack." She flumps down on the bed. "I can't believe I'd forgo all this for a campbed and cheap sheets," she says as her palms fan across the cashmere-soft counterpane. "Maybe I'll borrow a couple of pillows from here — if you don't mind?"

"Of course not, technically it's all yours anyway . . ."

She twists around, as if this thought is just occurring to her now. "I suppose in a way you're right. If only things were different and he could stay here . . ."

I blink back at her. Could she really be so callous as to oust me? First from the beach, now from the *bed?*

She reaches up and pulls a strained pose. "I'm actually thinking of changing my facial to a massage today because my back got so messed up last night."

So it's true. She's got the guy, now she wants the adjustable mattress and the Egyptian cotton too! I feel dizzy with disillusionment but instead of confronting her I go the other way.

"Tell you what, Jules," I say, voice tight with the agony of it all. "Why don't we switch beds? You stay here with Alekos and I'll stay at the shack with Loulou."

At least this way I'd get decent company for the night.

Her eyes light up with glee but her mouth says, "Oh no, I couldn't possibly ask you to do that."

"You're not asking, I'm offering," I say, martyr to the end.

It is her room after all. Besides, I'm hardly in need of a shower you can have sex in. And this way I could leave for Athens without any fuss at all, not having to explain myself to anyone.

"Well, it would just be for one night . . ." She feigns being won over.

"No problem, it's not like I've even unpacked yet." I get to my feet, eager to get away from her. The nausea has returned full force.

"Well, you hardly need to take your whole suitcase . . ."

"Oh, you know what it's like." I keep moving to avoid eye contact. "It's almost easier to take everything than try and predict what I'm going to need."

"Mmm," she concedes. "Obviously you can take the car. You know it's automatic."

"Thanks."

"Can I do anything to help?"

"No, no!" I trill. And then it occurs to me that we should probably check the arrangement with Alekos first. Or rather she should — I can't imagine ever speaking to him again.

"Don't worry about that!" she tuts as she changes into her robe. "Who's going to turn down all this?"

I look at the deluxe suite complete with live sex toy. She has a point.

"You know, I had the funniest thought today," she says as she twists her hair into a bun. "When I left work everyone thought I was getting married in Mauritius and now they're going to look at my holiday snaps and be like, 'Why is the groom holding worry beads?'!"

It now hits me quite strongly that this might be the last time I see Jules. I have enough trouble keeping in contact with people I like, and after everything that has happened here . . .

"I suppose I could be gone by the time you get back." I test the water, to see if she's going to offer any resistance to me walking out of her life.

"Okay, if you could just leave your key in reception for Alekos, just in case he gets here before I'm out of the spa?"

Wow. I know I'm in a sensitive state but is that really it? No stay for dinner, no making up for last night?

"I gotta go!" Jules comes over and gives me a sturdy kiss on the cheek. "You're a star!"

I want to correct her and tell her I'm the moon, actually, but in reality I am more of a third wheel, which is appropriate, I suppose, since I am currently in the country that invented it.

I can't believe I only arrived at the hotel twenty-four hours ago and here I am already preparing to leave. I go back into the vast bathroom and pack away all my toiletries, then squish the clothes I dislodged back in my suitcase and take a few photographs to look at ten years from now when this will just be another snapshot from my world travels.

Every time I step on to the deck, the view seems a little different — now the wind is blowing patterns across the ocean surface like dark paint spraying outward, there's a strange sense of foreboding as the clouds gather and even the water in the infinity pool gives a jelly-like shiver.

And then it dawns on me that Alekos could already be on his way over. Immediately I switch to fast-forward. There's no way I can face seeing him — he'll read me like a book and I don't want him knowing the affect he's had on me. I have to get out of here now!

I drag my own case over to reception — terribly gauche, I know, but I didn't want to risk waiting around for a buggy. I'd bundle straight into the car but I can't go directly to the shack in case he's still there. Best I find a hidey-hole somewhere in reception then as soon as I see him walking on through I can skedaddle.

"Would you like me to store that for you?" a super-swift bellboy enquires as I deposit my key at reception.

"Oh, yes please!" Far easier to be discreet without the giant case appendage. I gabble my details and then dart behind the nearest pillar — Alekos has just walked through the main entrance.

My god he looks rough. Well, I suppose he didn't get much sleep last night.

I watch as a little old man accidentally clips his shoulder in passing and Alekos looks ready to clout him. Jeez. I'm glad I stayed out of his way.

"Miss Selena Harper?"

What? Who's calling my name?

"Miss Selena Harper!"

Oh, for god's sake — it's the bellboy with my suitcase ticket. In my haste to hide I'd forgotten to take it.

"Quiet!" I want to shriek. But it's too late — Alekos has heard him now and stopped to look around.

"Miss —"

I reach out and grab the bellboy by his jacket tail, yanking him back behind the pillar with me and sssshhing him manically.

Alekos makes one more 360-degree turn, looks as if he might have imagined the whole thing, and then goes on his way.

Finally, I loosen my grip on the bellboy.

"I am so sorry about that!" I attempt a breezy smile. "I actually am ready to go *right now!*"

He couldn't look more relieved.

I feel weak with sadness as I pull back on to the main road. To lose the man of your dreams and your best friend in one day is phenomenally depleting. I can't help but suspect I need to become more discerning about both categories in future.

As I pass through the town square I keep my eyes directly on the road ahead, trying not to look at the bar where I had my firework cocktail or the bakery with the amazing cream pies or the grocery shop staffed by twin Bobby Balls.

274

I get all the way to the bottom of Alekos' road without incident, and then stall. I'm not sure I can do this after all. I edge a little closer but find myself puffing out my breath Lamaze style in a bid to keep from crying again. I'm afraid that if I walk in that door and see the place I mistook for our home I'll lose it again and this time I might not be able to stop.

Is this really over? I feel as if I'm experiencing some massive bolt of separation anxiety. Alekos may have been physically dependent on me initially but I'm the one who became emotionally dependent. And, as of now, emotionally abandoned.

For half an hour I sit there in the car, wondering what I should do for the best. I'm just about to start up the engine when my phone bleeps. Another text.

For one foolish moment I think it might be Alekos telling me it's all been a terrible mistake — he's broken it off with Jules and he's coming home to me!

But it's not, it's Jules.

"Alekos says he's already fed Loulou tonight, just give her half a can in the morning."

Ah yes. There we are — the coded love message I've waited my whole life for.

Well, at least I don't have to worry about Loulou this evening. If I want to I could find another hotel room and then nip over and see her for breakfast — I'm sure it won't seem anything like as daunting in the daylight. Especially when I have a getaway plane waiting . . .

My intention is to put Elounda behind me and head to Plaka for some comfort eating at the Pinenut, but as I draw level with Driros beach I find myself pulling in before I've even realised what I have done.

Yes, there's a risk it'll just make me feel even more woefully nostalgic, but this little nook has offered me so much peace the past few days, I just want to take a moment to say thank you.

I pull on a jumper and step out of the car. Whoah! If I thought the descent to the beach was perilous by day, it's even more hairy by night. I end up inching my way down on my bottom, feet first, running my hands over the rubble, ready at any minute to claw my fingers in like crampons. I pause before I step on to the gritty sand at the base. It is just so beautifully still here. For the first time since this morning when I saw Jules' note, I feel I can breathe.

It's a very different place without all the energy and sunshine of the day but I'm just as enamoured of its more subdued side. I used to love that twilight phase when the day was winding down, the air cooling, Alekos yawning, me packing up my unused laptop, knowing that I'd actually lived myself that day rather than just observed others.

I'm just deciding whether to place one of the plastic chairs under the tree or out on the jetty when I freeze. I am not alone — there's a body on the beach.

CHAPTER
TWENTY

"We should look for someone to eat and drink with before looking for something to eat and drink for dining alone is leading the life of a lion or a wolf."
— Epicurus

He doesn't look like he's been washed ashore — his clothes are dry and no limbs are skew-whiff. Plus, as far as I'm aware, dead men don't snore.

It seems an odd place to sleep, flat out on the grit, but I suppose plenty of people nod off on the beach by day, and he does have a hat over his face so perhaps he was dozing in the afternoon sun and accidentally slept through going-home time.

I creep a little closer. Hold on a minute — I think I recognise that hat!

"MSV?" Even though I'm using a nickname he's never heard, my voice is enough to stir him.

"Selena!" he startles, quickly shuffling upright and slipping his trilby back on to his crown. "You came!"

"You were expecting me?"

"Well, actually, I'd given up hoping." He gives his face a reviving rub. "I got here just before seven, but you'd already shut up shop so I didn't really think you'd come back. You probably thought I'd forgotten about dinner, right?"

Oh no. That would be me. I'm only now remembering the arrangement for him to cook for the Driros crew. Gosh, that seems a lifetime ago. Only yesterday I had him in mind for Jules, and look how outdated that concept is.

"My tour was late back and I couldn't let you know because stupidly I never took a contact number for you."

I nod empathetically. "I was thinking the same last night — and I don't even know your name!"

"Greg!" He grins. "And you're Selena, right?"

"Yes," I say, as I reach to shake his hand. "Pleased to meet you!"

We chuckle at our belated formalities and then he asks, "So what was going on last night?"

"Oh. It was my birthday and I ended up eating alone," I explain, hoping I don't sound too tragic.

"Really?" He looks concerned.

"Yes, it's a long story," I say dismissively.

"Well, clearly I have more than enough time to hear it."

"It doesn't have a happy ending," I warn him.

"Well." He gets to his feet, dusting himself down. "The night is young. My fridge is full. We could pretend tonight is your birthday if you like?"

"A second chance?" I smile, liking the idea of pretending the last twenty-four hours never happened.

"Why not?" He shrugs.

"Why not indeed!"

I can't help but give the moon a grateful glance as we climb back up the bank. I won't have any qualms about telling Greg my pitiful story because he's certainly a man who has known great heartache, although thinking about it, his situation does make mine look rather trivial in comparison.

"So did you walk here?" I ask, noticing I am the only car in the lay-by.

"Yes, I'm so close — just across the road and up the hill. The Elounda Carob Tree Valley Villas."

"I've heard they're gorgeous!" I coo, remembering Alekos telling me that they were pretty much his idea of a dream home.

"Well, my wife does have excellent taste."

"Except in men."

"Thanks very much!" he splutters.

"No! I mean, whoever this guy is she left you for. Oh sorry, I'm just making it worse," I cringe as I unlock the passenger door for him. "You can get me back plenty when I tell you my sorry tale."

"Does it involve Alekos?"

"Of course. And then we have the surprise arrival of my best friend." I hold up a corrective finger. "Former best friend."

"They hit it off?" He offers me a neat little euphemism.

"While I was sleeping. Not in the same room or anything," I hasten to add. "But it just felt extremely behind my back. Though really it's okay because I think she's just shown me what a bad idea he was."

"So one day you'll be thanking her?"

I nod as I turn on the engine. "Just not tonight."

Greg requests a U-turn and then directs me up a bumpity dirt driveway. I can't see beyond the beam of the headlamps but there appear to be wild fields all around us and at one point he reaches in his pocket and uses a remote to open a broad metal gate.

"Keeping the riff-raff out?"

"And the goats in," he explains.

We're on smooth tarmac now and approaching a series of eight or so hip buildings blending cool Cubism with traditional Cretan stone, each with their own cluster of carob trees.

"This really is stylish," I comment as he directs me to his driveway. "Even your low-life friends must have got a kick when you pulled up here!"

Greg chuckles to himself, remembering their first night. "We actually took the wrong turning into someone's private driveway, set all these dogs barking and then this crazy Greek lady ran out in her nightie and chased us down the hill!"

"Little did your pals know that that was the best offer they were going to get in Elounda!"

"I know," he laughs as we step from the car. "By the third night they were thinking of asking her out on a date!"

"Have you heard from them lately?" I ask. "More bacchanalian tales from Malia?"

"Yes, and you don't want to know." He shudders.

"You don't feel you're missing out at all?"

"Not with them."

"But you do feel you're missing out on something?" I persist.

He pauses and picks up one of the shedded carob pods, inspecting its brittle, withered surface. "It's silly really . . ."

"What?" I encourage him to continue, both out of curiosity and an instinctive need to try and fulfil other people's holiday dreams. Especially now that I'm so in need of distraction.

"I don't know. I suppose I thought my first time abroad might be a little more eventful."

I raise an eyebrow.

"I've probably just watched too many movies. And listened to too many Greek myths — they're not short on drama, are they?"

I shake my head. "Mind you, you have been abandoned by your friends and you've met me at the single-most tragic juncture in my life, so that's a start, isn't it?"

He concedes a nod, throwing the pod back into the bushes and continuing up the Flintstones flagstone path.

"Besides, if you're looking for a story to tell the folks back home, I think they'd probably rather you let your cooking do the talking — how cool that you can prepare an authentic dish for them from the country you just visited?"

"Is that a hint for me to hurry up and get my pinny on?"

"Well, I am a little peckish . . ." I grin.

"Duly noted." He stops suddenly. "I've just remembered — there is one pre-birthday-dinner requirement . . ."

"What's that?"

"You need to make a wish. Upon a star."

My head is about to tilt heavenward when he steps aside to reveal a glowing oblong of pale turquoise.

"You've got your own pool!" I gasp.

"Which is just as well, because you need to be floating while you're wishing."

"That's a new one on me!" I blink at him. "Does that make it extra-effective?"

"I don't know about that, but it's the best cure for the miseries. I do this every night — come on!"

Already he's kicking off his shoes and pulling off his T-shirt in that hair-rumpling way men do. One splosh and he's in, gliding to the centre. I watch as his facial expression becomes awash with serenity.

"Are you going to join me?" he asks, swishing water through his fingers.

The old me would make an excuse to opt out but this feels like an opportunity to hang on to some of the spontaneity Alekos encouraged in me. Besides, I don't want the last memory of me in a swimming pool to be the one where I'm thrashing around crying . . .

Because it's dark and he doesn't seem the type to stare, I venture in wearing my cotton camisole and knickers, then swill over and float beside him, listening to my own breathing in my waterlogged ears.

"I was going to try this earlier at the beach for the full natural effect," Greg explains, "but I find there's a hint of menace about the sea at night."

"You mean the niggling concern that some slimy beastie might grab your leg and yank you down into the depths, never to return?" I suggest.

"Exactly," he confirms.

I smile to myself — this is a man after my own heart. I loved that Alekos was such a fearless merman but I didn't like feeling a scaredy cat around him. It's good to be understood.

"So, pick a star, any star . . ."

"Ahhh," I sigh as my eyes dart around the assembled constellations. "There are so many to choose from!"

"No rush."

I take my time locating the one that seems to be twinkling just for me and then take a breath. "I wish Greg would come to Athens with me."

"Athens?" he chuckles. "When are you going there?"

I gasp, inadvertently splashing him in the face as I flounder myself upright. "Did I just say that out loud?"

"Did you not mean to?" He looks amused, blinking the chlorine from his eyes.

"Well, not really. I mean, wishes don't come true unless you keep them to yourself, do they?"

He thinks for a moment. "I'm not sure. Sometimes I think it might be easier to just ask for what you want."

He's got a point. I kept my deepest wish regarding Alekos to myself and look where that got me.

"So what do you think? About Athens." I dare to test his theory. "You said you wanted an adventure and I'd welcome the company . . ."

"When are you thinking of going?" he asks.

"Tomorrow."

"*Tomorrow?*" Now it's his turn to make waves.

"I know it's soon but you've got no babysitters to arrange, no work to ask for time off," I wheedle.

He looks quite flummoxed but I can see some part of him daring himself to be receptive to the idea. "How long are you going for?"

"Two nights, probably."

"Wow, that's a long way to go for a quick break — my guide today said it takes nine hours to get here."

"By boat," I clarify. "I was thinking of taking one of those new-fangled aeroplanes — they do it in fifty minutes."

"Really?"

I nod.

He thinks for a moment and then suggests we continue this conversation on dry land.

"Preferably in the kitchen." I give him another nudge as we pad wet footprints across the decking to the front door.

"Oh wow, Greg! This place is beautiful!" You'd think I'd struggle to get excited about any accommodation after the elite indulgences of the Elounda Beach, but the villa's interior styling is so fresh and enchanting I feel instantly revitalised. Amidst all the immaculate white (including shiny Perspex dining chairs and an outsize cotton sofa, plump with ten large cushions) my eye is drawn to the accent wall of softest hyacinth displaying the word "home" in raised white script.

"Oh, I love that!" I enthuse, discovering the lettering — like the whitewashed chandelier above and the foot-long candlesticks beside the fireplace — is also made of wood.

"There're more words upstairs!" Greg leads me to a bedroom painted with the same sugared-almond subtlety, only this time in sheer mint and showcasing the word "joy". I sigh mistily as he opens the door on to the balcony, allowing a gentle breeze to swell the veillike curtains, and then follow him through to the main bedroom. Its hue is pale Wedgewood with "dream" set at the head of a starkly modern white four-poster.

"Stunning," I murmur.

If my circumstances were a little different, I could live somewhere like this. The Cretan love shack was a tad too rustic. But to me this Greek chic is perfection.

"For you."

Though I have numerous clothing options in the car, I accept Greg's offer of a robe, and even opt for a towel turban so I can feel like a movie star swanning around her Mediterranean hideaway with her private chef.

I might even feel inclined to cook myself in a kitchen like this — sleek stainless steel appliances, dishwasher, juicer, marble-topped dining table with a teak alternative al fresco and, most charming of all, a picture window lined with three glass shelves displaying dainty jewel-bright vases of flowers.

"From the garden." Greg points through the window to the row of miniature rose bushes and then hands me a glass of wine. "So first things first — happy birthday! To the start of a whole new year."

I can't help but pull a face as we chink. "And what a start it's been!"

"Look at it this way," he encourages. "Things can only get better!"

"Actually, they already have!" I acknowledge as I take a sip of the chilled liquid. "This is all so civilised."

I turn back to the lounge to take in the details I missed on my first scan — including a parade of silver lanterns and an impressive stack of DVDs.

"Did you bring all these with you?" I ask as curiosity drives me to file through them.

He nods. "I know most people catch up with their reading on holiday, but there are still so many classics I still want to see."

"*Onassis*, the mini-series?" I hold up the case, giving him a dubious look.

"My mum insisted I take that." He cringes. "She's got everything Jane Seymour's ever done — she plays Maria Callas in that. Anyway! Talk to me about Athens," Greg requests as he continues with his food preparations. "What exactly did you have in mind?"

"Well, I just have one appointment at noon on Sunday," I say, not wanting to distract him with the details now. "How about you tell me what you would most like to do there!"

He stops mid-slice. "I suppose the Acropolis is old news to you?"

"Ancient," I tease before admitting, "Actually, I've never been."

"Really? Would you want to?"

"I actually think it's compulsory," I announce. "Let me check their website, make sure they don't have any weird holiday closings or anything."

I heave my laptop out of my bag. "Will I be in the way if I put it here?" I motion to the kitchen table.

"No, there's plenty of room. Besides, we'll probably eat outside — I thought the weather was going to turn nasty for a minute but actually it's warming up again."

"It is indeed." I smile as I scroll through assorted websites. "Oh my god!"

"What is it?"

I open my mouth and then close it. Is this for real? I lean closer to the screen as if this will authenticate the words before me. I can't believe it — I think I might just have found the "event" that will make Greg's holiday utterly unforgettable.

"Selena?"

"Mmm?" I stall — I daren't get his hopes up in case it's not quite as feasible as it sounds. "I'm just trying to find the ticket information."

"You're obviously in the right job."

"What do you mean?"

"Well, your face really lights up when you're looking up tour stuff."

"It's just the reflection from the screen," I lie. In this moment my own personal miseries have been leap-frogged by a burst of altruistic excitement. I want to squeal and do a little dance but I have to keep it all inside — this will be so much better as a surprise.

I tap feverishly, getting as much info as I can on this unique event without arousing suspicion. Talk about synchronicity — we are obviously supposed to be going to Athens together tomorrow. Beyond that I don't know but right now I'll take any kind of certainty, however short-lived.

"So listen. How do you feel about getting one-way tickets there? It's no more expensive and that way we can decide to come back when it suits us, depending on whether we like or loathe the place." I don't want to alarm him too much by telling him that I'm not planning on coming back at all.

"I put myself in your capable hands," he says smiling.

"Good man."

As I look at the hotel options I marked as favourites earlier, I try not to dwell on the fact that this is the second time in a week I've taken an impromptu trip with a man I hardly know but assure myself that at least my taste is improving — Greg seems to be one of those mythical nice men you hear about but never actually meet.

"Accommodation-wise, we could go for the Athens Gate Hotel," I inform him. "Walking distance from the Acropolis, simple, clean lines, rooftop bar . . ."

He comes and leans over my shoulder. "That looks good."

I reach for my credit card.

"Did you already get the flights?"

"Yes," I tell him.

"Well, let me do this," he offers, wiping his hands on the tea-towel and switching positions with me.

"More wine?" I offer the chef a top-up.

"Don't mind if I do," he says as he intently studies the screen. "Do you want to check this over before I click confirm?"

I scan the page. Well, he's marked two rooms so we are obviously travelling respectably. "Er, just one thing, when it says number of children?"

"Yes?"

"They mean travelling with you."

"Oh-oh!" He quickly makes the 2 into a 0, muttering, "Miss Know-it-all!"

"Is my dinner ready yet?" I jibe back.

The meal is delicious — golden flaky filo cheese pie and a couple of zesty salads — though Greg insists it's more like picnic food.

"I'd love to have done moussaka or dolmades but they're an hour in the oven and I thought you might expire if I made you wait that long!"

"Quite right!" I say as I reach for a slice of watermelon, even though I'm already fit to burst. "Are these your girls?"

Greg nods and hands me the photo I have spied. "Lily," he says, pointing to the eldest. "And Daisy." He shakes his head and sighs. "You know the thing she was most peeved about when we explained the divorce?"

I shake my head.

"That she wouldn't be getting a baby brother or sister to play with. She said Lily got to cuddle her and push her round in the pram when she was tiny and she couldn't believe that she wasn't going to get her turn."

"You know you can get those dolls that are the same size and weight as a baby? They even come with this weird rash . . ."

Greg chuckles. "I know just the one you mean! Tried that. Didn't fly."

"Or . . ." I say, on a bit of a fix-it roll, "my friend Roxy is about to give birth and she's not so very far from you. It's her first and I'm sure she'd welcome a little pram-pushing assistance once a month, not to mention your child-rearing expertise! I'm going to give you her phone number . . ."

As I start rooting through my bag in search of my phone, Greg gazes back at the photograph.

"It's strange," he muses. "It's like I don't really know who I am without them. I'm so used to being in father mode and now I'm here and there's no one to keep a watchful eye on or wipe ice-cream drips from their chins, well, at least not now my mates have gone."

I chuckle and then tell him, "As uncomfortable and unfamiliar as this all must be, it's probably just what you need. You're going to have more time apart from them — weekends, alternate Christmases, that kind of thing; this is a good chance to remember what you like to do."

"You're right," he sighs as he reaches to open our second bottle of wine. "Lately, when she's had them for the weekend, I'll just lose hours on the Internet. I justify it as research for work — I'm in webpage design — but, really, I'm just idling away the hours."

"Easily done. And all the more reason to find something to do that gets you out of the house, away from the screen." I scroll through my address book and jot down Roxy's number, determined for him to have it whether he wants it or not.

"Been reading up on your Greek myths?" Greg picks up the book I've set on the table.

I roll my eyes. "Yes, well, I'm sure it'll come in useful for a pub quiz sometime. Or one of those party games — If I were an Olympian, which would I be?"

He starts flicking through the pages. "So who would I be? From what little you know of me . . ."

I contemplate him for a while. "Would you be offended if I compared you to a goddess rather than a god?"

"Feel free — according to my friends I was emasculated long ago!"

"Well, I was thinking of Hestia," I tell him. "Goddess of home and hearth."

"Sounds cosy." He grins, until he locates Hestia's write-up . . . "Dedicated to peace and neutrality, didn't have any notable adventures, rarely roamed — well, that's me." He slumps further as he learns that few shrines were built in her honour.

"Well, that's not strictly true," I inform him. "Each and every home is considered a shrine to her."

His face brightens. "Well, when you put it that way . . ."

"And how did you manage to scoot over the bit that says she's was the kindest, most virtuous and charitable of all the Olympians?"

"Now you're making me blush!" He hides his face in his hands.

"Can I ask you a question?" I sit back in my chair, giving up on finding the phone for now.

"Of course."

"Well, in many ways, you have been living my worst fear and yet, divorce aside, you don't seem to have too many regrets, I mean about the lifestyle itself?"

"I don't," he says as he clears the plates. "But I suppose it would depend on the individual — what you consider success and failure. I may have led a little life by Onassis standards but I was happy. I hope I will be again. You can't regret happiness, can you?"

"Not for a minute," I confirm.

"It seems like domesticity represents something very negative to you. For me it was a choice and, admittedly, it doesn't come with all the historic baggage of being a woman being chained to the kitchen sink — a man getting to spending more time with his kids? The worst you've got to worry about is the perception of being a wuss or not being the main breadwinner. Tough for an alpha male. But not an issue for me."

"Alpha is a Greek word, you know . . ." I hear a voice in my head.

"I liked my job but I liked my kids more," Greg continues. "And it's not like I gave up a huge social life at work — I gave up a grey padded cubicle and a squeaky chair. And in return I got to hang out with two people who are a source of endless fascination to me."

"But what about all those household chores?"

"Well, all jobs have elements you don't enjoy. What is it with yours?"

"The paperwork, the early mornings, the guests who seem hell-bent on finding fault, no matter what."

"So for me the equivalent is ironing and plumping cushions. We've got a dishwasher and I order most of

292

the supermarket supplies online so that's hardly a hassle. Things are changing, you know! Only on *Big Brother* do you have to use a mangle as part of the laundry process!"

We decide to reconvene in the lounge area so we can splay out in a manner befitting our ever-more tipsy state. I get the feeling Greg hasn't really had the chance to talk through his feelings about the divorce of late, especially not with his Malia mates, so, for better or worse, I encourage him to let it all out.

"I feel like my life has shrunk," he tells me as he rests his head on the back of the sofa. "There were four of us, then three when she left, and now it's just me. And I know it's temporary and it'll be back to three in a few days but I had a whole family before and now . . . I don't."

My heart is heavy for him. Contrary to what I would have predicted for myself, his sense of loss hasn't come from a feeling that he's missed out, it's more to do with the depleted body count. He was part of a team. He felt complete. And now he's feeling less than . . . So strange, what people take away from us when they leave.

"I still expect her to come through the door," he continues. "I know people say things like that when people have died . . . But I'm having trouble accepting that she's gone. I don't understand why the kids weren't enough incentive for her to stay. It wasn't like things were bad between us —" He stops suddenly.

"What?" I ask him.

He looks slightly ashamed. "I almost wouldn't mind if she carried on taking him away with her on her business trips if we could still have her at home."

My heart aches for him. "But the difference is that now you'd know . . ."

"I could block it out."

I shake my head. "You can't live like that." I reach out and give his hand a squeeze. "I'm so sorry that you're going through all this."

He turns to face me, looking deeply apologetic. "I've totally depressed you now, haven't I?"

"Oh please!" I tut him. "It would be far worse if you were telling me jokes to try and cheer me up! This is just what I need — a good wallow in love's miseries!"

Greg looks at me and then makes an earnest suggestion: "Let's not take our miseries with us to Athens."

"Okay!" I smile, wishing it were as simple as not packing them. "We'll leave all our tears out to dry on the patio while we swan off to the Acropolis! Actually, I suppose we should talk timings . . ." I haul myself upright so I can think through the practicalities. "Let's see — we need to allow an hour and a half to get to the airport and another hour and a half before the flight, so we'll have to leave by seven a.m.!" I look at my watch. "Yikes! That's only five hours away! I should go!" I get to my feet, none too steadily. "Woah!" I reach back for the arm of the sofa.

"You know you're more than welcome to stay," Greg offers. "The sheets in the spare room have been changed since the boys left so it's all pristine and all yours!"

Hmmm. I have had too much to drink to drive. And this is a neutral space. I will miss the chance of sleeping with Loulou one last time but I won't miss waking up and going down to an empty kitchen — it just wouldn't be the same without Alekos grinning at me in a state of undress. I mean, who smiles that much first thing in the morning?

"That's very kind of you," I say, so grateful not to have to be alone tonight. Although the second Greg wends up the stairs, I have a little flash of "don't leave me!" anxiety.

This isn't like me. I am one of life's independents. I don't cling. What is going on?

I rouse myself sufficiently to get what I need from the car but as I step back inside the villa, I find myself confronted by the word "home". It seemed so comforting when I first beheld it; why does it taunt me now?

"Don't dwell, don't analyse, just sleep!" I tell myself as I hurry up the stairs, along the corridor, and slide into bed.

But within a few minutes of lying there in the filtered moonlight, I feel my emotions preparing to rush in on me.

"No!" I take a defiant breath — I can't risk another flood of tears so I raise an imaginary shield and prepare to deflect them with as much diligence as if I'm fighting the Trojan War.

"Joy, joy, joy!" I whisper to myself.

Just five more hours. That's all I have to get through and then I'll be on my way.

CHAPTER
TWENTY-ONE

Love is a serious mental disease.
— Plato

When I awake the next morning it occurs to me that tonight I will be sleeping in my fourth bed since arriving in Greece. But before I do, I need to revisit the first.

"So, if you follow me there, I'll run in and feed Loulou, leave the keys and the car, and then hop back in with you and off we go to Heraklion!"

"Got it!" Greg heaves a sportsbag on to the table and double-checks he has everything he needs.

"Excited?" I ask.

"I think the technical term is hungover." He grimaces. "That's the most I've drunk since I've been here."

"As long as you're not having any regrets —"

He shakes his head. "How can I miss out on the chance to travel with a highly experienced excursions professional?"

I give him a rueful look. "You know Athens doesn't exactly fall into my area of expertise."

"Well, then you'd better get studying." He grins, handing me his travel guide.

"I'll speed-read it on the plane," I tell him, taking a last slurp of tea. "Ready to go?"

I think I'm doing an excellent job of being chirpy and motivated but then we step outside and the unexpected view of Elounda Bay lurches my stomach.

In the bright morning light the colours seem almost hyperreal: the earth is hot-baked orange, the grass freshest green, the sea such an intense blue. And what is it about those mountains? They always seem so knowing. For a second I panic — I can't leave all this, I just can't!

"Alright?" Greg makes a gentle enquiry.

I tell him yes but my queasiness persists as I slide into the hire car and lead him back on to the main road. Can I really be exiting Elounda without even saying goodbye? Yes. I'll leave Alekos a note at the house and send Jules a text from the airport. It may seem a bit underhand but, even if my intention was to shock them, I don't think Jules will be too bothered — she's at that giddy stage where you just want to be with the man all the time and she'll be getting the deluxe bed without the guilt of thinking I'm sleeping in the servants' quarters. I won't mention Greg to them — seeing as I'm supposed to be the morally superior one, it'll hardly do to reveal that I picked up a man on the beach and am now running off with him for a dirty weekend in Athens. At least that's how it would seem to them.

"No need for you to come any further," I call across to Greg as I pull over at the side of the road. "I'll just be five minutes."

I step out of the car and begin the trek up to the shack. My jitters increase but they are nowhere near as bad as last night's hyperventilations. I have to admit that some masochistic part of me would like to see Alekos one last time but really, what good would that do? What's done can't be undone and it would destroy me if I had to see them together. All the same, I still feel a dip of disappointment to find the house empty.

Except for Loulou, of course!

"Hello, my darling girl!" I give her a full body rumple. "Ready for some breakfast?"

I open the cupboard and take down a tin of dog food. She makes a dismayed whine.

"You were hoping for leftovers?" I guess, opening the fridge to see if Alekos has set aside anything for her.

"What's this?" I say, nosing inside a big cardboard box. The contents are not what I was expecting. "Surely not?" I pull it out and set it on the side as Loulou's tail wags wildly.

It's a birthday cake. With my name piped on in Greek.

When did he get this? And why didn't he give it to me? I frown to myself, trying to remember the sequence of events the day I left . . . We went to the beach, he went to the doctor . . . hold on! Before he left he answered the phone to my mum — there's a good chance she would have told him she was ringing to wish me a happy birthday. But why didn't he say something at the time? Perhaps he wanted it to be a surprise. He did try and suggest we meet up that night, but Jules poo-pooed that. Even so, he still could have brought the cake over with my case. I wonder why he changed his mind about giving it to me — apparently he didn't even want me to see it because he dissuaded me from coming here to pack up my things. Suddenly I'm curious . . . I cross under the arch and head up the stairs to my former room.

"Oh my god!" It's littered with coloured streamers and somewhat deflated balloons. He did all this for me?

It makes it all the more mystifying why he then jumped into bed with Jules. Unless while I was busily falling for him, his feelings were evolving from lust to friendship. Maybe I'm the first female friend he ever had, hence the big celebration.

It's then I notice the envelope on the bed. I hurry over and, heart pounding, tear it open. The image on the card is of a glowing moon in a dark, shimmery sky.

"To my beautiful moon goddess," I read, clutching my heart. "I am honoured to be experiencing your birthday with you. I hope that I may make this evening as special for you as these past few days have been for me — *tonight we go dancing!*" And he has signed off, "From your Greek protector."

"Oh Aleko," I cry out loud, eyes brimming with tears. Loulou puts her chin on my knee, by way of comfort.

I'm about to slump into fantasies of what might have been if I'd only sent Jules a text saying, *I'm falling in love!* instead of making out that I needed saving — she hardly would have turned up if she thought I was mid-holiday romance — but then it dawns on me that Greg is patiently waiting for me.

I get to my feet. I can't ignore the facts — Alekos may have meant all this at the time but he went on to sleep with Jules and he hasn't even replied to my text from two nights ago. If he wanted to see me he could have easily made it happen. But he made his choice patently clear, again, last night. As lovely as the card is, I can't go idealising something that wasn't ideal.

All the same, I find myself tucking it into my bag as a keepsake.

I'm tempted to set the cake down for Loulou to snuffle through, but instead return it to the fridge before I set the house and car keys on the table, along with my brief note.

"Gone to Athens to do the interview."

Loulou gives the piece of paper a sniff as if to say, "That really is brief, isn't it?"

"I know," I shrug as I set down her food, "but I honestly don't know what else to say."

I feel even more of a wrench leaving now but I know this trip to Athens is the sane choice.

"Alright?" Greg enquires as I step into the car. "Well, obviously it's not alright, but is there anything I can do?"

"No, oh shit!"

"What?"

"Just drive!" I instruct, ducking down in the passenger seat. I've just seen Alekos' dad Petros strolling in our direction. I can't risk an encounter, however brief — he'd ask me why I was leaving and

301

even though I have a legitimate reason, I suspect he'd be able to read the underlying motivation.

"All clear," Greg announces as we round the corner.

"Sorry about that," I grimace as I sit back upright.

Greg can't help but smirk a little. "You're not dull to be around, I'll tell you that."

We have one more stop en route — Greg dropping off his spare villa key for his pals just in case they need somewhere quiet to recuperate from alcohol poisoning, STDs, etc.

As I lean out of the window to watch the parade of radioactive sunburns and sloganed T-shirts, a bare-chested guy pulls level with me on his outsize quad-bike.

"Hey — aren't you the watersports girl from the booze cruise?"

"Not any more." I attempt a smile.

Immediately I'm transported back to that crazy day with the never-ending parade and trade of sopping life-jackets, the subsequent raki dinner in Plaka, and then the idyllic moonlit beach. Enough! I have got to stop pining and reminiscing like this. It's over.

"Do you mind if I drive?" I ask Greg when he returns to the car. I really feel I need to concentrate on the road rather than stomach-churning memories.

"I would be delighted if you did!" He looks relieved. "Would it be awfully rude if I fell asleep?"

"Not at all. Drink some more water, have a kip and hopefully by the time we get to Athens you'll be feeling human again."

He smiles gratefully and then closes his eyes.

I hope the sleep does revive him. I want Greg to feel as good as he can — it's not every day a film fanatic gets the chance to walk on to the set of a movie . . .

CHAPTER
TWENTY-TWO

Let Greeks be Greeks, and women what they are.
— Anne Bradstreet

"That's such a trip-off-the-tongue name, isn't it?" I test my pronunciation skills as I attempt to read the official name for Athens airport. *"Eleftherios Venizelos."*

Rather more visitor-friendly is the metro system whisking you directly into the centre of town.

"It says here that it wasn't until they began excavations to make the city more traversable for the 2004 Olympic Games that they discovered not just the odd chipped vase, but also whole streets, houses, cemeteries, aqueducts — all buried!"

"Like an ancient underworld!" Greg enthuses.

"Exactly. And many of the artefacts are now displayed in their corresponding stations."

The Akropoli stop, where we're headed, is like a museum with genuine marble statues alongside the ticket booths and the kind of hip, blown-up photos and groovy lighting typically found in a design hotel. It is thus all the more of a shock when we step out into the present day and discover layer upon layer of cramped, shanty-shabby cubical living — endless shoeboxy blocks of flats stained with city life.

"Gosh." Greg grimaces. "It's like the modern Greeks looked at the architectural accomplishments of their predecessors and thought, We can't top that so what's the point in trying?"

But then raised up on a hill in the midst of it all and emerging like a sculpture hewn from a vast chunk of raggedy limestone are the unmistakable pillars of the Parthenon.

We both burst out laughing, unable to believe that we're so close to such an iconic structure.

"You know, Acropolis actually means high city," I tell Greg.

"So let's dump our stuff and get high!" he cheers.

It's so nice to be around someone so even-tempered and easygoing. The hotel is equally understated in latte, mink and muted heather tones. Greg checks into his room, me into mine. No propositioning. No ridiculing. No nakedness. I tut myself for adding to the statistics of women who fall for the wild womaniser type, thinking they can change him, thinking they'll be The One who makes him want to settle down. What a battle. Is that any way to live, fearing that if you have one less-than-alluring moment he'll run off with someone else? I'm glad I'm out of his reach now. I take a breath and await the sensation of returning to my saner self. This is more me. Culture. Shopping. Chaotic, dirty, impatient traffic.

It all rushes busily around me as we step back on to the street and yet instead of making me feel more at home, I feel the strangest pang for the simple soporific pleasure of the beach. It's just culture shock, I assure myself. That could never be enough for me — shingle and sea. It can't be.

"This way!" I swiftly lead Greg away from the exhaust fumes, down a leafy pedestrian street lined with pavement cafés, gift shops and kiosks crammed with all manner of portable snacks.

"If in doubt, just follow the crowds!" I give him my tip for getting to the major tourist attractions without the aid of a map. Unfortunately this causes us to contemplate an incline on a par with the approach to Zeus' cave. The man at the ticket office tells us about a more gentle route but I'm on such a mission to get Greg a glimpse of the film crew scheduled to shoot here today, I decide we should press on — literally pressing my hands on my thighs as we wrench upward in the garish midday heat.

"Are you sure you're okay?" Greg checks on my panting frame.

"I've survived worse," I say, taking a deep inhalation of pine needles and honey and sun-baked earth, before clomping determinedly up to the next stage.

"So here we have the Theatre of Dionysus," Greg pauses to consult his leaflet.

"Yes, yes, the birthplace of drama as we know it, where the tragedies of Sophocles and Euripides were first performed," I breeze through the highlights — one quick glance shows me that the open-air ledges that once seated seventeen thousand are decidedly free of men in berets with clapperboards so I continue pacing, calling back to Greg: "We can linger longer on the way down."

306

"But what if we come down a different path? There seems to be more than one route —" He stumbles around in the rubble, obviously a little overwhelmed by the scale of the place.

I reach out and steady him: "These sites have been here since the fifth century BC, they're not going anywhere in the next hour." The film crew, on the other hand, could relocate any moment . . .

"Well, if you're sure . . .?"

"Trust me, I have my reasons." I just wish I also had aerial vision. Perhaps it was rather naive of me to think this would be a simple game of hide and seek among the Doric columns — as if diva movie stars are going to just be scuffing up dust with the rest of us.

"It looks a bit of a building site, doesn't it?" Greg nods ahead to the cranes and scaffolding tattying up our vista as he muses, "Restoration and decay occurring simultaneously . . ."

"Mmm," I concur absently, continuing to scan the horizon.

We've now reached the sprawling plateau at the top of the hill, just a stone's throw from the most legendary pillars of all time, but Greg is preoccupied with the Porch of the Caryatids — six columns carved in the shape of voluptuous Athenian maidens.

"This was used as a harem during the Ottoman occupation." He's taken over the reading now, just as well since I am so distracted. "Do you think that's why it is known as the Erechtheum?" he enquires with a twinkle. "Apparently these statues are made of concrete, the real ones are in museums. In fact, there's one Caryatid in the British Museum along with the Elgin Marbles!" His jaw gapes. "Oh my god! I always thought they were literally talking about little glass marbles — they mean big Greek statues and, jeez, two hundred and forty-seven feet of a frieze that once decorated the Parthenon. No wonder there was such a scandal!"

I too am having a revelation — I've just spied one of those Meccano-style extendable make-up cases and a camera tripod. I feel an inner whoop of excitement — we've made it! All we need now is the popcorn!

"There's something I want to show you . . ." I go to pull Greg on.

"Can I at least take a picture here?" he resists.

"If you're quick," I tsk.

He cocks his head at me. "Are you this brusque with all your tour groups? I thought the idea was to savour the moment, really let yourself imagine what life was like —"

"Oh, for goodness' sake!" I despair, grabbing the camera out of his hand and taking an arbitrary shot of him and half a Caryatid. "I've told you, we'll do all that on the way down." I jog him onward, keen to keep pace with a man with a walkie-talkie and a swinging ID pass, though it's not easy to scurry elegantly on such uneven ground.

"Careful!" Greg cautions as I go to trip for the third time.

I know I'm rushing, I know I'm a little manic, but I'm worried that if I stand still I'll get engulfed by heartbreak again — I feel it creeping up behind me like a dark shadow, but if I keep moving and keep distracted I should be able to hold it off, though some strange part of me is looking forward to getting back to my room tonight so I can lose the brave face and let the tears flow.

Even thinking about that has my eyes turning glassy. So I take a deep breath and try desperately to latch on to the details of where I am right now.

I must say, in all the tours I've taken to crumbling ruins, this one seems to have inspired the greatest sense of occasion in terms of dress code. Of course there are the classic T-shirt-and-khaki-shorts brigade and I even notice one middle-aged lady in a swimming costume and a sarong flapping in the excitable breeze, but I also see a young woman in a fine-knit camisole with pearls and a clutch bag, and another in high-waisted, wide-legged navy pinstripe trousers with a red satin blouse. Perhaps they, too, heard about the filming and are hoping to be discovered?

While Greg gawps skyward at the classic symbol of Greek democracy in all its milky-gold glory, I am equally awed at the ground-level sight of the makeshift movie camp, complete with canvas-backed actors' chairs. It's just like the website said and, even though it's a peak-season Saturday, they haven't cordoned anything off from the public — we're right in amongst it.

All I have to do now is wait for the drachma to drop.

"Looks like they're filming something . . ." Greg notes casually as he checks through the shots he's just taken. "Probably some documentary for the History Channel."

It's time to unveil the surprise. "Actually, you're witnessing history in the making right now."

"What do you mean?" He looks up at me.

"Well, Mr Film Fan, this just happens to be the first ever Hollywood movie to be granted permission to shoot at the Acropolis!"

"What?" He looks befuddled. "This is a real movie?"

"Yes!" I throw my arms out wide and zing, "Ta-daaaa!" as if I arranged the whole thing just to amuse him.

He's still sceptical. "You mean with real movie stars?"

"Have a look around."

It's easier for me to spot the actors because I Googled the cast list last night but I want to see if Greg can identify the faces on his own. "That woman," he begins, pointing to a sophisticated blonde off to our left. "Wasn't she in *Schindler's List*?"

"And a little film your daughters might have enjoyed . . ."

"*The Princess Diaries*!" he exclaims. "She was Mia's mum." He clicks his fingers as he accesses her real-life name: "Caroline Goodhall!"

"Yes!" I cheer.

He looks around, ready for the next. "Alistair McGowan!" he gasps. "Just stood right there! He looks pretty tanned."

"I think he's playing a Greek guy."

"Who's the leading lady?"

I look around to see if I can spot her. And then, right on cue, the crowds part, offering us a total movie-star moment: there she stands, fair glowing in a turquoise dress, shins gleaming bronze, feet tilting forward in steep brown leather wedges, perfectly composed as a make-up artist finesses her glossy brown waves, tucking a lock behind her gold-hooped ear before staining her pouting lips crimson with what looks like a felt-tip pen.

"It's the lady from *My Big Fat Greek Wedding*." Greg grins.

"Nia Vardalos," I confirm.

"She looks beautiful," we both coo together as her face illuminates with a heart-spillith-over smile.

I know we both look instantly starstruck but she just seems so warm and engaging — look at her checking on everyone else, bantering merrily, playing with the scraggy stray that makes Loulou look ready for Crufts.

"My wife is going to freak. She loved that film."

"Ex-wife," I correct him.

"My ex-wife is going to freak!" he titters joyfully. "So what's this one called — hold on, let me guess. *Acropolis Now!*"

"No," I laugh. "Think romantic comedy."

He chews his lip in deliberation and then offers, "*Athens, I'm in Love? Kiss Me Aegean?*"

"No, but I like them!" I laugh, impressed by his wit. "It's actually all-too-relatably called *My Life in Ruins!*"

"Oh, that's great! *My Life in Ruins*," he repeats gazing back at the Parthenon. "And to think I thought I was just coming to see a heap of rubble. So what's it about?"

"All I know is there's a jaded female tour guide who is transformed by the love of a Greek man."

We both look at each other. I hadn't even made the connection until I said it out loud.

"Only you're not jaded," Greg observes. "At least as far as work goes."

"No," I agree. "And my leading man has run off with —" I hesitate. I can't even call Jules my best friend any more.

"A piece of set decoration?" Greg helps me out.

"Exactly."

Greg shakes his head. "I still can't believe this is happening — how did you know about this?"

"I literally only found out yesterday at the villa when I was looking up opening times — I did a quick crosscheck and up popped a press release announcing the filming."

Suddenly there's a loudhailer in our face, making an announcement in Greek.

We look a bit concerned until the man translates for us: "Remember to not look at the camera."

We frown back at him.

"Just keep walking in this direction."

"Oh my god," I grip Greg's arm, "I think we've just become extras!"

"I feel so Ricky Gervais!" he chuckles back.

As we wander onwards oh-so-nonchalantly, we find ourselves burrowing deeper into the film camp, so deep now that we are standing beside Nia and a man holding a big black umbrella to shield her both from the melting sun and the dusty wind. Greg edges off to get a better look at the tail end of "our" scene and I'm about to join him, fearing I may have overstepped the proximity mark, when the umbrella holder is summoned and, mistaking me for crew, enquires, "Could you?"

"Of course," I say, taking control of the umbrella.

I've read enough *Empire* magazines to know that certain stars forbid minions to look them in the eye but the second I'm in position she beams directly at me — I've never seen brown eyes look so bright and sparky and all too soon I hear myself gushing, "I love your dress!"

"Isn't it gorgeous? The costume department sewed it in two days!"

"It's perfect — the colour totally pops on you," I enthuse. "But I have to ask — how do you get around in those shoes?" I point to her wedges. "It's so precarious around here!"

"I know!" She rolls her eyes. "I fell down some stairs yesterday."

I look horrified.

"Just four steps but it felt like I fell for a month." She leans closer. "We have a deal that when filming is over we're throwing them into the sea!"

I laugh at the vision of this ceremonial offering and then fret that I'm getting over-pally. "I'm not disturbing you, am I?"

"No, no," she assures me. "I always say a set is like having a party and I love to host — I want to make sure everyone has finger food!"

She seems so happy and energised, but then again she is slap-bang in the middle of a dream-come-true.

"So how did you feel when you first heard you'd got the authorities to lift the ban on filming here?"

She smiles as she flashes back. "I instantly had a dream that the camera crane swung into the Acropolis and I woke up thinking. *I broke Greece!*" she gurgles. "Really, it was a tremendous sense of responsibility mixed with euphoria!" She still looks incredulous at her good fortune. "It was such a crazy wish!"

But it came true. "So it really does pay to wish out loud," I decide.

All of a sudden I feel like I'm visiting an oracle in this secret umbrella world and dare myself to ask about the concept of her character being changed by the love of this Greek guy, not that I have a vested interest or anything. But does she really think it's possible?

"I think we all change every day — I'm going to change as the result of meeting you," she asserts. "Every day, if you just take a moment to absorb what happened, you usually have changed in some way, but you don't always realise it."

I nod, definitely feeling these past five days have changed me, I'm just not quite sure what to make of it all yet.

She gives a little wave to a broodingly handsome man in a Brut-style denim shirt having his dark mane further ruffled.

"Is that your leading man?"

"Alexis Georgoulis." She gives an appreciative growl.

314

I smirk to myself as I see all the surrounding women eyeing him admiringly. Just like you-know-who. "What is it that's so appealing about Greek men?" I sigh.

"It's the way they own their sexuality," she answers without hesitation. "They just walk in a room and they're not afraid to announce their sexual beingness!"

I blink back at her — so it's not just Alekos. And apparently he can't help the way he is — it's a national trait!

"Nia!"

She's being called for her scene.

"Break a leg!" I say as she thanks me for the shade, and then fret that a) that's more a phrase for theatre luvvies and b) she may well do just that in those shoes.

"You're not the only friend of the stars!" Greg reappears holding up two autographs made out to his daughters.

"Does that say Ian Ogilvy?" I squint at the first.

He nods ecstatically.

"Big fan of *The Saint*, are they?" I frown.

"Nooo," he tuts. "You know he writes children's books?"

"No."

"Oh, we've read them all," he raves. "Daisy's favourite is *Measle and the Slitherghoul*."

I can't help but chortle at the title. "Was he nice?"

"I thought he'd be an old smoothie but he seems a real gentleman, almost shy. He's playing the husband of Caroline Goodhall."

"Is that the other autograph?"

He nods. "She told me a hilarious story about Richard Dreyfuss!"

"Hark at you!" I splutter.

"I know! I was just standing next to her and she started chatting to me like I was her guest at some fabulous Agatha Christie dinner party, she's just so classy!"

There's another loudhailer announcement, this one unmistakably requesting quiet on set so we decide to slope off to the outer edge of the Acropolis and sit on the wall where we can chat comfortably without messing up a multi-million-dollar soundtrack.

"Isn't it funny, you really can't tell the real tour groups apart from the actors," I say as we look back at the crowd.

"Except that group are clobbering Alistair McGowan with their handbags and rucksacks."

"Apart from that . . ." I grin. "That big grey boom thing really helps you spot where the star is, doesn't it? They may as well have a big arrow on a stick."

"Holding for the cloud!" we hear the next announcement and watch the white veil swish across the sun.

"Athens looks so different from up here, doesn't it?" I say, turning to survey the wondrous panorama.

There's still enough cardboardy-looking manila for you to think half the city was made from office supplies but now we get to see the roof gardens and restaurant terraces, the terracotta tiling and even the occasional dome.

Greg points out one of two lush green hills emerging from the city and I name them both — Lycabettus and Filopappou — trying to win back some tour-guide credentials.

"And look — you can even see the sea from here!"

I nod in the direction of the shimmering splay. To think that only yesterday I was listening to the guide at the Yachting Club Villas speak of the Athens coast and now I'm looking at it. What a difference a day makes, indeed.

I suppose you really never know what is around the corner, good or bad. One minute I'm on the ship, ticking over, slight sense of something missing but looking forward to seeing Jules, then she diverts to Mauritius which seemed like such a loss at the time but then I gained the amazing experience with Alekos, only to lose it again, thanks to Jules. She seems to have a knack for whipping things away from me lately. But then if that hadn't happened I wouldn't be here right now, making a nice man's dream come true. So maybe everything has worked out for the best.

I smile as Greg climbs a level higher to get a better look at the view, only to wince at a sudden high-pitched whistling-shriek.

"Oh my god!" Greg covers his ears. "Is that what they do here instead of yelling *Cut!*?" He looks over to where the crew are packing up their equipment.

"Actually, I think it's directed at you!" I spot an official making "get down off the wall" gesticulations.

"Oops." He blushes, jumping back on to the sandy earth.

"Well, at least you can say you got whistled at on holiday!" I console him.

"I can say a whole lot more than that now." He smiles earnestly as he turns to face me. "Seriously, Selena, I couldn't have wished for more than this. I just hope I can repay you in some way."

"You already have by coming here with me."

"Oh." He waves my words away, like it's nothing.

"Honestly, I don't know how I would have got through the day without you." My eyes are prickling now. The thought of wandering Athens alone with my sorrows is too grim to contemplate.

"So you know what I do when my girls need cheering up?" he asks as he smudges a baby tear from the corner of my eye.

I shake my head.

"Take them shopping. And not for anything tasteful!" he hastens to add. "The most fun thing to do is to pick something ridiculous that will make you smile every time you look at it. And from what I saw of the giftshops on the way here . . ."

I nod understanding. "I know just the place!"

CHAPTER
TWENTY-THREE

"Friends are as companions on a journey, who ought to aid each other to persevere in the road to a happier life."
— Pythagoras

The old district of Plaka may be tourist central but it is also pristine and characterful, its paved streets home to a multitude of gift shops, cosy cafés and skinny cats slinking between the open-fronted restaurants wafting fragrances of stewed lamb and caramelised onions. The only slight drawback is that the name of the area puts me in mind of Alekos, but then doesn't everything?

Fortunately, I am soon tuning in to Greg's challenge — the Grecian sandals in trendy metallics and embroidered cheesecloth smock tops both make me smile but perhaps aren't ridiculous enough. I have more luck with the Demis Roussos-esque crinkle kaftans and colourful pom-pom slippers — I buy a pair in a donkey brown and lime colourway that I definitely find amusing and Greg gets pink and purple for his girls. For himself, he can't resist a set of amber worry beads and a T-shirt printed with:

> *To Do Is To Be* — Socrates
> *To Be Is To Do* — Plato
> *Do Be Do Be Do* — Sinatra

This is just the overstimulation I need. Everywhere I look a different Grecian god gurns back at me — I pause beside a display of masks with facial features fixed mid-cackle, snarl or moan, all crying out for a water feature to be piped through their lips.

"I think my mum has that urn!" Greg laughs, handling a piece of the black pottery painted with animated figures.

"Mine too!" I giggle. "It's funny, when you're a kid you think these things are precious family heirlooms akin to museum pieces and then you see them in their country of origin for under a fiver!"

"I suppose back in their day they were really unusual," Greg decides.

"Maybe even tasteful."

Next door is a shop selling nothing but natural sponges, another has beauty products made from olive oil including one poorly named "Heavy Leg Cream". If I had stayed in Elounda and stared at the sea, all my emotions would have been reflected back to me; here I am fascinated by the array of products — not least the satyr-shaped bottles of ouzo.

"Do you think you pour the drink out of the penis like a spout?" I cringe. "That's just not right."

All of a sudden Richard Dreyfuss bursts from a shop in full gladiator costume, goofing around at full volume with a young co-star.

And to think I worried about us ever finding the film crew — now we can't avoid them.

After they yell "Cut!", I hear a member of the crew sympathise with the Oscar-winner that he has to act

320

like an idiot in front of dozens of gawping tourists and nonplussed locals but he's having none of it.

"I'm not embarrassed." He shrugs chirpily. "They pay you a lot of money, you can do anything!"

Much as we'd like to stay and gawp, hunger urges us to sidestep the cameras and ponytailed men dangling assorted ropes and wires and proceed back up Ariadnou Street in search of a restaurant table that won't be appearing at our local Odeon.

"What about here?" Greg stalls beside a quaint corner taverna.

I'm instantly enamoured of its trailing vines and tartan-blanket-clad tables and pronounce it "Spot on!" Though when we sit down, the street is so slanty we actually have to perch with a foot out like a strut to avoid toppling over. I'm not exaggerating — when the waiter pours the beer there is no need for him to tilt our glasses because they're already set at an angle.

"Ready?" He prepares to take our food order.

"We'd like the fish soup," we decide.

"With or without the fish?"

Greg and I look at each other.

"The first, the cheaper one is made with fish stock," the waiter explains. "The second has actual pieces of fish in it. Is good. Is swordfish."

"With," we confirm.

Greg chinks beer with me and then takes a rousing breath. "This has to be one of my all-time best days. I mean, how often can you say you bumped into Richard Dreyfuss while you were out shopping? I don't know how many times we've watched *Jaws*."

"You and your girls?" I'm shocked.

"No, me and the guys!" he laughs. "You know, they said they would come back to Elounda for the last night. You have to come over and tell them everything we saw or they'll never believe me!"

"Um." I look awkward.

"What?" He looks confused and then his shoulders slump. "You're not coming back with me, are you?"

I shake my head. "I can't. I have to keep going."

"But where will you go?"

"I haven't quite decided yet. Maybe New Zealand."

"Gosh!" Greg baulks. "When you go, you go!"

I smile weakly. Just thinking about the trip leaves me drained.

"You don't look entirely convinced," he ventures.

"I'm just a little bit lost at the moment," I sigh. "If there was a rehab facility for the broken-hearted I'd check right in, but in the meantime . . ."

"Perhaps, if you decide to go back to England, you could come and stay with me for a bit?"

"Really?" I brighten. Now there's a new option!

"Marcia has the girls for another week towards the end of the holidays, or you could come while they're there. Aside from the vomiting they really are delightful!"

I chuckle. Suddenly I think how nice it would be to have someone to bring home those dolls in traditional dress I always find myself drawn to when I'm abroad but never have anyone to buy them for. With this prospect on the horizon I could start today.

322

"That really would be lovely," I tell him, warmed by his friendship.

The soup is surprisingly filling with whole potatoes bobbing in the tasty broth but we still manage a fig ice cream as we wander the backstreets and snoop around the intriguing Anafiotika neighbourhood — cut directly into the Acropolis bedrock, it's like discovering a secret world of cliff-dwellers, only they live in little whitewashed houses with graffitied walkways rather than caves.

I innocently reach out to stroke a potted geranium petal but find myself getting a flash of Alekos running his fingers through every basil bush we would pass. It's time to go back to the hotel . . .

The sky is a misty dark violet and the Parthenon glows gold with its evening floodlights as we take a last look back.

"What a great day!" Greg yawns as we enter the hotel.

Despite my wobbles I, too, have a satisfying sense of a job well done. And what with our early start, we both feel entirely justified settling for an early night.

I don't even switch on the main light as I enter my room, just head for the bed, grateful for the exhaustion because it means I only have the energy to read Alekos' card once. Though, inevitably, I do tuck it under my pillow . . .

In the night I dream that Alekos and I are the romantic leads in a movie, but every time we are about to kiss, the director yells, "Cut!"

And the director looks a lot like Jules.

I sigh as I drag myself upright the following morning and wonder how long this pernicious grasp on my heart is going to last? Even when I'm having a good time with Greg I can feel it tightening and tugging me back. I've felt a degree of this before, generally when I'm leaving a place I've formed an emotional bond with — sailing away from mysterious Venice or the island bonhomie of St Lucia. But it's been a while since I felt this for a person.

I want to hate Alekos for sleeping with Jules but it was certainly one way of keeping his word about "no funny business" with me. Apparently I should have made him promise not to get it on with my friends either. Or any other woman for that matter. How very reasonable of me — I don't want you but I want you to want me and no one else! I shake my head and snuffle at myself as I get to my feet and fling back the curtains to blinding sunshine.

Closing my eyes I let the glare infuse me, absolutely determined not to let self-pity ruin my last day in Greece.

Fortunately, Athens continues to be on my side and presents us with one of the most gorgeous locales of any coastal town I have visited — the harbour of Mikrolimano.

"Holy mackerel! When the concierge said we'd have our choice of fish restaurants, I wasn't expecting quite so many options!" Greg laughs as we contemplate the curve lined with fishing boats and at least twenty

324

equalsized dining rooms opening directly on to the water. They all seem to have been part of some large-scale *Changing Rooms* project — each "room" has its very own distinctive style — a mermaid fantasy with iridescent shells next to white wicker and monochrome stripes, leopard print and purple velvet alongside shabby chic and glass mosaics . . . In essence, something to suit every colour palette, star sign, age group and financial disposition — from tatty old-school trestle tables to fine dining with a besuited greeter who hands out a business card as you pass. We opt for a pared-down nautical theme made hip with Sixties-style white mouldings.

"I can't believe we're going to eat lying down," Greg laughs as we slip on to a pair of padded sunloungers just millimetres from the water's edge. "This is so decadent!"

As the waiter takes our order across the street to the restaurant kitchen, we lie back and take in the comfortingly traditional view.

It's a little unnerving to feel so full and so empty at the same time. But I know I'm in the best possible place — there is something about the fluidity of water that suggests ever-altering possibility. It's like the situation I find myself in now: I didn't predict this so why worry myself about the week to come, even if I do have to make a decision about where I go next by tonight.

"The water really glitters like diamonds in the sun, doesn't it?" Greg sighs. "I think the next time I'm feeling blue at home I'm going to take myself off to the nearest beach."

"And where would that be?" I ask.

"Morecambe," he replies.

And then we both burst out laughing.

"Ah, here are our starters!" I cheer, beholding a heap of deep-fried fish no bigger than your little finger, which you crunch whole.

Greg takes one daintily by its crispy tail, goes to speak and then halts himself.

"What?"

"Nothing."

"Go on."

"No, I was just going to ask if you'd heard from anyone in Elounda since we left but I'm sure you would have said if you had, so then I thought it's best not to mention it if you're not thinking about it. But now I have. And so you will be and —"

"It's fine." I put him out of his misery. "I actually got a text from Jules this morning. She sent it last night but I'd switched off the phone at nine p.m." Now I'm rambling.

"So what did she say?"

"Just, *When are you coming back?* And she offered to pick me up at the airport when I return."

"Hmmm, someone's feeling guilty. I take it she has no clue that you're doing a runner?"

"Not yet." I sigh. "Half of me feels like I'm being a cow but the other half feels entirely separate from her now. Do you think it's odd, the way I've just switched off? She was supposed to be my best buddy!"

"I think you're hurt and your trust has been tampered with and you're doing what you have to do to cope."

I smile at him. He really is turning out to be an ideal friend. "Thank you for being non-judgemental."

"I'm not judging *you*," he confirms. "I do have a thought or two about her, however . . ."

"Really?" I cock my head.

"I know you say she didn't know she was muscling in on your action and that she's on the rebound, but her behaviour does strike me as a tad selfish and unsisterly."

I go to agree but then our main platters arrive and I go the other way. "Well, we're none of us perfect, are we?" I shrug. "I'm sure whenever we're back in England it'll be like none of this ever happened."

"End of subject?" Greg raises a brow.

"Well, she can take my man but she's not messing with my meal!"

As we eat we first talk briefly about New Zealand and then our respective parents — apparently Greg's never liked Marcia.

"It's so annoying when they're proved right, isn't it?" I tut as I dab my chin with my napkin.

"Ah, but the beautiful thing about having children is that you can never regret the relationship that brought them into the world!"

I chuckle. "That's true. You wouldn't want them any different, would you?"

He shakes his head.

"What do you wish most for them," I ask, "in terms of future relationships?"

"Well, that's a long, long way off . . ." He takes a sip of wine and mulls over the question. "It's funny, isn't it? In every other aspect of their lives I'd wish for them to reach for the stars but all I can think in terms of relationships is that I hope they don't get too hurt."

I nod. "I know what you mean. Who even believes in great love any more? It's so easy to get stymied by the fear of the pain."

"Which happens to be a very real fear and a truly horrible pain," Greg concurs. "Oh god, listen to us!" He grimaces. "How are you going to get through an interview with a couple of believers in this mood?"

"Don't worry, they'll do all the work and if it's anything like all the others, I'll come out with my faith entirely restored and little birds tweeting around my head."

"Excellent — and then you can convince me that happy endings do exist."

"Deal!"

We enjoy ten more minutes' peace, and then move on to the assigned interview location — Zea Marina, just a few minutes' taxi-ride down the coast but distinctly more yachtie than fishy with a jostle of white masts jutting from gleaming, freshly hosed decks. Greg pauses to admire a sharp fifty-footer, so sleek and stark, banded with smoked glass like a pair of wrap-around shades.

328

"This is so St Tropez!" Greg raves. "Or so I imagine . . .?" He looks to me for confirmation.

"Well, St Tropez is certainly very ritzy and picturesque, but it doesn't offer quite such a sweeping vista!" I raise his gaze from the port, out to sea.

Greg virtually stumbles back at the sight of the vast and majestic coastline, leading the eye all the way back to the high-rises of central Athens.

"I love it here!"

"Me too!" I agree. Possibly because this marina seems to be more about boats and less about being seen in the right restaurant — I think I like it even more than Mikrolimano. Especially when I notice that one of the yachts is named *Wounded*.

"Will you be using this as the backdrop for your interview?" Greg enquires.

"I hope so, though the sea breeze can play havoc with the hair!" I note, releasing a strand of my own from my mouth.

"Are you nervous? I mean, these are friends of Alekos, aren't they?"

My heart does a little flip. I hadn't even thought of that. "I don't know how well he knows them . . ." I say, trailing off. "But I'm sure it'll be fine. Generally, it's just a case of winding them up and letting them go." I look at my watch. "The interview will probably take about an hour and then I allow half an hour for faffing. Are you sure you're going to be alright here?"

"Are you kidding? I may have a little wander but most likely I won't even budge from this spot," he says, settling himself on the nearest bench.

"Okay, I'll see you right back here around three o'clock. Any problems, call me."

"Aye, aye, Captain!"

He looks so sweet and content sitting in the sunshine. "Maybe you'll even find a millionairess!" I tease him as I turn towards the apartment the couple described over the phone.

"I can feel myself getting richer just sitting here!" he calls after me.

CHAPTER
TWENTY-FOUR

A heart that loves is always young.
— Greek proverb

"*Kalispera!*" I give my minimal Greek an airing as I press the buzzer on the front of the building. "This is Selena!"

"Welcome, welcome!" The door springs open and Nikos and Athina greet me with a fierce hug and kiss, muttering excitedly to each other in Greek, as though they had a bet on what I'd look like from my voice.

I go to close the door behind me but they peer past me demanding, "Where is Alekos?"

Did they really expect him to escort me? Perhaps he was planning to. It's not like I discussed this arrangement with him at all. "He's still in Elounda," I tell them, hoping they'll still be alright talking to me. "Working at the beach."

"Oh, oh, he had to work . . ." They nod, satisfied with the reason, making some reference to Angelos still being away. "So, come, come!"

They bundle me up two flights of stairs and then they step back, insisting I enter the apartment first, to get the unobstructed benefit of their pride and joy — the wall-to-wall lounge window showcasing the dazzling marina, even more photogenic from this height.

"Oh, that's just perfect!" I gasp, especially since this means no hair dancing — and what my couple lack in height they certainly make up for in follicular abundance: him with a dense grey sweep, her with a chestnut cascade.

"We didn't know which seating you would prefer?" They show me a line-up that looks like we're ready to play musical chairs, back in the Fifties. I suspect all their furniture has been inherited, everything is delightfully mismatched and yet there is a charm from the woven rugs on the laminate flooring to the photos and religious artefacts in cheap frilly gold frames on the walls.

"Well, nothing too big to block out the view," I say, dismissing the velvet armchairs. "Can I have a look at you on these, if it's not going to be too uncomfortable?"

They quickly oblige my choice of kitchen stools with little base-of-spine backs.

"That's great, you can't even see them. Now I might have to shine some light on you to make sure you don't become silhouettes with all that bright sunshine behind you . . ."

The last thing I want is for them to come off like documentary criminals or teen prostitutes keen to conceal their identities — this is supposed to be a celebration of their love, not a covert operation.

"Would this help?" Nikos offers me a torch.

"Um, do you have anything bigger?"

Suddenly every lamp, candle and bulb is paraded before me.

It takes a bit of adjustment but we finally get the balance right, with the help of my handy portable reflector disc purloined from one of the ship's photographers.

"You both look lovely," I compliment them on their Sunday best and glowing complexions — I can still feel the silkiness of their skin from our initial embrace. They both have an earthy, grounded quality to them but when they start to relax and joke with each other I see Alekos' twinkle in Athina's eyes.

"You could almost be related!" I tell her as I marvel at the resemblance — especially in those distinctive green eyes.

"We are!" She laughs. "He's my nephew! He didn't tell you?"

"No." I frown, feeling a little foolish.

"Yes, yes, he used to live with us during the school year." Nikos points to the wall and I home in on a photo of a chubby teenage Alekos in a whole different kind of uniform to the one I'm used to seeing.

"He is a different shape now, of course."

"Yes he is!" I smile at his cuddliness and then feel a pang: how I wish I could turn back the clock and find myself here for tea after a maths lesson — I could have been his childhood sweetheart!

"Would you like a little wine?" Nikos offers, jolting me back to the present day.

I hesitate. It's likely to make me feel worse but I say yes anyway and watch with amusement as Athina goes burrowing beneath the sink and siphons golden liquid from some hidden contraption.

"*Yamas!*" I say, chinking glasses with them. "So, shall we begin?"

"Are you hungry?" Athina checks, luring me over to a pot on the stove. "My mother's recipe . . ." She makes me try a spoonful of what turns out to be a mix of carrots, celery and rice.

"From Macedonia."

It is utterly delicious, her tip being that the vegetables are cooked in oil, not boiled in water. I explain that I've already eaten but suggest we might film a minute or two of them enjoying the feta and tomatoes cut in big ragged chunks, for a bit of local flavour.

After my night at a neutral hotel, it is strange to be in this homely Greek environment and it makes me feel close to Alekos again which has good and bad aspects — usually when I do my interviews, I sit with a rapt look on my face as the story unfolds of how the couple met. Initially I try not to direct them too much or ask too many questions as I like them to be able to tell it their way and I love watching how they interact, taking it in turns, overlapping each other, beginning and ending where the other left off or seeing who focusses on which detail. But today, instead of feeling inspired, I just feel sick to my stomach with envy. I want what they've got! I want to be embedded in someone else's life, I want my fingers to still be entwining with his in forty years. I think it's because I felt so recently like I had a shot at it myself that it's all the more poignant.

Several times I have to zone out, nodding encouragement without even listening as I try to hold back my tears. The fact that Uncle Nikos periodically uses a phrase just like Alekos makes it all the more excruciating. Why did this ever seem like a good idea?

As they talk I wonder if Alekos suggested them because their story begins in a similar way to ours — in as much as he was too pushy and she was resisting because she'd heard he had a reputation. But then it goes a whole lot deeper with hardships and enforced separations that really tested their devotion. Ultimately I get sufficiently drawn in that I forget my pitiful plight although, come the end, I'm still in need of a tissue.

"Well, that's a good sign!" I tell them, trying to jolly myself up. "If you can reduce an old cynic like me to tears, you'll be a big hit!"

"You're not as cynical as you think you are," Athina tuts.

"Aren't I?"

"Well, of course, we just go by what Alekos has told us . . ."

I want to ask, "What has he told you?" And more importantly, "Why has he done what he's done?", but it's not appropriate.

"You want to see some more photographs? I think I have some in the bedroom drawer." Athina tinkers off before I can stop her.

"You look a little sad when you look at his picture," Nikos comments, catching me glancing back at the teenager.

"I just miss him, I suppose."

"But you'll be back there tomorrow?"

"No," I shake my head. "It's time for me to move on." Again.

"Why?" he splutters.

I shrug noncommittally. I didn't come here to bad-mouth their nephew.

"I don't understand." Nikos seems to require a reason.

"He's with my friend now." I crack.

"*With?*" His brows knit together.

"Yes, *with*."

"No, no, no, no!" He's having none of it.

"I feel the same way but it is what it is."

"When did this happen?"

"Three days ago. She turned up unexpectedly, they met at the beach and by that night they were together."

"It's not possible. That is not Alekos."

Athina has returned and Nikos brings her up to speed in Greek. She is equally incredulous. I don't know why they are acting so surprised. He must show a very different side of himself to them.

"He never rushes into affairs," Athina insists.

"Never," Nikos confirms.

"Even at the cost of having people say that he is cold or arrogant or a heartbreaker or gay!"

"I hadn't heard that last one," I say.

"Well, it's amazing what women will say to explain away the rejection."

"Ever since —" Athina stops herself. "The reason doesn't matter, all you need to know is that he does not jump on the bed quickly."

336

I smile at her phrasing. "Well, perhaps if you saw my friend it would make more sense. She's absolutely stunning. All men —"

"It's not the looks," Nikos dismisses my rationalisation. "You see this boy?" He taps the photo frame. "He became very good at judging people's characters — imagine when he shed his weight and the girls rushed to speak to him . . . He could see the difference in their eyes. He went out with a few of the pretty-pretty girls for the novelty but all that did was clarify his position. And then —"

Nikos and Athina exchange a look.

"Is it really so awful?" I'm starting to get concerned. "Whatever it was that happened?"

"We should have tea," Athina decides, while Nikos takes up the story.

"A few years ago, he started to see this woman but very quickly he realised it was a mistake. He tried to step away gently, with honour, but she became hysterical. Refused to accept the situation. He tried to be more firm with her — It is over. They have no future. And then she went to commit suicide."

I gasp out loud. "Oh my god. Did she live?"

He nods. "But for a while that was not a certainty."

"It really put a burden upon him. He had many nightmares." Athina leans in the doorway. "He didn't do anything wrong — you can't be held responsible for someone else's emotions — but it doesn't take long for the story to get twisted. Yes, people agree that her action is a comment on her instability but people also wonder, *what did he do to provoke her?* He was so

337

cautious after that, didn't want to get involved with anyone in case they also turned that little bit crazy . . ."

That's actually really scary. I think how I'd feel if I was in the same position — some guy you're in a casual situation with decides they'd rather die than live without you. Even if you know that you did nothing wrong, you would still be shaken up and question yourself.

"So of course the girls continue to throw themselves at him, they ask him out, they try to take him to the bedroom and he turns them down and that's when he starts to hear stories coming back about himself — that he's heartless and arrogant but really he's just being careful."

It takes me a moment to get my head around all this. He certainly did turn down a number of women on the ship. I saw that with my own eyes a few times. But how can they explain how he was with me?

"The strange thing is," I begin, "I found him too full-on. He didn't seem cautious with me at all."

"Well, he'd done his research, he felt he could trust you."

"And he knew you were leaving the ship, he didn't want to lose you. He had a limited amount of time to win you!"

"Hold on!" I need to backtrack a little. "How do you mean research? Is there some dossier on me that I don't know about!"

Athina comes over and sets down our respective tea cups. "Let me see, you'd never eaten crab before you came to Alaska, you have a dream of learning to tango in Argentina and your favourite mode of transport is a floatplane."

"How do you know all this?" I'm actually quite freaked out now.

"When Alekos is in love, he has to speak about it. He would ring us and tell us all the things that you'd said in your excursion talk."

"I never saw him there." Although, granted, the theatre auditorium does seat several hundred and you can easily loiter at the back by the door, completely out of view. I've done that myself when I know I can't stay for the full duration of the talk and I don't want to look like I'm walking out midway through because I'm bored.

"When he couldn't get there in person he would watch in his cabin," Athina adds.

Of course. I'd forgotten about that — all our talks are broadcast on the in-house TV channel.

"He really used to watch me?" I can't help but be flattered, especially when I've lost count of the number of people who've dropped off during my talks.

"He said you were his favourite show!" Nikos laughs. "He loved the Q&A session at the end, especially when the questions were completely unrelated to the topic of the day. He couldn't believe how patient you were with everyone."

"So if he came across as overly familiar, it's because he felt he already knew you," Athina confirms. "He trusted you. And he knew he wanted you. And that was that."

"And what if I didn't want him?"

"He's Greek." Athina rolls her eyes. "It's not going to strike him as a likely obstacle."

I chuckle and then all too quickly my smile fades. "So if all this is true — and I'm not doubting you — then why is he now with Jules?"

Here we draw a blank.

And then my phone bleeps. It's Greg. Poor guy, I've already been an hour longer than I said.

"I am so sorry to come here, upset everyone and then leave!" I apologise as I get to my feet. "Please don't worry about this. Love is very unpredictable. These things happen."

They are still shaking their heads and muttering as I pack up my equipment and tell them again how wonderful they were and how grateful I am that they agreed to this project. Even if my love mission has backfired in the most spectacular way.

I'm at the door now but reluctant to let go of Athina — something tells me that the second the lock clicks she'll be on the phone to Alekos.

And he won't thank me for that. But I didn't say anything out of place. I simply explained he'd chosen Jules. No malice, just the truth.

I hover on the pavement outside their apartment. Part of me wants to ring on the doorbell again and say, "Well? What did he say? Did he tell you the reason?" But then I realise that the last thing I want to hear is what Jules has that I don't.

Besides, Greg is calling again.

"Hello," I strive for ebullience as I stride towards our meeting spot. "Sorry I'm so late. I'll be there in —

What? You went where? And now you have no clue how to get back . . ." I trail off.

I can't believe it — I don't know how I've done it but in under seventy-two hours, I've managed to lose two men.

CHAPTER
TWENTY-FIVE

Fate leads him who follows it, and drags him who resists.
— Plutarch

I sit down on one of the waterside benches and fold the map out on to my lap. "Right, let's start with street names."

"They're all in Greek!" he despairs. "No neat little translations beneath them. I'm guessing this isn't a prime tourist trail."

"Okay, well, landmarks then, anything that distinguishes the area?"

"I don't know — every road seems to have big skips and dusty clumps of building falling into them. It's definitely seedier than where we started, more chaotic and careworn. I'm still getting a mariner vibe but now it's more Popeye and Bluto than Onassis and Callas. Oh and here we have a small street urchin who seems absolutely outraged that I don't want to empty my wallet into his palms. *No!*"

"Piraeus," I gulp, instantly getting visions of the bloodied bandages and stray dog that plagued my last visit. Not the ideal destination for a travel novice on their own. And the last place I'd ever want to return to. "I think the best bet is for you to just jump in a taxi and get them to drop you back here at the marina."

"That was my plan twenty minutes ago but every taxi I've seen is chock-a-block and —" His voice is drowned out by the penetrating honk of a ship's horn, no doubt making him jump but blasting home a very particular realisation to me: I am not the same person as I was fourteen years ago! Ships are my friends now and I am perfectly capable of guiding my charge to safety.

"Greg!" I begin by calmly commanding his attention.

"Yes?"

"Can you see the water from where you are?"

"No, but I'm just approaching a surprisingly posh restaurant — the first that doesn't look like the cook is waiting behind the door to clout you with a ladle — I could ask in there?"

"Get them to point you in the direction of the main port," I instruct, getting to my feet, now in search of a taxi myself.

"Will do, hold on . . ."

There's muffling and clinking and a small misunderstanding over the kind of water he's interested in — bobbing with boats rather than ice — and then he's back out on the street.

"She said it's just around this corner and — yes! yes! — I see ships!"

"Big ships?" I enquire.

"Huge!" he gasps. "Like blocks of flats with funnels and anchors!"

"Okay," I breathe, encouraged. "Now you want to look for a landmark of some kind so I can locate you. But not a ship in case it sets sail."

"Basically there's just miles of metal fencing, a security hut . . . Hey, what about a gate number — E10?"

"Perfect!" I like the simple precision of his choice. "Stand right by the sign and don't go anywhere. And if anyone else asks you for money don't say no, say *ohee*."

"*Ohee*?"

"Yes, just in a more gruff, stern voice."

"*Ohee*," he repeats, dropping a couple of octaves.

"That's it. Now don't move."

As the lemon-yellow Mercedes switches between derelict backstreets and congested main arteries I'm amazed at how far Greg has walked. And how adventurous he's been. I just hope this hasn't knocked his confidence too badly — perhaps I can convince him this is all just another movie set — yesterday Acropolis, today apocalypse.

"Here, here!" I blurt as I spot the outsized sign for E10, reluctantly emerging from the taxi cocoon and removing my necklace as I do so, just in case . . .

I have to dodge a gang of growling cars and mob-like pedestrians but there's no missing Greg — and it's not just that he's paler and more anxious-looking than the general ensemble — the man is holding a giant orange lifesaver ring.

"Selena! Oh thank god!" He rushes to embrace me, clunking me slightly with the hard casing. "I'm such an idiot, I'll never wander off again, I promise!"

"Don't be silly." I wave his apologies aside, relieved I'm not getting the blame for letting him go out to play unsupervised. "But what, pray tell, is with the ring? Were you afraid someone might throw you in the water?"

He rolls his eyes. "I went into this marine supplies shop to get off the street for a bit and the shop assistant was watching me so intently I felt compelled to buy something!"

"You couldn't have just picked out a fish-hook?"

"Well, actually, I was tempted by this sonar fish-finding watch — it has a radius of seventy-five miles and transmits images of the fish on to the LCD screen on your wrist." He shows me a photograph in the brochure he had scrolled in his pocket.

"Have you had a complete nightmare?" I ask, genuinely concerned for his sanity.

He takes an assessing breath. "Well, there was a point where I could see my life taking a very wrong turn . . ." He flinches as he steps out of the path of some swarthy men with porcupine-esque stubble. "Have you ever seen *Never on Sunday?*"

I shake my head.

"It's this great black-and-white film from the Sixties about a feisty prostitute working the port here. She sleeps with all the shipyard workmen and visiting sailors and I had horrible visions that would end up being me!"

I giggle at the picture he paints of himself in a pencil skirt swinging a dinky handbag and assure him, "Don't worry, we'll get you back to Lancaster, virtue intact!"

"I have faith," he says as we stroll onward in the direction of the metro. "The woman who played the prostitute went on to become the first female Minister of Culture for Greece!"

"What, for real?"

"Yes, her name was Melina Mercouri. I'm sure she would have been an excellent candidate for your love story — she met an American director when her first film took her to Cannes and they spent the next thirty-nine years together, until she died. In fact he wrote, directed and played opposite her in *Never on Sunday*."

"Wow, you really know your film trivia, don't you?"

He shrugs happily. "So how did you get on with your couple?"

I open my mouth — where to begin? Do I really want to rehash more stuff about Alekos? This is Greg's holiday after all, not a counselling session. "Fine." I decide I'll tell him all later. "It went really well."

"Good. So now what?" He looks expectantly at me as we pause beside the overpass that could return us to civilisation.

I would have thought I'd want to make a speedy exit before my old stray dog pal sniffs me out but I can't help but feel drawn to the water's edge.

"Do you mind if we have a little ship-side stroll before we head back?"

"Not at all," he indulges me. "This is like a home from home for you, isn't it?"

I nod and yet find myself questioning if that is even true any more — are cruiseships home to me or just another means of escape? Part of me yearns to walk trance-like on board and be spirited away as if my time in Greece were just a dream. But another part feels resistance — *Not again, don't make me go round again!* It's probably simply that it's too soon — just eight days since I disembarked in Vancouver. How different things were then . . .

"I really can't get over how vast they are." Greg's gaze climbs the balconied levels. "How many cabins would you say are there?"

"On Celebrity *Summit*?" I muse. "You're looking at about a thousand."

"So double that to get the number of passengers?" Greg queries.

I nod. "And throw in another thousand for crew . . ."

"Wow," he reels, "three thousand people on one ship!"

"That's nothing! Royal Caribbean are building one that's going to accommodate nearly five and a half thousand guests!"

"What?" he gasps. "That's more than the population of the town where I grew up!"

"You're going to like this one." I turn his shoulders to the right. "See the *Costa Atlantica*? That's an Italian line and the deck names are all inspired by Federico Fellini!"

"Really?" he pips.

Nothing like a film-related fact to cheer him up.

"But I'll tell you what gives me the biggest kick," I say, taking a seat on one of the giant painted bollards. "They named one of the ships in their fleet *Costa Fortuna*!"

Greg chuckles back at me. "And do they?"

"Actually, they're considered 'mainstream', so not too pricey. Celebrity are premium and Crystal, over there with the seahorse insignia, that's luxury."

Greg smiles and teases, "You really know your cruise trivia, don't you?"

"What can I say? I know people think it's a naff way to travel but when I think of the places those ships have taken me and all of the people I've met on board, it's been the best part of my life."

Greg takes a deep breath. I think he's going to say something profound about how we each have to find our own unique path and that we should be unconcerned with anyone else's judgements but instead he whispers, "Is it true that they have male escorts on board to dance with the single ladies?"

I roll my eyes. "Yes, but it's nothing untoward — they're all highly vetted silver foxes. Mind you, I did meet this one chap, seventy if he was a day, he'd be waltzing away one minute and then the next thing you knew he was down on the floor demonstrating a yoga position — in his suit, no less, feet behind his ears —" I stop suddenly.

"What is it?" Greg gasps. "Your eyes have gone all googly!"

"It's just . . ." I stumble forward, squinting into the sunlight, trying to be certain. "I've never seen it before, at least not in person . . ."

"Seen what?"

A smile creeps over my face and I feel an excited fluster as I breathe, "I think it's *The World*."

Greg frowns. "Do you mean you think the world of it?"

"No, *The World* is the name of the ship." I turn to him, eyes bright with excitement. "This, my friend, is the Holy Grail of the cruising fraternity!"

"It doesn't look anything special." He shrugs as he assesses the simple white lines of the vessel I'm pointing to.

"It's not the look, or the size," I explain. "What makes it unique is that the cabins are actually people's homes with their own furniture and ornaments and full kitchens with ovens and biscuit tins — just like an apartment!"

"You mean people actually live on the ship?"

"Technically, yes, but it's actually unlikely to be their *only* home. In fact, I did hear that the typical resident has nine 'second' homes!"

"Nine?!" he hoots. "Wow. So I'm guessing these residences aren't cheap."

"I had a friend who went to work on board and she said the prices start at about half a million."

"But what's the advantage of *owning* a cabin? Why don't they just book on a Crystal cruise for a year?"

"Well, for one thing, *The World* tends to spend longer in each place than the average cruiseship. On my ship you'd be lucky if you got an overnight, it would mostly be a morning arrival and a late afternoon departure, but *The World* will dock in Rio to coincide with the carnival and they'll be there for five nights, or you get to spend three nights in Cannes during the film festival, or nearly a week in Russia, so you can get into the country and do some exploring."

"So you definitely get to see more of each place."

I nod. "And I suppose their clientele are in less of a rush, not trying to cram everything into a two-week vacation."

"Rich retirees?"

"I think they are in the majority but also consider the amount of business people who now have portable offices. They have faxes and Internet on board so you can be doing multi-million-pound deals from the middle of the ocean!"

"And you can come and go as you please?"

"Exactly!"

Greg pulls a face. "I'd feel a bit odd about my possessions sailing around the world without me. I mean, I have enough problems finding my house key half the time, imagine the added stress of trying to keep track of your home!"

I chuckle. "Oh I love the idea of it! 'Henry, I'm bored. Where's the residence today?' 'Let me see . . . currently in Libya about to set sail for Italy.' 'Lovely! Let's catch up with it in Genoa, shall we?' 'How long do you want to stay?' 'I don't know, a couple of countries, maybe even a continent if we're having fun!' Don't you just love that? I've always wanted to go on board."

"Well, why don't you ask your friend?"

I give a nonchalant shrug. "We've lost touch. Shame, really, she was great — Cherry by name, cherry by nature. I got a few emails when she first transferred but then she just sort of vanished . . ."

"Bermuda Triangle?" Greg's eyes widen.

"Maybe," I humour him. I've actually never been there myself; subconsciously I suspect I'm saving it for my last voyage. I think it would be a fitting end to my life — of no fixed abode, even in the afterlife! "Shall we walk on down to the end?"

We stroll past all manner of sea vessels emblazoned with local brandings — Hellenic Seaways, Minoan Lines and the smaller, fleeter Flying Dolphin.

"So do you still have her number?" Greg enquires.

"Who?"

"Cherry."

"Why?" I blink at him. "Do you want it?"

He tuts me like I'm being deliberately obtuse. "I meant for you to call now . . ."

"Ohhhh," I laugh. I'm so used to filing people away when they leave the ship. I never really expect to see them again.

"Seeing as we're in such close proximity, it's got to be worth a try!" He tilts his head. "Or is there some reason you're reluctant?"

"No, I mean, it was a little bit strange how she left." I turn to face him as I explain how she persuaded her boyfriend Dom to come on board as a DJ and then promptly buggered off to *The World*.

"Oh!" Greg looks a little taken aback, possibly drawing some parallel to his recent split. "How did he react to that?"

"Well, you can imagine he was pretty shocked — she basically dumped him for a sexier ship. But fortunately he got on really well with Jules —"

"As in the home-wrecker of Elounda?"

I smile. I can't help but delight in the disparaging remarks he makes about Jules, even though I know they are just to make me feel better. "She totally took him under her wing and they ended up together. Right up until last week, actually."

Greg stops in his tracks. "Cherry's ex was the guy she was going to marry?"

"Yes," I confirm.

"And how long ago did this all kick off?"

"About a year, I suppose."

"I wonder if she has any regrets," he ponders out loud.

"I don't know about Cherry but I'd say Jules is regretting ever getting involved with him. Not that I've heard the full story there . . ."

Greg is quiet for a moment and then says, "Sounds like you all took it a bit personally, her leaving so suddenly . . ."

"Well, of course it happens all the time, people coming and going, it's part of ship life; I was just surprised that she didn't say goodbye." Though I realise as I say it that I've just done the same thing to Jules.

"Not even to you?"

"No. Maybe she was ashamed about what she was doing and she just wanted to disappear. I know all about that feeling, so I can't hold it against her."

"But you said she emailed . . ." Greg is like a dog with a bone.

"A few times, yes. But it wasn't the same — you know when you're tiptoeing around a subject, you can't really relax? We didn't reference the situation at all. She didn't even ask after him, just told me about her new job." I shrug my shoulders.

"So maybe you don't want to call her?" Greg studies me for a few moments. "What's that smile for?"

"I was just remembering this game we used to play — everyone would write down a body part on a piece of paper and put it into a hat, along with the names of various staff members, mostly ones we'd never met. Then we'd each get a pairing — the ship's doctor and knee, the maître d' and nape of neck etc. — and we'd have to go up to them and find an excuse to touch them in the appropriate place."

Greg raises an eyebrow.

"I know, it was silly but we used to get so giggly. She really was ideally cast as Entertainments Officer, there's just something infectious about her energy."

Greg cocks his head, giving me a significant look. "So for old times' sake?"

I hold his gaze. "Why are you so keen?"

"Well, if you got to meet up then I could be the hero who reunited two friends, as opposed to the complete twonk who got lost the second he was let off the leash."

I laugh at his reasoning. "Okay!" I reach for my phone and start scrolling through my address book. How can I advise Greg to embrace opportunity if I don't do the same myself? "It's ringing!" I tell him, aware that my heart is now pounding. Could she really be just an anchor away? "Voicemail," I mouth, preparing to leave a message. "Cherry, this is your long-lost shipmate Selena! It's possible I'm spying on you right now! We're at Pireas, beholding *The World*, so if you're on board get the captain to honk the horn. If not, text me back and let me know where you are. It would be great to catch up."

I snap my phone closed. Wow. Ordinarily I'd be straight on the phone to Jules, especially since Cherry was her friend first, but I feel decidedly uninclined to speak to her right now. Besides, nothing will probably come of it, so what's the point?

"Fancy a coffee?" I ask as I notice Greg eyeing a passer-by's polystyrene cup.

"I'm desperate for one — I didn't quite have the nerve to go into any of the cafés," he admits. "Every time I approached they gave me such strange looks."

"Well, I suppose it's the nautical equivalent of walking around with a traffic cone," I remind him of his fluorescent appendage.

"Perhaps I should have dunked myself in the water and pretended I'd just been washed ashore!"

"We could still try that look if you like!" I jest, pretending I'm about to nudge him into the water but instead I hurry him back across to the landlubber side of the street.

The chain café with the clearly displayed menu and price list and English-speaking staff is in sharp contrast to the locals' joint I was too intimidated to enter the

354

last time I was here — another reminder that nothing stays the same, except perhaps the preparation of the coffee — even though the place is doing a roaring trade in *café frappé* we see several Greeks favouring the traditional coffee prepared in a tiny long-handled copper pot, sitting beside the till in a nest of hot ash. It's a strange sight — like seeing your mum's teapot on the counter in Starbucks — but one that intrigues Greg.

"Let's try one of those!" He surprises me, until he adds, "That's what Zorba would have drunk!"

"You know that would be a fun way to choose your future holiday destinations?" I begin as we take our moulded plastic seats on the upper level. "You write a list of your favourite flicks, look up the filming locations and then retrace the steps of your movie hero! It would be something fun to do with the kids too, like San Francisco for —"

"Is that your phone?" he interrupts.

I scrabble in my bag. "Oh my god, oh my god, *it's her!*" I squeal. "Cherry?"

"SELENA!"

"No way!" I jump to my feet, rushing to the window. "Are you really here? We're just across the road at the little red café on the corner!"

Greg looks baffled by the squeaking that ensues and it's only when I get off the phone and translate that he understands Cherry is indeed just metres away.

"I can't believe we caught her! They sail again tonight but she's on her way right now — we're going for cocktails at the bar where Onassis took Maria

Callas!" I zing, reeling. "And it's all thanks to you and your wandering feet!" I reach across and hug him for the second time today.

"You mean it's a good thing I led you here?" he asks, chin wedged in my shoulder.

"Absolutely!" I set him back in his chair. "Your feet are obviously guided by destiny! In fact —" I contemplate him for a moment before formally announcing, "I hereby relinquish my role as your shore excursions guide."

"Wh-what do you mean?" He looks aghast. "Are you leaving me here?"

"No, no!" I laugh. "I just meant that I am no longer the boss of you!"

"So we're a team now?" he asks hopefully.

"A team!" I confirm, as we chink our tiny cups of authentic Greek coffee.

CHAPTER
TWENTY-SIX

An open enemy is better than a false friend.
— Greek proverb

"There's going to be more shrieking, isn't there?" Greg braces himself as we prepare to meet Cherry.

"I can't deny it." I smile, straightening his collar. "Funny that when men greet each other they get all deep and gruff and back-slappy whereas women flap their hands and squeak."

"My wife never did that," he notes, bemusedly.

"Well, then, you're best shot of her," I only half joke. "All the best girls pogo and get overexcited."

"Selena!" Right on cue a girl with flailing arms hurtles towards me.

"Cherry!" I exclaim as we collide in a hug worthy of a WWF smackdown.

"Oh here we go," Greg mutters, no doubt wishing he could borrow a little of the pastry from the next table to wedge in his ears.

Us girls do a merry little dance as we babble busily over each other, "*I can't believe you're here/it's been too long/you look so fab/this is crazy!*"

And she really does look well. Back on the ship her bob was a perfect crimson bubble, all she needed then was a green stalk sprouting from her crown and she really would look like her namesake. Now her hair is more of a shiny oval, as vibrant as ever and an exact match for her lipgloss and nails — I happen to know that she has a selection of ten shades to choose from to accommodate the fickle ways of red hair dye! It's funny, though Jules is the more model-esque, Cherry has always been more of a pleasure to behold, her greatest beauty secret being her joyful nature — just looking at her makes you smile.

Once we've stopped dancing and grabbing each other's hands, Greg steps back into frame, complete with lifebuoy.

Quick as a flash Cherry quotes our favourite line from *Sex and the City*, channelling a lusty Samantha: "Seamen, twelve o'clock." She jiggles her eyebrows.

"I pray when I turn around there are sailors, because with her, you never know!" I giggle back.

"So who's your man overboard?" Cherry looks quizzically at Greg.

I duly make the introductions.

"Wow, you really come prepared for a sea voyage, don't you?" She grins at him.

"Actually we flew here." He looks awkward. "Do you think it's time I let it go?" He gives me a pained look.

"Don't worry, we can pop it straight in the car," Cherry offers. "It's right outside, if you don't mind chatting while I run an errand?"

"Of course not!" I pip, happy to fit in with her schedule. "I just can't believe you drive here!"

"Are you kidding? I leave that to Konstandinos," she says, introducing us to a besuited man standing proprietorially beside the kind of sleek, black vehicle you have to check for diplomats before you slip on to the leather seats.

"Wow, *The World* really is in another league," I coo. "So where are we headed?"

"Kolonaki, it's basically the designer district of Athens. You're going to die when you see this shoe store —"

"Is this errand for a billionairess?" I enquire gleefully.

"Actually, the shoes are for me — don't look so shocked!"

I try to tone down the surprise on my face. "It's just that you were always so scathing of label queens!"

"Oh, I still am, and wait till you see all the clones on the street — high blonde ponytails, huge black sunglasses, right forearm crooked at forty-five degrees to show off the latest designer handbag . . ." She titters. "But Richard has got me into supporting *local* designers, the point being you can buy Chanel or Prada anywhere in the world but when you come to Greece you want to see their unique vision, right?"

I nod.

"He's made me realise that they'll go out of business if everyone forgoes them in favour of the big-name chains. I mean, we were in Florence the other day, which as you know is tiny, and where there used to be one-off boutiques there're now three Zara stores a stone's throw from each other. And that's a Spanish brand. You go to Spain and it's H&M every other shop, and they're Swedish! Now I'm all for international relations but you also want to try and keep hold of a little national identity!"

She makes a good point. I just have one key question: "Who's Richard?"

"You don't know, do you?" Her pupils dilate as she says the words, "He's my fiancé!"

I should be happy for her — and I make all the outward signs that I am — but inwardly I feel a stab of injustice. She casts Dom aside, swans off to *The World* and within a year is all loved up and proposed to? Not that I want to be engaged but it's the principle of the matter. Maybe that's why Greg and I get on so well — I'm so much more comfortable with disillusioned spurnees.

"So what's he like, this Richard?" I ask.

"I can honestly say I never met a nicer millionaire!" she giggles.

"You mean you're with him for his money?" I can't believe how much she's changed.

"Don't be silly." She swats me playfully. "He's an absolute riot. I think I've finally met my match in cheekiness. I just wish you could meet him but he's working all day. Oh! Have you guys seen the changing of the guard?"

We shake our heads.

Cherry consults with Konstandinos and the next thing we know we're stepping on to Syntagma Square outside the Tomb of the Unknown Soldier.

In front of the carved marble edifice stand two little beach huts, or so they seem, with a pair of matching soldiers in the most distinctive of Greek uniforms:

360

beige jackets fitted at the torso and then flaring to the mid-thigh with a full pleated skirt over white woollen tights with black garters. Their shoes are clompy, almost clown-like clogs sporting outsize pom-poms, and their natty red caps have a long black tassel dangling from temple to waist like a single hair extension.

"This is the most bizarre uniform I've ever seen!" I whisper.

I suspect that the only thing that stops people giggling is the fact that they are carrying blade-tipped rifles and they themselves look like they've been carved from giant tree trunks.

"Do you think they grow them specially for the job?" I can't help but enquire. "I haven't seen any other Greek men anywhere near this height!"

"Well, they are considered the army elite," Cherry informs us.

"The Evzones?" Greg enquires.

"That's right," she confirms. "Basically, they are a ceremonial unit here to guard parliament. Here come their replacements now." She directs our vision to the left where another statuesque team approach.

My eyes widen as they commence their changeover ritual with a slo-mo step in perfect synchronicity, first lifting their left legs, extending them outward, pointing the toes and then stamping their feet to the ground. The same follows with the right legs. And so on. It looks as if the are imitating a stalk or, more specifically, John Cleese's Ministry of Silly Walks.

"Is this for real?" I gawp.

Cherry nods respectfully, adding, "I do like a man in tights!"

As the one nearest us positions himself beside his sentry box he lifts his foot almost to eye level and I notice they actually have nails hammered into the soles of their shoes, for maximum concrete clicking, I presume.

"Which reminds me . . ." As soon as we've grabbed a few snaps, Cherry bundles us back into the car, taking us from the ridiculous to the sublime in the shoe department.

The boutique she had raved about couldn't be a better ad for specialist shopping. Even the exterior sets the mood with its scalloped canopy, potted topiary and flat-screen TV running black-and-white movie clips of the female icons of the Fifties and Sixties — Audrey Hepburn, Jackie O, Sophia Loren — whose style is emulated within.

"The designer used to be a stylist for Greek *Vogue*," Cherry tells me as we step inside. "His name is Vassilis Zoulias and he has an amazing eye for detail — I even love the wrapping they use: yellow with herringbone tweed print, isn't that striking?"

I nod as my eyes dart from the shoeboxes to the framed photos of starlets emerging from planes and swirling in premiere frocks and settle on a magazine cover featuring Elizabeth Taylor at the Acropolis — it gives me quite a thrill to think I was there myself just yesterday!

362

And so to the shoes themselves . . . each artfully lit wall cube features two or three exquisite designs — sunshine yellow strappies, calamine pink slingbacks, African Queen jungle-print courts and then my favourites — pointy-toed deep emerald-green satin with a black bow.

"Are they too expensive to touch?" I whisper.

"In pounds we're talking from about a hundred and twenty up — I know people who've paid more at Hobbs."

"Would you like to try them?" The assistant tempts me further.

"Well —"

"Oh go on, I want to give mine one more go." She smiles at the assistant who duly presents her with a glossy red pair with polka-dot detailing. "I can't decide if a matching handbag is a step too far?" She frowns, stepping over to the display.

"Erm, do you mind if I have a quick nose in the bookshop across the street?" Greg asks to be excused.

"Of course!" we chorus.

The second he is out the door Cherry grips me. "Quick! All the goss, I'm dying to know!"

I take a deep breath. "For starters we're not an item. We just met on the beach a few days ago, but he's been an absolute godsend."

"But what were you doing on a beach in Greece in the first place?" Cherry is impatient for information.

"Well." I bring her up to speed on the situation with Alekos, including my foolish infatuation, but falter slightly as Jules comes into play. Not least because Cherry looks chilled at the mere mention of her.

"Jules is here in Greece?" she quakes.

I nod.

She tuts herself. "It's silly. It shouldn't matter any more, especially not now I'm with Richard, but it still stings to think of her with Dom."

Talk about greedy! She casts Dom aside but resents it if he hooks up with someone else? I'm glad the assistant is approaching with my dream shoes because I really don't know how to respond.

"You know, it took a long time and a lot of therapy to get that image out of my head," Cherry says, lowering herself on to the chaise.

"What image?" I frown. Did she have some kind of guilt issue from abandoning him?

"You know why I left the ship, don't you?" She looks up at me.

"Because you got a better offer from *The World*," I reply.

"Because I caught Jules and Dom together. In the thalassotherapy pool."

"Doing what?"

Cherry rolls her eyes.

"*No!*" I gasp.

"She never told you, did she?"

I shake my head as I sink down beside her. "I had no idea."

"Well, that explains a thing or two . . ." Cherry trails off. "So where is she now?"

I feel my world tilting even more off-kilter as I say, "With Alekos."

Cherry looks horrified. "With the man you've just told me that you were madly in love with?"

"Yes."

"Oh my god, she's done it to you too!"

For a second we sit there too shellshocked to even play Cinderella. Until I remember the facts of my situation. "Actually, it's not the same," I gulp, trying to get a grip. "Jules didn't know how I felt; I'd sent her all these texts ridiculing Alekos and saying I wished she were there to torment him. Look . . ."

I file through some of my backlog and read them out loud to her.

"So you never mentioned that your feelings changed?"

I shake my head. "Well, there is one here that says: *They say everything looks better in the sunshine — is that why Alekos is looking better every day?* But that could just be dismissed as lust."

"Go on."

My heart sinks further. "I don't remember sending this one . . ."

"Read it," Cherry urges.

"*I'm having secret thoughts of rearing one of Roubas' puppies with this man!*" I look up at her. "That's his father's dog . . ."

The more I read the worse it gets.

Cherry slumps back on to the velvet. "My therapist said it wouldn't be the first or last time she'd do it. Apparently it's not about the guy, it's about wanting what you've got. She said it's strangely common among women who are looks-based personalities. Society tells them they can have anything they want because they're beautiful. And then when they see another woman happy in love when they're not, they get all indignant — I'm the pretty one! That should be me! And so they set about getting it for themselves, regardless of the cost to the friendship. Their only aim in that moment is to win — to prove that physical attractiveness is the greatest trump card, because without that, they will feel utterly worthless."

Could this really be true? I'm too dazed to process what Cherry is saying but I get the gist — Jules did it on purpose. She knew how I felt and she did it anyway.

"Do they not have your size?" Greg makes a tentative approach, trying to find a reason for our wretched state — when he left us we were all twittery and frivolous.

"It's not that." I pull him on to the chaise beside us. "You know the home-wrecker of Elounda?"

He nods. We've just about updated him when the assistant approaches, no doubt curious as to whether any more friends will be joining us on the chaise.

Cherry looks at her watch. "I suppose we really should be getting a move on. They're perfect." She hands the assistant her pair. "What about you, Selena, are you going to treat yourself?"

I sigh, thinking of New Zealand and how my sister's lifestyle is more hiking-boot-orientated. "I'm not sure I'll have an appropriate occasion —"

"Nonsense!" Cherry cuts in. "Your next formal night is only a couple of months away — Oh my god!" She

366

suddenly grabs my arm. "Why don't you two have dinner on board with us tonight! You could wear them then!"

"I thought you were sailing?" I frown.

"We are, but why don't you come with us?"

"Hold on." Greg looks concerned. "Wouldn't we have to buy an apartment to do that?"

"Not at all," Cherry chuckles. "You'd be our stowaways!"

"Oh, I don't know . . ." Greg looks fretful.

"I'm only teasing!" she nudges him. "You'd be our guests — we have a three-bedroom residence so you'd even have your own rooms!"

"A three-bedroom residence?" I marvel, realising I never did get the full story on her situation with rich Richard. "Do I take it you're not in entertainments any more?"

"Well, I like to think that I'm as entertaining as ever but no, I'm no longer staff on *The World*. I help Richard run his business — doubled his profits in the last six months, if you don't mind! So what do you think, shall I call ahead and arrange the passes? Or do you have other plans?"

I look at Greg. This is rather more of an adventure than either of us was expecting.

"Where exactly are you sailing to?" Greg has the sense to enquire, not that the destination particularly matters to me.

"Chania."

"Chania?" I repeat, wondering why that port name is ringing a bell.

"It's where Nana Mouskouri was born," Cherry informs me, as if that will end my niggle.

"That's not all . . ." Greg looks awkward.

"What?"

"You know what island it's on?"

Cherry shakes her head. "No, but I can check the schedule —"

"No need, I went there earlier in the week."

"Not Crete?" I blanche.

He nods.

"Oh well, then forget it." Cherry folds her arms defiantly. "There's no way I'm going there while Jules is at large. I'll stay here in Athens with you guys and then catch up with the ship in Istanbul."

"Good idea!" I confirm as we trade credit card slips for our precious parcels.

"Is it?" Greg challenges as we head for the door.

"What?" We turn back to face him.

"You're just going to let Jules off the hook?"

We blink confusedly at him. "I don't see what purpose it would serve to confront her now."

"Really?" he says.

Cherry and I look at each other and then back at the man who appears to be challenging our righteous indignation. "What are you saying?"

"Just that Jules must be counting her lucky stars right now. She steals your guys and what do you do to retaliate? Disappear! You couldn't make it any easier on her if you tried."

"It's a matter of self-preservation!" I protest.

"What about the next woman she does this to? What possible incentive is there for Jules *not* to do this again?" He raises an eyebrow. "I'm not saying it's an easy situation — when Lily was getting bullied in the playground my first instinct was to get her into a new school but what kind of message would that send? I didn't want to teach my daughter to run from her problems, we're a whole nation of confrontation-avoiders and I see that backfiring in the worst way."

"So what did you do?" I ask.

"Presumably, you went to the headmistress?" Cherry surmises.

"Well, actually, Lily persuaded me to let her try something else first . . . She went back to school and faced down the bully, having positioned her friend so she could do a secret mini-movie of the whole thing, and then came home and uploaded it on to YouTube. Of course the bully didn't care what the other girls thought of her, she even thought it was great advertising — showing her at her scariest — but her comeuppance came a week later courtesy of her twelve-year-old boyfriend Jason. He'd been off with flu and when he came back he dumped her on the spot. She spent the next year trying to win him back with do-gooding. It really was quite amusing in the end."

"So you're saying that confronting Jules is the morally right thing to do?"

Greg shrugs as he holds open the door for us. "I'm just offering my opinion. What you do with it is up to you."

As we step outside I can't seem to raise my eyes from the pavement. "I hate to be a wimp about this but I don't think I can go back there. I know I should feel all fired up but I don't, I just feel weak."

Cherry reaches for my hand. "What if I was there with you?"

"I'd be there too," Greg offers.

"And Richard," Cherry adds. "I know I can count on his support."

"Oh no!" I panic. "I don't think you should let him anywhere near Jules!"

"I'd like to see her try with him!" she scoffs confidently.

"Careful what you wish for," I caution, heaving a sigh. "Really, Cherry, it's great of you to offer but you've got no reason to get involved in this now — your life has moved on."

"It's not just about me, I'd do it for you and, like Greg says, for the next girl. *So there isn't a next girl . . .*" she clarifies. "Besides, perhaps this will spare you a few months of therapy — it could be the fast track to some closure!"

"I'm not sure that seeing Jules suffer would make me feel any better about Alekos," I grumble.

"But you know what would feel good?" Greg pips. "Standing up for yourself."

"God!" I throw up my hands. "Would you stop talking so much sense?!"

He grins back at me. "You said yourself you've always wanted to visit *The World* . . ."

"And you do need to get back to Crete . . ." I concede.

"So are we all in?" Cherry looks expectantly at me.

"Come on then," I link arms with them both, "I think it's time for us to set sail on the good ship *Revenge!*"

CHAPTER
TWENTY-SEVEN

"The strong do what they have to do and the weak accept what they have to accept."
— Thucydides

"I feel like I'm going undercover as a rich person," Greg gulps as we approach the pre-boarding security desk for *The World*. "Do you think I should have worn a tie?"

"You'll be fine," I assure him as I surreptitiously study the genuinely wealthy residents ahead of us, wondering how they made their respective fortunes. They look normal enough. No instantly apparent differences between them and my regular cruisers. Then again, I suppose it's too hot for furs and too early for tiaras.

"These are the guests I called about." Cherry smiles at the security guard as he takes custody of our passports, exchanging them for a sticker. A little yellow sticker. Surely it should at least be gold?

I have to admit, I was expecting to be greeted by scalp-tingling chandeliers and shimmering opulence but in fact the lobby area is decidedly understated. Yes, the reception staff are suitably glossy and charming but the bar area has an almost corporate business look to it. I wouldn't be surprised if that besuited gentleman sipping sparkling water started to make a flip-chart presentation.

By way of utter contrast, Cherry begins our tour at the ship's Banyan Tree spa and we are instantly transported, via a dark, fragrant corridor, to Asia. My hand reaches to pick up a leaflet for Jules but then halts over the wafting incense. Maybe not.

We continue on past the gym, on to the two-table casino with hip white leather stools and spangled curtains that look ready to reveal a magician. The bar at this level is far more fun with a low ceiling bristling with fibreoptics — fine wispy threads pulsing neon sea anemone colours. There's a small circular dance floor, about the size of one swirling skirt, but I'm guessing it could hold a dozen or so tightly clasped slow dancers.

"Cute, huh?" Cherry grins. "This is a lot smaller than she's used to . . ." she explains to Greg.

"Oooh, I wish we had one of these!" I gurgle as we discover the deli and adjoining grocery. "Special K! Kettle Chips —"

"Are we moving?" Greg blurts suddenly, looking alarmed.

"Yes," Cherry confirms with a check of her watch. "We're just setting sail now."

"Oh my god! I'd forgotten we were on a ship!" He laughs at himself.

"Come on, let's get up on the top deck so you can really take it all in."

"I can't even get my head around the fact that there are lifts on a boat!" he chuckles, amazed as we press the call button.

"It's the little mail boxes that get me," I say, noticing that each room has one — just as a regular apartment would.

"Want to take a quick peek inside?" Cherry offers, noticing the maid entering a few doors down. "This is one of the rentable rooms so we're not snooping on anyone's home."

We can't resist and discover it resembles a sleek, modern hotel room, all glossy beige wood and clean Scandinavian lines. In fact, now I come to think of it, the overall look of the ship is very much Ikea for Billionaires.

"So this is a studio, the smallest option."

"But it has its own balcony?" I peer out on to the wooden deck.

"They all do, every last one. Of course, ours happens to have a Jacuzzi . . ." She twinkles.

"On the balcony?" I gawp. "So you can sit in it at night under the stars as you're sailing along?"

Cherry nods. "You could sit in it while you're in port, too, but that would just be weird."

"So although this living space is relatively small, you really have the rest of the ship as your playground."

"Exactly!" Cherry grins at Greg. "It's so quiet on board you can always find a public area and have it all to yourself."

"So go on, then, tell me: how much are we talking here?" He braces himself for her response.

"About four hundred thousand for this. I think ours was eight."

"Wow."

"But think of all the airfares you save!" she reasons.

"I think it's brilliant," I pip. "I'd never leave!"

"But isn't this your life already?" Greg frowns in confusion.

"Let me tell you, my room on the ship doesn't have its own espresso maker and a bathtub with a view of the ocean. The only personal object I can squeeze in is a picture of my mum and dad Blu-tacked to the wall."

"Remember that Ukrainian musician's cabin?" Cherry prompts.

I roll my eyes. "He was so talented you'd think they'd have him in the penthouse suite, but it was just a humble house band so he's tucked away in this little cell with big ol' pipes running through it. No windows. You had to duck and weave just to get in. Completely claustrophobic."

"It wasn't really a room at all," Cherry decides. "Just a sectioned-off area with a door on it. Anyway, onward and upward."

We pass through an Internet area with a *Matrix*-esque contraption that looks like a cross between a recliner and an exercise machine with the computer no doubt set at some ergonomically accurate angle. I consider slotting myself in to try it out but I'm not sure I'd ever get out of it again.

"Fresh air," Cherry cheers as she leads us on, pushing open the door leading on to the delightfully breezy deck. She points up a level. "That's the only full-size tennis court on any cruiseship!"

"Really?"

"It's to do with the guest/space ratio," she explains. "On any other cruiseship it would be an extravagance to dedicate that much space to two or four passengers but here they don't have those kinds of restrictions. There's plenty of room and far fewer passengers, so why not?"

"Why not indeed!" I nod, noticing that the court is a non-traditional blue, presumably because it can be.

"And you've got golf up there too?" Greg observes. "I wonder how many fish get concussed by misplaced golf balls . . ."

"Well, you're not going to believe this, but the balls actually dissolve into fish food."

"They do not!" I hoot.

"It's true, they're biodegradable. This is actually the greenest ship going. The World Wildlife Fund were protesting our docking at one port so the captain invited them on board to check us out and on the next visit they were there again, only this time with welcome banners!"

"That's impressive," I acknowledge, thinking how interested Alekos would be in the environmental element. It makes me feel quite churny thinking about him, realising that I can no longer share any thoughts or moments with him.

"Who fancies a cuppa?" Cherry takes me by the arm, noticing I need reviving.

I presume we're headed back to the deli but in fact she's saved the best to last.

We actually have our tea on the bridge. I can't believe guests are allowed to freely view the nerve centre of the ship, but then again, I suppose on this vessel guests are so heavily vetted, and if they did accidentally break the multi-million-pound navigation system, you know they'd be able to pay for a replacement.

"So when are we going to meet Richard?" I ask, realising that since we're moving, he must be on board.

"Here he comes right now." She beams.

My jaw gapes almost as wide as the drawbridge that lowers to allow swimmers full access to the sea when the ship is anchored. I was expecting someone a bit old-fashioned suity with a heavy flicked fringe but in fact he's gorgeous with close-cropped tawny hair, the clearest aqua eyes and perfect gold-dusted tan. As he steps closer I notice he has the cutest chin dimple à la Kirk Douglas.

"Welcome!" he cheers. "It's so lovely, aaggh —"

"Oh my god!" Greg and I cry in unison as he trips, about to crash headlong into the tea china.

"Oh Richard, I wish you wouldn't do that!" Cherry rolls her eyes as he halts millimetres short of devastation. "Ever since we saw that documentary on stuntmen last week . . ."

As we make introductory chit-chat I can't help but wonder what hideous flaw he must have to balance out being rich, handsome and fun.

"So!" He claps his hands together suddenly. "Let me run through our restaurant choices for this evening . . ."

He certainly has a lot of energy. Perhaps to the extent of being insensitive?

"So what will it be?" He looks expectantly at myself and Greg as he completes the list.

"Well . . ." We exchange an uneasy look — Greg with his dress code concerns, me with my general fatigue.

"Allow me to offer you one other dining option," he says, leaning in conspiratorially. "How about room service?"

My face instantly brightens. So much for him being insensitive.

"Would I still need a tie?" Greg frets.

"No, but you will need pyjamas!"

Ten minutes later we're standing before Richard's extensive wardrobe getting kitted out with brand new, handmade silk pyjamas courtesy of his last trip to Gibraltar.

"He thinks they make great presents so he always stocks up," Cherry explains as we marvel at the range of options on offer.

"Navy for you, my good man." He hands a pair to Greg. "And silver for the lady —"

"No, give her the black," Cherry diverts him. "That way she can still wear her new shoes!"

Now this is fun — all four of us gleaming luxuriantly by candlelight, us girls in stilettos, the men in velvet slippers. Better yet, it really does feel like we are in someone's home. Unlike the studio, Richard and Cherry's three-bedroom apartment has been completely personalised with artefacts and framed photographs from their trips around the world, alongside the gleaming Bosch appliances in the large black-marble kitchen.

"I can't believe you have a washing machine in your cabin!" I chuckle as Richard presents each of us with a Martini accessorised with an authentic Greek olive.

"Right!" He then bears down from the head of the table: "Regarding the comeuppance of Ms Jules Webb, I think we need a strategy!"

I look at the alert faces around me, still not quite believing the team operation this has become.

"If we just turn up and have a go at Jules, she'll simply get huffy and leave."

"No lynch mob?" Cherry looks slightly disappointed.

"Quite the opposite," Richard continues. "I think we should invite Jules and Alekos for dinner — start the evening off nice and refined."

"They're staying at the Elounda Beach," I attempt to make a contribution. "I happen to be familiar with all the menu options there . . ."

"Hmmm, I'm sure the food is divine but I don't think it's the kind of place we'd want to cause a scene . . ."

"So there's still a chance of a cat fight?" Cherry brightens.

Richard rolls his eyes at his fiancée. "Ideally, we need somewhere that offers an opportunity for Jules to make a move on one of us guys —"

"Excuse me?" Cherry baulks.

"Don't worry, we won't let it get further than a proposition — it'll just have so much more impact if we can catch her in the act."

"I don't know." I grimace. "I mean, she's only been with Alekos a matter of days; she might not be ready to move on."

Richard's confidence doesn't waver. "If our assessment of her motives is correct, she'll drop him the second she sees you girls with new toys."

"Which would also double as a neat little comeuppance for him." Cherry gives me a significant look.

"I've got a suggestion for the venue." Greg holds up his hand, requesting permission to speak.

"Yes?"

"My Carob Tree Valley Villa — there's a kitchen and lounge, outside dining, pool area, balconies, an upstairs to take a little tour of . . ." He gives a subversive wink.

"He's right, it's perfect," I concur. "It even comes with its own caterer!"

"Really?" Cherry gawps.

"You're looking at him," Greg mumbles.

"Great!" Richard claps his hands together. "If you do the grub, I'll supply the booze."

"Beware!" Cherry issues a general caution. "Richard is the sneakiest topper-upper I ever met!"

"Secret of my success!" He puffs his chest. "I really have no business acumen or seduction skills, I'm just a very deft pour! Anyway, we'll get everyone a bit tipsy and see whether she makes a play for me or Greg here," he says, reaching to give him a manly jiggle of the shoulder.

"I'm not sure that's entirely fair." Greg looks uncertain.

380

"Well, I don't think Jules exactly plays fair, do you?"

"No, I mean in terms of setting her up to choose between you and me." He heaves a sigh. "You've got the looks and the money and the jet-set lifestyle. I'm a recently divorced house husband on his first holiday."

"Who happens to be one of the loveliest people I've ever met!" I exclaim.

"But we're talking about someone quite mercenary here," Greg reasons. "She's not going to go for lovely."

"This isn't for real, you know?" Cherry reminds him.

"I know," he pouts, "I just want to feel part of the game."

"How about I write you a cheque right now and make you a millionaire too?" Richard offers, ever the good sport.

Greg laughs. "Well, if you're offering . . ."

"Or better yet — we swap identities!" Richard gets highly agitated. "Oh, I like that — I get to be Greg from Lancaster!"

"Oh no!" Cherry winces at the terrible accent he subsequently attempts. "Please stop!"

"No?" Richard looks crestfallen.

"Maybe it's a little bit too ambitious," Greg concedes.

"Not necessarily . . ." I'm probably going to regret complicating things but I open my big mouth anyway. "If you're serious about switching, Greg can still be from Lancaster, but now he is primarily based on *The World,* where he met his lovely fiancée Cherry. And Richard, your hometown is still Lymington, in fact, that's where you live now as primary care-giver to two gorgeous daughters — Lily and Daisy."

"And I'm your new beau, right?" He grins at me.

"Well . . ."

"Absolutely." Cherry gives her seal of approval. "All the better for making Alekos suffer!"

Richard rubs his hands together gleefully. "This is going be a blast!"

Greg still isn't convinced. "I'm not sure I know how to act rich."

"Give me your watch!" Richard instructs as he removes his Rolex, ready to trade. "That's always a good place to start. Plus your wardrobe could be a bit more yachtie. Come on, we're pretty much the same size, let's get you into some resort wear!"

As we watch the two men scuttle off to play dress up, Cherry shakes her head. "I think Richard thinks he's going undercover for the CIA."

"And Greg thinks he's getting in character for a movie!"

"Thank goodness we get to be ourselves — victims no more!"

I chink glasses with her and drain the last of my Martini.

"So how are you feeling?" Cherry asks, tone softer now.

I sigh. "Honestly?"

"Honestly."

"The ridiculous thing is I still miss him. It's like some part of me hasn't heard the news that it's all gone pear-shaped."

She nods understanding. "When I first got to *The World*, I had this sudden panic that I'd imagined the whole thing — of course, Dom would never do such a thing to me!"

"How does she do it?" I marvel. "I mean, I can pretty much imagine *how*." I pull a face. "Aren't you at all nervous about sending Richard into the lair?"

"I'm more worried about poor Greg!" she titters.

"This has turned out to be quite a first holiday for him," I smirk.

"You don't think there's any way your friendship could —"

"Nooo." I shake my head. "And that's not disappointing in any way — I like things just the way they are between us."

"Okay, well, just don't give up hope — I know it's silly to even say it when you're feeling so disillusioned, but good things can come out of the blue. I'm living proof of that."

"Actually you are!" I grin, ready to put a positive spin on the situation. "I may have lost Jules and Alekos but I've gained you and Greg!"

"And Richard," she reminds me.

"Ah yes, my new fantastically good-looking boyfriend!"

"Hey, don't you go getting any ideas now!" Cherry teases as the doorbell dings, announcing the arrival of dinner.

Two hours later my belly is full, my eyelids heavy, but my heart is still fluttering nervously at the prospect of tomorrow's showdown. Not least because it involves seeing Alekos. I can't even imagine what it will do to me to see his face again.

"See you chaps in the morning — breakfast on the balcony?" Richard suggests as we prepare to go our separate ways.

"Sounds lovely!"

I give Greg a goodnight hug but pull Cherry aside for a quick recap.

"So let me just get this absolutely straight," I say as she sits beside me on my latest bed. "First thing tomorrow I call Jules and Alekos and invite them to dinner at Greg's villa. Meanwhile, the four of us transfer from the ship to Elounda, arriving a few hours ahead of them to set everything up."

"Correct."

"Greg and Richard are keeping their own names but switching identities?" I continue.

"Precisely." Cherry nods. "This way we'll see whether Jules goes for looks or money."

"My money's on the money," I tell her. "She's just had looks with Alekos."

Cherry sighs and takes my hand. "You really did like him, didn't you?"

I give her a wobbly look.

She shakes her head sadly. "I can see we're going to have to do some major psyching up for this. If Alekos doesn't ever know that you really liked him then your dignity will be intact. Right now it's seeping out of every pore."

"I don't know how to stop it!" I say, brow crumpling in frustration.

Instantly her arms are around me. For the past two days I've been squishing everything down, trying to hold myself together for Greg's sake, but all it takes is for Cherry to say, "Go on, treat yourself to one last cry!" and it all comes chugging up and out again. The devastating hurt and disappointment. The anger, the injustice, the overwhelming sense of humiliation and loss.

"This is why we're going back," Cherry says, stroking my hair as she rocks me gently back and forth. "We're doing this for every girl who's ever been cheated on."

CHAPTER
TWENTY-EIGHT

In baiting a mousetrap with cheese, always leave room for the mouse.
— Greek proverb

"Positions, everyone!" Richard alerts us as a vehicle pulls up outside the villa. "We have company."

As Greg dims the lights, Cherry secretes herself in the laundry room under the stairs (so she can make her entrance at the most impactful time) and, as the one person linking everyone, I prepare to do my welcome hostess duties.

I'm not looking forward to greeting a loved-up Alekos and Jules so I take a bite of *dakus* so any facial distortions can be put down to chewing rather than the contempt and revulsion I'll actually be exhibiting.

"Oh!" I stall just one step out the door. At the end of the tealight-lined pathway there is a distinct absence of red hire car, just Alekos stepping from a dusty motorbike on to the tarmac. I look around him. "Where's Jules?"

He switches back to inspect the bare leather seat and then throws up his hands. "Oh no! She must have fallen off!"

"*What?!*" I gasp, rushing over, before it dawns on me that he's winding me up.

"I'm sure she's on her way." He shrugs, sounding clipped and detached. "I brought some sargos fish," he adds, holding out a plastic bag of silvery items. "I just harpooned them."

"Really?" I accidentally sound impressed. "Actually, I can still see the mask mark on your face!" I reach to highlight the indentation at his temple, but he flinches before I even make contact, ducking back to retrieve a box of beers from the bike's lockbox.

Hold on a minute! Isn't it me who has cause to be all surly and cold with him, not the other way around? What's going on? And why is my heart still looping at the mere sight of him?

"I won't be staying long," he informs me as I bid him follow me inside. "I just wanted to say goodbye."

"You're leaving?" I startle, turning back to face him.

"No, but you are."

Did he just evict me from the island? "I am?" I ask, unable to hide the disappointment in my voice. As hard as it was to return to Elounda today, I had such a rush of affection for this place . . .

"Well, your ten days are up now, aren't they?" He shrugs. "Jules said the two of you will be returning to England tomorrow."

Did she now? Something has obviously gone seriously awry between those two. Maybe that's why he's so grouchy. I know it's not part of the plan but I wonder if I should just confront him outright about the whole sordid saga, while I have the chance?

I go to step towards him but a pair of arms pulls me back into a clinch. "I was getting lonesome in there without you!" Richard nuzzles into my neck.

"Oh, er, darling!" I exclaim, improvising badly — I don't think I've ever called a man darling before in my life.

"I don't believe we've met?" Alekos bristles at this foreign presence.

"This is Richard!" I fluster, still squirming within his all-too-firm grasp.

As they nod at each other another male head appears around the patio doors.

"And that's Greg," I say, as he waves a welcoming oven glove.

"How many men have you got in there?" Alekos snorts.

"Just the two tonight," I trill, carelessly.

Alekos grunts something in Greek but I don't get a chance to request a translation as he's marched on ahead asking if he can have a look around the villa — apparently this is one of the plots he has been considering for his own villa purchase.

I'd follow him in but the guest of honour has just pulled up.

I take a deep breath. Much as I want to pluck out Jules' eyelashes until she confesses all, I have to act as if I am completely oblivious to her treachery.

"Thank god you're back!" Jules crushes me with what I've always interpreted as a heartfelt hug but I now consider brute force. "It's been an absolute nightmare since you've been gone — is he here?" She pulls back suddenly.

"If you mean Alekos . . .?"

She nods.

"He's inside," I confirm.

She tuts agitatedly. "It's just like I warned you — you sleep with him once and then he completely loses interest. I'm just glad it was me he messed around not you."

I blink back at her. Is she going to try and spin this so it looks like she's done me a favour?

"What are you talking about!" I give her a playful smack. "I thought it was all steamerama between you two . . . When I left, you were planning a cosy night in with room service and the infinity pool!"

She rolls her eyes. "I know! Probably one of the sexiest hotel rooms in the world and he's too sullen and hungover to —"

"Hungover?" I interrupt. That doesn't ring true. "Are you sure? He pretty much has a two-drink maximum . . ."

"I know!" she scoffs. "Lightweight! He really needs to work on that because, let me tell you, he's a damn sight more fun drunk. And what's with this rule of only having one employee out on the boats at any one time?"

"What?" This is the first I've heard of it.

"Something to do with the insurance, apparently, so off he goes every hour whizzing around the bay and I'm sat like a lemon on the beach."

"I thought you liked lying on the beach doing nothing."

"Not with a twelve-year-old boy for company! Thank god for his sister, I don't know how I would have got through the nights were it not for her."

"You've been hanging out with Brooke?" This situation is getting more bizarre by the second.

She nods enthusiastically.

"I thought she was only fifteen?"

Jules shrugs. "She's very mature for her age, kind of like a teenage Diana Dors."

"I'd heard she was a bit of a looker . . ."

"Oh my god, she has all the boys at her mercy!" Jules simpers. "We went to Agios Nikolaos with a big gang of her friends . . ." She gives me an ooo-eee look. "It's a lot livelier than this place. No wonder you took off to Athens first chance you got!"

"So are you ladies joining us or do we have to bring the party to you?" Richard appears on his second rescue mission of the evening.

As predicted, Jules' eyes immediately get a glint. "Now you look like a man who can mix a mean cocktail!"

He grins back at her. "And you look like a woman who's knocked back a few in her time!"

She emits a girlish tinkle, too keen to indulge him to take offence.

"So what's it going to be?" He raises his eyebrows expectantly.

"Why don't you choose for me?" she purrs submissively.

"Okay," he says, leading her to the kitchen. "Let me get a proper look at you . . ."

She does a slow turn, showing off her backless dress.

"I'm thinking sour . . ." He strokes his chin. "Or just a little tart?"

No wonder he's in charge of the cocktails, he seems to have a gift for stirring. I quickly stick my head in the freezer on the pretext of getting the ice.

"What do you say to a simple Screwdriver over a measure of ouzo — A Screw You Over, if you will . . ." he says, fearless in his ribbing. "Cherry?"

"Oh no, I don't like those," she says, accepting her custom-made drink.

"Oh, I wasn't referring to the maraschino variety," he titters, motioning for her to look behind her.

"Hello, Jules." Cherry the person is right up in her face.

"Top up!" I grab Jules' glass before it smashes on the floor.

The two of them contemplate each other — one looking stricken, the other defiant.

"Surprise!" I whimper in the background.

"Why didn't you tell me she was here!" Jules hisses at me through gritted teeth.

"Oh, don't look so perturbed," Cherry tinkles, oh-so-sweetly. "I'm not going to glass you! In fact, I want to toast you — if you hadn't stolen Dom from me then I never would have met Greg . . ."

Right on cue he pops up and blesses Cherry's forehead with a kiss. "I really am terrifically grateful," he enthuses. "I was seriously thinking of giving up my apartment on *The World* until she came along —"

"You own an apartment on *The World*?" Jules cuts in, unable to curb her knee-jerk envy.

"Well, technically it'll be *ours* in a month — we're getting married!"

Jules' mouth gapes further.

"So you see, you did me a huge, *huge* favour!" Cherry smirks.

I can almost hear Jules thinking, "That wasn't part of the plan!" To the point that she doesn't even quite know how to respond — giving Richard the perfect opportunity to swizzle the stick a little more.

"In a way you also did me a favour," he layers on the torment. "If you hadn't hooked up with Alekos, then Selena wouldn't have been free to come to Athens and fall into my arms."

Jules' head swings back in our direction. "You mean, you two are together?"

We nod decisively, even though I am now painfully aware that Alekos is watching.

"Well! Who knew I was such a matchmaker!" she brazens. "You see, Aleko, I do serve some purpose beyond funding the spa community!"

Wow. There's tension all round. I check how Alekos is doing and find him looking positively murderous now.

"Everything alright?" Cherry dares to enquire.

He glowers back at her and then finally growls, "You cooked Greek food?"

"What?" She frowns as he heads for the kitchen table.

392

"Er, actually, that was me!" Greg owns up, somewhat timidly. "I hope that's okay. I always like to try out recipes in whatever far-flung country I find myself and it turns out that Greek is my favourite so, really, any tips are most welcome . . ."

Alekos stares him down for a full ten seconds before caving. "Let me try your saganaki . . ."

Meanwhile Richard invites Jules for a tour of the pool area and Cherry pulls me into the loo to do a gleeful little dance.

"That was brilliant!" she squeaks. "Did you see the look on Jules' face when she heard I was marrying money! It's so true what they say — living well is the best revenge! I just never knew I'd have the added bonus of rubbing her perfectly exfoliated nose in it!" She reaches out to embrace me. "And what about Alekos? He's like a Greek Heathcliffe or something! Is he always that surly?"

"Not at all," I sigh. "You should see him when he's laughing or" — I get all misty — "underwater."

Cherry gives me a quizzical look and then shrugs. "Well, whatever happened with Jules, he's definitely not into her now."

"I think it was a one-off thing," I confirm. "And she made some reference to him being drunk but that's still no excuse, is it?"

"Maybe she drugged him; I wouldn't put it past her."

"Don't get my hopes up!" I complain and then sigh. "I suppose we should get back out there . . ."

"Yup, let Phase Two begin!"

We emerge one by one, trying to be discreet, but no one is even looking. I can see Richard and Jules still talking in the garden and Greg and Alekos now seem to be getting along quite nicely, in a culinary kind of way.

"So I could add a few more pinenuts to this?" Greg is actually taking notes.

"And a very small pinch of cinnamon," Alekos advises. "You know these are actually Selena's favourite —"

"What are?" I perk up, hearing him say my name.

"The courgette blossoms," Alekos mumbles, continuing to avoid my gaze.

"Well, then, you have to try one of mine while you can." Greg offers me the tray. "Not sure I'll be able to get the right flowers back home!"

"And where is home for you?" Alekos leans back on the counter, helping himself to an olive. "When you're not going around the world on *The World*?"

Greg opens his mouth but no words are forthcoming.

"Where do you call home?" Alekos rephrases his question, thinking that might help.

"Well," Greg begins, "that's hard to say. Because I have several properties. Seven, in fact," he blabs, completely overdoing it.

"You own seven homes?" Alekos repeats.

"Yes," Greg confirms with a definitive nod. And then his face falls as he realises Alekos is waiting for the list. "Oh, let me see now . . . there's one in Geneva," he offers tentatively.

Alekos nods. "I've never been there."

"Really?" Greg perks up. "It's very swish. And Swiss, obviously," he laughs, all-too-earnestly.

"Where else?"

"Um, a villa near Madrid, a ranch in Montana, a penthouse in Moscow . . ."

From the curious collection, I suspect he's trying to think of the most land-locked locations, least accessible by cruiseships. Also, apparently, beginning with the letter M.

"A macadamia plantation in Paraguay," he continues, "and, er, a castle in Scotland."

"A castle?" Alekos' eyes widen.

"Very small, nothing fancy."

"And the seventh?"

Poor Greg looks wrung out.

"It's like naming the Seven Dwarfs," he bleats. "There's always one that eludes me . . ."

"I think Cherry mentioned somewhere in Dubai." I try to help him out with the first place that comes to my mind.

"Oh, I know it well, my uncle moved there." Alekos brightens. "Whereabouts?"

Greg shoots me a *thanks a lot* look.

"Sorry," I mouth back.

"Um. Cherry, sweetie?" Greg summons assistance. "Our place in Dubai, what's the name of the area . . .?"

"Dubai?" She frowns.

Surely I can't have picked the one place she's never been?

Greg heaves a sigh. "You know, Alekos, the truth is that home for me is wherever my princess is!" He pulls her close.

"Oh, you're so sweet!" Cherry tweaks his nose. "Now why don't we go and offer these delicious morsels to the rest of the guests?"

"Good idea!" Greg cheers, keen to escape the interrogation scene.

Alekos continues to study him as he scurries off, commenting, "He seems rather jumpy."

"Well, you know when you're the host of a party . . ."

"I thought Richard was the host?" Alekos corrects me. "This is his villa, right?"

Oh what a stupid idea to switch their identities! So much more trouble than it's worth and it's not even Alekos we're out to deceive!

"Yes, yes, you're right, but Greg has been in charge of the cooking and that's very stressful. Especially when there are such discerning palates at large . . ."

He nods, taking my point. "Perhaps it's best I cook the fish for him, then?"

"Oh yes, that would be very considerate," I agree. "What can I do to help?"

I want to stay close to Alekos. I need to get to the bottom of exactly what happened between him and Jules. Whatever it was, it's over now. Which isn't to say it's forgivable, a man sleeping with your best friend is the most fundamental deal breaker, but there's something fishy going on, and not just with the sargos.

"You are familiar with this kitchen?" he enquires.

"Well . . . a little."

"Could you find me a baking tray and a sharp knife?" he says, reaching for a lemon from the fruit bowl.

Amazingly there is no "Oop, pardon me!" clashing as he descales and I clean away the debris or "Sorry, I just needed to reach for the . . ." as he unstoppers the olive oil and I hand him the appropriate brush. We seem to be oddly streamlined, even in this area where I have so little expertise.

"That's it," he says as he slots the tray in the oven. "They'll be ready in under ten minutes."

"Gosh," I gasp. "I always thought cooking fish would be so complicated — I could do that!"

"Yes, you could," he confirms and then gives me a sideways look. "What did you think of the courgette blossoms?"

I may be mistaken but it feels as if he has deliberately singled them out to trigger a memory of our day at Zeus' cave.

I take another forkful and then whisper, "Not quite as good as the ones we had at that taverna in Lasithi — maybe they need your magic card?"

He very nearly smiles but then, just as quickly, looks cross.

"Aleko, what —"

"Do I detect the aroma of fresh fish?" Richard appears, master of interruption.

I take a step back so he can get a full view of Alekos' handiwork through the oven door. "He caught them himself!" I boast on his behalf.

"Oh, that's fun, isn't it?" Richard yars. "I used to love doing that as a kid."

I see Alekos check his expression — did he just patronise me?

"I hear you're quite the little merman!" Richard continues with his baiting.

"I do love the ocean," Alekos replies in a measured tone.

"I'm quite keen on watersports myself. Selena tells me your brother has a business here?"

Alekos nods. "If you come down to the beach tomorrow, I would be happy to set you up with whatever you need."

"That's very generous," Richard concedes. "But you know what would be more fun?"

Alekos looks guarded. "What?"

"If we went tonight."

"In the dark?" I hoot derisively.

"I take it you've never been monoskiing by moonlight?" he quizzes me.

"No, and I very much doubt you have." I give him a "remember your role" glare. "Besides, I don't have a death wish — you may as well do it blindfold!"

"Oh, that's fun too."

Is Richard for real? Or is this all part of the game? I can't tell.

"But you're missing one key factor that only occurs once a month," he says, leading me to the window. "It's a full moon!" The blinding globe of white cannot be denied. "That's really the only night to do it, wouldn't you agree, Aleko?"

"It is certainly the brightest night," he concedes.

"But surely it's still way too dangerous?" I fret as I notice Alekos' jaw take on a competitive jut. "I really don't think it's a good idea. Those inky waters . . ."

"Well, it's up to Alekos," Richard shrugs, "it's his town. His equipment."

Richard looks at Alekos, Alekos looks at Richard.

"Perhaps we'll have a race, just to make it interesting . . ."

I roll my eyes. Men! "How are you going to do that?" I despair. "For a start, we'd need two speedboats!"

"We'll borrow one of my father's."

"Well, then, we'd also need two drivers." I point out the next obstacle.

"I'll do it."

"Cherry!" I exclaim. Has the full moon made everyone lose their minds?

"Trust me, I've driven more speedboats than cars this past year."

"Well, then, that's settled," Alekos confirms.

"Only I think we should mix up the teams," Richard decides. "I'll take Cherry. Alekos, you can have Selena."

I feel like a daughter being bequeathed to a man for an arranged marriage, only that wouldn't be nearly such a daunting scenario.

"You know I can't do that, look what happened last time . . ." I grimace.

"You'll be fine," Alekos assures me, without actually meeting my concerned gaze. "You won't make the same mistake again."

"Really?" I can't believe how much his vote of confidence means at this time, even though my stomach is already running through the full range of nautical knots.

"If you're absolutely sure."

"I'm sure."

"Let him show off for you!" Cherry hisses as she guides me back into the lounge.

"Who?"

"Alekos, of course! He's obviously beaten down by this whole Jules saga; he needs to feel like top dog again."

"Speaking of which . . ." I look around me. "Where did Jules and Greg go?"

"Ahhh, she suggested they take a little tour of the villa." She gives me a knowing look. "They've been upstairs for some time."

"Gosh, I hope he's alright," I wince, envisioning him pinned to the bed with re-appropriated coat hangers. "Do you think we should check on him?"

"I'll nip out and loiter under the balcony to see if I can hear what's going on," Cherry decides, grabbing Richard as she does so, yelling, "We need to talk team tactics!"

400

I hang back, watching Alekos prepping the now-cooked fish, quite happily until . . .

"What is it?"

His face has suddenly darkened at the sight of something outside the kitchen window.

"Has one of the goats escaped?" I go to peer myself but he stops me, quite roughly.

"What?"

He studies me anxiously, gripping my shoulders.

"Speak to me!" I search his eyes for a clue. I've never known him act like this before.

"It's probably all quite innocent . . ." he begins.

Fighting against him I wrench around and see Richard and Cherry flicking each other with water from the pool. In between kisses.

"Oh!" I bite my lip.

"You don't seem surprised?" He frowns.

"No," I reply.

"Or upset?"

"No."

Alekos thinks for a moment and then looks concerned. "Is this some kind of swingers party?"

"No!" I laugh. "Nothing like that. If anything it's more of an entrapment party . . ."

"Entrapment? What do you mean?"

Suddenly the pinger goes off and Greg comes haring down the stairs looking a little flushed. "That'll be the stifado!"

"Is it done?" I ask him as he clatters assorted pans and plates.

"More than ready," he replies, giving me a highly significant look.

I take a nervous breath. The time has come.

"Can everyone gather in the lounge?" I call. "Jules, you too!"

While Greg arranges the stew bowls and spoons on the lounge table, Richard hands each of us a glass of freshly popped champagne.

"A toast!" We follow his lead of holding our glasses aloft. "In fact, perhaps Alekos would like to choose the sentiment, seeing as we are all visitors to his fine island."

A pair of assessing eyes flit around the group — to Richard and Cherry, then Greg, Jules and even me — before he decides which cause to champion. "To honesty!" he announces, not without a hint of sarcasm.

We're all a bit uneasy chinking to that, duplicitous to a man.

"And friendship," I add before our glasses meet.

We all take an elongated slurp.

"And what would you like to drink to, Jules?" Cherry enquires, eager to set the ball rolling. "Your next boyfriend, perhaps?"

Jules gives Alekos a dismissive look before smirking, "Why not?"

"Have you decided who it's going to be yet?" I challenge her. My heart is thumping wildly as I say the words. Confronting someone is terrifying, especially with an audience. Even more so when up until a week ago you considered that someone your best friend.

"How do you mean?" She gives me a dubious look.

"Well, is it going to be Greg or Richard?" Cherry feigns bubbly intrigue. "We're all dying to know."

Jules' jaw tightens. "You're still angry with me about Dom —"

"No, no," Cherry corrects her. "I'm angry with you about your behaviour tonight."

"Tonight?" she gasps. "What have I done now?"

"Hmmm," Cherry muses. "Shall we begin with your attempts to sabotage Selena's new relationship?"

"Oh yes, let's!" Richard enthuses.

"What are you talking about?" Jules flushes.

"Well, let me see . . ." He tilts his head jauntily. "I have been introduced to you as Selena's beau and yet earlier, when we were outside by the pool, you told me that Selena has been on a complete man rampage since you arrived, after anything in trousers."

"Jules!" I sputter, horrified.

"What?" She looks wide-eyed at me. "I just meant you were ready to meet someone, that's all!"

"Why would you lie like that?"

"Who's lying? Do you deny that when we arrived at the Elounda Beach you were ogling every man from the hedge trimmer to the hotel manager, gurgling 'Ooh, he's nice! He's nice!' "

"I meant for you!" I despair. "You're the one who turned up out of the blue demanding an instant fling!"

"You know perfectly well I'd already made my choice, however ill-advised." She throws a grudging look at Alekos but he's too withdrawn to be affected.

"Yes but —" I stop myself. Now is not the time to blurt out that I didn't want her to be with Alekos because I wanted him for myself.

She raises an eyebrow at me.

I take a breath. "I didn't think he was right for you."

Now that has him riled. But just as he's about to speak, Richard steps in. "We're getting sidetracked!" he says, turning back to Jules. "You also asked if I was the same guy who gave Selena a business card on her birthday saying, 'Thanks for an unforgettable experience!' And went to great pains to point out that it was inscribed with three hearts."

"Three octopus hearts!" I blurt. "It was Graeme's card!" I look to Alekos for support. "Remember me texting you to say that he and Emily were in the Veghera bar that night? Besides, if I were out on the pull, why did I invite Alekos to dinner that same night?"

Jules looks caught out. She didn't know about that.

"You got my texts, right?" I prompt my alibi.

"Not until the next day." Alekos looks rueful. "But yes, you did invite me over."

"I don't know what you're all making such a fuss about!" Jules huffs, deep in denial.

"You told me that you'd always had a thing for men with chin dimples," Richard persists, determined to get her to crack.

She rolls her eyes. "It's not my problem you took that as a come-on — sounds like wishful thinking to me."

"You sat on my lap out on the balcony and put your hand down my shirt," Greg suddenly blurts.

Now Jules is really thrown. She can't believe the men are turning on her like this.

"The seats were metal," she forages around for an excuse. "They were too cold for me to sit on in my thin dress . . ."

Greg doesn't even wait for the rationale about the hand. "You said that while the others were having their monoski race you'd like to show me the Jacuzzi in your hotel room."

All eyes are upon her now. Her face turns to puce.

"I don't have to stay here and listen to you twisting everything I say and do!" she smarts, reaching for her handbag. "I'm leaving!"

"That's right, Jules — why don't you go and have another spa treatment?"

"I'm going to need one!" She takes Cherry at her word. "It'll take a deep tissue enzyme scrub to rid myself of all your negative auras!"

I can't help but snort at the woman who so wilfully sets about destroying other people's relationships. "You know what, Jules? You can get wraps till you're mummified and microdermabrasion till your face is raw, but I'll tell you one thing — you're never going to be beautiful on the inside."

Finally a human reaction — it may be barely discernible but her eyes get suddenly glossy and I see her swallowing hard as she exits.

We all stand in silence, staring at the door.

Finally Cherry attempts to make light of an agonising situation. "Well, I don't know about her but that was the best detox I ever had!"

"Hear, hear!" Richard cheers. "Here's to detoxing your life of people who don't have your best interests at heart and treasuring the ones who really care!"

Alekos and I exchange a look, not really knowing which category we belong in as far as the other is concerned.

"You did the right thing." Greg reaches to console me, suspecting quite rightly that I'm a little shaken up. "I know it feels mean but at least there's a chance now this will get through to her enough so that she'll think twice the next time."

I nod. I expected to feel triumphant — the villain has been unmasked! But actually I just feel sad. I can't believe my judgement was so off. And not just about her.

"Come on! Don't let this be a downer!" Richard tries to rouse our spirits once more. "Look at all this lovely food."

But suddenly no one has an appetite.

"You know what we need?" He refuses to let the slump get to him. "Moonlit monoskiing!"

CHAPTER
TWENTY-NINE

There are only two remedies for the suffering of the soul —
hope and patience.
— Pythagoras

What I really want to be doing now is sitting under a
Cretan arch with Alekos, getting to the real crux of
what went wrong. Not dragging him around the bay at
the end of a rope, much as I might think he still needs
a good dunking for sleeping with Jules.

I can't believe he's still so tight-lipped about the
experience — when everyone else was calling Jules on
her stuff I thought perhaps he'd pipe up and say,
"You're right, guys — she did a number on me too!"
And then all would be revealed and I'd graciously
forgive him and we could be reconciled. But he said
nothing. And though at certain points he looked like he
was experiencing some recognition or enlightenment,
ultimately his expression remained dark and brooding.

I look at him now strapping on the black lifejacket
and extra-grip gloves then loosening up his arms in
preparation for the race. He's probably wondering how
the hell he got caught up in all this madness. Of course
it doesn't take much to trace everything back to me. No
wonder he wants me gone.

"Ready?" he asks, eager to get the final chore over with.

I can barely muster a nod. Trudging towards the speedboat we look like Team Despondent next to Cherry and Richard's Team Euphoria.

"How did we let them talk us into this?" Alekos wonders out loud.

"Never underestimate the persuasion skills of an Entertainments Officer," I explain. "Even if they are now retired."

"Okay, we need to ride out for about ten minutes to get to the best stretch of water," Alekos advises. "So just follow us."

"Aye, aye, Captain!" Richard is as exuberant as ever, reaching to give Alekos a sporting "may the best man win!" handshake.

Meanwhile I'm taking one last shot at convincing Cherry to call the whole thing off. "Are you sure Richard's not going to hurt himself?" I wheedle, trying to appeal to her protective girlfriend sensibility.

"Don't be silly — he's an old pro," she dismisses my concern.

"Do you know for certain he's even done this before?"

She leans close. "When I say he's an old pro I mean it — he was the Hampshire monoskiing champ two years in a row."

"What?" I reel back. "Well, how is that going to make Alekos look good?"

"Don't worry, we've got it all sorted . . ." She winks and taps the side of her nose.

"He'll know if he fakes a fall," I caution.

"It's all going to be fine," she assures me. "Come on, let's get going!"

Alekos instinctively goes to take the wheel but I tell him I need the practice, especially since I've never driven at night before.

"Lights?" he suggests as I pull away from the jetty.

"Oh yes, please!"

It hadn't occurred to me that the boat would have headlamps just like a car. Nevertheless, I am aware that I'm driving like one of those people who refuses to believe that the world is round — right now it seems far more likely that the sea will end abruptly and we'll tip over the edge into oblivion.

"You know there are no walls or lamp-posts to hit out here," Alekos reasons. "You can go faster."

This really is a test of nerves. I know I can't inch along like this indefinitely or Alekos will never be able to rise up on to the surface of the water. Gingerly I push the lever forward.

"There you go," he encourages. "Now when we get to the spot and I'm in position I want you to hit it and then keep it at around thirty-three miles per hour. If for any reason I fall —"

"Don't fall!" I beg.

"I won't. But if I do, just pull back the throttle and turn the boat to the right to stop smoothly. Then slowly — *slowly* — come back around to get me. You'll have to be very careful because it won't be easy to see me and I don't want you to run me over."

I roll my eyes. Great. That would be the perfect end to the perfect day.

"Any questions?"

I only have one: "Why did you do it?"

He frowns back at me. "Why did I do what?"

"*Why did you have sex with Jules?*" I yell, ostensibly so I can be heard over the noise of the engine but mostly because I've bottled up my reaction to this for too long.

"Well?" I pout. Why is he still saying nothing? I demand a response! "Look, obviously I know now just how full on and manipulative she can be, and she mentioned you'd had a drink and of course she's stunningly attractive and yes, I suppose you could argue that I had been rejecting you, but after that moment we had in the infinity pool at the hotel . . ."

Only now does his face change.

"The way you held me and moved me through the water . . . I thought — I mean, did I imagine . . .?" Suddenly I feel horribly out on a limb.

"No," he says, so quietly I have to strain to hear his words. "It was real."

"But then *why*?!" I implore, utterly exasperated.

He contemplates me for a second and then says, "You're not going out with Richard, are you?" nodding to the boat powering alongside us.

"No, and for the record, Richard is actually the millionaire businessman from *The World*; Greg is the father-of-two renting the villa. I wondered if you might recognise him from the beach?"

He shakes his head.

410

"He had problems boarding the kayak on my first day?"

"Oooh." His eyes narrow. "The one with the silly hat?"

"Well. Yes. Anyway, I'm not going out with either of them, it was all just part of the ploy to catch Jules out."

He nods, taking a moment to process the information.

"I'm sorry you had to get caught up in it all. I didn't realise you and Jules were no longer an item or I would have spared you."

"We were never an item," he says sternly.

"Well, it certainly looked that way for a while." I pout.

"Well, apparently not everything is as it seems," he grizzles.

Right, that's it! I can't stand any more of this evasive, ambiguous talk — I cut the engine and turn to face him down.

"What are you doing?" He looks confused.

"We're not going anywhere until we sort this out."

"Oh really?" he challenges me, hackles rising.

"Really," I confirm. He's not the only stubborn person in this boat.

Alekos makes a thoroughly Greek grunt and then stares moodily out to sea — it's only when Richard pulls up to find out what is going on that he decides he has nothing left to lose.

"Just give us five minutes," Alekos requests.

Finally he faces me. I can almost feel the effort it takes for him to heave his heart up on to the slab.

"I never wanted you to leave with Jules," he begins, speaking like the telling of his side of events is one big chore. "I wanted you to stay with me. But your friend needed you — or so I thought — and so I backed off," he says matter-of-factly. "I went home after work to pack up your things as promised and then I started to get really . . . sad." As he continues, his voice gradually becomes infused with more emotion. "I thought, what if this is it? What if she's never coming back here? It felt like we were breaking up before we'd even begun."

I feel a little pang as he sighs, "I wanted to reach out to you, to tell you how I was feeling, but you already had Jules pulling on you emotionally, I didn't want you feeling torn." He looks into my eyes for the first time. "But when I came over and it was just you and me, I couldn't resist pulling you into the water and having you in my arms — just in case I didn't get another chance." He smiles wistfully. "It felt so good. All I wanted then was for you to feel cherished and cared for and connected to me somehow."

My eyes prickle with tears. "I did," I tell him in a small voice. "I felt so close to you then." All the more agonising to feel this distance right now.

Even though I know something wicked this way comes, I bid him continue.

"Well, then Jules came back from the spa and my only thought was to get out of there, to get out of the way. And take those good feelings home with me."

I nod, remembering feeling the same thing, convinced that moment would be enough to carry us through.

412

"So I went back to the house," he continues. "I looked at the cake I'd bought you and the card and the champagne —"

"I don't remember seeing any champagne . . ."

He grimaces. "Well, that's where it starts going wrong. I decided to open it anyway. Actually it was Loulou's idea — a toast for the birthday girl," he attempts a little joke. "So I had a glass. But that just made me miss you more. So I had another. And that got me thinking, What if this really is it? What if we never get to recapture what we had here? I mean, I liked you on the ship from afar but having spent this time with you and having you smile at me, really at me, not just through the TV screen . . ." He shakes his head. "So I have another glass. And then it's the end of the bottle and I crash out." His head seems to grow heavy. "The next thing I know there's a knock at the door. I answer it, all groggy, and there's Jules."

I can't help but bristle. That conniving, covetous harlot!

"She says she has jet lag and no one to talk to — you were asleep and she was hoping I might still be up. I tell her I was in bed myself. She asks if she can join me . . ."

"Just like that!"

"Just like that."

"And you said yes?" I despair.

"No, of course not. I tell her no. I tell her that I like her friend. More than like . . ."

My heart tweaks.

"But she told me I was wasting my time. She mentioned a couple of the things she told Richard about you ogling the men at the hotel and the thing with the guy's business card on the bedside table."

"And that's all it took?"

"Actually no," he clips, suddenly cold. "It was the texts that did it."

Now it's me experiencing a chill. Suddenly I get why he's been so mad at me, so desperately hurt — Jules showed him the texts I'd sent her! And you can bet it was the early ones.

I slump forward, head in my hands remembering phrases like *He couldn't be of less consequence!* and *I'm just here for the taramasalata.*

"Aleko, you have to understand that was right at the beginning of the week — I was still in defence mode."

"You called me a bully."

"I was wrong. You're not a bully, you're encouraging. You've made me try so many new things . . ."

"And sleazy?"

"Well, you know I had issues with that at first but Nia Vardalos has made me realise you can't help it," I try a little cheekiness. "It's just your natural Greek sexuality."

"Did you say Nia Vardalos?" He looks at me with utter bewilderment. Which is an improvement on the looks he's been giving me the rest of the evening.

"It's a long story . . ." I mutter.

Alekos sighs. "You can imagine how I felt to see those words from you — this woman I absolutely adored, this woman I wanted to believe was starting to have feelings for me, mocking me behind my back."

I hang my head in shame.

"And then here's this other woman who seems desperate to be with me, offering comfort . . ."

I close my eyes, picturing how she would first soothe him and then make her move . . . How the hell am I going to convince him that my feelings genuinely changed, that I really did fall for him? "Wait!" Suddenly I scrabble for my phone. "Look, I can show you the texts I sent her *after* that!" I say, remembering doing this very thing in the designer shoe shop in Athens.

"Are you guys done yet?" Cherry calls over to us, as Richard reverses back to get level once more.

"Hold on!" I plead.

"What are we waiting for?" Cherry howls.

"One minute!" I turn back to Alekos. "Look at this one: *Contrary to my initial impression, he really is an officer and a gentleman!* and this: *I'm having secret thoughts of rearing one of Roubas' puppies with this man!*"

He gives his first full smile of the evening — could I be getting through to him?

"I like that idea!" he concedes.

"That's just the tip of the iceberg. Now we're talking again I can tell you how I *really* feel!"

"GUYS!" Richard and Cherry shout together.

"Let's just get this out the way," Alekos decides. "Then we'll talk."

Oh god, I can't bear it! Still, maybe it's for the best — maybe the monoski spray will sluice away all his anguish and mistrust and he'll come back on board all revived and receptive!

"Here I go."

"Good luck!" I bleat as he plops into the water.

"Ready?" Richard calls across.

I watch Alekos bob up, smooth back his hair, and then brace himself for the sudden surge. "*Ena, dio, tria . . .*"

"GO!" yells Cherry.

And we're off.

I can definitely feel a difference driving the boat while yanking an appendage. I look back to check that all is well and can just about make out Alekos swishing back and forth, board juddering beneath his feet as it rides the waves, sending wild spumes of white spray flaring in his wake. His body tilts perilously close to the water as he takes each turn, one-handed no less! Aside from his amazingly controlled technique, it is an outrageously sexy manoeuvre.

I check ahead of me and then, when I'm confident I'm on course, take a peek over at Richard, who's throwing similarly daring yet elegant angles. So far the guys have been going from left to right in reasonable synchronicity, but I can't help but worry that they might clash if they fell out of time. Perhaps I should just edge over a little bit?

All of a sudden I sense something is wrong. I hear voices calling out to me. Alekos is down.

"Shit!" I cut the power.

Right, what did he say? Turn to the right and then creep slowly back. Do not run over his head. Oh god, I just know it was my fault, I should never have tried to veer, I've obviously thrown him off his stride and now Richard won't get to do his trick, or whatever he had planned, so he'll be mad at me too.

"Aleko!" I call into the night, instantly irritated — this is hopeless, I can't see a darn thing. Why oh why did I go along with this? "Aleko?" I call again. Still nothing. Please don't say I've already concussed him. I can't even judge how far on I went after he dropped. "ALEKO!" I try bellowing louder. Again nothing.

I see that Cherry has stopped her boat and I quickly reach for my mobile.

"Cherry! I've lost him!" I panic as she answers.

"We'll come and help you look."

"Careful!" I squawk caution. "Make sure you don't run him over."

I am trying desperately hard not to freak out but I start to fear that Neptune got a taste for Alekos when he jumped off the cliff on the octopus day and has now decided to keep him for himself.

"Please give him back to me!" I find myself praying. "Please."

I climb out on to the front of the boat so I can study the lit water. What's that I see? I lean over as far as I can but it's just out of reach. I'm going to have to move the boat forward a tad. When I turn back I see a dripping figure looming over me.

"Oh my god, Aleko!" I stumble back.

"Looking for something?" he deadpans.

"You!" I exclaim. I go to hug him, so relieved he's alive, but he steps away from me.

Surely he's not still mad?

"What is it?"

"My hand," he says, wincing as he tries to flex it.

"Oh no, please don't say you've messed it up again! Was it my fault, when I turned the boat?"

He shakes his head but flumps down on the seat, obviously a little shaken. "Is that your phone?"

"It's Cherry," I tell him, quickly answering. "Yes, yes, he's back on board."

"I'm fine," he says, waving away any potential concern. "Tell them we'll see them back at the villa."

"Okay. See you there." I snap the phone closed. "Richard says thank you for cutting things short — he was starting to get a bit peckish."

Alekos snuffles a smile and then looks up at me, eyes brimming with remorse. "Selena, I'm sorry I slept with Jules — I wish it had never happened. *Really*. Even at the time it felt wrong —"

"Don't worry about that, it's in the past now," I shush my patient as I crouch by his side. "I'm just concerned about your hand, how bad is it?"

"Well," he expels a long sigh. "That depends."

"On what?" I frown, confused.

"How bad would it have to be to get you to stay?"

My face illuminates with hope. "You think you might need my help again?"

He nods. "A bit of unbuttoning here, a bit of melon slicing there . . ."

418

As a grin spreads across my face, there is so much I want to say but, instead, I ever so gently lift his damaged hand to my lips. First I kiss his fingertips, then his knuckles, then his wrist.

I feel the rest of his body slump in submission as he informs me that the pain appears to be spreading up his arm. By the time I get to his elbow his supposedly injured hand is at the back of my neck, entwined in my hair and pulling my face up towards his.

We kiss. Mouth to mouth. Heart to heart.

Dizzy from all the anticipation, I take a moment to set myself just far apart enough to watch with delight as all the desire and admiration and sparkle returns to his eyes. Once again I find myself beaming.

"You love me a little bit, don't you?" I tease.

He tuts at me. "I love you a lot."

And then he pulls me closer and shows me, and the stars above, just how much.

CHAPTER
THIRTY

What we achieve inwardly, will change outer reality.
— Plutarch

One year on . . .

Here he comes again. Striding purposefully towards me
in precision-pressed naval whites complete with rigid
black epaulettes, soft white loafers and a patent peaked
cap with nifty gold insignia. Even his Mediterranean
tan and onyx-glow eyes look like they've been officially
issued in a bid to create the ultimate cruiseship pin-up,
all perfectly offset against an opulent ocean backdrop.

This time I don't run. I let him come all the way up
to me and scoop me up into his arms and kiss me.

"Perfect!" My sister cheers. "Now with you wearing
his cap!"

"Honestly! Don't you think you've taken enough?" I
groan, even though I can think of worse ways of
spending my time.

"Alright," she says, taking one last snap before
returning her camera to her bejewelled formal night
clutch. "I just wanted to make sure I had enough
mementos — this has been the best holiday ever!"

It has indeed been a great week — cruising around
the beauty spots of New Zealand, catching up with

420

Mum and Dad, doing my *Love Makes the World Go Round* presentation and then padding back to Alekos' cabin at night.

Naturally I'll feel a wrench leaving my family tomorrow, but I also can't wait to get back home to Elounda. We have one of the Carob Tree Valley Villas of our own now. Well, we had to stay somewhere when Alekos' brother returned from the mainland!

The other significant change is that we had to hand back the car and switch to Alekos' motorbike. Initially I was terrified. "I'm not a horse!" he would cry as my thighs gripped tight each time we squeezed through a narrow passage or overtook another vehicle. I used to ride with my eyes closed and my head buried in his back. But now he'll pick me up in town and I'll step on the back with a bag of groceries and sit upright and look all around me and love the sensation of the wind ruffling my hair. Of course sometimes I want to touch him, so I'll lean my forearm across his shoulders or stroke the back of his neck or rest my hands on his thighs but, whatever pose I adopt, it always seems to make me smile. I never knew that it was possible to commit to one person and one place and yet feel so free.

I think the most liberating thing has been letting go of my old fears. I've made such damning comments about Shirley Valentine and yet I realise now it wasn't becoming *her* that I feared, it was her beaten-down alter ego Shirley Bradshaw. Shirley *Valentine* was a role model — a woman who dared to shake off her shackles and open herself up to a whole new life. So now when

I catch myself in comparison-mode I feel proud. And when I do my share of the household chores, I don't see myself with a poodle perm and a nylon housecoat, I think of myself as Hestia, goddess of the home!

Mind you, the film still continues to affect me — the other day, watching it with Alekos for the first time (he chuckled at every twitch of Costas' moustache), it made me think of Jules. Husband Joe was rotten to his wife and yet when Shirley found a joyful new existence, she didn't dump him, she stood her ground, gave him a chance to reflect upon his behaviour and then felt compassion for the misery that he had become and invited him to join her. Well, I wasn't about to invite Jules out to Greece any time soon but I was curious about her well-being — rumour had it that she'd gone back to the cruiseships and then, just a few weeks ago this was confirmed by my Czech mate Jindrich . . . I'd had secret hopes that she'd embarked on some kind of voyage of self-discovery since the great Carob Tree showdown last year but I wasn't prepared for him telling me that she was now working in the kids' department. Apparently she told him that corralling the under-tens uses even more calories per day than her fitness classes and it's helped her let go of any attachment to being perfectly groomed, on account of having her hair tugged and that flawless complexion drawn all over with face paints.

She also told him to pass on a message to me to say that she hoped I could one day forgive her and that she now only talks to single men, although she's still trying to work out what she personally finds attractive without

422

that trigger of coveting what someone else has. Which sounded surprisingly self-aware for her.

Cherry is sceptical about Jules' redemption but that's okay. We'll see how it goes. Besides, it turns out Cherry makes a much nicer best friend! She's even lined up some of her wealthy neighbours from *The World* for my new customised tours of Crete — she and Richard had their honeymoon at one of the Elounda Beach Yachting Club Villas and now all their friends are hooked! For them I devised the deluxe package and a while back I got a chance to test out my family tours on Roxy and baby Rihanna and Greg and his two girls. At least that was my excuse for inviting them out at the same time. I knew he'd never call her under his own steam. They've been together two months now. I'm beginning to think Alekos was right about the magic of Elounda. I wonder what will happen when Kirby and Lana come to stay? They say they can't wait to see me and Alekos together so they can gloat about being right all along and, by the way, they still want to know what he's like in bed!

Michelle and Hazel want to come out too.

It's funny. When you stand still for a moment, it seems the world has a chance to come to you.

Like now, as I lean on the balcony rail in the balmy breeze, taking a moment before dinner, Alekos finds me and snugs up behind me. It's been such an adventure since we got together and yet the biggest journey for me appears to have been learning to trust someone. I always hoped that one day I'd be able to shake off all those bad relationships, all those disappointments,

really let those panicky tears and paranoias go. It's been a gradual process but I can feel my heart getting stronger — and a little bolder — every day we are together.

"Can you believe how much has changed since our first cruise together?" I marvel out loud.

And yet some rituals stay the same ... when we arrive in Heraklion a few days from now we'll stop at the monastery — Alekos will cross himself there, I'll save my prayers for the Monday booze cruise — and then we'll continue on to the cliff-top vantage point where we will pause and survey the bay. Only now it won't just be him getting misty-eyed at the view.

"Go on!" he'll urge me as his hand warms the back of my neck.

And that's the point at which I'll look up at him and heave a big happy sigh and murmur his favourite words, "Home, Sweet Crete . . ."